THE SEVEN SUCCUBI

THE SECOND STORY OF HER MAJESTY'S OFFICE OF THE WITCHFINDER GENERAL

PROTECTING THE PUBLIC FROM THE UNNATURAL SINCE 1645

D1824600

Also by Simon Kewin

Stories of
Her Majesty's Office of the Witchfinder General

The Eye Collectors

THE SEVEN SUCCUBI

THE SECOND STORY OF HER MAJESTY'S OFFICE OF THE WITCHFINDER GENERAL

PROTECTING THE PUBLIC FROM THE UNNATURAL SINCE 1645

SIMON KEWIN

Elsewhen Press

The Seven Succubi

First published in Great Britain by Elsewhen Press, 2022
An imprint of Alnpete Limited

Quotes are included from: *Bleak House*, Charles Dickens, 1853, London: Bradbury & Evans; *The Mabinogion*, from the translation by Lady Charlotte Guest, London: Longman, Brown, Green and Longmans, 1848; *Macbeth*, William Shakespeare, 1623, London: Edward Blount and William Jaggard; *Malleus Maleficarum*, Henricus Institoris, 1487, from the translation by Rev Montague Summers, London: John Rodker, 1928; Wikipedia, entry can be found at https://en.wikipedia.org/Cyhyraeth. Quotes from documents in the internal archives of Her Majesty's Office of the Witchfinder General that are no longer, or have never been, in the public domain, are used with permission.

Elsewhen Press, PO Box 757, Dartford, Kent DA2 7TQ
www.elsewhen.press

British Library Cataloguing in Publication Data.
A catalogue record for this book is available from the British Library.

ISBN 978-1-915304-01-8 Print edition
ISBN 978-1-915304-11-7 eBook edition

Designed and formatted by Elsewhen Press

MALEFICOS VIVERE NON PATIERIS

Nihil obstat: Dorothy Aphrodite Coldwater
Imprimatur: Campbell Percy Hardknott-Lewis KCB DL,
Lord High Witchfinder of All Wales

CONTENTS

For Richard Bawden

1 – The Dark Room

Remember that many who succumb to the lure of
the dark arts lack the character and self-discipline
to resist the siren call of their illicit powers. In their
strength is their weakness; they reveal themselves
when they think they are beyond our reach and do
not fear us. That is our opportunity. That is how we
will know them.

–Earl Grey, Witchfinder General, *Office of the
Witchfinder General Handbook*, 1999

It was a moment of idle curiosity that sealed the fate of
Maude Woebegone.

She'd been *so* damned careful, used her powers
sparingly. She never worked an incantation for the simple
convenience of an easier life. Hardly ever, at least. Oh,
she might hurry herself to the front of a queue from time
to time by planting distracting ideas into the heads of
those ahead of her, or she'd fritz someone's phone with a
flicker of St Elmo's Fire if they were talking too loudly
on a train. She might even, at a pinch, persuade the rain
to pause for a moment and have a good think about what
it was doing before choosing to unload upon *her*. But
those were all little things, cantrips rather than full-on
spells. Magic that, surely, barely registered on the
thaumometers of the operatives of the Office of the
Witchfinder General, unless they happened to be standing
very close by.

And why would they be pursuing her, anyway? They
should be out there catching the *real* users – the ones
summoning demonic presences, or intoning the chthonic
syllables of death spells to murder or extort or gain
personal power. People who climbed the greasy poles of

politics or business by killing or incapacitating those above them. She would never dream of working magic that was so ... extrovert.

Well, hardly ever.

Now, lying in the King-sized bed of her room in the *Gwesty'r Ddraig Goch* – The Red Dragon Hotel – in the bustling centre of Cardiff, she shut her eyes and exhaled a long, slow breath of relaxation. It had been an exhausting day, during which she'd worked hard to keep her powers in check. She would allow herself the briefest, slightest relaxation. A bit of harmless fun. The Office obviously had a significant presence in the Welsh capital: the famous Hardknott-Lewis himself, Lord High Witchfinder of All Wales, would be perched up there in the Black Tower of the castle, peering disapprovingly over his flock. She'd walked around the castle walls that afternoon, admiring the carvings of the Animal Wall, forcing herself to stroll as if she didn't have a care in the world. His imagined gaze upon her shoulders had weighed her down like a heavy overcoat.

But nothing had happened. She was in the clear, wasn't on any sort of witch watch list. She was just a regular person come to Cardiff for a concert at the Tramshed and a bit of sightseeing. Sure, the band she'd come to see were *Summoning*, a name Hardknott-Lewis no doubt thoroughly disapproved of, but they were a harmless metal act, with no actual incantatory power to their lyrics. She'd checked, just to be completely sure. Not a single entity had manifested when she'd tried intoning the spells the band had scrawled across their album covers.

She was safe. There was no risk to what she was about to do. It was a little like surfing the stations on a TV. She reached out with her mind's eye and began to channel-hop, flicking from room to room, eavesdropping on what was occurring around her. A hotel was always a good place to do a bit of idle people-watching; you got a snapshot of so many lives, all neatly parcelled up in room-sized boxes.

Next door, a young couple were sitting in

companionable silence, each reading their own book, there with each other but happily lost in their own worlds. Sweet, but dull. On the other side of her, a single man lay on his bed seeing but not really watching the television. His mind was a fuzz of unfocused anxiety; his thoughts circled as he stressed over money, the job he hated, the girlfriend who'd left him, money again, what he should do with his life. He was thinking about watching one of the hotel's adult channels, finding the brief oblivion of a lonely orgasm, but had decided he couldn't be bothered. She felt sorry for him; he was not in a good place. There was nothing she could do.

In the suite below her, an older couple were sipping cups of tea after a busy day's shopping. They were laughing at some shared joke, and thinking about a stroll around Cardiff Bay after dinner. The evening promised to be dry, and Cardiff was a cosmopolitan place these days, relaxed. No one would give two guys walking arm-in-arm a second glance. From room to room she drifted, dipping into this life and that, tasting the strife, passion, joy and boredom of the collection of people who happened to be there in that hotel on that night.

Then, two floors above her, her wandering attention hit a solid wall. Intrigued, she pushed a little harder. Whoever was in that room was another user, and, what was more, they'd erected magical barriers to keep questing interlopers out. *Powerful* barriers. She pushed harder still, seeking a slit by which she could slip inside. The walls, iron hard, continued to repel her.

Her disembodied mind circumnavigated the exterior of the room, studying it from every angle. It was so easy to miss slivers where pipes and cables entered a room, or to leave cracks around windows and doors. But whoever was inside had been very thorough, making sure there were no flaws in the warding incantation. And the question was, why? It was so much safer to hide in anonymity, as she did. Magical barriers would keep intruders out, but they were also a great way of broadcasting that a practising magic user was inside. And that they were up to something that they did not want the world to see.

Maude knew she should withdraw, return to her own body and let the intriguingly-locked room go. If the operatives of the Office did spot what was going on, and came looking for the perpetrator, she didn't want to be anywhere nearby. What she wanted was to be an innocent member of the public, an oblivious bystander.

But she'd been so good, so careful all day. And there was no sign of anyone coming. And the area of effect of the magic she'd have to use was small. The Black Tower was half a kilometre away, and what were the chances that an operative would happen to be studying this particular hotel, right at this moment?

Small. *Tiny*. She would give it another push. The truth was, she was intrigued. It was so hard to gain magical knowledge with the Office's obsession with suppressing the mystical arts, and this was something new. The walls were dark – like the darkness inside a sealed sarcophagus in an abandoned crypt on a moonless, winter night. They were *solid* dark, as if the user had chiselled out sections of midnight and slotted them into place to form a room.

The magic required for such a feat was *cool*.

Maude pulled her disembodied essence back a short way, mustering her strength, then threw herself at the barriers, pitching all of her suppressed, frustrated power into the effort of it for one, brief, glorious moment of release.

Unexpectedly, the wall vanished as she battered at it, admitting her, sending her sprawling in a conceptual heap as her thunderbolt charge was met with no resistance. For an instant, she was disorientated. The room blazed with light, so bright that it blinded her. There was someone else in the room with her; the user who'd worked the powerful warding. They were making no attempt to conceal themselves.

Maude tried to recover, flee back to her body, but she was held by the other user's gaze, pinned like a butterfly on a card. Panic fluttered through her. Using all her strength, she attempted to make the distant fingers of her body's left hand move, send an SOS SMS to the few other users who knew her and who would recognize the code words. But, before she could press OK, the walls flashed back into absolute solidity, and they were a guillotine, severing Maude's mind from her body, slicing through the mystical ties keeping her two aspects connected. The pain of the break howled through her, but she had no throat to scream with.

The figure in the room moved nearer Maude's disembodied soul, apparently perfectly capable of perceiving her despite her incorporeality. She was a woman, although no one that Maude knew. The raw magical potential coiling off her was like steam rising from an overheating reactor core. She towered over Maude. She *loomed*.

There was a voice, too: well-educated, almost aristocratic in its tones. Mainly, the unknown woman sounded bored, as if Maude were nothing more than an irritating inconvenience.

"Hello, little bird. Come fluttering around to peck at me, have you? You should have stayed safe in your own cage."

Maude's cry rang only in her disembodied mind. She threw herself at the walls again, desperately, but she was a maddened fly bouncing off solid stone, and there was no possible hope of breaking through.

The user who had trapped her sighed a bored little sigh of resignation before uttering the first syllables of her death spell.

2 – The Visitation

With regard to the bewitchment of human beings by means of Incubus and Succubus devils, it is to be noted that this can happen in three ways. First, when women voluntarily prostitute themselves to Incubus devils. Secondly, when men have connexion with Succubus devils; yet it does not appear that men thus devilishly fornicate with the same full degree of culpability; for men, being by nature intellectually stronger than women, are more apt to abhor such practises.

–Henricus Institoris, *Malleus Maleficarum*, 1487

I was relaxing after a hard day's witchfinding, draining my third bottle of Kingfisher, when the buzzer on my flat door rang.

We have good security: our residences are kitted out with all the latest technology in an attempt to keep the forces of darkness at bay. It's unobtrusive – we're supposed to be nothing more exciting than local government workers after all – but it's most definitely there. My front door was reinforced steel, and I was pretty sure it also had some form of m/tech woven through it as a ward against the ineffable. I'd run my thaumometer over it a couple of times and picked up a definite flicker of something disguised within. Strictly speaking, of course, we weren't supposed to use or rely upon any such forbidden sorcery, but that was one of the grey areas, right there. Better to bend the rules a little and keep the witchfinder alive. Fight the bigger fight.

The video camera built into my door was perfectly normal electronic kit, although top-end: high definition with motion detection and facial recognition. Most likely the caller had rung by mistake – perhaps a taxi driver looking for a pickup at one of the other apartments in the once-grand Cardiff townhouse in which I lived. I wasn't expecting any deliveries and I hadn't invited anyone around. Briefly hoping that it might be an unexpected social visit – from DI Zubrasky perhaps – I picked the camera's video up on my phone.

It's fair to say that the screen revealed just about the last person I expected to see on my doorstep on a windswept, wintery night. The Crow – Campbell Hardknott-Lewis, the Lord High Witchfinder of All Wales – was bundled up in a black overcoat, a red scarf plumped around his neck to keep out the chill. He held his hat in one leather-gloved hand (it was possibly a fedora, but I'm not an expert) so that I could see his face clearly as he looked directly into the camera.

His expression was … calm. It didn't help. Alarm thumped through me, as it always did when I encountered the Crow. It wasn't just your normal fear of meeting the boss and having to be on your best behaviour – recent events had kicked off a whole extra dimension of anxiety. I had employed forbidden powers in the apprehension of Peter Warder and Evangelina Mormont. Hell, I had *killed* Warder by unleashing a torrent of sorcerous energy at him, without any understanding of what I was doing or how I was doing it. I was a *user*. There were no grey areas wide enough to cover what I'd done, no extenuating circumstances that could justify such actions in the eyes of the Office. I was one of the people I was supposed to spend my days hunting down. The fact that I paid in sweat-drenched nightmares, and a sense of dread that sometimes felt like it was a fist clutching my heart, counted for nothing.

I'd responded by doing what most people do in such situations: bumbling on in the vague hope it will all resolve itself by some mystical means. But I knew I was kidding myself; I couldn't change what I was, and I was firmly in the category of things the Office considered *unnatural*.

I was *fairly* sure Hardknott-Lewis didn't know the truth, although he'd admitted to having concerns about my family background – a catalogue of users and practitioners, it turned out. He'd even revealed that he knew I had, as he put it, *potential* myself. Well, yeah – he was damned right about that, although, unaware of the truth at the time, I'd denied it. I reassured myself by repeating the mantra that, if he knew the truth, I would *not* still be walking the streets of Cardiff – or any other town, come to that. I'd be safely locked away in the frozen limbo of Oblivion, never to trouble the waking world again.

I also repeated to myself that I clearly shouldn't be pursued because I was a good guy. Okay, so maybe everyone thinks that about themselves, even the ones who aren't. But users like Mormont and Warder clearly wielded their powers for evil. I wasn't like them. Magus law made no such distinction – magic use was magic use – but I was benign, right? I didn't go round killing people unless I had a really, *really* good reason. I wasn't so different from, say, the warding magic woven into my door, there only for good.

It's fascinating the efforts the mind will go to in order to try and resolve the irreconcilable. I know perfectly well what cognitive dissonance is, but, ironically enough, if you'd asked me, I'd have assured you I was not experiencing it.

Two months had passed since Faebrook Folly, and my life as a handsome, keen-eyed witchfinder had simply continued. I'd taken a week off, then got on with my life. Sometimes, whole hours could go by without me spiralling into anxiety about my position. But now here was the Crow on my doorstep, just him and me, late at night. As to what he suspected and what doubts lingered within his steel-trap mind – that I didn't know. But he had never, ever come to visit me at home before.

"Hello, Danesh," he said through the intercom, his voice calm, the familiar Welsh music in his vowels. At the same time, his idiom was always so formal that it sounded like even his spoken words were properly punctuated. I had never mentioned this to him.

"I apologize for the intrusion at this late hour," he continued. "May I come in? A matter of some urgency has arisen that I would very much like to discuss with you."

There was only one thing I could do: maintain the pretence, let him in. What other options did I have? A night-time flit across the Cardiff rooftops? If I didn't fall and break my neck, he could easily muster forces to surround and capture me. And then he'd sit me down and stare into my eyes and ask me, with a disappointed look on his face, precisely why it was I had run…

I pressed the button that granted him access, then spent the next thirty seconds desperately attempting to tidy up the clutter – *detritus* might be a better word – of my single-male-living-alone life. I had never been to his home – I had no idea where it even was – but I imagined leather armchairs, oak bookcases, maybe a grandfather clock picking its way through the dusty seconds. Something, in short, far-removed from the teetering mountains of pizza boxes and take-away curry containers that filled the floor between my sofa and TV. It looked like I'd been trying to model the buildings of some shanty town or bombed-out city in my sitting-room. I threw them all into a black plastic bin-bag, feeling bad about not recycling them, then crossed to open the inner door.

The Crow seemed to fill my room when he entered. How did he do that? He was a tall man, wiry, his movements like those of the strutting bird. He peered around the room, and it felt as though he were examining every nook and cranny of my frightened little soul. He carried a brown leather briefcase in his hand. It matched his shoes perfectly, I noted. Maybe he had a range of such bags, one for each outfit, and his butler picked them out for him each morning.

I think I managed to sound calm as I spoke.

"Lord High Witchfinder, welcome to my humble lair."

If he disapproved, he didn't show it. He'd been in

plenty of grim and disgusting situations over the years: charnel houses and ritual summoning circles and the bloody scenes of supernatural struggle. My flat was bad, but it wasn't *that* bad. He nodded his welcome, set down his briefcase, shrugged his way out of his heavy coat, then looked around somewhat helplessly for a place to hang it. I took it from him and added it to the pile on the single, already overwhelmed, hook on the back of my door.

"Please, sit down," I said. "Can I make you tea? From a teabag, of course."

"Tea would be lovely, thank you. Strong and black."

"I, ah, I only have mugs." In the grand old manor I imagined for him, he only drank from the finest bone china cups. Probably served him by that butler upon a tray with a silver creamer and sugar bowl.

"A mug is splendid, thank you," he said. "It fits more in, does it not?"

I thought he was going to refuse to sully himself with my scruffy furniture, but he sat down, placing his gloves in his upturned hat on my little table. With his perfectly symmetrical tie and those polished brown leather shoes, he looked like some precious enamel badge sitting among the dusty tat of a junk shop window. I became suddenly aware of how scruffy everything of mine was, although Hardknott-Lewis had said and done nothing to make the point.

He studied the teetering pile of video game cases upon the table, his brow furrowed as he tried to make sense of the titles. He picked up the top one and considered it with an air of fascination, as if he were examining some incomprehensible alien artefact. It was, I noted, *War of the Witch King*, a title and a game he was not going to approve of. I dreaded to think what he made of the lurid artwork. I hurried away to boil the kettle before he could ask me about it.

When I returned, his tea and my coffee held on a tray that I'd surprised myself by finding down the side of the microwave, he was standing again, studying the books in my bookshelf, head slanted on one side. I watched as his gaze skimmed over the copy of *The Picture of Dorian Gray* given to me – anonymously – by Sally Spender. Her little act of both reassurance and invitation. If the Crow noticed it, he didn't say anything. Perhaps there were so many books he found troublesome – fantasy books, horror books – that he failed to make the connection.

Sitting again, he sipped at his mug, then gave that little satisfied gasp of delight all tea-drinkers make. Then he set his drink down and considered me.

"You must forgive me for intruding upon your private time, and I am aware that this is all somewhat unorthodox, but the matter I wanted to discuss with you is somewhat delicate."

This was not a good opening. Perhaps this was what he did if he suspected something about one of his people: afford them the dignity of a quiet, private conversation before escorting them through our part-time broom cupboard into Oblivion.

My throat had gone dry. I was grateful for the coffee. "Is it about the new case?"

He'd sent me a MORIARTY message just before I'd left for the evening, mentioning a Code 27 he wanted me to look into the following day.

"This is a different matter, something outside our normal routine. The fact is, I wanted to discuss a matter relating to your thesis, and I thought it best if our conversation were held, shall we say, *in camera*."

"I don't … I don't understand."

"Off the record," he said. "Between you and me."

That was puzzling too: surely his office at the top of the Black Tower was utterly secure? And as to my thesis, I'd written it as part of my induction process into the Office, carrying out research that now seemed very basic. I hadn't looked at it since.

I took another sip of coffee. "I'm sure I got all sorts of things wrong."

He lifted his briefcase onto his lap. I couldn't see the

digits he entered into the combination lock, but there were a lot of them. The catches clicked, and he lifted out a bound sheaf of papers that I recognized.

"Actually, I think you were on the right lines with your central analysis. I would not necessarily say that you are our resident expert in the area of succubi and incubi, but, then again, you probably know more than most. We are, as so often, stretched thin."

I had written thirty thousand words on the parallels between the classic succubi and incubi of the middle eastern and western tradition – highly sexualized demons in female and male form respectively – and certain entities in Indian folklore, apsaras and yakshini. To be honest, my conclusions were that the comparisons weren't particularly helpful to either culture. I think I'd been keen to work on a theme that bridged the two strands of my mixed parentage. I was pretty sure I'd managed to misrepresent both traditions equally well. Which is something.

I'd also expressed the view that the highly sexualized representations of succubi found in the texts told us more about the writers than the demonic entities – there is more than a hint of the erotic fantasy to some of the depictions. A clear misogyny too, with the female blamed for the triggering of unwelcome feelings of sexual desire in the (usually male) author.

Hardknott-Lewis slipped on his small, round reading-glasses and leafed through the pages. "I think you tackled the whole subject most capably, given your understandable lack of direct experience of the area and the restrictions placed upon your access to source material."

I had limited my analysis to the theoretical succubus as I'd obviously assumed they didn't actually exist. Now I wasn't so sure.

"Succubi are real?"

"They are, regrettably, just one more example of the very real threats that we protect people from. We may quibble over their precise nature, but certainly entities of this sort do exist, most assuredly. They are rare, although they appear to be more common than they were, a fact that I put down to wider sociological changes. They are, fundamentally, sexual in nature, using the act of congress to gain influence over their victims."

I doubted anyone had used the word *congress* to mean sex for about a hundred years, but I chose not to mention it. Instead, I tried to think back to my somewhat hurried researches on the subject.

"The classic succubus takes semen from her male victim and passes it onto a friendly incubus by some unspecified means, who then uses it to impregnate a human female."

Now the Crow lifted another book out of his briefcase. I recognized the stained red leatherwork on the cover, the gold lettering. It was one of our copies of *Malleus Maleficarum* – the Hammer of Witches, the fifteenth century tome that had supposedly greatly influenced the original Witchfinder General. It had once been the Office's handbook and bible (if you'll excuse the word). Things had moved on these days, and we were a little – a little – more progressive, but the book was still referred to at times.

The Crow had marked a page with a cloth bookmark. The ancient parchment creaked as he opened the book.

"So Institoris asserted, although there is much that is puzzling in his account. For one thing, he says there are three ways that the bewitchment can take place, then only lists two."

I read the passage he was referring to upside-down. I remembered it. Hard to forget a section so calmly mentioning the intellectual superiority of men over women. Yeah. Different times. I'd love to have got Institoris and Lady Coldwater together in a room for a little chat.

"Perhaps the book was redacted?" I suggested.

"I think, on balance, that it just does not make sense a lot of the time. The whole business seems to be unnecessarily complicated, and nor does it explain how the cambions resulting from the process end up bearing the demonic taint, given that only human gametes are involved."

Of all the ways I'd imagined my evening panning out, a discussion of demonic semen-swapping with Hardknott-Lewis had not been high on my list.

"Cambions?" I said. "I don't recall what they are." I probably never knew, in truth.

"They are the resulting children. They are changelings; human/demon hybrids with unnatural powers. Sometimes they are described as completely normal in appearance, and sometimes as rather twisted in nature, although I assume there is some element of the fear of illness and deformity in that. The word, though, is fascinating, coming from a Celtic root meaning crooked."

He had a habit of wandering off into etymology, and of describing his revelations as fascinating when clearly they're nothing of the sort. I nodded my head in an *interesting* kind of way and tried to make sense of where he was going.

"Have you encountered a cambion, or are you pursuing a succubus?"

A weak smile washed over his features unexpectedly at that. It disappeared rapidly.

"A cambion? I don't know. I suspect not, given the timing. I don't believe I've been that lax. But, as to me pursuing a succubus, I am afraid it is rather the other way around."

It took me a moment to grasp what he was driving it. The possibility that the Crow had a love life – a sex life – was simply one that had never occurred to me. I mean, I would have conceded the possibility on a strictly conceptual level, but that was as far as I'd have gone. He was a fine physical specimen for his age, but it was like imagining your parents writhing in the throes of passion. And a succubus – that was a whole different level of disturbing. Unwelcome visions flicked through my brain of a naked demonic form, very definitely female, writhing on top of his stretched-out body. The succubus gasped and her – its? – tongue was noticeably forked as it flicked out, and…

I pushed the images aside. Whatever had happened, it surely wouldn't have been like that. And as to Hardknott-Lewis, I had no idea where his predilections lay: whether he had a partner or even what gender set his manly pulse racing. If you'd asked me, I'd actually have guessed he was rigorously celibate, seeing sexual desire as a weakness; something to be overcome with a strict regime of physical exercise. Sort of like the opposite of me, who, while also currently celibate, very much saw sexual desire as something to be relished and enjoyed, if only the damned opportunity would arise.

But you never knew. I'd read the accounts of his earlier days in the Office. He'd certainly gone about his work in a passionate way. Perhaps he was the sort of person who formed attachments rarely, but then did so with absolute, unswerving devotion. Perhaps, in the grand manor I imagined for him, he shared his evening meals with a Lady High Witchfinder – or (I wasn't sure how the terminology would work) another Lord High Witchfinder. At the end of the day, sipping fine brandy, they sat and discussed the finer points of the day's events, commenting wryly upon the features of this demonic attack or that undead horror.

"Are you saying you've been the, ah, subject of an, attack by a succubus?" I asked. We were getting into very dangerous waters very quickly. Cooperating with demonic forces was very, very high on the Office's Big List of Forbidden Things. And if there had, indeed, been congress, didn't that imply some degree of cooperation? A certain … bodily willingness?

And, more than that, why the hell was he telling me any of it?

He paused for a moment – uncharacteristically unsure of himself – and then lifted a third work from his briefcase.

"I went to see Lady Coldwater today in order to obtain a copy of this book. She has a whole shelf of them on Level -1."

"She allowed you to take the book away?" I was impressed. Our librarian hated to lose any of the books in her charge, even temporarily. Especially those on the closed levels. Level -1 was the deepest I'd ever been into the Vault, the floor Oliver Auchter had been hidden on, under Lady Coldwater's protection.

"A certain amount of negotiation was required. Technically, I am her superior and she has to do as I ask." The sparkle of amusement in his eye made it perfectly clear he understood the true situation perfectly well. The Lady did as the Crow asked only if she happened to think it was a good idea.

"Right," I said, trying to sound convinced.

"The relationship is an … ongoing negotiation, and I obviously respect her tradition. That is the modern way, is it not? Things were once so black and white, but now we relish our grey areas. There we are. It was imperative that I saw the book again, however."

He held out a modern-looking hardback with the picture of a red dragon flying upon spread wings on its cover. On the spine, there was a stylized picture of a dragon's head, flame licking from its fanged mouth. The sort of image you see adorning pub signs up and down the country. The book was called *The Red Dragon, a Bestiary of Modern Britain* by one Dr Miriam Seacastle.

"Are you familiar with it?" the Crow asked.

"I heard mention of it but couldn't obtain a copy. In fact, I was assured that none survived."

"No, well, Dr Seacastle rather overstepped the mark when she produced it. Her earlier works were harmless enough, fanciful and extremely inaccurate, but her Bestiary was the product of a great deal of solid research and investigation. It is a short volume, little more than a collection of notes, some of them fanciful, but there is much in the book that is precise. Not only that, she makes several rather inciteful remarks about actions taken by the Office over the decades. Again, some are wide of the mark, others are accurate. We obviously could not allow any of them to enter the public domain."

"The Office suppressed the book."

A pained expression passed across the Crow's features. "We acquired all the available copies of it and took steps to ensure no more were produced."

He handed it over to me. It had a section for each entity described: a line-drawing followed by a paragraph or two of explanation. The details it contained were scant, but I knew enough to see that some, at least, were accurate. Possessed statues were in there, as were malevolent spirits, both of which I'd come into contact with recently. There was also a short piece on the Pestilential Presence, although the drawing accompanying it was highly inaccurate. The reality was *way* worse.

The last page caught my eye: in the acknowledgements section it expressed gratitude *for her invaluable insight* to none other than Dorothy Aphrodite Coldwater.

"The Lady was involved in writing this?"

"She was a consultant on it, filling in a few details here and there."

That at least explained why the book was considered much more dangerous than Seacastle's other works – which, according to the book's backmatter, had lurid titles like *Nightmares and Other Beasts*. If the Lady had provided details, the chances were they were completely accurate.

"How did she come to be involved in the book?"

"Dr Seacastle, I can tell you, is also a member of the Pale Sisters. I assume our esteemed librarian agreed to help in order to warn people of the dangers posed by some of these entities."

"Which the Office could not allow."

"Even if her intentions were benign, we obviously cannot permit such works to circulate, especially when they contain a great deal that is reliable. People do dabble. Officially speaking, none of the entities described in this book exist: they are made-up stories and myths, or people do not know about them at all. They are the monsters of children's books or, forgive me, video games." He waved a hand over my pile of cases. "They need to remain as precisely that. Fanciful, ridiculous, even childish."

"I imagine Lady Coldwater wasn't impressed at having the book restricted."

"She was not, but we were able to come to an … understanding that we found mutually acceptable. She agreed not to offer Dr Seacastle any further academic input, and the remaining copies of the book were housed within the Office's various libraries rather than being destroyed."

I was willing to bet that Lady Coldwater had continued talking to this Dr Seacastle, but I chose not to say so. I turned to the entry on the succubus, marked with another slip of cloth. Seacastle had also provided a modern interpretation of the entity, concluding with:

> Many accounts exist of the emotional and physical harm inflicted upon those who are attacked by the succubus. It is easy to understand why: while physical exhaustion doubtlessly accounts for some of the damage, the wrecking effect upon intimate human relationships and upon the victim's peace of mind or even sanity must be considerable. Guilt can be a powerful and insidious enemy. It is a sad fact that, unchecked, such liaisons can lead inexorably to the victim's demise.

Hardknott-Lewis was watching me carefully as I read. Was it my imagination or was there a slightly, well, haunted look in his eye?

I trod carefully. "These attacks … you have direct experience of them?"

He remained as matter-of-fact as ever. He might have been discussing his weight-lifting regime.

"I have experienced a series of episodes involving an entity that I now believe to be a succubus. They were vivid, but I confess I ignored them at first, assuming them to be illusory, mere hypnagogic dreams. My imagination reacting to events witnessed."

"But now you believe the attacks are real?"

"They have become somewhat more … assertive."

"Assertive how?"

"Danesh, this may seem an odd request, but would you be offended if I stripped to the waist and showed you my back?"

3 – Reading the Runes

The sigils of power used in the various incantations and summonings I have described are often referred to as *letters* in the so-called *forbidden alphabets* – but, in truth, the analogy is flawed. The runes are, more accurately, *logograms*: characters that represent whole ideas, objects or entities. The most obvious parallel is with the lettering system used in Chinese writing – or with the hieroglyphs that occasionally emerge from the mysterious sands of Egypt, carved onto the walls of ancient tombs – as opposed to the small number of simple sounds to be found in any latter-day western alphabet. These arcane sigils have power because they resonate with the fundamental forms and laws of Creation. It is possible there may be an infinite number of them, with those that are currently unknown existing *in potentia* in some shadow realm: written, as it were, in black ink upon black paper set upon a table in an unlit room. It requires only for someone to learn them, or stumble across them, to unleash their hideous power...

–Samuel Bedfellowes, *The Old Ways*, 1847

I grimaced as I sipped the weak *coffi* (I'm picking up Welsh words, but embarrassingly slowly) that the Office's machine invariably served up. Hot water would almost have been preferable. The stuff always looked like it might have some taste to it, but it never did. It wasn't the disappointment that killed you – it was the hope. I'd read the instruction manual from cover to cover, hoping there was a way to persuade the mechanism to put more actual coffee in its coffee, but I hadn't been able to wring any sense out of the words.

Back at my desk, I began to leaf through the notes that had arrived that morning, spelling out the details of the Code 27 the Crow had assigned to me. He could have had everything scanned into MORIARTY, but he liked the old-fashioned approach. The bundle of papers was even tied together with a red ribbon, meaning that my first job was to get everything digitized so I could do useful things like searching and cross-checking. The job didn't look like it was going to amount to much. No doubt someone high up in the *Heddlu*, the Welsh police, had circumvented normal procedure and had asked Hardknott-Lewis to look into a little matter that they wanted to wash their hands of. And so, it had come down to me.

At the bottom of the sheaf of notes and papers, I found the other reason for Hardknott-Lewis resorting to old technology: as well as details on the official case, he'd included, without any comment or explanation, a series of sketches he'd made with swift, firm pencil lines on sheets of artist's paper. He had a good hand: with a few lines he was able to conjure up a series of powerful images. I studied each in turn, finding that I was holding each sheet of paper by its edges as if afraid of touching it. They were all of the same entity: a hypersexualized female form, her breasts bare and her mouth slightly open in rapture. He had depicted her vulva, his own body meeting hers, with a few lines of shaded black, nothing more. Nevertheless, there was something decidedly pornographic in the images and the way they were posed; they seemed like the worst kind of exploitative fantasy art: all those female warriors in unsuitable armour, the witches and fairies wearing very human lingerie. If they hadn't come from the Crow, I'd have dismissed them as adolescent nonsense.

But, in truth, I was already having some trouble concentrating: Hardknott-Lewis's story had been circling around in my head all night like a pack of wolves just beyond the glow of the fire. His confession troubled me on many levels: the thought that he, of all people, was vulnerable was something I found oddly disconcerting. And, an attack on him was also an attack on all of us. I had my difficulties with the precepts of what the Office did, clearly, but I could also see that much of its work was vital. Without us to keep the forces of evil in check, we faced pandemonium. Maybe even *literally* pandemonium. A couple of years before my arrival in the Office, according to the folklore, an abandoned mediaeval summoning circle deep in an abandoned slate mine in the north of Wales had quietly reactivated thanks to the alignments of the spheres and the seasons and begun to vent gibbering, chittering imps through from some hellish dimension. The outbreak had spread substantially before being properly contained, helped by the fact that the area had been largely abandoned by humans. A couple of isolated cottages and one farmstead bore the brunt of the incursion, before the Crow and a few others sealed up the breach and returned reality to its proper order. According to local reports, there'd been a nasty outbreak of a cholera-like disease in the off-grid water supply, nothing worse. According to Office chatter, we'd come close to buckling.

Then there was the fact that Hardknott-Lewis had chosen *me* to be his confessor. I assumed I was the only one who knew, but was it also possible this was a test he put everyone through? If it were, he'd gone to extreme lengths to make it convincing. The marks on his back had been red and livid: gouges rather than scratches. They were also very definitely fresh, overlaying the palimpsest of old wounds and scars that he carried with him. If it was a test, if he'd done that to himself to make his story convincing, then he was even less a person I needed as an enemy than I'd thought. For one thing, you'd need a specially-designed tool to inflict such wounds. Maybe a four-pronged gardening implement with a long handle. Something that would have taken real effort to create or acquire. It didn't bear thinking about.

But, whatever the truth of the situation, he'd stood in

my room the night before, stripped to the waist, and there had been the livid lines scarred diagonally across his back. I'd barely known what to say. In the end I'd gone with, "Do they hurt?" It had been a pretty stupid question to ask.

He'd shrugged his shoulders, his sculpted musculature flexing impressively beneath his scarred skin.

"They sting."

Even in such an awkward situation, he hadn't been able to resist the opportunity to make a point about the work of the Office. Or perhaps he was trying to make sure I stayed true to the faith.

"They are another powerful reminder of the dangers we face, are they not? We may read a message here, if we wish: namely that there are abominations out there ready to cause us untold harm and distress. Even I, well-protected and wise to the ways of the unnatural, even I have been attacked. Forgive me if this sounds like arrogance, but I believe the entity that did this had to be very strong. I was not, at the time, able to resist it and it is, as we speak, currently unchecked."

"Have you had the scars looked at?" I asked. "By someone medical I mean?"

"I adjudge that viral or bacterial contamination is the least of the dangers, but I have taken to bathing in a weak antiseptic solution twice a day to kill any infection."

Ouch. That had explained the faint chemical tang, at least.

"And you experienced, I mean you saw … the creature that did this, can you describe it?"

"I will make some sketches to show to you if you would be willing to assist me with the matter."

What else could I say? "Of course. A magical attack like this needs to be taken seriously."

"Quite so. I am in London tomorrow, but perhaps we could discuss things further upon my return?"

"Yes. Forgive me, Sir, but if this conversation is private, then is this an official investigation? It'll go onto my case list in MORIARTY?" It certainly hadn't been there when I'd left for home that evening, and he had never assigned an investigation to me in such a way before.

Hardknott-Lewis half-turned his head to talk to me over his shoulder, but he didn't look directly, sparing me the stare of his piercing eye. "I'd be grateful if we could leave this off the system for now. There are reasons for me wanting it to remain, let us say, somewhat unofficial."

If anyone else had come to me with such a request, I'd have been duty-bound to report it immediately. As it was, after a moment of hesitation, I'd said, simply, and even though I really did not, "I understand."

"Excellent," he'd replied. "Thank you, Danesh. I will get dressed and leave you in peace. We have talked in the past about the dangers posed specifically to you by the resurgent English Wizardry as a result of your recent actions against them and, of course, as they see it, because of your background."

"You think they're behind this?"

"It is possible. I'm keeping an open mind."

The group had gone quiet since events at Faebrook Folly. With Peter Warder and Evangelina Mormont gone, we had no idea about the identities of any of its members. They remained a shadowy threat. Whispers from the underground – quite literally the underground, sometimes – suggested that they were still active and planning the next move in their campaign, but we had no idea what or when that would be. We had no idea if we were facing one or two lone crazies or a well-organized sect of powerful users.

We also had no idea who, if anyone, was giving them their orders – although there was also talk of a figure called the *Warlock*. Whether he was real, or more Office myth, no one knew. Some had once believed that Mormont was the Warlock; that she'd taken that title as well as *Sorceress* because, well, she liked cool titles. It seemed unlikely now. Assuming that the Warlock figure even existed.

"You should take extra precautions," the Crow said.

"They will be coming for all of us, sooner or later. They will want to harm me because that weakens the Office – a classic decapitation strategy – but you, if it *is* them, they especially despise. I assume you have suffered no … incursions like those I have experienced?"

"No."

"Good, good. The first thing we have to ascertain is how widespread these attacks are."

Widespread was an interesting word.

"Do you know of other cases?"

He'd hesitated uncharacteristically before replying. "I have heard a hint, nothing more. You recall that I had other business to attend to in Herefordshire while we were at the Ndidi murder scene?"

"You were pursuing a succubus?"

He was knotting his tie back up with a practised sequence of hand movements by this point. "Not directly. I was discussing a possible pattern of attacks with an English colleague. We agreed to pursue our own enquiries and reconvene."

"But this colleague has also been targeted."

"I will know more about the matter tomorrow. The situation appears to be suddenly developing: in the past, the attacks I suffered were weak, to the point that I dismissed them as imaginary, as I say. This latest assault was too overt and too powerful to ignore. Something has changed. But I'll speak to you again when I know more. And … thank you, Danesh. This is a delicate situation."

And with that, he'd left me alone.

Now, my best guess was that he'd been killing two birds with one stone by coming to my flat: seeking my help as some kind of expert on succubi, but also testing me to see how I reacted. Perhaps he'd come to me precisely because he had doubts about me, and wanted to see if telling me prompted any change in behaviour from those assaulting him. People he perhaps feared I might be in league with. Despite the betrayals I *had* committed, it troubled me to think that he might have such doubts about me.

Whatever the truth of the situation, I clearly needed to get up to speed on succubi as rapidly as possible. Hardknott-Lewis had consented to loan me the Seacastle volume after I'd promised to return it to Lady Coldwater once I'd finished with it. I'd skimmed through it in the early hours of the morning, but there were still many gaps in my knowledge. I was only just coming round to accepting the idea that succubi were a real threat. So often, the dangers we face are nothing like the figures of popular myth. I guess the truth seeps out sometimes.

I studied the sketches the Crow had provided further, looking for any clue or detail I might have missed. The succubus wore no clothes or jewellery that could have been used to trace her – it? – down in some way, and had no obvious distinguishing marks like a tattoo or scar. This was certainly a succubus from the western tradition, nothing like an apsara or a yakshini. Did that tell me something about Hardknott-Lewis, or about the summoner responsible? There was also something both beautiful and inhuman about its face. There was an avaricious cruelty to it. Had that been there or was it simply Hardknott-Lewis's reaction?

It troubled me more and more that he'd apparently been complicit. He had been an active partner in these acts. Once perhaps, back in the bad old days of the twentieth century, we might have gotten away with shifting all the blame onto the female partner and condemning her for being so helplessly desirable. It wasn't like that now – but where did that leave Hardknott-Lewis? He said he'd been helpless to resist, but if he *were* a willing partner, he'd committed a serious magus law offence, and I had to report him. His mention of visiting London had given me a thought, though: perhaps I could ask to speak privately to Earl Grey himself in order to spell out my suspicions.

Maybe, even, Earl Grey knew all about the Crow's supposed test and was expecting me to do exactly that. Which meant not to do so would be condemning myself. On the other hand, I still felt a strong loyalty to the Crow, despite all my betrayals. Going over his head felt wrong.

The other possibility was that he had committed no crime, because he really had been under the sorcerous control of the succubus as he claimed. There was a defence there; we didn't find people guilty of magus law crimes when they were the unwilling victims anymore. Perhaps I could cover myself by making notes in MORIARTY to that effect, stating that I'd decided to believe his story.

Damn, this was difficult. I had to tread carefully.

I scanned everything I had into MORIARTY, cataloguing the sketches under an innocuous tag that made no mention of Hardknott-Lewis, instead inventing a bullshit code name for the subject. I added my thoughts, though, spelling out my doubts and dilemmas. It would do for now. Then, gratefully, I went back to the other items I'd been given. Before I spent any more time on the succubus case, I needed to keep up with my day job and tackle the official case assigned to me.

A Code 27 is a *non-specific weird encounter* – and is, in fact, one of the commonest categories of shouts we receive. Code 27s cover a multitude of sins – or, put another way, they're too vague to be of much use to anyone. If you didn't know where else to put something but suspect there might be something a bit weird going on, you bung it into a Code 27 and move on. There's a page in MORIARTY with over three hundred of them, all marked as unsolved/no further action required. Every now and then someone reviews them, looking for patterns, but they rarely uncover anything useful. They're something of an Office joke. I'd bored Olwen more than once on pub crawls telling her that my love life was basically a series of Code 27s.

It was the sort of wisecrack that fell a bit flat if you weren't talking to another operative.

I went to find her now to see who was around to accompany me. Since events at St John's Churchyard Gardens and my fun near-death experience with the malevolent spirit, we'd been very keen on the *two operatives* rule when we didn't know what we were facing. Problem was, of course, that we very often didn't have even one operative available. The UK governments obviously had to cover up any funds they directed to us for fear of being discovered and/or laughed at, and the smaller the amounts involved, the easier the cover-ups were. Somewhere in the bowels of Whitehall, there were some very clever and creative accountants spending their days in disguising Office expenditure as something else completely. The rumour was that we were currently kept afloat via the invention of a pair of completely fictitious nuclear submarines. The fact that no one ever saw them was proof of just how advanced the vessels were. We, meanwhile, funded almost but not quite adequately, triaged and did the best we could. Like all the emergency services.

These days, Olwen was very often deployed in the field tackling lower-level threats and intrusions. She'd be ascending to the dizzying heights of *Acolyte* soon enough. To free up resources, we were experimenting with an automated system for receiving calls and alerts from the *normal* authorities. I hadn't tried calling it, but I assumed it was as useless and irritating as every other phone menu system in the known world. Perhaps you had to type in the code number of the mystical menace you were being threatened by, then sit and listen to some recorded minor chord music while the system found someone for you to talk to.

In the end, I decided to check out the Code 27 alone. The notes Hardknott-Lewis had provided were vague, but I could tell from his even-more-understated-than-normal language that he considered the call to be a low-level risk. I did take care to fully log where I was going and what I was doing within MORIARTY beforehand. In the unlikely event that things did go sideways, someone would come looking – and, hopefully, get to me just *before* the gibbering nightmare from the dimensions of madness laid a tentacle on me.

It took me forty minutes to schlep through the busy

pedestrianised streets of Cardiff city centre to reach the
docks. I moved with the tides of shoppers, occasionally
cutting across the currents to escape the flow into and out
of stores. The people around me looked bored, happy,
weary, cross – all the normal range of human responses.
It was good to see. I saw no one glancing around warily
for fear of being attacked by some chittering demon or
slithering revenant. These were possibilities that did not
appear to be entering the heads of my fellow Cardiffers
(to use the demonym). Which was good. We in the Office
were doing our job, because people had no idea we were
there.

Towards the water, a low winter sun shone from the
sky with a cold intensity. It found gaps between the
buildings and shone straight into my eyes, blinding me,
blinding everyone. People became mere indistinct shapes
glimpsed through eyelashes. The cars creeping warily
along were a rumble and an array of gleams, nothing
solid anymore. Down by the bay, the whole town seemed
to be dissolving into cold light.

Shielding my eyes against the light, I pressed on. The
Crow had provided a precise location: an empty
warehouse in one of the more run-down corners of what
had once been *Bae Tigr* – or Tiger Bay in the English.
Mermaid Warehouse the place was called. Someday soon
it would no doubt be converted to high-end flats or an
interesting assortment of ethnic eating outlets. For now, it
slumbered away as an old warehouse, echoing with the
cries of long-departed dock workers. The walls were tall,
looming over me, but the windows were dark and
everything looked quiet. The only sound was the
welcoming background thrum of the city idly humming
away to itself. The occasional wail of an emergency
vehicle. I'd take a quick look around the old building to
check that nothing untoward was taking place, then I
could get back to further studying Dr Miriam Seacastle in
the warmth and comfort of our luxurious offices.

I was circling the building, looking for a door in the
austere brickwork, when my phone rang. My Office

device, its number known only to fellow-operatives.

Olwen was calling me.

"Hey, Danesh," she said.

"Hey. Are you back at base? I only just left."

"I'm in the field. Literally in a field, as it happens, with Digbeth. And I see that you're attending a call all on your own."

"What is it you're facing?" I felt a bit protective of Olwen, even though she was only a few years younger than me. And Digbeth – I didn't know him that well. Kept himself to himself, but my impression was that he'd do anything for a quiet life. How much use would he be if it came to trouble? I honestly wasn't sure.

"Code 23," said Olwen.

Code 23: unidentified ritual activity. It was another category that potentially covered a wide range of activities, from the mundane to the seriously malign.

"Anything we should be worried about?"

The wind whistled down the phone from Olwen's end, making her words hard to make out, and I had to get her to repeat what she was saying.

"Don't think so. A couple of walkers found some rabbit entrails strewn around in a rough circle and got a bit freaked out, imagining all sorts of satanic rites. It's probably just foxes. Or kids. And stop changing the subject; we were discussing you."

"I'm flattered you're keeping tabs on me," I said. "Or maybe slightly creeped out."

"Yeah, sorry. The system pings me when someone logs an action, and if I'm honest, I haven't worked out how to stop it yet. We don't have much of a signal out here so the notification only just came through. Is what you're doing wise?"

"Technically, I'm *reconnoitring* rather than *attending*. That's allowed, yeah?"

"That's bullshit, and you know it."

"Any sign of spookage and I'll get out of here, I promise."

"Kerrigan should be free in an hour. He's heading off

to a *Nazi Hunter* job, but it's nothing that should detain him long."

Nazi Hunter. Office slang for operatives devoted to pursuing your evil magic users and necromancers and the like. Once, there'd had been a whole department dedicated to such threats. These days, we were all Nazi Hunters when the situation demanded it.

I thought about waiting, but too many other things were whirling around in my mind, things I wanted to focus on. "I'm not going to be in any danger poking my head through the door of an empty warehouse."

"Have you ever actually watched a horror movie, Danesh?"

"I've watched *every* horror movie. I have a fully-functioning light, and I promise to keep looking behind me so the masked crazy doesn't lay a hand on my shoulder at precisely the moment I'm not expecting it."

Olwen's sigh was loud through the phone's speaker, like she was breathing into my ear. "I don't like it Danesh. There's too been much weird stuff going on lately."

She seemed to want to talk.

"There's always weird stuff going on," I said. "That's what we do."

"Sure, yeah, but it feels worse, like everything is mounting up. I don't know, kinda … connecting."

"Hardknott-Lewis must have given you the talk about the dangers of seeing patterns where there are none."

"Oh, several times, but sometimes we see faces in the flames because there *are* faces in the flames. You know this. There's too much happening at the same time right now: Hardknott-Lewis heading off to London again, English Wizardry, all the apparently-random calls on our time. The things that happened to you, the continuing situation at Caerlech: maybe it all adds up to something."

I found myself smiling into the phone, although she obviously wouldn't have been able to see it. She was our resident expert on a lot of up-to-date AMM (anti-magical monitoring in the jargon) – and, like all disciplines that involved extensive use of social media, it tended to induce feelings of anxiety or even paranoia. Olwen was working on algorithms that monitored peoples' posts looking for patterns of disturbance or threat – and she'd reported increasing mention of nightmares around the Cardiff area of late. It all fed into her feelings of disquiet.

"Honestly, I think what we're seeing is within normal. Normal for us, that is. I used to think the same, that some unnamed horror was just around the next corner, ready to devour us all. It's easy to let everything get on top of you."

"Yeah, I guess." She didn't sound convinced.

"Let's talk about this after work," I said. "I'll buy you a pint and we can sit in a secluded corner of a run-down pub."

"Well, it is time you explained properly to me about DI Zubrasky and this mysterious Sally woman. There's definitely something going on there you're not telling me."

She meant romantically, not in any dangerously magical way. Didn't she?

"Nothing to tell, but you're welcome to ask."

"Just don't go and get yourself killed before you pay for my drink, yes?"

"You have my word. Where exactly are you, by the way? Where is this field?"

"Gotta go. I'll explain later. Just … don't die. Or *undie*, come to that." She rang off.

I smiled to myself as I slipped my phone back into my pocket. She was a worrier, our Olwen. Which completely made sense to me. Frankly, I'd worry if anyone in our line of work *wasn't* a worrier.

I turned my attention back to the grim warehouse. I'd found the door now – or at least, the ground-level door: weirdly, there were several on the first floor, with no obvious way of reaching them. Handy for the local giants, I guessed. The place certainly looked deserted, and the tiny windows were surely not big enough to squeeze through. I could see no sign of anyone breaking in. The door was solid, securely shut, but I'd been provided with the seven-digit code required to gain access. There was also a key, but I wouldn't need it. The security guard who'd contacted us had left the place unlocked while we investigated.

Another mournful wail echoed around the buildings as another emergency vehicle raced to an RTA. Except, there was an edge of something different in the sound that sent an involuntary shudder down my spine. There was a note of infinite sadness to it – and almost, I thought, a hunger. It sounded organic, the call of some voracious hunter stalking the docks of Cardiff.

I ignored it. Weird sounds bounced around the city sometimes, echoing off the walls. It seemed to be very nearby, just around the corner, but I figured that was an illusion: my primitive hindbrain conjuring up demons in the darkness.

I looked around, just checking that I was alone, wasn't being observed by anyone or anything lurking in the shadows. Olwen would have been pleased with me. The air breathing off Cardiff Bay was icy, seeming to suck the heat out of my fingers and toes, and the weak winter sun was already fading into the gloom of twilight. I was alone. With numb fingertips, I typed in the security number and got it right on only the second attempt.

The report we'd had was from a security guard who'd heard voices coming from within the echoing building. This actually wasn't particularly unusual: homeless people sometimes sheltered in such places when they could, especially during the winter – and who could blame them for that? It also wasn't unknown for groups of youths to break into deserted buildings to drink copious amounts of cheap lager. The security guard had searched the premises and had found no sign of anyone, apart from some graffiti plastered across the walls.

She had, however, insisted that she'd heard voices in a language that she couldn't identify, but that always seemed to be calling to her from somewhere else in the building. She'd step into a room that the voices had been coming from, only to find … nothing. In the end, spooked, she'd left and called the police. Who, in turn, had no doubt sighed and shaken their collective heads and put it through to us.

Most likely, the security guard was hearing echoes coming at her from outside. Or from inside her own head: perhaps she'd been working too hard for inadequate pay and was in need of a good, long break. Yeah, that was probably it.

My phone providing a bright pool of light around my feet, I stepped inside. The good news was that the building had power. The bad news was that only the essential circuits were on – mainly, security and fire-detection. I hadn't mentioned this to Olwen, but I'd have to descend a narrow, shadowy staircase if I wanted to switch all the lights on. I decided against it: as well as my phone, I had a head torch, which I slipped on now. They could be disconcerting to use: if you heard a sound in the darkness and turned your head, the darkness remained behind you. The darkness *moved* to stay behind you.

The warehouse was, indeed, deserted. I stood in a cavernous space stretching from front to back of the building. A line of bulky steel pillars ran down the centre of the room supporting the floors above. There were other rooms I couldn't see into though: at some point in its history, the building had been divided into multiple smaller spaces, perhaps with some thought of turning it into offices or the flats I'd imagined. The inner doors, I knew, were unlocked.

I headed towards the nearest one when the first whispers came to me. It sounded like someone was directly behind me. Despite all my former assurance, I spun around in alarm, heart thundering. There was no one there. Of course there was no one there. I was alone in the empty building. Except, I could still hear the whispers: odd snatches of sound with no words in them, coming at me. I couldn't even say what language, if any, was being spoken: certainly not English, Welsh, Hindi, or any other tongue I had some familiarity with. Were they even words? Possibly not. They were guttural grunts more than anything. Whispers, cut-off growls of rage. The word that came to mind was *bestial*. They didn't appear to be random, though. I began to pick out repeated patterns of sound, the same phrases repeated over and over.

Like, yeah, a chant. An incantation.

The sounds did something to the hairs on my forearms and the back of my neck, actually making them stand on end like in all the good books. There's a word for it: horripilation. It suddenly seemed like a very apt word. The temptation to get the hell out of there was strong, and the reaction of the security guard to do exactly that suddenly made sense – but I was a (fairly) highly-trained Acolyte in Her Majesty's Office of the Witchfinder General, and a few spooky sounds didn't rattle me. I ran *towards* them, not away. That's what we do.

And, the chances were – this is what I told myself – there was probably a perfectly rational explanation. That's what people always say, isn't it? It was, I don't know, the pipes making weird gurgling sounds. Wires in the walls picking up and amplifying radio messages from local taxi firms. Echoes from outside. Hell, maybe there was a black metal band rehearsing somewhere nearby and the demonic utterances were just the lead singer practising his death growl. Which, I had to say, he'd pretty-well perfected.

Then I held up my phone to illuminate the far wall, the point where the sounds were coming from, or echoing from, and I saw what was covering it. Runes from the forbidden alphabets. I'd seen something like them several times – deactivated versions during my training and then the real things in the spell circles inscribed round the bodies of Evan Cornwallis and Martha Ndidi. Hardknott-Lewis himself had laboured to disarm and erase the latter set, explaining their malevolence and making sure I left the room before beginning his work.

The sigils on the wall in front of me, however, were a whole different level of disturbing. The others had been static, hinting at unnamed horrors while just being marks on the floor. These ones were alive – or, at least, they were *moving*, and giving a very clear impression of being alive. Or, I don't know, of yearning to be alive, to steal the life from anything they touched. They crept across the flaking paint of the wall as I watched, replicating, growing. It was like watching some colony of bacteria down the lens of a microscope, or a swarm of something insectoid.

As with the sounds, there were repeated patterns in the runes, like the lines of some incantation repeated over and over. I recognized some of the basic forms of the letters – often, the more powerful runes are enhanced or combined versions of simpler patterns. The sigils in the spell circles around the murder victims had been mainly to do with containment and sealing. These, from what little I could tell, were the opposite: more to do with release. With tears in the fabric of the worlds and the opening of ways. If I had to guess, I'd say someone or something had been summoned through the veils, or had hacked their way into our world across the aether.

The forbidden alphabets have tongues that go with them: arcane, ancient languages that have the guttural sounds required to properly render the runes. Our everyday languages simply don't have the range of raw noises. I hadn't yet learned any of those chthonic syllables – such knowledge was well-protected – but what I was hearing sure sounded like they *could* be from such a tongue.

These, clearly, were what the security guard had heard. Perhaps the infestation had only been minor at the time, or perhaps she hadn't even found it. Perhaps she'd convinced herself it was only graffiti, and wasn't moving. It's surprising how often people convince themselves that things they're seeing with their own eyes aren't really there because, rationally, they couldn't be.

But clearly, we needed to seal the building off, get the Crow in to put a stop to the spreading plague. Wooden doors weren't going to halt it: it was creeping across every surface it could find, and it was growing in scale with every passing moment. Outside, the city of Cardiff stood waiting, oblivious to the threat. The innocent people of the city – and all the others – would have no idea what was happening to them until it was too late.

I scanned my circle of light upwards. The runes were there too, spreading onto the ceiling like a living rot, the whispering and chittering from them louder and louder with each moment. They were creeping over the floor, as well, writhing across the stone flags, seemingly drawing themselves as they went, and it was very hard to escape the notion that they were sniffing me out, coming for me. A vision of a last remaining tiny circle of clear floor flashed through my mind, me standing in it as the vile, evil, live runes crept and crept towards me.

I ran for the door.

Then I stopped, thinking that I should record some images in case they'd be of help to Hardknott-Lewis. I did not want to report that I had simply fled, and the Crow needed to know what he was dealing with. As I had at the Cornwallis murder scene, I held up my Office phone and began to capture images and audio of the profane symbols, getting as close to them as I dared, wary of them suddenly leaping at me. Because, I didn't at all know for sure that that wasn't possible.

I took five, ten seconds of video. Then the phone buzzed, like a message was coming in. Great timing. But instead of stopping, the device began to rumble more and more violently in my hand, like it was trying to shake itself free of me. Confused, I glanced at the screen to see what notification was there – and saw what was really going on. Somehow – I don't even want to think about how – the runes were there on my phone. Physically *on* it: not pictures, but actually creeping off the screen, around the sides and back, edging towards my hand.

One touched me, the tail of one of the strokes like an outstretched tentacle, and a burning sensation flashed up my arm as though I'd been touched with a red-hot brand. At the same moment, alarming, blaring images washed through my brain: screaming mouths, mangled limbs, splashes of blood. I glimpsed a wide, deep pit, dark and bottomless, and there was something down there, something vast and terrible and seething with rage, and then I was falling forwards into the pit towards it. It wasn't anything like one of my disorientating episodes, my blackouts. This was solid, visceral. A physical assault. This was the runes, their magic attacking me.

It was at that point that I dropped the device and, as we say in our MORIARTY reports, vacated the premises.

4 – Holdfast

We call the magical enchantments we work *spells*, and of course *spelling* is also used in the mundane world to mean using the correct letters to make up everyday words. This is not coincidence; the two senses are irredeemably intertwined. Spelling a word incorrectly is bad because your meaning might not be clear and you could end up conveying a wholly unintended idea to your reader. It's the same with magic – only, potentially, much worse. Magic based on the runes of power have to be spelled out – literally spelled out – very, very carefully, or else, again, your meaning might not be clear. This time, the harm could be very much greater; the effect upon reality may be far from that originally intended. Perhaps catastrophically far. A word of warning to the reader of this tome, then. Take no shortcuts. Learn the runes and their meanings carefully. Study them. Study the effects of combining them. Use them sparingly and with hesitation. Be very, very sure that you know what you are doing before beginning to draw out even the simplest of them.

–Bleddyn Williams, *Spellbook*, 1982

I slammed the door of the warehouse shut and breathed in the sweet, sweet Cardiff air. The alarming visions that had flooded through me were gone, leaving only a heaving sickness in my stomach. I held up my hand expecting to see terrible wounds, but I was unscathed. I had got out in time.

Okay, first things first. I needed to know how widespread the outbreak was. I circumnavigated the building as rapidly as I could, sprinting around its perimeter studying the walls and floor. I'd assumed that the runes were spreading outwards from the old building, but what if they weren't? Maybe I was only seeing the outer edge of some larger infestation covering a much greater area. Maybe whole swathes of the oblivious city were, even then, succumbing to the magical rot spreading across it.

The good news was that I could see nothing on the ground anywhere around the building – yet. There was some graffiti on the walls, but it appeared to be mundane, expressions of love or else words that made no sense. I was under no illusions, though: the containment wouldn't last for long. Doors and walls would provide no barrier. I also wasn't seeing what was underground: pipes and drains and ducts would connect this building to other buildings. Ultimately, to all other buildings, and the runes had clearly demonstrated their ability to move onto and through wires and technological devices. For all I knew, they were already seeping along the drains and water mains and phone lines. They weren't going to get very far if they quested southwards or eastwards, out into Cardiff Bay; I doubted even potent magical runes could survive those waters. But any other direction, into the populated city centre – that had to be fertile ground. If the runes had sniffed me out, tasting my life-force in the aether or whatever the hell it was, then the prospect of a third of a million Cardiffians would be irresistible.

Perhaps the outbreak was already widespread, and the rising tide of nightmares that Olwen had reported was real after all. If things got very bad then we'd have to step up our response, maybe even evacuate an area of the city. These were powers we used very rarely, but we had them. We also had various excuses lined up and ready to go if some mass outbreak of lycanthropy or demonism struck: fumes from a chemical factory fire, the danger of explosion from some industrial unit.

Maybe you've heard the news stories.

Back at the entrance to the building, keeping a good

couple of yards of clear ground between me and the door, I called Hardknott-Lewis. I still had my personal phone – the very one that Sally had added her own name to by some mystical means, tagging herself as *Goddess*. We were under strict instructions to keep our work and personal lives separate, which meant leaving no clues or messages about our Office work on our own phone, but this was another injunction I had failed to comply with. I still had a number for Hardknott-Lewis from the days when he'd contacted me in my last year of university. At the time, of course, I had no idea who or what he was. He was in my phone as *Scary Serious Guy*, a label I probably should change. Although, now that I did know him better, it still seemed about right.

I had no idea if the number still worked for him, but it was time to find out. It rang for only a moment before he picked up.

"Danesh, this is a surprise. Your memory for my old telephone number is impressive."

Right. The Crow came from an age when people actually remembered such things. It was a useful mistake – better he think I'd remembered than failed to wipe his details from my private phone.

"Apologies for calling you directly," I said. "But something's come up. Something troubling."

"Have you been able to glean useful information from the sketches I provided?"

After he'd left my flat the previous evening, I'd dug out the box of photocopied textbook pages and sheaves of notes that I'd accumulated during my work on my succubus thesis. I'm not going to lie; I hadn't read all of them as thoroughly as I should have. This time I had: I'd been up until two in the morning refamiliarizing myself with the whole subject. There were still lots of gaps in my knowledge – but I knew a bit more.

"A few possibilities," I said, "but it isn't that." I filled him in on everything I'd found inside the warehouse. There was a moment's pause as he considered everything I'd said. The fact that he wasn't immediately clear on what to do was, in itself, troubling.

"Are you sure there is no sign of these runes anywhere else?"

"I've searched the immediate area and can't see anything. The warehouse is definitely the epicentre."

"Well, perhaps only the centre, although there are, of course, numerous tunnels and caverns and drains beneath the streets of Cardiff that animated sigils could use to travel. It is impressive that you would think of that. You say the runes are moving; can you be absolutely sure on that point?"

He'd trained us to be observant, to report what we experience calmly and diligently. I tried to clear my mind and recall only the facts.

"Absolutely. They were visibly moving across surfaces, and they were very definitely replicating."

"You said you thought that they were coming for you."

"In truth, I can't be absolutely sure of that; it's possible that I was spooked and that the runes were simply spreading in every direction. I can't prove that they were aware of my presence."

"Yet you are convinced that they jumped the gap to the electronic realm. That your phone became ... infected?"

"That's definitely true. They were crawling off the screen."

"Well, they are magical in nature; perhaps we should not be so surprised at such an outcome, although I have never heard of the phenomenon before. You felt their touch as a burning sensation in your hand. My first concern is for your well-being: is it possible that you have become tainted in some way?"

I held out my hand to study, splaying my fingers wide, half-fearing to see the runes spreading up my arm like malevolent, moving tattoos. There was nothing.

"I seem to have escaped unharmed."

"Interesting. Well, that is good. You were able to resist them somehow."

What did *that* mean? "I dropped the phone pretty quickly when I felt their touch."

"Of course. Who wouldn't?"

"There's something else," I said. It had only just occurred to me.

"Go on," said the Crow.

I had to tread carefully. Like I say, I was supposed to know basically nothing about the forbidden alphabets, but I'd picked up a few clues here and there, and I'd taken the opportunity to pick up all the scraps of knowledge I could from the books I had access to in the library. I'd had to fill in time while I was waiting to speak to the Librarian somehow.

"I'm obviously no expert, but I got the impression that the runes were maybe to do with the opening of gaps in reality. Tears and rends in the fabric that keeps the different realms apart. Perhaps of summoning something through into our plane."

There was another pause before he replied. It seemed to go on for a long, long time.

"There are certainly runes of that nature, Danesh, although of course you will not be familiar with them."

"I think I saw something similar at Faebrook Folly, when Evangelina Mormont and Sally Spender disappeared into the portal." I hadn't – or at least, if I had, I hadn't made the connection, but the Crow didn't have to know that.

"You did not mention this in your report."

"It's a detail that's just come back to me. Perhaps I'm mistaken, and all I'm doing is piecing together scraps of unrelated information, but it occurred to me that these runes could have something to do with the – thing – that attacked you." I decided it was probably best not to talk openly about succubi on the phone. I mean, if a keyword like that did raise alarm bells anywhere, it would probably only be referred to us anyway. But still.

"You are suggesting that the summoning of the entity that attacked me took place in that warehouse."

"It's a theory."

"An interesting theory. The location you are in … you need to be careful there."

"It's deserted. I can deal with a few muggers."

"That is not my concern. That site has history, like St John's Churchyard. A tradition of manifestation and haunting activity. Of unquiet souls. There used to be a chapel there, too, a rough sailor's one. It is long-gone but its foundations will still be there beneath the ground. Or maybe the roots go deeper, down to … whatever prompted them to build a chapel there in the first place."

"I'll be careful. I know what I'm doing," I said, although I was thinking more and more that maybe I didn't. "Something else – when I first went in there, when I first came into contact with the runes, I caught a glimpse of something. Like, a vision. I don't know if it's relevant."

"What sort of something?"

"There was a vast pit, and there was something huge and terrifying living inside it. It was reaching up for me, yearning to reach me."

"I see," said the Crow.

"Do you know what that was?"

"Not by name. There are entities that dwell in the aether, huge and dreadful to our perceptions. Perhaps it was one of those. As I say, that place is a focus. This entity you glimpsed might have been attracted there because the veils are thin, or, equally, its presence on the other side might be the reason the site is unquiet in the first place."

"Right."

"We need to find out what has been taking place in that building in, say, the last three weeks," the Crow's voice said. "Someone on *this* side carried out the summoning ritual."

"I'll look into it." If the fanatics of English Wizardry were behind this, then it might be the breakthrough we'd been looking for.

"Excellent. First, we need to secure the area and put a stop to the outbreak. The timing of this is unfortunate; events are moving here in London and I need to stay for a little while longer."

"Although, if my theory is correct, then the timing makes complete sense and it's all related."

"Work on that but keep your mind open as well. Go and speak to Lady Coldwater; she has much relevant knowledge about such magics. She may know how to counteract the runes before I can get back to Cardiff. In the meantime, I shall speak to the regular police about erecting a cordon around the building. We can use our usual excuse of a suspected gas leak. Can you remain there until they arrive?"

"Of course."

"Make sure no one goes inside. That includes you. And if you see any sign of the symbols spreading across the ground outside the building, call me back immediately."

"Can I ask how long you'll be in London?"

There was another pause, and I had the impression he was glancing around a room at the faces of people he was meeting.

"I am not sure," he said. "A day or two. Actually, my intention was to contact you and request that you come and join me tomorrow. There is much taking place here that it would be useful for you to see."

Useful for whom? I wondered. Then another thought occurred to me. A deeply troubling one. You know that sensation when apparently unconnected scraps of knowledge fall into place and you see a pattern? That. I had suddenly seen one possibility of what was going on here: the Crow's suspicions about me, his trip to London, and now his summons. London was where the Star Chamber of the Office would meet: Hardknott-Lewis, as the Lord High Witchfinder of all Wales, Earl Grey, overseeing all of Britain and the British Isles, and then the other five: the heads of Scotland, England, Ireland, the Isles and the Overseas Domains. The Star Chamber was the ultimate decision-making body of the Office. There was no appeal to a higher authority, and its actions and processes were completely secret and undocumented. The chamber certainly had the power to, say, banish a rogue Office operative into Oblivion for crimes against magus law, and no one could stop them.

Was that it? Was that what was going on here? Was I to be given some sort of hearing before being despatched to that living end? It would explain Hardknott-Lewis keeping me active as an operative. Perhaps he'd simply been gathering evidence all this time.

"Danesh?" he said. "Are you there?"

But, again, I couldn't refuse to go. I couldn't run. Not only would it be futile, it would be a clear admission of guilt.

I managed to get a reply to emerge from my throat. "I don't like leaving with all this going on."

"No, I understand, believe me, but sometimes it helps to step back and consider the bigger picture. See if you can at least secure the site today with the Librarian's help. If you can, come up to town tomorrow. You could fit in a visit to your mother while you're here. I understand that she has been poorly."

Poorly, yes. Magically cursed and now, thanks to Lady Coldwater, being magically cured.

"That would be good," I said. "I'll wait for the police then get back to the Librarian."

"Excellent. And, Danesh?"

"Sir?"

"You will be sure to wipe this call from your phone's history, yes?"

"Of course."

I waited twenty minutes for the police officer to arrive – which was an impressively short space of time. Presumably Hardknott-Lewis had talked to some high-level colleague in the *Heddlu* to put things into motion. A sleek, black unmarked car purred to a halt, and after a moment, a plain-clothed officer climbed out. I say *plain-clothed*, but he'd also taken the trouble to slip his stab vest on over his shirt. Couldn't say I blamed him, although it wasn't going to be much help.

I knew him: it was the DI in the know who'd met me outside St John's Churchyard Gardens before my encounter with the malevolent. He was a tall, powerful man, and his bulky vest only served to enhance the effect. His broken nose still gave him that tough-guy, prop-forward appearance. I wondered if he'd chosen to leave it askew to give himself a more fearsome appearance and make his job a little easier when it came to facing people down.

As last time, I wondered why the police had despatched a DI to do what was, basically, a stand-around-and-guard-the-entrance job – something surely more suited to a uniform. The answer was probably to do with that phrase *in the know* – I don't know how many police officers in the Welsh service know of the Office or had heard hints about the array of supernatural threats we face, but it probably isn't many. Perhaps this DI and Zubrasky were all they had at anything like street level. Perhaps getting promoted to DI was a part of the trade-off in having to deal with us rather than carrying out proper policing.

"It's WA Shahzan, isn't it?" he asked as he locked his car and ambled towards me in an *I'm calm, everything's under control here* sort of way. If he was irritated at being despatched to an apparently-deserted warehouse, he didn't show it. Perhaps events in St John's Churchyard had given him a little more respect for us. "I'm DI Evans."

"Thanks for coming."

"You're back on your feet, then. Last time I saw you they were carrying you out of that churchyard."

"It's fair to say things didn't go quite to plan."

"Yes, I got that impression. If this is racially insensitive then tell me to piss off, like, but you looked as white as a blanket of snow on the Brecon Beacons when they carried you out. What happened to you in there?"

After events in the warehouse, it was calming to have a conversation with a normal human for a time. We had a few moments. And, a plan had occurred to me, and I wanted to know if I could trust this DI Evans.

"Best I don't say too much. Basically, an unquiet spirit took a strong dislike to me."

"Did it now? Bastard thing. Well, it's good to see you back on your feet."

"You don't seem surprised that … such things can happen. How much do you know? I mean, how do you even end up being aware of us and what we do?"

Evans looked amused. "Oh, I've guessed more than I know. I've seen a few things over the years, things that didn't make sense. You know how it is. I asked questions and got ignored. I asked more and got ignored more. Most people would turn a blind eye, I suppose, but I kept on, and eventually someone higher up took me aside and had a little word with me. Told me all about you lot and what you do. My fault for being so bloody single-minded."

"Does what we do trouble you?"

"You don't get far in the police if you let things trouble you. Plenty of things happen in Cardiff on a Saturday night that trouble me more, I can tell you."

"Can I ask, are there many others besides you and DI Zubrasky?"

"Don't know for sure; it's all a bit hush-hush, like. Don't take this the wrong way, but I think a lot of the higher-ups are a bit embarrassed by the whole thing."

"And you're not?"

He looked amused. "I'm here to protect the public. Simple as."

"How is DI Zubrasky?" I hadn't spoken to her since reporting my break-in at Sally Spender's house. I tried to sound like I was only making polite conversation, but in truth, I'd idly hoped that she might be the one who turned up in answer to the Crow's call.

Evans didn't appear to be fooled for a moment, judging by his grin. "She's currently investigating the hotel haunting case, or my guess is she would have come."

"The what? I haven't heard of it."

"Just our name for it; I'm sure it's nothing unnatural. Someone was killed in a hotel room and a few people reporting hearing spooky noises at around the same time. And there are some odd details in the case; the person attacked was alone, everything locked up and no sign of any one breaking in."

"Death by natural causes? Suicide?"

If he was annoyed at my patronising attempts to tell him how to do his job, he didn't show it.

"That was our first reaction, but there are one or two details that suggest the victim was attacked."

"That actually does sound like we should be involved."

"If it comes to it, she'll be in touch, I'm sure. You'd be surprised how often people claim or believe something supernatural is going on when really, it's just a matter of some bastard getting their revenge on someone they don't like. Half the buggers probably even believe what they're saying is true."

He glanced an experienced eye over the warehouse. "So, there's something similar to your unquiet spirit in there, is there?"

"This is a very different threat. Again, probably best I don't go into too much detail."

"Are the public in danger?"

"They might be in time, yes. For now, we need to make sure no one goes in."

"Is there anyone inside?"

"I don't believe so. I didn't search the whole place, but if there is anyone in there, the chances are they're beyond our help."

"Right. Lovely. So, what's the plan?"

I came to a decision. Technically, I was in breach of the rules, and the Crow had directly ordered me not to re-enter the building – but, on the other hand, there *were* now two of us, in compliance with Office regulations. Sort of. If you squinted from a distance.

"I'd like to go back inside to retrieve something. Something we can study and perhaps find a way to counter the threat."

"What is it you need to retrieve?"

"A phone. I dropped it when I was attacked." If I could retrieve the device, it might give the Lady something she could work with. And, to be honest, I felt more and more ridiculous that I'd let go of the thing and fled.

"Attacked by what?" Evans asked, getting effortlessly to the essentials of the matter.

I was very aware of how this sounded even as I said it. "Attacked by ... writing."

If he found my statement ridiculous, he didn't give his feelings away. "Writing?"

"Runes. Magical and malevolent runes of power."

He nodded his head, as if this was run-of-the-mill stuff in Cardiff. "Zubrasky said you were mostly worried about the runes at those two murder scenes."

"Sigils drawn by someone who knows what they're doing wield a lot of power, and these are considerably more dangerous than the sets found at the murder scenes. It's possible they're alive in some way. They're certainly malevolent, and they're also spreading. They're definitely harmful if they touch you."

Evans glanced to the building, then back to me. His police-trained matter-of-fact pragmatism didn't waver as he planned out the operation in his head.

"Okay, where did you drop it?"

"Not far inside the door."

"So, we open up, charge in and grab it before these evil letters know what's going on?"

"We need to neutralize the runes covering the phone, too, make it safe for transportation."

I took three items of equipment out of my backpack. Unlike the regular police, we don't walk around with our weapons and gizmos in plain view. I held up the first one for him to see: a small brass contraption about the size of a large marble and carved into an icosagon. A twenty-sided polygon. The fact that it was oddly like a gamer's D20 in appearance was simple coincidence: the device was shaped like that because it could be rolled. A sphere would have rolled further, but you'd have no control over how far the thing travelled across a surface. With a bit of practice, you could position the polyhedral devices just where you wanted them. Symbols were carved onto its twenty surfaces. Touching a particular set of five of them at the same time would activate the device – something you didn't want to happen by mistake. The other symbols – see, I'm trying not to use the word *runes* here – are for controlling the field generated by the device: the size and shape of the affected area as well as its duration. I'd deployed just such a device to freeze Sally Spender's alarm so I could break into her house.

"This is a *holdfast*," I explained. "When it's activated, it generates a containment area that freezes anything inside into stasis. Anything: solids, fluids, your internal organs, it makes no distinctions. If I can position it near my phone and get the timing right, then the runes that have infected the device should be held long enough for me to get it back to base."

"*Should*."

"Yeah. Should." I showed him the other two objects: a simple grabber arm with a telescopic arm and a cloth bag. "With luck, and if I shape the containment field correctly, I'll be able to pick up the held phone with this and place it in the bag for transportation. Once the field is created it isn't going to get any larger. I'll probably get a chunk of frozen air molecules as well, but that's no problem."

"And this bag is also mystical in nature, is it? Some sort of magical holding container?"

I showed him the interior of the bag, like any stage magician performing a track. "Actually, no. The bag is just a bag. I use it to put my shoes in if they get wet."

"And what's going to stop these evil bastard runes from, I don't know, attacking us while we're in there?"

"Hopefully speed. They move, but not particularly quickly. I might have to play hopscotch, leap between clear spaces on the floor to reach the phone. If there's no way through, then we might need to think again. I don't know, some sort of long stick or something."

I had another idea. I pulled a small plastic baggy out of my backpack.

"Earplugs might help, too. There's a verbal component to these runes; they utter syllables that may well be some sort of malign incantation. If we can blot them out, it might help."

Evans took the two nubbins of orange foam that I held out for him. "And what do you want me to do?"

"Stay by the door, on the outside. Keep away from the symbols if they come for you. If I get attacked or lose consciousness, I'd be really grateful if you could grab me and haul me out of there."

"Got some rope in the car, useful for all sorts of things. We could tie it round your waist so I could pull you back if needed."

I nodded my assent. It made sense. I also gave him my private phone, turning off the lock temporarily. I showed him the Crow's number. "If I don't get out, phone this person and say what's happened. He'll understand."

"He's in the know?"

"Oh, he's so in the know that he basically *is* the know."

The massed chittering sound from the runes hit me like walking into a crowded Cardiff pub as I reopened the door, despite the earplugs. In the short space of time, the outbreak had grown. Had my presence had something to do with it, exciting the runes into action? Whatever the truth of it, we urgently needed to stop the outbreak.

The light was fading now, the short day already over, but Evans, being the proficient and well-equipped officer that he was, had a strong light to shine inside the building. He was admirably calm as he surveyed the scene.

"They're moving. And … it's like they're talking." He had to shout to make himself heard.

"Just be glad you don't understand what they're saying," I called back.

"I know slurred and indistinct threats when I hear them."

My phone was maybe five metres inside the doorway, right where I'd dropped it. Runes crawled across it like primordial trilobites thronging an ancient seabed. The floor was also thick with them, but there were one or two gaps the symbols hadn't covered yet. I should be able to tiptoe my way over to the phone if I could get it secured by the holdfast.

I sized up the throw, feeling the weight of the twenty-sided sphere in my hand. I set up the device by pressing the various symbols on its surfaces: area of effect, delay before triggering. I had three of the devices with me, but time was short. I needed to get this right.

I practised the throw once, twice, then made the roll. The holdfast skittered across the floor – too fast, I thought, but then the rough surface of the floor, maybe even the runes, grabbed at it, slowing it down. It rolled to a halt directly up against the phone.

"Nice throw," said Evans.

"All those years of playing Dungeons & Dragons at university weren't wasted after all."

A light blinked three times from the holdfast, and then the shaped zone of stasis I'd dialled up appeared, engulfing the phone perfectly.

Nodding at Evans, feeling oddly like I was a deep-sea diver or some unfortunate worker entering a breached reactor core, I stepped into the warehouse, jumping from blank space to blank space like a character in some archaeological adventure movie evading traps. I managed to reach the phone without the poisonous runes touching me. Although, was it my imagination, or were the writhing, twisting shapes writhing and twisting more hungrily? Maybe. I ignored them. Working quickly, terrified I'd fumble and drop either grabber or bag to the floor, I reached out to snag the frozen lozenge of air in which the phone was entombed. It took a few goes, the grabber frustratingly awkward to manipulate, the patch of space centred on the holdfast weirdly slippery, but in the end I had it. Trying to move quickly and carefully at the same time, I pulled the object nearer to me, across several of the malign sigils, before sliding it into the bag.

I had it. I stood and turned to pick out the steps I'd need to reach the door and safety. Evans was framed in the rectangle of the doorway. His features were indistinct in the shadows, but I thought I caught alarm there.

Studying the floor again, I saw why. The gaps I'd used to step my way across had closed up, the runes writhing on top of each other. The rustling, oddly insectoid sound was louder than ever, like I was standing in the middle of a locust swarm. A hungry, two-dimensional locust swarm.

"You're going to have to run for it, Danesh." Evan's voice was reassuringly calm. And he was right. Just as I'd glimpsed in my imagination, I was standing in the middle of a sea of the twisting, chittering runes, and they had me surrounded.

"Run, Danesh. Run now."

I ran, leaping into the air as I did so in order to limit the number of times my feet had to touch the ground. Evan was winding in the rope attached to me like a sailor reefing a sheet in a storm, his arms working hard.

Something else happened, too: I jumped, and this little light came on in my head, a light that was somehow shining through my body and my legs. Something clicked within me, and I jumped *really, really far*, covering the five metres between me and the door in basically a single bound. Which, from a standing start, is obviously impossible. And that was because I wasn't jumping; I was once again working magic. It was poorly controlled, unexpected, a reflex – but definitely happening. I could feel the power of it fizzing through me as I hurtled through the air towards the door. I could feel the air streaming into my face.

I landed on Evans and we crashed in a heap on the cold, hard flagstones outside. He jumped to his feet, offered me an arm to pull myself up, but there was something guarded, suspicious in his gaze as he looked at me.

But he said nothing. Maybe he thought what I'd done was normal for an Office operative. Instead of asking, he turned his attention to the bag, still clutched in my hand.

"You got it then."

"I need to get this back to base quickly, before the holdfast wears off."

Evans kicked the door shut again with his boot. "I'll keep an eye on the place until you're back."

He peered back into the bag. Something was troubling him. "You lot are all about fighting the use of magic. But this holdfast device of yours; it's magical in nature. I don't get it. And just now, when you leapt for the door. That was something an ordinary person could never have done."

I resorted to cliché while my breathing returned to normal. "Sometimes we have to fight fire with fire."

That appeared to amuse him. "How do you tell the difference?"

"What difference?"

"Between the good fire and the bad fire. Fire is fire in my experience; it all burns the same."

It was a good question. A very good question, one that was a little close to the bone right then.

"It's all in the training," I replied.

5 – The Bookwyrm

Once, the idea of microscopic creatures – creatures we cannot see but that can, for example, move from person to person causing disease – would have been dismissed as madness. Many scientists did indeed ridicule the notion of tiny "animalcules" as fanciful. Today, of course, we know that the microscopic legions are vast and hugely varied. The point is this: what we know now does not define everything that we *can* know. We are stumbling about the cave with our guttering torches, slowly exploring, but the cavern is vast and there are passageways and levels in it that we haven't yet even glimpsed. At best, we may catch distant whispers echoing out from them towards us...

–Dr Miriam Seacastle, *Red Dragon, a Bestiary of Modern Britain*, 1999

The LED on the electronic lock down to Level -1 of the Book Vault glowed quietly green as I swiped my badge over it. The quiet *click* that lock made when it was opening was one of my favourite sounds.

I'd assumed my access to the restricted level – where Lady Coldwater had her desk, and where Oliver Auchter had been hidden away – would have been rescinded after the eye collectors case was wrapped up. But quietly, without fanfare or any sort of notification or induction process, I'd apparently been granted permanent access. Whether this was at the insistence of Hardknott-Lewis, or whether the Lady had decided I was sufficiently trustworthy, I didn't know. I'd decided not to mention it, in case someone saw a mistake had been made and my access was revoked. I hadn't spent long down there, for fear of annoying the Librarian, but I'd delved into a couple of matters as background on assigned cases.

I'd also, twice, checked to see if my card allowed me access to Level -2. It did not. I *had* ascertained how many levels there were in the library, if the titles on a locked set of index card drawers behind the Lady's desk were to be believed. The Vault went down to -5 – where, if Office legend were to be believed, a single, cataclysmic volume of magic was locked away in high-security isolation, probably never to be opened under pain of Armageddon. The three levels between there and where I now stood housed books that were more and more esoteric, more and more dangerous, the deeper you went.

I strode down a shadowy passageway between floor-to-ceiling oak bookshelves, past thousands of restricted and forbidden tomes, all containing clear hints of equally-forbidden lore. I ignored them all, fearing the wrath of the Lady if I stopped to idly browse, although my gaze slid across the spines, picking out titles where I could.

Finding the book you wanted down there was never easy. Hardly any of them were digitized, and couldn't be searched, not even from MORIARTY. The Lady did not approve of making texts easy to work with – quite the opposite. I hadn't yet worked out her cataloguing system, but it certainly wasn't standard Dewey Decimal. For one thing, I doubted that system had the categories our library needed. *Demonic Summoning*, *The Raising of the Dead*, *The Forbidden Alphabets* – these were not classifications you needed much of in your local public library. So far as I could tell, the books in the Vault were arranged completely randomly, although there were little brass plates every few paces, each of which displayed a sequential seven-character code. Each book presumably had its set of coordinates, and if you wanted a particular volume, and could persuade Lady Coldwater of your absolute need, she'd consult a card-based central index to identify which aisle and shelf your book sat on. You *could* browse and find what you wanted eventually – but by then she'd be at your back, blades drawn.

These thoughts were interrupted by odd sounds reaching me, getting louder and louder as I made my way towards the central desk. More so than libraries, our Vault genuinely *is* very quiet. Normally, the only noise to be heard is the creaking of the wooden floorboards as you walk across them – a fact that had always struck me as odd, given how hushed and ordered the library was. This time, though, I could definitely also hear the sounds of fighting: grunts of effort, the thumps of heavy blows on soft bodies, the clear *clang* of steel blade striking steel blade. These were not sounds normally heard in a library, not even ours. I broke into a run, the bag containing the *held* phone with its cargo of malicious runes banging awkwardly against my side. Was the Lady under attack? I hadn't seen her for over a week, and I knew next to nothing about her habits and routines. Was it possible something had crept – or been summoned – into the Vault? I didn't know for sure that there weren't other doorways into the place. I drew my handgun from its holster across my chest as I ran, selecting the standard ballistic bullet from the six available.

The sounds led me directly past the hexagon of desks where the Lady normally sat and worked, the spider at the centre of the web, and onto the heavy wooden door with its lattice of ironwork on the far side of the room. One of the rooms through there was, or had been, Oliver Auchter's safe house. Was he still there? Did all this have something to do with him? The outer door was ajar, a fact which was odd in itself. I burst through, kicking the door open with my gun held ready. Perhaps a bit over-the-top, but you have to take your pleasures where you can. Beyond the door lay the corridor with the three other doors leading off that I remembered from visiting Auchter. Two were shut, but the third, the one directly ahead, was cracked open. The sounds, loud now, echoing off the hard walls, were coming at me from there.

Not pausing to come up with any sort of plan, I threw myself at the door, kicking it wide as I burst in…

…to be met with the annoyed frown of Lady Coldwater, a katana held in her two hands as she stood, poised, beside the mannequin she was practising her combat-techniques against. Sweat trickled down the sides of her face, and her work-out top was soaked with it. In a rack against the wall were the other weapons she'd been practising with: an impressive assortment of staves, clubs, blades and throwing-weapons. There was no one else in the room.

"Danesh," she said, her chest heaving from her exertions but her gaze level, focussed. "Can I help you with something?" The tone of her words was clear: she had better things to do than to help me. Many, many better things.

"I thought you were being attacked."

She swept a stray lock of grey hair behind her ear. "I'm honoured that you ran to my defence, but there is no need, I do this every day to hone my combat techniques. Don't you?"

"I try to," I lied.

"You should," she said, clearly not taken in. "You have some skill, and youth is on your side, but you need to practise constantly. Practise, practise. Work at it every day: the slightest edge could make all the difference between surviving and succumbing the next time you have to fight for your life. Have you brought my book back? The Seacastle volume that Hardknott-Lewis borrowed and then gave you to return?"

She didn't miss a trick. Fortunately, I'd picked it up from my desk on the way down, having drawn out everything useful I could from it. I held it up for her to see.

She took a step closer, something in her stance threatening as if I had mortally insulted her. The tone of her voice dropped a note.

"I assume you've looked after it? No dog-ears, none of the pages stained in any way?"

"Of course." I knew well enough that she protected her books as fervently as a mother lion protecting her cubs. I held the book out for her to see.

"You're not wearing gloves, I see."

"I was very careful, I promise you."

The offering had the desired effect. Her tense, combat-ready stance relaxed, the tip of her katana falling from my eye-line. "Leave it on the central desk, and I'll return it to its proper location." Her eyes narrowed as another thought occurred to her. "Is this about your mother?"

The Lady had promised to do what she could for my mother to attempt to rescue her from the magical curse that she'd been struggling under for many years. She'd eventually asked *some friends from Gravesend* – I assumed, another chapter of the Pale Sisters – to help her, administer the magics required to slowly soothe the disturbances in her head away. I also assumed that Hardknott-Lewis knew nothing about the arrangement, a situation I was happy to maintain. My mother, suffering with the burden of her strong magical curse, would probably be consigned to Oblivion if the Crow were involved. Magus law was very clear on the matter.

Whatever the Gravesend people were doing, it appeared to be working. These days, when I spoke to my mother on the phone, she seemed tired, often sad, but not delusional. She no longer confused me with Az, my dead twin. Her memory seemed to be slowly improving – or, at least, her forgetfulness wasn't getting any worse. Her sadness I took to be a good sign: she was coming to terms with everything that had happened. She was healing. It would take time, of course, and perhaps she'd never fully be better, but she was more and more herself. I tried to visit her whenever I could – and the Crow's suggestion of a visit to London was certainly welcome.

I said this to the Lady, expressed my gratitude. As well as my hope that we could keep the affair as a private matter.

The Lady shrugged, as if none of it was of any great importance. "I think that's for the best. Was there something else? You could have returned the book without interrupting my training, you know."

I held up the bag containing my frozen phone.

"Actually, yes. Something has come up, and our glorious leader tells me that you're the only one who can help with it."

"The Lord High Witchfinder said that?"

"More or less."

"And what is in the bag? More books?"

"My phone."

"Do you perhaps need assistance unlocking it? Or finding Settings? I was under the impression that people of your generation are rather good at such things."

"I'm afraid it's worse than that," I said. I filled her in on everything that had happened. She was our librarian, yes, but as a Pale Sister she was devoted to eliminating evil and destructive magic from the world. And the expression on her face told me very clearly how she felt about the runes I described.

"We need to find the counter-enchantments immediately," she said, "wipe out the spell before it spreads. It is possible that whatever was summoned by these wayward runes is still there, in the circle. All you saw was the backwash, the overspill. Once that's done, we need to find out where the runes came from, who it is that knows such terrible magics, and put a stop to *them*, too."

"Do you know how to read words written in the forbidden alphabets?"

She actually wrinkled her nose in disgust. "I recognize many of the major forms and I'm able to pronounce two or three hundred of the syllables if I have to, although they give me a sore throat and quite often a migraine, too. I am, however, no expert. There are rather a lot of runes – possibly, according to some, an infinite number – and it actually isn't healthy to memorize them. They have something of a tendency to … take on a life of their own, as you have discovered."

"There must be something we can do."

"How long do we have before your holdfast wears off?"

I checked my watch. "Seven minutes."

"Good. Fortunately, there is one down here who is an expert on the runes. And, indeed, on many things. Possibly, if you believe everything he says, on all the things."

"*Down here* … there's someone else living down here in the Vault? Who is it?"

For once she smiled, enjoying my confusion. "I suppose that depends on what you mean by *living*. Follow me, we need to go down a level."

The door down to Level -2 wouldn't have looked out of place as the entrance to some dank, dripping oubliette in the dungeons beneath a mediaeval castle. I think it was oak – not that I'm an expert, but it looked like it should have been – the ancient wood a rich brown turning to an ashy grey as if the door had once been outside, exposed to the rain and the sun. A latticework of serious-looking iron bars ran vertically and horizontally across it, like a cage had been built around a normal door. Four of the horizontal bars had handles on them: they slid sideways to lock into the frame. Four very modern padlocks secured these four ancient bolts. There was also, for good measure, the familiar card-reader: the very one that I'd tried out and that had found me wanting. The doorway sat in the far corner of the room from the entrance up to the ground floor. To reach Level -2, you had to cross the entire floor and therefore had to pass Lady Coldwater, roaming Level -1 like Cerberus guarding the entranceway to Hades.

"It's a serious-looking door," I said.

"Yett."

I didn't follow. "Yet what?"

"It's not a door, it's a *yett*. That's what they're called. You should read more, you find out all sorts of useful things in books, you know."

She had the keys to the door – the *yett* – on an actual large, iron ring of the sort used by jailors in all good fantasy and adventure films. I chose not to mention how satisfying this was to me as she unlocked each bar and slid it across. I'd expected squealing and grating sounds, but the locks and bars opened effortlessly. She'd kept the mechanisms well-maintained.

Finally, she touched the card held in the lanyard around her neck to the reader, and the mechanism released with my favourite soft *click*.

"Follow me. Don't touch anything. Especially don't read anything or take anything."

We passed through the doorway and began to wind down a set of spiral stairs, a rough rope strung around the central spine providing us with something to grasp onto.

"What's down here?" I asked

"Books," said Lady Coldwater. "Obviously."

I expected to find some dank, dripping underground cavern, green slime on the walls, maybe a manacled skeleton or two, but, when the lights began to glow to the Lady's touch on a switch – dimly, no doubt to protect the books – I saw that Level -2 had smooth concrete walls with no sign of slime anywhere upon them. The air felt dry on my face: some mechanism was keeping the environment well-suited to the precious books. The scent of paper and leather was coloured by a faint chemical tang in the air. Something else to do with protecting the books, I assumed.

The nearest bookshelves, however, were more along the lines of what I'd hoped for: six rows of ancient-looking wooden racks filled with weighty tomes. The shelves had desks and pews built into them, resembling something you might find in a church. Oddly, the books had been placed on the shelves with their spines inwards and the edges of the pages outwards, and a thin black chain dangled from each, tethering it to a heavy iron bar running the length of each shelf.

"Do these books have to be chained up so they don't escape?"

Lady Coldwater cast an appreciative eye over them – perhaps as she might a collection of dangerous animals in her possession.

"Of course not. Very, very few of them, at least. The

books themselves aren't dangerous; it's what's written in them that is the problem. The things that people might do with what's written in them."

"You can't see what the books are called. They're the wrong-way round."

"Which is a good thing, but that isn't why the books are arranged like this. This is a mediaeval chained library recovered from a monastery in the borders between Scotland and England, and this was how the Monks kept the books. They're chained because the books were so precious; you could only read them at the shelves. The entire thing was transported here in the 1950s when the monastery in question was … cleaned up."

"When you say, *cleaned up…*"

"The Monks were from a reclusive order, closed to the outside world. It's fair to say that their investigations had taken them to some very dark corners over the centuries. We – the Pale Sisters I mean – found out about them and the Office agreed to rehouse the books in safety. Another example of our fruitful cooperation."

She led me past the chained books to an isolated display-case standing alone in an open space. It was also wooden, but with a glass top. Inside lay a single book, its binding red leather. The cover was stained and mottled, with no title visible upon it that I could see. Was there a hint of trepidation in the Lady's step as she approached the case? Maybe I was imagining it.

"Here we are," she said.

"It's another book?"

"As I say, it's always what's in the book. Let me show you."

She unlocked the display-case with two separate keys and hinged the glass lid upwards. She fished a pair of white cotton gloves from another of her pockets, paused for a moment as if she were psyching herself up to defuse a bomb, then opened the book.

It was one of those beautifully illustrated tomes that mediaeval Monks devoted their whole lives to creating: hand-written and illuminated with colourful decorations and depictions of fabulous beasts. The colours were vivid: purples, reds, shining gold. The opening letter of each page was rendered in highly-decorative calligraphy, all loops and curls, and I could see that a creature like a stylized dragon or demon had also been drawn on each, weaving its tail around the lines of text that followed.

"It's beautiful," I said.

"Less so if you can read what's written. Do you have any Latin?"

"Very little."

"Good; it won't make much sense to you then. The monks who wrote this book had long-left the path of wisdom."

"It's one of the chained books?"

"It is. Every couple of weeks I take one of them and place it in this case."

It was like she was feeding some dangerous beast, a beast that only she could see. It made no sense.

"Why would you do that?"

"Let me show you."

She continued to turn the pages, the ancient paper – I suppose it was actually vellum – crackling as she did so. She moved slowly, as if expecting to reveal some wonder or horror on each successive page.

Finally, she stopped. "There it is. Lean a little closer. Do you see it?"

I leaned in, as instructed, playing her game. The book was open at yet another page of cramped, Latin text. The Monks who'd written it didn't appear to have bothered leaving spaces between the words, which had to make deciphering the text a challenge. The representation of a small dragon, its body all curving, intertwined lines like the knotted shoots of a bramble, or the silverwork of a master jeweller, was there in the upper-left corner. It had been painted with breath-taking care, each tiny scale painted in gold or silver. Its eyes were shut, as if asleep, but the features on its face were so vivid it could have been alive. It curled around the words as if guarding treasure.

I was about to ask what, precisely, I was looking for

when I saw it: the dragon was moving. Two tiny, stylized puffs of smoke lifted from its nostrils, to rise up the page and fade into nothingness. The creature's sides – as colourful as any stained-glass windows with the sunlight streaming through them – were slowly inflating and deflating. The little drawn creature was animated there in the ancient book. It was alive.

"I don't … what is it?" I breathed.

The Lady's voice was a whisper, as if she were afraid of startling the creature. "They have many names: archaeon is one, bookwyrm is another since they appear to enjoy taking on the form of a dragon such as this one. They're often to be found in the really old libraries. This one came here with the chained books."

Bookwyrm. There'd been an entry on the creature in the Seacastle volume, although I'd skimmed over it.

"I've never heard of anything like this."

"No."

"You believe it will be able to read the runes?"

"They are … conceptual creatures," the Lady said. "Beings of pure thought rather than flesh and blood. They inhabit ideas; they don't really live in the physical world at all. Where they come from, I don't know, but what few there are have found their way to libraries because they love words; it's the perfect habitat for them. Words encode high concentrations of human thought. This one will have been roaming around in these book for centuries, absorbing the meanings and ideas contained in the words on the pages."

I dreaded to think what Hardknott-Lewis would have made of such a magical beast ambling around in his Vault.

"I don't see how this bookwyrm is going to get at the runes, unless we transcribe them into a book somehow."

"The creatures are ancient, but they're not technophobic. You forget that paper books are simply a convenient technology too; a way of storing large volumes of data. I believe a computer, a mobile, will be no different. The creature should be able to jump the boundary. More than anything, they're inquisitive little souls."

"And if it can't *jump the boundary*?"

"Then we'll think again, print your pictures off, perhaps. I believe I'm correct, though. I heard of a case of an archaeon taking up residence on the internet. To them, all those computers and datastores are just another library. Once you can read the language you can extract the sense."

I dreaded to think what an ancient creature like a bookwyrm would make of humanity by absorbing everything to be found on the internet.

"Are you sure the creature knows the letters of the forbidden alphabets? Will it be able to speak this language?"

"If you believe what they tell you, they speak *every* language, understand more or less everything. They are somewhat arrogant creatures, but their wisdom is vast. Now, give me your phone. I want to ensure it's properly isolated before your containment void, your *holdfast*, wears off. The last thing we want is for these runes to spread into the Vault."

She took the phone from the bag, still frozen inside its chunk of stilled air, and placed it next to the book in the display case. Then she closed the lid once again and … did something. I saw a rapid lick of her hands, moving in a very deliberate pattern. Very clearly, she'd worked some spell to seal the phone away inside the case. I chose not to say anything.

"These bookwyrms … how do you communicate with them? If they're purely conceptual entities, they can't hear us talking at all."

"They pick up echoes of our presence – something like seeing ghosts for them, I believe – but to converse properly there are certain spells, the working of which allows us to enter their domain for a time. If they do not wish to grant you access, then you don't get in, but if they are amenable, they will talk. The creatures are fickle, but they can be useful. I will give this one a chance to study your phone, then attempt to … seek an audience."

Once again, she was spelling it out before my eyes: she

was a magic user, openly weaving spells. Unlike the Office of the Witchfinder General, the order to which she belonged (or, officially, *had once belonged*) saw a clear distinction between benign and malign magic use. Office policy asserted that all magery was corrupting – although that didn't stop us using m/tech devices like the holdfast. Grey areas. Supposedly it was more acceptable to use preconfigured devices, whereas the Lady was wielding spells of her own. It was, clearly, absolutely forbidden, but I wasn't going to say anything was I? She knew plenty of incriminating details about me, too. We were complicit in our betrayal of Hardknott-Lewis, the Office, and everything I'd vowed to stand for.

It was best if we simply kept everything quiet.

Inside the display case, the illustrated dragon was moving, making a little show of sniffing the air. It appeared to know that some fresh source of knowledge had been given to it. It picked its way across the page, prowling across the lines of scrawl like a series of stepping stones from one side of the ancient tome to the other. We waited in silence until, finally, the holdfast's incantation expired. The molecules in the frozen chunk of air began to move again, and my phone fell to the surface next to the book. The runes crawling off its screen moved again, winding across its surface like the tendrils of some plant.

I glanced aside at the Lady. An expression of disgust passed across her features at the sight of the runes. She saw something of what they were about.

"Is the bookwyrm safe?" I asked. "Won't it be infected too?"

"It can't be harmed. It doesn't exist in the same universe as the runes. It is only exposed to the *idea* of the runes."

Now the little dragon had reached the edge of its page. It sniffed the air, although I could see no reason for it doing so; it was a very organic gesture. Perhaps taking on the form of a wyrm affected its behaviour – something like sculptural determinism for possessed statues. The creature leaned off the page, a forked tongue flicking from its vividly-coloured snout. The runes wound and looped nearby, reaching towards the bookwyrm. Finally, the two met, touching across the gap between them. The runes crawled over the body of the bookwyrm like some hideous disease, but the little creature appeared unconcerned. It flowed onto my phone, circled once, then became nothing more than a pixelated image on the screen. I couldn't be sure, but it was either licking the runes – or eating them.

"How long will it take to get an answer?"

"An hour or two. Or a week or two. Bookwyrms don't like to be hurried. Tell me where this warehouse is and I'll meet you there. Let's say three o'clock."

It was around midday now, so that worked. The Lady rarely ventured out of the Vault, but she was fearsome in the field when she needed to be. I'd be glad to have her with me.

I told her the whereabouts, and she noticeably stiffened.

"Do you know this place?" I asked.

"If it's where I think – yes. It's a nexus. A point of weakness in the walls between the worlds. Many bad things have happened there over the years. Some places should be sealed off and never used again."

"Will the two of us be enough?"

"That depends on what the archaeon finds, and what the runes are doing. Is there anyone else who could accompany us?"

Olwen and Digbeth would be out for hours yet. The others were scattered around South Wales on various operations, although there was Kerrigan, attending his Nazi Hunter job. I'd picked up his request for backup on MORIARTY; he'd decided there was a low-level risk to what he was facing. I could join him, help wrap his case up, then bring him with me to meet the Lady at the warehouse.

We just had to hope the runes stayed nicely in their box and didn't spread out onto the streets of Cardiff before then.

6 – El Encantador

The sorcerer, the enchanter, the cunning man, the wise woman, the alchemist, the seer, the expeller – all are to be treated with likewise suspicion. For most, lacking the strength of mind, untempered by the necessary discipline, the whisperings of powers beyond the veil are too much of a temptation. While it is undoubtedly true that the benign can appear superficially to be ill-intended, it is also the case that, beneath the skin of the seemingly good, the apparently saintly, there lies all too often a rotten heart pumping out only blackened blood.

–Sister Anna Dottery, *The Pale Sisterhood*, 1886

Kerrigan's Nazi Hunter job turned out to be less troublesome than I'd feared. He was staking out a supposed rogue enchanter in the suburbs of Cardiff, the part of town where the city sprawls off down the coast to meet up with the tendrils of Newport coming the other way. All I knew was the name of the user he was pursuing – *El Encantador* –from which I'd summoned up an image of an extravagant wizard with flashing eyes and a goatee beard. He wore deep red robes and whispered spells that conjured up poisonous spiders or dancing flames. His lair would be some deserted church or gothic townhouse nestling behind high iron railings and overgrown gardens where blowsy flowers filled the air with their heady scents.

The truth ended up being rather more mundane: a drab, square, pebble-dashed meeting hall in the heart of a housing estate. I squeezed the Mini into a gap between two people carriers. The hand-drawn sign on the hall door only increased my sense that there was nothing much here to trouble the Office: El Encantador was a children's entertainer, performing *magical tricks and incredible illusions* for a midday audience of young families. It was hard to imagine anything less threatening to the natural order of the world. The poster also told me that the show would be over soon. I could grab Kerrigan and fill him in on the way back into Cardiff.

Inside the little hall, the audience was strictly segregated into two groups: at the front, near the stage, fifteen or twenty children sat cross-legged. On the other side of the divide, at the back, were the parents and grandparents and aunts and uncles, taking the opportunity to sip a cup of tea and have some welcome peace. There was basically no contact between the two sets of people: kids and parents were enjoying time with their own peers.

It was immediately obvious that the show wasn't going well: the children were laughing and rolling around, paying little attention to events on stage, occasionally punching each other or pulling each other's hair. The adults, I was glad to see, weren't doing any of that.

El Encantador wore the flowing purple robes and pointed hat that all real magic users prefer. Not really – although, if they did, it would make our lives a hell of a lot easier. He also carried a short wand with the required black with white tips, and his hat was adorned with silver stars and moons. I watched as he lifted this to reveal a white dove perched upon his head. That got a subdued snigger from some of the kids. It was also hard to miss the fact that he was balding, with bushes of greying hair above his ears and smooth scalp between.

Didn't the dove's claws scratch, I wondered?

Kerrigan saw me and worked his way through the throng. He was carrying a plastic cup of tea but was also, I saw, filming the performance on the stage with his phone – his personal phone, not his Office one. He carried on recording as he crossed to meet me. There was no mistaking the sheepish look on his Viking-warrior features. He was embarrassed at calling me out to such a place. He was dressed in his habitual uniform of jeans and rock band tee-shirt. Despite his berserker appearance, he actually favoured groups from the softer end of the spectrum, all bouffant hair and eye-liner. It always amused me. But then, tee-shirts from your harder death metal acts weren't going to be very acceptable within the Office. He'd been good to me during my recovery from the eye collectors case, making sure I wasn't overdoing it. That was Kerrigan: team-player, decent bloke. But a small part of me, also, wondered if Hardknott-Lewis had told him to involve me, keep an eye on me.

Paranoia, probably.

He spoke before I could say anything. "I know what you're thinking, laddo."

I said it anyway. "I'm fairly sure that real users don't advertise the fact with a nice, colourful poster."

"Ah, he's clever, see. That's what he wants us to think." He studied me more carefully. "What's happened? You didn't just come to provide back up, did you?"

"Can we talk outside?"

"Give me two minutes. I don't want to miss anything."

I could spare a few minutes, especially if it meant having Kerrigan with me back in Cardiff. DI Evans was under strict instructions to call me if anything suspicious manifested outside the warehouse, and so far I'd heard nothing.

"You're enjoying the show that much?" I asked.

Kerrigan's glance went back to the kids by the stage. "Thing is, I've brought Jac along. Thought I'd kill two birds sort of thing and give his mum a bit of time to herself. He's started school part-time, but he's off today."

Right. Things were beginning to make sense. Jac was his older boy, five or six years old. I could see the lad peering at us over his shoulder, his hair cropped short and a cheeky grin on his face. If Kerrigan had brought his beloved son along with him, then he really wasn't worried about getting into a magical fire-fight.

I played along. I liked Kerrigan. "Your son, yes. Excellent cover for our operations."

"Exactly what I thought," said Kerrigan, grinning through the jungle of his beard.

"You're filming it for him?"

"Promised him I would. Proper little witchfinder he's turning into. Wants to study the performance to work out the tricks."

"I'm impressed you can drink coffee while holding a phone."

"We have a three-month-old at home. I can do *everything* one-handed."

Now, the magician was working some subtle close-up magic using an unfeasibly complicated wallet, making money or cards or some such disappear and reappear in unexpected places. The children were becoming more and more unsettled, their neat lines breaking down, half of them not even watching him. Wallets were boring. This magic show was boring.

El Encantador looked up, scanned the crowd, and I caught a definite hint of panic in his eye even from the back of the room. Panic and something else, too: anger, perhaps, that his life had come to this. It was maybe even fear. Fear that this was all his life would amount to. He was about as far from a genuine, dangerous user as it was possible for someone to be.

"Tough audience," I said.

"You have no idea."

"I assumed entertaining kids would be easy."

Kerrigan shook his head in a pitying, wise-old-elder kind of way. "There speaks someone who doesn't have children. Take my advice, enjoy your freedom while you still can. You and me – OK, not you and me, any normal adult – they know there's no such thing as magic, right, so they love it. They enjoy being deceived; they enjoy trying to work out how the trick is done. Jac though, kids his age, they *know* the world is a magical place. They're not disillusioned yet. Producing some doves out of thin air isn't going to impress them, believe me. In their heads, this sort of thing happens all the time. Things are constantly appearing and disappearing. People, food, toys, you name it. Their whole world is a fantasy. How do you impress an audience like that?"

"Okay, how do you?"

"Beats me," said Kerrigan softly, his eyes on the far end of the room.

At least El Encantador appeared to realise his tricks weren't landing. He slipped the wallet into a handy pocket – apparently wizard robes had pockets, which had to be useful – and stepped back to wheel a curtain on a frame to one side of the stage. Then he wheeled an identical device onto the other side. Finally, he held up his hands as if to work some dire enchantment and spoke in a booming voice.

"For this next trick I need a volunteer from the audience. Who would like to come up?"

The arms of roughly half the audience shot in the air – including Jac. The other half – that would have been me at that age – studiously kept their arms down and avoided all eye-contact.

"Let me capture this," said Kerrigan, "then we'll talk. Won't take a moment."

El Encantador picked one of the volunteers, a boy, and invited him onto the stage. He then produced a cake and broke into some patter about it being dangerously magical. If anyone ate it, it would turn their poo sparkly pink. This detail elicited an amused response from the audience. Now he had their attention. Then, for reasons that were not completely clear, he put the cake on a little table behind the right-hand curtain and hid it from view. He made a little show of fussing around with something at the front of the stage, leaving the young boy alone by the curtain. To howls of amusement, the boy peeped behind the curtain and then, plucking up courage, finally unable to resist the cake, stepped through.

After a few moments, El Encantador pretended to suddenly notice the hullabaloo. He turned to look at the curtains, puzzling over the whereabouts of the boy. When he asked where the boy had gone, the audience, showing no solidarity with their former comrade, pointed at the curtain and shouted in delight that he was behind there, eating the cake.

The magician milked it for some time, claiming not to believe them, then finally relented. In pretend fury, he marched to the curtain and pulled it aside to reveal the intact cake on its stand but no sign of the boy.

There then followed a whole back-and-forth with the children as the magician refused to believe them, in best pantomime style. Finally, he pointed to the other curtain. Did they mean that one? Was the boy there? Of course, he was not. He could not be. And yet, when El Encantador finally threw back the left-hand curtain, there the boy was, somehow transported across the stage, a chunk of cake gripped in his hand and smearing his mouth. To the watching children, the revelation was about the funniest thing they'd ever seen.

"How the hell did he do that?" I asked. The floor was solid; I could see no mirrors or other curtains the lad could have hidden behind. There were no doors in the back wall that the stage wizard could have used to perform the switch. "Is there something going on here after all?"

Kerrigan only shook his head. He leaned over to whisper. "You don't come to many kids' magic shows, do you? Relax; that was textbook. Boy's a plant. Twins probably, playing along."

"Right, yes."

"Come on, I've recorded enough. Let's talk."

Kerrigan followed me into the car park. "Go on," he said when we were alone, "tell me what you're up against."

I filled him in on recent events – missing out all the details of the bookwyrm and the Lady's magic use. When I was done, Kerrigan puffed out his cheeks, then stood and shook out his long hair before knotting it back into a ponytail.

"If her ladyship is meeting us, then it has to be serious."

"It did not look good, I have to tell you."

His previous jocularity had gone from his features, to be replaced by the steely determination he kept for serious field operations. "Right you are, that trumps El Encantador. I'll drop Jac off at his mother's, and we can go do some real work."

I couldn't resist. "And leave this dangerous wizard running free?"

Kerrigan grinned. "I'm not *just* here for some free child care. I haven't completely got you here under false pretences. The thing is, I did a bit of background research on this wizard, like, looked into his name. His real name."

"He's not really called El Encantador?"

"He's *really* called Hywel Williams from Swansea. A web designer who does a bit of kids' magic on the side. I think he probably saw the name on a trip to Spain some time and liked the sound of it. He used to call himself Wizard Dizzy, but he's obviously trying to be a bit more professional, like."

"Right, so, I don't get why we're here."

"The name, Williams. It's cropped up a lot in our records over the years."

Kerrigan was as Welsh as the Welsh hills; he obviously knew how common the name was.

"Did you find anything on Hywel?"

"There were a few flags on his father and grandfather, both of whom liked to don the robes and pull rabbits out of hats, but that's about it."

I couldn't resist. "Father and grandfather. Seems we have a magical dynasty on our hands. Nothing else to go on?"

He ignored my hilarious sarcasm. "The only other suggestion was from ten years ago. There was a bit of a ruckus in Swansea; a possible sighting of our old friend the Lurker in one of the old smugglers' tunnels. A family were slaughtered in their home nearby, ripped to shreds they were. In the end we had to invent a gas explosion and reduce the place to rubble to get rid of the evidence."

"Williams was involved?"

"He lived a short distance away. It's conceivable he was dabbling, attempting to call the creature up from the depths and it all went pear-shaped and got a bit murdery."

"Or it's a complete coincidence."

Kerrigan stroked his beard, but I could see from his grin that he knew we weren't really going to find anything. A moment later, the clatter of footsteps told us that the show was over. Back inside, the kids came running back to find their adults. Kerrigan's face lit up as his son told him excitedly about things we'd just seen for ourselves. As we headed outside, I scanned the crowd, looking for the twins who'd been stooges in the teleportation trick, but there was no sign of them.

I guessed you had to be careful not to spoil the illusion.

I did catch a glimpse of El Encantador, though, by the rear entrance of the little meeting hall, the door to the kitchen. Silver beer kegs were piled up beside overflowing bins, and he was sitting on one of them, leaning backwards against the wall. He still wore his hat, but it was pushed back off his forehead. He was vaping, staring into the middle-distance. He seemed to sense my gaze upon him and looked up. The hunted expression was still there on his features. He looked drained. Why did he do this to himself?

I tried to convey my appreciation of his show with a nod of my head and a smile, and Kerrigan and I headed for our cars.

7 – Forbidden Alphabets

We dealt with an adjunct to the matter of the possessed children at the Tiger Bay orphanage today. More and more, I am convinced that there are certain points on the surface of the Earth, certain odd corners, where lines of force cross or the walls between the worlds are unaccountably thin. We uncovered one such today, in the crypt of a rough chapel built in times past within the bay area. I do not like to think what grim gods have been worshipped in that unholy catacomb, but I am in little doubt that this location was, in fact, the source of the ensorcellment that so afflicted the children, rather than some foreign sorcery from a cargo ship as I had previously supposed. We did what we could to seal the portal, employing both magicks and the strong iron of chains and padlocks.

–Isaac Shackleton, Lord High Witchfinder,
Personal Journal (written in private cipher), 1888

Back at the warehouse, Evans had been magically replaced by Zubrasky. She was leaning against her car, arms folded, watching me with an amused expression on her face, as we approached.

"Hello, Danesh."

"DI Zubrasky. Do you know Kerrigan?"

She acknowledged my colleague with a nod of her head. "Our paths have crossed. Glad you could finally get here. Wouldn't want these dangerous letters of yours to get out of hand."

"Any sign of them manifesting outside the building?"

"Manifesting?" She obviously knew what the word meant, but she did enjoy taking the piss out of our arcane terminology. Which, fair enough.

"Appearing."

"There's nothing. I've checked all around."

"Has anyone come near, attempted to gain access?"

"You're the first. No one's gone in, no one's come out. We had a couple of people wandering around about an hour ago but judging by their Torchwood tee-shirts, they were lost Dr Who geeks. They didn't even look at your warehouse."

"Okay, good."

"The sound coming from within though: it's louder, I'd say. It's like there's a room full of crazy people in there having an argument. I take it you've found a way to neutralize the threat to the public?"

"We're just waiting on one other agent who will have the answers we need."

"Three of you. Wow. This must be a *seriously* dangerous threat we're facing here."

I ignored her barb. I hadn't heard anything from the Librarian; she was not one to log her activities in MORIARTY or, indeed, to follow any proper procedures. I caught Kerrigan's look, and he wandered off a few paces to mutter into his phone in an attempt to find out where Lady Coldwater was.

Zubrasky was watching me, although I couldn't make out her expression in the low light. Let's go with a combination of fondness and admiration. I hadn't spoken to her since she'd helped me with information about the taxi that Sally Spender had taken to set her trap for Evangelina Mormont.

"Evans told me about your hotel ghost case," I said.

"Oh, he did?" Her voice gave me the clear impression that she thought he shouldn't have.

"Anything we should be concerned about there?"

She paused before responding. "I don't think so."

"You don't sound sure. Someone died in a hotel room."

"Which happens surprisingly often."

"But there were unusual noises."

"Have you ever been in a hotel?"

"I got the impression from Evans that there was a bit of a locked room mystery going on."

She hesitated again, clearly in two minds about what to tell me. I wasn't police, so she wouldn't normally say anything, but I *was* law-enforcement. Of a sort, depending upon what you meant by *law*. And maybe she thought she might need me at some point.

It would have been nice to think so.

She decided to fill me in on a few facts. "A young woman called Maude Woebegone was found dead in a room. As you say, locked from the inside, no sign of anyone else being involved. Normally you'd think suicide or an overdose maybe, but this felt different."

Felt was an odd thing for her to say. She was normally only interested in hard evidence. She had no magical abilities, latent or manifest.

"Different how?"

"The toxicology results rule out any kind of overdose, or any kind of dose come to that, and from the autopsy we know there was no auto-erotic asphyxiation going on. That tends to be men, anyway, right? She'd had a few bouts of mild depression, but so far as we can tell, nothing that would have led her to attempt suicide, and no known recent flare-ups. She'd come to Cardiff for a gig, a bit of fun. Nothing that should have led to her death."

"You must have established a cause."

"That's where it starts to get a bit unusual. The post-mortem couldn't find one. She was young, healthy, physically fit, with no underlying health conditions. She'd just made herself a cup of tea and she was lying on her bed and she just … stopped."

"Some medical condition we don't know about or they didn't find. That happens."

I could see Zubrasky nodding her head in the low light. For some reason it felt like she was trying to convince herself when she replied. "Maybe. Something else, though. In her last moments, she was trying to send a text. We unlocked her phone using her fingers. She appeared to be in a hurry, or distracted, or unable to see what she was doing, because she was mostly typing nonsense. Yet the lights were all on in the room."

"Nonsense like misspelled words or words you didn't recognize?"

"Just nonsense. No encryption going on that we can spot."

"They could be pre-agreed code words."

"Who does that? She worked at a veterinary surgery; she wasn't some kind of spy."

"If you want us to take a look at them, see if we can pick up something, we can. I assume the evidence is all logged in HOLMES?"

"Of course. Which also means you have full access to it without any of us knowing, yes?"

It did – but I wasn't supposed to admit it.

"I'll arrange access," I said. "Maybe it's nothing, though. Maybe the unidentified health condition was affecting her muscles. She was in agony, or her vision was affected. Who was she sending the text to?"

"She hadn't picked a recipient."

"Anyone suspicious in her contacts?"

"No one that raises any flags with us."

"I'll check on those, too."

"I don't like it, though," Zubrasky replied. "It seems too easy to leave her as an open verdict and move on. If someone did this to her, I want to know about it. Maude was young. She was only a year or two younger than me."

I'm sure Zubrasky pursued every criminal she came up against with equal vigour, but clearly the lonely death of this young woman was troubling her. Zubrasky was good at her job: tough, rigorous, but also compassionate. She hadn't lost her idealism despite everything she'd witnessed. She was the sort of officer you wanted on your side.

"There's probably not much I can do," I said, "but I can come and look at her, look at the crime scene if you like. If it can wait a couple of days."

"We've extracted all the evidence we can from the room; there's nothing to see there. You might be able to get something from her though?"

She was talking about an Assay: the ability that adepts like our pet necromancer Gilroy had of conversing with the vanishing souls of the dead. It was possible I could persuade the Crow to allow it.

"How long has it been since she was killed?"

"Four days."

"That's a long time. The … process we carry out; it needs to be done as soon after death as possible."

"So you always say. We only found her yesterday."

"I'm simply stating facts. We can try, but there may not be much we can pick up after all this time. And my boss; he's wary of allowing this to be even attempted. I think he's worried that it will become routine in every unexplained death."

"So, maybe that wouldn't be such a bad idea. Most killers are known to their victims."

"But you couldn't use such evidence in a criminal court."

"But it would give us leads so we could track down evidence we could use."

I couldn't argue with her because she was right. The Office insisted on only using magic when absolutely necessary, but more and more that seemed like a flawed approach. Also, I felt like I owed Zubrasky several favours at this point in our professional relationship.

Also, also, the fact was I wanted to be in her good books. Was that wrong? When she smiled and looked into my eyes – when I could see her eyes – it was just a little bit like the sun rising in the morning. My own feelings confused me. When I thought about Sally my heart went fluttery, but then here I was with Zubrasky and something similar was happening. A non-professional relationship between us was maybe never going to work out given our respective roles but, hell, I'd damn-well like to find out for sure. She'd never shown me anything beyond banter and polite friendship in the past, true, but maybe I was as much to blame for that as she was. And verbal sparring: that was something. Who bothered to do that with someone they didn't care about? In a dysfunctional male way, banter was an expression of love, right?

"I'll see what I can do," I said. "I can't promise, but I might be able to get it sanctioned."

I thought she was going to place a warm hand on my arm, thank me fondly. That didn't happen. I pressed on anyway. Maybe it was the imminent danger; the desire to seize life while I still had it.

"I was thinking, also … perhaps we could meet up outside of work some time. Grab a coffee, or a proper drink."

"Seriously?"

Not the response I'd been hoping for. "Seriously."

"You ask me this now?"

"It's taken me all this time to summon the courage."

"The last time we spoke you were asking me to break the rules and track down information on a woman called Sally Spender. So far as I could tell she was simply a civilian with no magical connections whatsoever. Someone you were pursuing."

Right. Sally's cover had been very good. What did Zubrasky think: that I spent my working day trying to arrange my romantic life?

"It was a professional matter, I assure you. She was tied up in the *eye* case."

"Which you would say."

"It's true."

"But you can't tell me anything about her."

"No."

"Did you find her?"

"I did."

"And, is she still around? What's the situation here, Danesh? Are you trying to get off with her? Or me? Or both of us at once?"

She was asking a good question. A question I really needed to sort out for myself. There were days when I was so filled with desire – lust, I guess – that it all got a bit unfocussed, a bit broad-brush. I needed to get my head together. I needed to grow up.

"I mean, not both of you. Not together, I mean. I honestly haven't seen her since that day, but I believe she's still around."

Which was true. *Someone* had sent me a copy of *The Picture of Dorian Gray* with *Borderland Reading Group*, written in a familiar script, and it seemed likely that it could only have come from Sally. Which meant that she'd survived her leap across the aether, defeated Evangelina Mormont, and returned – although in what state, I had no idea. I also had no idea where she was now. I'd checked on her house in Cathedral Road, as well as her flat opposite it, a couple of times, but there was no sign of her, no sign of anything magical or unnatural going on. No sign of anything *anything* going on.

"I don't know, Danesh. There are too many things you can't or won't tell me. That doesn't seem like a good basis for a relationship."

"I get it. I just thought we could go for a drink, nothing heavy. I know I can't always be completely open about what I do, but you can't either, can you? What's your alternative, only date other police officers?"

"How do you know I'm not?"

I didn't. I'd made no attempt to research her in any kind of intrusive way. I'd already done too much of that.

"I don't. Look, I'm sorry I asked. This clearly isn't the ideal time."

She may have smiled at that. Her voice definitely softened a note. "Actually, it is sweet of you to ask. I'll think about it, okay? Things are a bit complicated at the moment, workwise and otherwise, but ... yeah, a drink might be nice. Just stop treating me like a useful police contact you can tap up and nothing more."

It was maybe as good as I could have hoped for.

"Yes. Right. Will do. Sorry."

She stood up straight and looked at something behind me.

"Is she your other agent?"

Over Kerrigan's shoulder, I could see Lady Coldwater was approaching. I could understand the scepticism in Zubrasky's voice. The Librarian looked like a small, frail woman who'd wandered away from the shops and was now lost. She was even – and I thought this was a nice touch – pulling one of those two-wheeled shopping trolleys from, like, the 1970's. Zubrasky probably calculated that there were tins of cat food and loaves of bread in it. My bet was on arcane weaponry and spellbooks.

"That's her. Probably best if you let us handle everything from now on."

"Casting me off again once you've got what you want from me?"

"That isn't…"

"I'm kidding. Trust me, I have plenty of better things to be doing. Sort out that investigation into Maude and let me know. As to the other thing … I'll text when things are a bit calmer, okay?"

She nodded at Lady Coldwater, climbed into her car and purred away. Kerrigan, the Librarian and I stood in a little circle while we discussed tactics.

"Did you discover anything about the runes?" I asked.

I was wary of what Kerrigan knew about her, but the Lady, clearly, didn't give a damn.

"Enough, I think. They're definitely summoning runes, some enchantment that has boiled out of control. Probably the user working them didn't fully understand what they were doing. The containment aspects to the spell are there, but they're broken and ineffectual, lost in the noise. Still, that suggests someone was at least trying to hold what they summoned. The runes should have held for a time. It's possible that the thing, whatever it is, is still there in the eye of the circle."

"Any idea what it might be?" Kerrigan asked.

"Hard to be sure. Something malign. Demonic."

"Could it be a succubus?" I asked. Kerrigan's glance of puzzlement was hard to miss. He knew nothing about the Crow's little problem.

"Perhaps," the Librarian replied. "The only way to be sure is to go in there and find out. We either destroy the entity, whatever it is, or send it back through the tear that it crept through."

"Can we do that?" I asked.

"We have to try," the Lady replied.

Kerrigan said, "What makes you think it might be a succubus? That's a bit of a leap."

"I heard a rumour of something," I said. "A hint that one might have been seen."

"First I've heard of it," said Kerrigan.

"It's way short of anything concrete. Barely worth mentioning."

He didn't sound convinced. "Yet you mentioned it. You need to log any threat, any whisper of a threat, laddo. You know this."

"Sure. I will. Let's see what we find in there first."

I caught the appraising glance the Librarian threw at Kerrigan at that point.

She said, "I have brought along some … protection for us to use."

"Protection?" I was imagining – what? – a magical ring maybe?

"A counter-rune. The letters of the forbidden alphabets can often be negated, reversed by their antirune, the same strokes and lines drawn in mirror-writing. I haven't had time to perfect the actions properly, but I believe I can grant us some sort of defence."

I didn't look at Kerrigan, not at all sure of how he would take this. The Lady, meanwhile, held up her finger to my forehead, holding it there like the barrel of a gun. "May I?"

"Will it sting?"

"A lot less than the runes in that warehouse if they engulf you. Stop whining and hold still."

I dutifully did as I was told. She pressed her fingernail hard into my skin and performed a complex sequence of movements. A tingling sensation ran across my skin and into my brain, like ice cream brain-freeze, but it soon dissipated. The Lady glanced at Kerrigan again, unsure whether he would allow her to mark him. After a moment, with a shrug, he acquiesced.

"Very good," the Librarian said. "I have already placed the antirune upon myself. I estimate we have about half an hour before its effects dissipate. There's something else, too. Whoever carried out this summoning left a signature of sorts in the runes. A *cartouche*, we call them. They're common enough if you know to look for them. Sometimes it's put there deliberately, like an artist signing a painting they're proud of, or a graffiti artist's tag, but most of the time it's inadvertent. A fingerprint left in the paint. With summoning spells like this it's usually deliberate: the enchanter putting something of themselves into the spell in order to bind whatever is pulled through to their will."

"Then you can identify the individual who worked this spell?" I asked.

"Given time, perhaps. It isn't anything as clear as a name written in the runes. It's a matter of tracing associations through the old books to work out where the magics involved came from, who first unearthed them. It's like tracing the etymology of words through the archives. Certain words are used only in certain locations. A county or a valley or even a village. After a while, though, you see patterns, and you can guess who a particular enchanter acquired their knowledge from. A forebear or a teacher, perhaps. But the whole process is imprecise. It doesn't help that these people use invented identities, give themselves ridiculous titles. *The Angel of the Dark Abyss* and other such nonsense. I may be able to work something out eventually."

When we had the luxury of three operatives, standard Office procedure was for two to go in and one to hold back to act as a reserve and/or raise the alarm if things didn't go to plan. I was still wary of Kerrigan getting to know things he shouldn't. He was my superior, and the decision was his, but I knew he'd listen to my suggestion.

"Lady Coldwater, shall we two go inside while Kerrigan maintains the perimeter?"

The Librarian switched on a keyring light and unfastened the straps on her shopping trolley. She pulled out two short, curved blades, good for close-combat stabbing and slashing. She was ambidextrous and could fight with two swords at the same time if needed – I'd seen her do it more than once. The swords had runes of their own etched all along them, and their pommels were ornately carved into ugly, leering faces like those of gargoyles. They were, pretty obviously, ensorcelled blades.

"Fine by me," the Lady said.

I could see that Kerrigan was having doubts about the plan. He was the sort of guy who preferred to tackle risks himself rather than let others face them. He led by example. But he was also good at giving acolytes like me the freedom to develop.

"I'll give you fifteen minutes," he said. "If you can't resolve the situation in that time, come out and we'll think again."

Maybe he suspected more about Lady Coldwater than I'd thought, and simply preferred not to ask too many questions. He strode away to check around the building, make sure there was no sign of the runes creeping out through any gaps.

The Lady, meanwhile, reached into her bag and pulled out two silvery rings, woven in complex organic patterns. Each had a single gemstone, red as a drop of blood, embedded in it.

"There's also these. Put one on."

"What are they?"

"Do you have your Stebsen's with you?"

Stebsen's – a Stebsen's Ward, another m/tech gizmo that we're supposed to carry with us at all times. It's a string of small round discs of metal that can be worn as jewellery or sewn into clothes – I had mine woven into a belt – that's intended to act as a sort of magical shield, bouncing back any attack directed at us. The devices only work against certain sorts of incantations, and that makes them worse than useless in many ways. You don't dare rely on them; you have to assume that the spell being flung at you is one the device doesn't protect you from and act accordingly. We were supposed to carry them with us at all times, just in case, but we rarely did.

"I don't."

"Well, these work along similar lines. They should offer us some protection. These are artefacts that the Office of the Witchfinder General doesn't know anything about; they're a little more powerful. They might help."

"You don't sound very sure."

She slipped hers on. "I'm not."

I took my ring and slid it over the knuckle of my finger. "What is it? A +3 Ring of Protection?"

She ignored my question. If I expected to feel anything, see the world through the blue glow of a protective shield perhaps, I was disappointed.

"You must have some idea about what we're going to face in there," I said.

"The bookwyrm was able to decipher some of the runes. I left it working on the others. I believe we're looking at some sort of wraith-like entity rather than a demon such as a succubus. A creature of death. Are you familiar with the banshee?"

"Of course."

"There are hints that a creature akin to one of those has been pulled into our world."

"Why would anyone do that?"

The look on her face was inexpressive. "Some people are complete bastards. Let's go. Try not to touch any of the runes. Try not to stand still for too long if you do come into contact with them."

We both strapped on head torches so our hands would be free. I drew my clothcutter blade from its scabbard on my ankle and pulled out my handgun from its holster. I rotated the barrel so that the matching round was selected. The bullet worked like the blade, making it, in theory, capable of reopening any cracks in reality and sucking whatever it struck back through the tear.

Tooled-up and ready, we went in.

Zubrasky had been right: the noise from the runes was very definitely louder. It was like standing inside some cramped aviary whose air was filled with screeching, flapping birds. The stone flags and whitewashed walls were coated with multiple layers of the runes, creeping over each other, no gaps between them. We were going to have to run across them to get anywhere.

"The basement," the Lady shouted. "I've studied the floorplans. There are stairs on the far side of the room leading down. Follow me."

She hared off, leaping across the ground as if she were stepping across the snapping heads of crocodiles in a lake. I stayed close. As before, the runes were definitely aware of our presence on some level. They swirled more urgently, and began to form lines – sentences, I guess – that quested around for us like tentacles. I lengthened my stride in a desperate attempt to limit my contact with the ground.

We reached the door on the far side of the room unmolested, but it was locked. Thick layers of the runes were creeping from underneath and around the sides of the door. They were definitely coming up from below.

I pulled out a *sesame* and attached it to the lock. It was the sort of device I'd used to gain access to Sally Spender's house: an m/tech gizmo that operates by temporarily translocating everything within a prescribed sphere into another dimension of reality. Handy for making locks vanish, and a thousand and one other uses about the home. I gave it a three-second delay, and then we stepped back to let it do its thing.

I felt a sharp, burning pain in my left shin, like someone had touched me there with the tip of a red-hot poker. The runes had crept over my boots as I stood at the doorway and found my exposed skin. I shouted something, hopping and kicking in a ridiculous attempt to get the runes off me, as if they were some flying insect. As I did so, the sesame triggered. A small sphere of the door and wall, including the lock mechanism, vanished. It would return in a minute, but by then we'd have the door open.

I kicked the door wide. Inside, a set of bare concrete steps led down into the ground. I tried to ignore the throb in my ankle; we were going to get caught by the runes, that was clear. This time, at least, there were no alarming visions of monstrous forms in pits. The Lady's protective ring appeared to be doing something. The sting was still there, but there was no sign of the rune on my flesh. We had to keep going, get to the heart of the outbreak.

The cellar of the warehouse was dank, the air heavy with moisture and an acrid stench that caught at the back of my throat like a physical lump. The floor was uneven, flags of stone tipping at odd angles as if something was trying to burst through from beneath, and the walls were also rough stone. The place looked old, perhaps the basement of a former building upon which the later warehouse had been built. Rusty iron columns were set at regular intervals around the room, supporting the floor above. Every surface was coated with the creeping runes, so many of them that individual sigils could no longer be picked out. The noise in the confined space was deafening.

The Lady touched my arm, directing my attention to the far wall. The runes there were … doing something. I watched as they writhed and threaded through each other, and I began to see the features of a face: shifting, indistinct, but unmistakable. It was large, filling the whole wall. I had to defocus my eyes to see it, like looking at one of those random-dot stereogram images.

I had to shout to be heard. "You see it?"

Lady Coldwater nodded. "The features of the enchanter who worked the spell. Either that, or it's the target."

I didn't recognize the face, but it was hard to make out, constantly shifting. I could read an expression of – what? – malevolence there. Ideally, I'd have taken pictures for later comparison, but that clearly wasn't going to work where the runes were involved.

Directly beneath the face, I now saw, there was a section of ground that had been fenced off with a set of iron railings. The rectangle was roughly the size and shape of a plot in a graveyard. We needed to keep moving. Both my ankles were now red raw from the repeated contact of the runes.

The Lady had seen the railings, too. We ran towards them, to find that they were, in fact, another set of steps leading even deeper, these rough stones rather than concrete. The runes clustered thickly across them, flowing up them like an unnatural flood. Lady Coldwater, her twin blades held ready, went first, while I followed closely behind, the barrel of my gun pointing over her shoulder.

Downstairs, the lights of our head torches dancing about the sub-basement, it was immediately obvious that here was the core of the enchantment, the summoning circle in the eye of the storm. I didn't need to see the runes spinning around the floor, I could *feel* the grim magic coiling off them, triggering a reaction of revulsion in the pit of my stomach. It joined up with a stench of rot and burning metal to become a sensation of wrongness filling me.

I caught a glimpse of another doorway in the far wall, too. It looked even older: an arched entranceway built of rough stone blocks. But the entrance was tiny, half my height, as if the people passing in and out of it had been children.

I put it out of my mind. A storeroom, maybe, nothing more. I had more pressing things to worry about. Directly in front of me, the darkness in the room seemed to twist, fold in on itself, and then a figure stepped out of that nowhere into my reality.

I say stepped. Slithered might be a better word. I'm not one for judging people by their appearances, but I was damn sure I wasn't going to hang around and assume the best here. The writhing horror held within the circle was a creature of death and decay, there could be no doubt. It was skeletal, wraith-like, but ghostly impressions of flesh or perhaps cloth flapped around on it as it moved. It was about my height, but it was also raised a few inches off the ground, as if the floor it had walked upon in some other realm of reality was at a slightly different elevation.

It screamed, the sound a grating whine that sent spikes of pain through my brain. The creature was held by the runes surrounding it, but it was struggling against them. They wound around and through it, like chains, but the creature wrenched at them, stretched them to breaking-point. Perhaps it was this that had made the runes multiply as they worked harder and harder to contain the beast they had summoned. Had it tried to materialise again and again, or had our presence in the sub-basement finally lured it into our world?

Impossible to know; we could worry about that later. Lady Coldwater danced around the perimeter. Her features wavered through the strange energy of the circle, but I could see her well enough for her to catch my gaze. She nodded her head, telling me to be ready. We would attack from two angles at the same moment.

She nodded, and we struck, the lady scything her twin blades through the air before lunging, me firing my clothcutter round at the writhing form in the circle. Discharging my gun in an enclosed space like that was dangerous, but I figured there was no way I could miss.

Blades and bullet struck, and they did their work, opening up a rent in the fabric of reality. The swirling runes began to spiral inwards, drawn into the breach to be ejected into whatever plane of reality existed on the far side. The chittering, screeching sound had become so loud I'd stopped hearing it. Now, it added a note of fury to its cacophony, as if the sigils were fighting back, reluctant to be banished from our world.

The entity, too, reacted. Sensing what was happening, seeing the two of us attacking it perhaps, it renewed its struggles to escape the runic bonds thrown around it. What happened next was probably our fault: we'd weakened the forces containing the creature, and it had a moment, a brief moment, when it could burst free of them, escape the rift our weapons had opened.

It did precisely that, leaping from the circle, seeming to grow in size as it flew directly at me, a keening wail of delight and hunger coming from its misshapen head. I'd heard that sound before, or one very like it: outside the building, the siren call I'd convinced myself was just some *ambiwlans* racing to an accident. Here in this enclosed space, I felt the sound in my teeth, the harmonics thrumming in my rib cage. There was a discordant note of wrongness to it, of malevolence, that instinctively made me want to flee.

Instead, I fired my remaining rounds at the entity, angling my shots upwards, conscious that I'd lost track of precisely where Lady Coldwater was. The rounds – each with their own particular magical effect – struck the entity but seemed only to infuriate it more. It swam against the growing flood of the runes as they were sucked into the rift behind it, but there was no stopping it. It lashed out a claw at my face – then howled with agony.

I glimpsed a silver blade slice through its skeletal torso. The Lady. She was standing on the other side of it in an attack pose, twin blades held poised as she picked out the next spot to strike the creature. From its reaction, I could tell that the blades weren't merely wounding it. The spells worked into them were also having their effect.

The entity whirled away from me to face the threat of the Librarian. She was quick and wire-strong – but even she wasn't quick enough. The creature leapt at her, ravening for her, and this time it was going with the flow of the runes, throwing itself back across the circle.

It cannoned into Lady Coldwater. She landed expertly, spinning around and springing back to her feet in one fluid movement, but the creature was quicker still. It lashed out a claw and caught her in the side. Her elegant stance crumpled as she fell to the floor in a cry of agony. She was suddenly helpless. The creature, the demon – whatever the hell it was – was going to slay her, devour her, drag her screaming into its own dimension.

I wasn't going to let any of those things happen. I still held my clothcutter blade, fizzing with its own Office-approved magic. I leapt for the creature, blade held out in my two hands, and buried the knife in the back of its skull.

The entity paused for the briefest moment – everything paused for the briefest moment – and then it began to writhe and shake. It was also shrinking, like it was being pulled into the tiny rip in reality and no longer had the strength to resist. The runes flowing around the walls and across the floor into the tear were a torrent now. The creature's wail rose in pitch as it was sucked in. In a moment, it had shrunk to the black point of a full stop and had gone.

I staggered towards the Librarian, desperate to get her and myself away from the breach. She'd climbed to her feet and was clutching one hand to the bloody wound in her side where the creature's claw had struck her. She was still with me, though; I caught the look of recognition and understanding in her face. We had to get away.

She hooked one of her arms over my shoulder, and we made for the stairs. It was like walking into the teeth of a gale, like battling against an avalanche. The runes were a tsunami wave, flooding down the stairs from the levels above, desperate to draw us in, take us with them. Leaning hard into it, pulling ourselves along with whatever handholds we could scrabble for, we edged step by step away from the breach. Up the first flight of stairs, then across the floor of the basement. With each step, the pull of the breach lessened, but with each step, also, we weakened from the effort of what we were doing.

In the end, it was Kerrigan that pulled us out. In clear breach of all Office protocol, he'd entered the building when he saw that something was happening. Our strength was giving up, and I was beginning to think that perhaps it wouldn't be so bad to let go, let myself fly from this world and all its troubles, when I felt his strong grip grabbing my shoulder. He seized the Lady with his other hand and hauled us upwards, back into the light.

We fell, all three of us, utterly exhausted, onto the lovely, *lovely*, cold tarmac of the Cardiff street.

8 – Cyhyraeth

The original Banshee (*bean sí* in modern Irish, from *ben síde* in Old Irish, meaning "woman of the fairy mound") lived in the Irish countryside, although similar entities have also been identified in other parts of the British Isles where the Celtic past retains a toehold: particularly Scotland, Wales and the Isle of Man. The creature is often to be found in close proximity to a tumulus or earthwork (hence the Irish name), although they can also reside in close proximity to rivers or lakes.

–Dr Miriam Seacastle, *Red Dragon, a Bestiary of Modern Britain*, 1999

Early the following morning, on the way to *Caerdydd Canolog* for my train to London, I dropped into the office to check on Lady Coldwater.

She had, inevitably, ignored all our requests that she go to a hospital to get her wound looked at. Kerrigan and I had helped her down into her lair, then she'd dismissed us. It was pretty clear to me what was going on, if not to Kerrigan: she was going to use some Pale Sister healing incantation to knit her muscles and skin back together. And, if she could do that, the question running around in my head was obvious: why weren't we all doing that? Not just Office operatives, I mean, but all of us?

I found her at her desk on Level -1, head in her hands as she pored over the pages of three separate tomes laid out before her. The pool of light from her lamp picked out the gold of her glasses but left the rest of the room deep in shadow. When she looked up at my approach, I could see that, whatever healing magics she'd employed, they hadn't fixed her up completely. She had her right arm in a sling, and she winced visibly as she slammed the heavy books on the desk shut. There were also two bottles of pills on the desk: two different sorts of painkillers, one of them morphine based. Both were open.

It didn't look like she'd slept. She was wearing the same clothes, right down to the patch of dried blood staining the side of her knitwear where the entity we'd banished had clawed her. Anyone else, I might have asked how they were. Somehow with Lady Coldwater, I knew not to.

"I brought your ring back," I said as I stopped a few yards from her, wary of invading her personal space too much.

"Keep it," she said, not looking up. "I rather think you might need it."

That didn't sound too hopeful, but I was grateful.

"What was that thing in the warehouse? You said you thought it was some kind of banshee?"

Now she looked up from her book to consider me. "I don't think it was. A related entity, perhaps. Have you heard of a *cyhyraeth*?"

My Welsh was still poor; I'd picked up a few words but little more. It was a failing, something that embarrassed me. This word, while unfamiliar, definitely sounded Welsh.

"Can't say I have. Does that name mean something?"

"It literally means something like *skeleton, a thing of flesh and bone*, but it also has the sense of *wraith* or *portent of death*. They're something like wights and something like banshees, often glimpsed or heard when a particular person is about to die. I believe that is what we witnessed."

It all seemed like a pretty good description of the entity we'd encountered.

"It damn-well nearly portended our deaths."

The lady waved a hand in annoyance. "Yes, yes, but we were simply in its way. I don't think it was brought here to bring about our demise."

I thought about the attacks on the Crow, and about

English Wizardry's wider project to discredit or destroy the Office.

"Are you sure about that?" I asked.

"Do you have reason to believe this thing *was* summoned as a trap for us?"

"Who else?"

"That's what I was trying to work out before you distracted me."

I thought about what she'd said. If the entities were portents, harbingers of death, it seemed odd that one had been consciously summoned. Unless someone was trying to seriously spook their intended victim, scare the hell out of them. Or maybe the entities were self-fulfilling prophecies: maybe, if they found themselves wailing in the vicinity of some poor soul, heralding their demise, the creatures then did all that they could to bring that demise about. Maybe even demons didn't like to look ridiculous.

"Have you spoken to the bookwyrm again?"

"I attempted it, but the creature refused my intrusion. They can be like that. They like to show off when they have important knowledge to impart, but they also like to be left alone when they're busy."

She said the latter with a frank gaze, and I didn't need to be a brilliant young paranormal investigator to work out what she was really saying. I needed to know just a couple of things, though, before I headed off to the Big Smoke to meet up with Hardknott-Lewis.

"Do you think you're going to be able to work out who summoned the creature, and who the intended victim was?"

She sighed and rubbed her face with her hands for a moment, a gesture of tiredness. "As I say, it's possible. The bookwyrm has no more information to go on because all the runes were sucked into the rift. It only has the few you captured on your phone, along with all the vast knowledge it has accumulated from other sources over the years."

"But, in time."

"In time, yes. Perhaps."

"Is there any possibility that that thing was a succubus? Or related to a succubus in some way?"

"Why are you suddenly so interested in succubi?"

"It's an area of personal interest," I lied. "They're what I wrote my thesis on when I was inducted into the Office."

She would know that, of course. She wasn't convinced by my explanation, maybe, but she was too exhausted to argue the point. "Well, I doubt it. Succubi and incubi are overtly sexual creatures, their bodies conjured and arranged to appeal to our erotic predilections. I don't know about you, but that thing was about as far from sexy as it's possible for a creature to be."

She had a good point. "It wasn't, I don't know, some kind of root form that shifts to attract its intended victim?"

"I've never heard of such a thing. Are you saying you have?"

"No, just a theory."

"Well, if I find out anything like that, I'll be sure to let you know."

"I'm going to London today," I said. "I'll stay at my mother's, see how she's getting along."

"That's good to know." My statement seemed to remind her of something. "And what of your injuries? Your legs were badly spellburned by those runes. The life-leeching element of them gave them a vicious bite. If you hadn't been protected by the antirune and the ring, I don't believe you'd be standing here now talking to me."

"I'm fine." I was. When we cut open the rift in reality and the runes had poured through, the ones attacking my feet and legs had been sucked off me, too.

"No after effects?" She sounded surprised. I did not ask to look at her legs, but I became aware of a pot of some lotion or elixir on the floor near her chair. My guess was she had been, as she put it, spellburned, and was still suffering the consequences, despite her defences.

I lifted the leg of my jeans to show her my pristine ankles. "No after effects."

She peered down at me calves over the top of her reading-glasses. "Interesting."

"What is?"

"I'd expect to see burns, marks. I assumed I'd have to work counter-incantations upon you to stave off the effects of those runes, but you appear to have natural resistance to them. A natural magical immunity."

Another neat thing – but also another thing I didn't need Hardknott-Lewis to know about. At least the Librarian didn't look troubled by the discovery. Not in the least. "It's possible that growing up around your mother, your long-term exposure to that magical curse I mean, has given you this natural resistance. As I say, interesting."

She knew a lot about me, knew I was compromised, but she didn't know the full extent of my magical abilities. I chose not to illuminate her. I left her to her researches and her books.

I decided to drive to London rather than play bus replacement service bingo on the trains. Soon I was battling along the M4, *en route* for Newport and for the Severn Bridge. The faces of the people in the cars around me were as inexpressive as ever; it struck me how mindless they all looked, sitting there and staring glassily out in front of them at the unfolding road. They looked like zombies. I had to assume they weren't.

So often, storms rushing up the Bristol Channel mean that taking the bridge between Wales and England is like driving into a turbulent cloud, the sidewinds vicious, but for once the air was clear and open. The winding river and the English shore stretched out around me. It felt a little like I was flying. The older Severn crossing ran a short distance away to the north, and it was strange how insubstantial the structure looked from the side. The car lurched around a little in the airs sweeping up the river, and I returned my attention to the road ahead. The plan was to park at my mother's house in Dulwich so I could spend the night there and see how she was doing. That would give me the afternoon to meet up with Hardknott-Lewis and attend to whatever it was he had planned for me. I needed to make good time.

I was well into England, zipping past the junction I'd taken to get to Faebrook Folly a few months previously, when the Crow phoned.

"Danesh? Is that you?" He had the tendency of people of his age to sound ever-so slightly amazed with telecommunications technology when it functioned and he reached the person he was trying to speak to.

"Hello, sir."

"Where are you?"

"Coming up to Reading."

"I read your report on what took place at the warehouse."

I had filed the details in MORIARTY the night before – leaving out, obviously, anything incriminating to either me or to Lady Coldwater.

"I think we managed to maintain the outbreak without causing wider damage."

"Excellent, excellent. I wish I could have been there, but it sounds as if the Librarian was able to help."

Lady Coldwater would not, I was fairly sure, have deigned to log any kind of report. Partly, the Crow was speaking to me to find out what she'd done.

"In the end it came down to basic Office work: infiltrating the site and reopening the tear in the fabric of reality so we could dismiss the summoned entity."

"But the Librarian … you said she was able to identify the entity? She thought it was a cyhyraeth?"

"She wasn't completely sure."

"Interesting. I have some small experience of the entities. You did well to banish it before it could walk the Earth."

I did my best to sound professional and intelligent. "I've been trying to work out why someone would summon one, given that they're essentially banshee-like harbinger entities."

"They can be grim protagonists in their own right. Your

speculation that they will attempt to bring about the death they are foretelling may well be accurate."

"So, they're like a sort of spectral assassin? You summon one to portend the death of your intended victim, and the entities then go about achieving that very thing."

"I suppose it's possible. The other option is that the thing simply slipped through the cracks opened up when some other entity was summoned."

"The succubus."

"Perhaps."

"This cyhyraeth, though," I attempted the pronunciation and failed badly, "it would still be foretelling someone's death, wouldn't it? The wailing, moaning sound it made is exactly that from what I've read. The victim hears it three times on three separate days, and on the third day it's the end. Maybe, I don't know, it imprints on the first person it sees and pursues *them* if it hasn't been given a named target."

"How many days have you heard it?"

"One, I suppose. Several times yesterday."

"Which doesn't mean that you're the intended victim. I presume many people will have been in the area."

"I suppose," I said, not feeling particularly reassured.

"We would be a lot further along if we knew who the target was," the Crow said, "although the only way to be absolutely sure would be to release the entity from its holding circle, which I couldn't recommend as a strategy. You said there was a face in the runes."

"One I didn't recognize and haven't been able to match to anyone. It certainly wasn't me."

"Good, good. Have you had a chance to look into who might have been in the warehouse recently?"

"I've kicked off a few enquiries. I'll chase them up as soon as I'm back in Cardiff. The Lady said she might be able to work out who the summoner was from the specific runes used."

"It is someone powerful, wielding great arcane knowledge, but not so powerful that the spell didn't run out of control."

"Unless that was precisely what was supposed to happen," I said. "The cyhyraeth was incidental and the user intended the runes to spill out once the rift was opened up. I'm obviously not familiar with the workings of such spells, but I imagine there's a way to complete them or seal them, and this wasn't done here."

There was the expected pause as the Crow grappled with how much he should reveal to me. "There is a component to such incantations that, properly worked, prevents them from running out of control. By not including this, the summoner unleashed a magical chain reaction. Fortunately, for us, rather a slow one. If the outbreak had been left for another day or two – well you experienced the effects of the runes directly. Imagine if tens of thousands of people had come into contact with them."

I didn't reply for a moment as I executed a tricky manoeuvre. Three lorries had decided to overtake each other, and since their speed limiters were set to almost exactly the same number, the blockage took long, long seconds to resolve itself. A small, small part of me wished I could wield magical influence, suggest to the drivers to stop blocking the motorway to let me past. It had to be very tempting if you had the ability.

"Yes, doesn't bear thinking about," I said eventually.

"You have suffered no ill effects?"

"None. I guess I wasn't in contact with the runes for long enough."

"Interesting."

It was the very word the Librarian had used. The Crow said it in a way that made it sound like he was secretly suspicious. Was he correct to be, and my (mostly) latent magical abilities had protected me? Or was I simply projecting my own anxieties onto his words?

I moved the conversation along.

"We should pursue the possibility that English Wizardry are behind this. This could be the work of the Warlock."

"Do you think that's likely?"

Honestly? I didn't know. The Librarian had described the cyhyraeth as something like a wight, and my brain had immediately made a connection with *white*, and the xenophobic intent of the sect. But perhaps that was pushing things too far.

"Again, it's a theory," I said. "Perhaps they're stepping up their activities."

"Well, let's bear it in mind. We have no proof that there even is a *Warlock*, let alone who it might be. English Wizardry are a danger to us, most certainly, but regrettably they are not the only one. What are your plans when you reach London?"

"I'll drop the car off at my mother's and be in Whitehall for two o'clock."

"Ah, yes, that's actually why I contacted you. There's been a change of plan. There are some things I would like you to see before we convene the Star Chamber. Can you meet me at Aldwych instead?"

The word *Aldwych* sent dread thumping through me. This was the London Underground ghost station that we'd repurposed and used to house Evangelina Mormont before her ultimate removal to Oblivion. All my fears about the Crow's real purpose for inviting me along resurfaced. Were they intending to imprison me even before they could meet to discuss me? Or perhaps the Star Chamber had already deliberated, and I'd been found guilty. The chamber wasn't like a criminal court; there was no right of representation or a fair hearing or any other such liberal nonsense. There was no right of appeal. For all I knew, they'd found me guilty and Hardknott-Lewis was effectively asking me to make my own way to the jail.

But, as before, what option did I have? If I refused, if I ran, it would only confirm their fears. Fears that, I had to hope, they didn't actually have.

"The ghost station?" I said.

"Come to the entrance on the Strand and you'll be admitted."

"I'll be there. Have you managed to discover anything

else about the succubi attacks? Are they more widespread?"

"That's one reason I'd like you to come to Aldwych. We are still piecing together what is taking place, but the attacks upon the Office do seem to be more widespread than simply an assault upon me."

"The runes in Cardiff. The cyhyraeth and the succubus. Do you think it's possible they're all part of a wider pattern?"

He sighed, as if disappointed at the wickedness of the world. "It's not impossible, Danesh, that's all I can say for sure. Regrettably, there are many people who wish to sweep us away, who would unleash their own version of magical chaos onto the world if they could. Weak and ignorant as we are, we can only fight the good fight. I'll see you at Aldwych."

"Sir," I said, and hung up.

I let out a long breath of air. Cars drifted past me in the unending motorway flow; lost in the conversation, I had slowed down. Aldwych ghost station. For all I knew, I would go in there and never leave. This might be the last time I saw London, saw my mother. Saw *anything*.

The urge to leave the motorway, turn around and head off somewhere else was strong.

I kept driving eastwards.

9 – Ghost Station

The origin of the name for our little cabal of free thinkers remains under a certain amount of dispute to this day. Lord Mortimer asserts that the idea was his – and, moreover, that it was not in any way a joke, but a serious attempt to put the group onto a proper and formal footing. Albany Greylag, however, maintained for years afterwards (until his untimely end at the cursed hands of the Witchfinder General) that the coinage had been his – and that it was, indeed a joke; a reference, obviously, to the Order of the British Empire (an award which, it should be pointed out, nearly a third of the founding members of the OBV had been awarded). Whatever the precise origins of the name, it is indisputable that loose groupings of our kind have existed for many centuries in these isles. As the twentieth century rolled on, the need was felt to exert control over the nation in more formal ways as compared to the rather wilder methods used in former times.

–Arnold Enderby Smithwick, *Annals of the Order of the British Vampire*, 1929

There was no sign of my mother at our family home. I had a key, so I let myself in to leave my overnight bag there.

I took the opportunity to poke around the house I'd grown up in, peer into each room. Memories happy and sad flashed through my mind. Some rooms had barely changed in all that time: same wallpaper, same ornaments, the same pictures on the wall. Az was eight when he died, which meant I could recall several of our joint birthday parties from before that age. Afterwards, the day was obviously a difficult one for everyone, and although we tried to celebrate, it never really worked out. But now I saw the two of us, full of giggling delights, rampaging around the house with our new birthday presents – I was in a Star Wars phase, he'd gone for dinosaurs – thundering up and down the stairs as my X-wing relentlessly pursued his triceratops. Happy memories.

I was impressed, also, at the state the house was in. On previous visits – before the intervention of Lady Coldwater's colleagues – the place had slowly been succumbing to a tide of clutter and detritus. Books and broken furniture and unemptied shopping bags covering more and more of the floor, the actual living space my mother had to move around in slowly reducing. She would do odd things, too, as if knowing vaguely what a room was supposed to look like without being able to get it quite right. She would hang her garden spade on the coat-rack or carefully pile her unwashed crockery upon the bookshelves. There was none of that now: the house was tidy in a lived-in sort of way, everything in its place, the floors vacuumed and the surfaces dusted. The sight filled me with a curious pleasure. In the old days, much to the frustration of my former self, my mother had been an absolute stickler for cleanliness and tidiness, berating us if so much as a single shoe was left in the middle of the floor. Now, the sight of all the order was wonderful to see.

I left a note explaining I'd headed off to work and would be back in the early evening – making no mention of my fears that I might never be returning – and set off through the familiar streets for East Dulwich and a train up to London Bridge for the Jubilee line. I could have taken a bus, or maybe even blagged a space in the underground car park at the Whitehall office and driven – but this was a route I'd taken often as a lad, heading up into the city for some gig or a night out. I wanted to reproduce the journey one more time.

I was met outside the rear entrance to the abandoned tube station on Surrey Street. A large concertina door in the red brick façade said *Entrance* over it – which I took to be a noun, not a verb or a command. Towards the top of the building, more writing saying *Piccadilly Rly* in black on white gave a clue to the building's former function. Beneath my feet, I knew, were extensive tunnels – the station had once connected to the Piccadilly line, and it was still possible, if you tried, to walk through the darkness to reach the lines where tube trains still whooshed and racketed along.

A black guy was watching me as I approached the doorway. I didn't recognize him. He kicked himself off the wall he was leaning against and walked to meet me. I'm no expert in couture, but I could tell his suit was individually tailored, fitting him like an elegant glove. It seemed to stretch and flow with him as he strode towards me. It made me, in my cream chinos and pastel shirt, feel scruffy. The newcomer was powerful-looking, had clearly been working out, although his preppy glasses made the overall effect more Clark Kent than Black Panther. To mix my superhero universes for a moment.

"You're Shahzan?"

We don't carry visible badges or insignia to tell the world who we are. I fished out my OWG card from an inside pocket.

He glanced at it, nodded. "I'm Lincoln Umenyora. Earl Grey asked me to come meet you here."

He hadn't shown me his credentials, which seemed odd. That was the convention. I didn't recognize his name; he had to be fairly new. A recent arrival from university, perhaps.

"You're from the London office?"

He considered me for a moment like it was a stupid question – which it probably was – then with an exaggerated sigh pulled out his card to show me. He was also an acolyte. He seemed hostile for some reason. Maybe he was just having a bad day. Maybe he was just a Londoner.

"Is Hardknott-Lewis inside?" I asked.

Another pause, like he was making it very clear how much he resented my presence.

"Follow me. I'll take you to him now."

He unlocked the door and heaved it to one side. The old metal squealed in complaint. There was light on inside, revealing one of the wide, tiled corridors so familiar from London's tube network. There was no one else in sight. Lincoln closed and locked the door behind us, and we walked in silence to the lift that would take us down into the depths.

By the way the lift clanked and juddered as it descended, I could only assume it was one of the originals. Lincoln kept his gaze directly ahead, looking at the door. The station, I knew from my brief researches, had had a chequered career. It had been used in the twentieth century, but had never been particularly busy. There were three lift shafts, but only one had ever been used. In World War II, the station had been used to protect Londoners from the bombs of the Blitz, as many stations were. There were photographs on the net of people bedding down for the night between the rails. The station had also been used to house precious items from the British Museum, including the classical Greek sculptures that people call the Elgin Marbles.

That, perhaps, had been how the Office had ended up in possession of the station. When the museum treasures were brought back above ground, we were given the rooms to house artefacts of our own – those we didn't want to ever be visible to the public. The station was watched over in the same way as the Possessed Statue Warehouse was. The platforms were still occasionally used by film crews to shoot scenes, but there were deeper vaults behind locked doors that only we had access to.

The lift finally clanked to a halt and, after a long pause while they had a good think about things, the doors scraped open. We walked to the end of the deserted platform, green and cream tiles covering the curved walls and ceiling. Distantly, down the tunnel, I could hear the rumble and squeal of trains running on interconnecting lines, see the spark of arcing electrical connections.

They called these places ghost stations because they were abandoned; no trains stopped there (although at some stations they still passed through, and the passengers got a glimpse of the deserted platforms). But the supernatural sense of *ghost* seemed more fitting as we strode along the platform. Perhaps it was because I was used to tube stations being busy. The odd acoustics weren't helping; our footsteps echoed back at us off the hard, curved walls. I could easily imagine the people who'd once walked there – Edwardians, those escaping the blitz – as if something about them still lingered in the place. So far as I knew, that was completely fanciful: we dealt with hauntings, for sure, but none had ever been reported here. It was all in my head.

Lincoln led me to the end of the curving platform, then hopped down onto the rails. I hesitated to follow. I watched a brown mouse scurry away from us into the darkness of the receding tunnel. The ground was grimy, oily, peppered with fag ends and scraps of paper. It didn't look like any kind of high-security magical containment facility. Which, I guessed, was part of the point.

"The rail's off," he called up to me. "It's perfectly safe."

"You're sure there are no trains coming?"

Lincoln didn't respond and headed off into the tunnel. After a moment, overcoming all the instructions I'd ever been given as a boy about riding the tube and staying well away from the edge, I climbed down to follow.

After maybe a hundred metres, we came to an apparently insignificant door built into the curving wall of the tunnel. Like everything else, it was coated in grime. A sign upon it said *No Unauthorised Admittance*. It was locked, but Lincoln had both the required keys – and also the eight-character code he had to type into a little keypad.

Once inside, he flicked a switch, and harsh, white lights flickered on. There was another locked door ahead of us, this one looking more recent and robust. The walls were suddenly smooth concrete, no blemish or stain. Still saying nothing, Lincoln carefully locked the outer door, then began to open up the inner one. Through this, once he had it open, lay a third door that resembled the sort of heavyweight, blast proof door you see on bank vaults in films. He had to put all his weight into hauling it open once he'd released the locks. Once again, when we were through, he took great care to lock everything up behind us.

We emerged into what appeared to be a control room, overlooking a large, square vault in the centre of which was a steel cage that might have been designed to keep a wild beast in check – except that there was something like a medical couch inside it, with strong restraints built in, and a bank of machines and computers to which someone had once been hooked up.

"This is where Mormont was kept?" I asked.

Lincoln nodded. "She was here for three years, until we put her into Oblivion."

"Hard to see how she could have escaped from this."

"Hard to see how she could have escaped from Oblivion, either, but she did. If your story is to be believed."

That was a weird thing to say. He clearly had something he wanted to say.

"You think I made it up?"

For the first time, he looked troubled, and hesitated before replying. "Sometimes, I don't know what to believe."

"You can go and see she's not in the Oblivion dimension anymore, right?"

He nodded, looked down at the ground and back up. "Sure. I believe she got out somehow, and that you met up with her. All the rest – the stuff with Warder – that I'm not so sure about."

"Warder was a friend?"

"We joined the Office together."

Right. That explained his hostility towards me.

"I'm sorry," I said. "He was, truly, working for English

Wizardry, him and Mormont. Maybe his friendship with you was genuine, but you have to consider the possibility that it was a cover story."

"He was a good guy."

I was suddenly very conscious that I was alone and on unfamiliar territory. I was, in short, on Lincoln's manor, and I hadn't come prepared for any kind of trouble. Was it possible Lincoln was tied up with English Wizardry? It seemed unlikely, given his ethnic background, but stranger things happen. People were good at living with contradictions.

"You must have read my case report about Faebrook," I said, keeping my voice low and relaxed.

"Sure. Mormont, though … you seemed very convinced Peter wasn't under her thrall."

Thrall was a tricky word in magus law. It has a strict legal definition which I for one can never remember, but the essence is fairly straightforward: if you're under the thrall of some user or possessing entity, then you aren't responsible for your actions. Ah, but the grey areas. It's always the grey areas that get you. How strong does the thrall have to be before it excuses what you do? Is control easier if the person welcomes it? How did you even prove something like that is going on?

Lincoln, though: it sounded to me like he was missing a friend and mad at those who were responsible, in some way, for what happened. I got that. There'd been no doubt about Warder, no mistaking the look of hatred in his eyes as we'd faced off – right before I'd unleashed my magical death ray. Thralled people tend to have a glassiness in their eyes, even a sense of confusion as they see what it is their body is doing. There was none of that with Warder. He was *there*, mind and body.

"He tried to kill me," I said. "He was working to restore fine old white English magic to its rightful place and replace all the troublesome foreign influence that he thought had debased the one true way. I'm sorry, I know he seemed like a nice guy, but he was the enemy. In more ways than one."

Lincoln looked like he wanted to say more, but instead he turned away. "Come on. I'll take you to Hardknott-Lewis."

We walked down a flight of plain, concrete steps, through more security doors, and across the floor of the space housing Mormont's one-time cell. It was a grim place to be incarcerated. She'd been heavily sedated and shouldn't have known anything about it – except that, somehow, she had used her powers to exert influence upon the outside world. From what I'd gathered, several attempts to influence her warders had been picked up – hence the decision to move her permanently into Oblivion.

Although, as we then found out, it hadn't been permanent at all.

The Aldwych entrance to that dimension is a lot more impressive than ours: instead of a broom cupboard that becomes a portal when the spheres are in the right alignments and the right incantations are intoned, this was a permanent entrance. It's a semi-circular tube tunnel, presumably another part of the underground train network that had never been used and that had been repurposed by the Office. A shimmering wall of silvery-grey indicated that the portal was active.

Hardknott-Lewis emerged from Oblivion then. He half-stepped, half-fell through the magical wall. For once, his hair was dishevelled and he was breathing deeply, as if he'd been running. His skin was a ghastly white.

He gasped out his words. "Danesh. You are here. Give me a moment."

I'd never been into the Oblivion dimension, but I knew that it was inimical to life; it slowly drained you when you went in there, sucked you to a husk. The longer you were inside, the more of your strength was leeched away. After an hour or so, you basically became a permanent resident, held forever as a lifeless, frozen image of your former self.

"How long were you in there?" I asked when he'd recovered a little.

He stood up straight. "Too long. There were certain

things I needed to see. How Mormont escaped for one thing."

"You could have gone in from Cardiff."

There was only one Oblivion dimension, with multiple portals. I knew it was a mistake to think of our plane of existence and the other as being somehow parallel, overlaying each other. From my limited understanding, that was far too simplistic. Oblivion was, effectively, infinite in extent.

"I prefer to keep our portal closed as much as possible. Here in London, they have a somewhat more relaxed attitude." He glanced at Lincoln as he spoke.

Lincoln simply shrugged. "I have other matters to attend to, Lord High Witchfinder. Do you need me for anything else?"

"No, please. Will you be in Whitehall later?"

"It depends. There's a Code 16 in Tottenham that is taking up a lot of our time. It's proving hard to root out."

Code 16 – *poltergeist activity*. They could indeed, from my own experience, be persistent little bastards.

"Well, we had better let you head off and tackle that," said Hardknott-Lewis. "My thanks for waiting, we can see ourselves out. We will hope to see you later in Downing Street."

"If the Christ allows."

Christ. London Office rhyming slang. *Jesus Christ, poltergeist*.

I could see that Lincoln was uncomfortable with just leaving us alone in the ghost station. My guess was that he thought of it as his territory, a part of the London office. Perhaps he'd been charged by someone higher up to keep an eye on us. But Hardknott-Lewis was his superior and his clear instruction couldn't be refused. Saying nothing more, Lincoln turned and left.

I began to speak, but the Crow held up a hand to quiet me as he peered down the corridor. After a minute or more, he lowered his hand.

"There. I believe we are now alone. What were you going to say?"

"Did you work out how Mormont escaped?"

"I found exactly what I expected to find. There is no way to escape from Oblivion. She was definitely there, and a strong-minded individual such as she could remain conscious for longer than most, but sooner or later her mind, her energy, would have dissipated. She would have crept into the cold torpor of near-death. The logarithmic approach to the zero-point without ever quite getting there. Even she couldn't fight against the metaphysical forces of an entire dimension of reality."

"We assume Warder took her out using the Faebrook Folly portal."

"I wanted to check that, but, yes, I believe that must be correct. The particular nature of Oblivion does make for a somewhat convenient escape mechanism. When she was isolated in her grim little cell up there, she could be watched and monitored, and anyone trying to free her would have had to come in to this ghost station. Once she was inside Oblivion, anyone with a portal could, in fact, have freed her."

"That doesn't sound very secure. Oblivion is supposed to be inviolate, the ultimate prison."

"Under normal circumstances, it is. The scale of the dimension is vast, truly vast. Too huge for our tiny minds to properly comprehend, I fear. You would have to know the precise coordinates of the soul you are looking for, otherwise you would have no chance. Simply blundering in and searching would be like trying to find a needle in a void the size of our entire universe."

"But Warder knew where in Oblivion she was."

"Yes. Except Warder … he simply was not that powerful from everything I know of him."

"Lincoln seemed to think Warder was under Mormont's control. That she was using him as a puppet, pulling his strings."

"That cannot be; even she can't have done that from inside Oblivion. I think … I think there is something else going on here."

It seemed, at least, that all my fears about being lured

to Aldwych so I could be pushed into Oblivion for my crimes were unfounded – for the moment, at least. Hardknott-Lewis had summoned me here for other reasons.

"You suspect a wider conspiracy?"

The Crow straightened his tie – which didn't need straightening – and stared into the Oblivion entrance as if able to see things there. "To be honest, I am not sure. There are certain indications but I have nothing more certain yet."

He glanced back at me and seemed to come to a decision about something. "You have never entered the Oblivion dimension, have you?"

"I … no."

"Would you like to look inside now?"

All my fears went clanging back through me. Was he simply being polite about despatching me through the portal? Trying to avoid any unpleasantness?

"There's no need. I can see it's taken its toll on you."

He smiled ruefully. "The place does rather sap you after a while. But we could peep inside and it would extract no terrible cost. I think it might be useful. It would be … illustrative."

What did that mean, I wonder? Was he about to abandon me there, or was all this some kind of coded warning? Whatever the truth, again I didn't really see how I could refuse. And I was intrigued to know what Oblivion was like – assuming I was able to leave again.

I nodded my assent.

"Excellent," said the Crow. "We only need to remain inside for a moment. Let me … activate the opening again and we will pass through."

He was already doing things with his hands, as if he were gripping something invisible and pushing hard against it, forcing it backwards. He was muttering syllables beneath his breath, too. He was, clearly, working an incantation – something that felt very, very wrong to see. I knew what his response would be if I mentioned it. He'd look pained, and agree, and give me another history lesson on the Assizes powers that the Office was allowed to wield to defeat greater evils. And I really didn't need to hear that again.

After a few moments, the shimmering wall began to shift and swirl. A whining noise, becoming louder but also more high-pitched, filled my ears, and the silvery-grey wall turned to an incandescent blue, the same blinding shade as the portal that Sally and Mormont had disappeared into at Faebrook Folly. The door was open.

I glanced aside at Hardknott-Lewis.

"After you, Danesh," he said, as if simply asking me to step into an office ahead of him.

After only the briefest pause while I tried to convince myself I was doing the right thing, I stepped through the fell gateway and into Oblivion.

10 – Oblivion

Special care must be taken when Mormont is transferred from her holding cell through the Oblivion portal at the Aldwych Station facility. Once inside, even she will not be able to withstand the debilitating effects of the dimension, but those around her will certainly be susceptible to her powers and glamours as she is moved. This is a maximum-security action; Mormont must be considered a severe threat at all times. For the first hour of her incarceration in Oblivion, she must be monitored and considered active, even if appearances are to the contrary.

–Earl Grey, Witchfinder General presiding, *Rulings of the Star Chamber*, 2020

I stood on a wide icy plain.

No, not a plain: a grey frozen lake, all colour leeched from it, no details anywhere. Somewhere far beneath my feet was a deep, wide ocean of cold water. I was inside a world sketched in pencil lines, leaden and drab. No hills or mountains rose in the distance to break the line of the horizon. I couldn't even see a horizon, as if the surface I stood on wasn't a sphere but flat. A plain stretching infinitely away in every direction.

It was also bone-achingly cold. You know how it feels on an icy evening in the winter, when you step outside and you can *feel* the heat being drained from your body? As if cold is a negative force in its own right, not merely the lack of warmth. That was how I felt standing there, feeling the heat being pulled through my feet, sucked out of my mouth with each exhalation.

I was already panicky, breathing rapid. I clutched my

arms to myself. I swear I could feel the frost forming over my features, but it wasn't only a physical cold. I went through long courses of counselling and support after Az's death, and one thing I learned was to be aware of my emotional state, to spot when my thoughts were turning self-destructive and do something about it. These episodes happened very rarely to me these days – but I could immediately sense my mood deteriorating as I stood in Oblivion. It was as if my life-energy, my soul, was being sucked out of me along with the warmth of my body.

I turned around, looking for the doorway so I could step back into the warm, welcoming light of London before I froze to a statue of ice.

There was no doorway. I was utterly alone.

I did what any modern person would do at this point: pull out my phone so I could call for help, feel connected. A ridiculous thing to do, of course. No signal in Oblivion.

I began to move, out of instinct as much as anything. *Keep walking, keep warm.* If I sat down or lay down, I'd never get up again. Distantly, I began to pick out tiny details in the drab plain: the vertical lines of sticks jammed into the ice here and there, scattered at random angles. I set off for the nearest one, wary of losing track of where I'd entered the Oblivion dimension, but having no landmarks to get a bearing off.

The stick was an iron bar, its spiked end hammered into the ice. Something protruded from the ice just beneath it, a small mound of black.

Then I saw the eyes, peering out at me from the ice. Open eyes. Whoever this was, the rest of their body was entombed in the ice, but they were alive.

If *alive* was the right word.

There was a little oval plaque welded to the pole, with letters engraved upon it. They said, in a curling, extravagant script, *Johannes Devereaux*. A name I'd never heard before.

I expected Devereaux's gaze to follow me as I moved around, but it didn't. That was almost worse. I could see the dim light of awareness deep in his eyes, but he wasn't alive to move to watch me.

I began to notice more and more of the spikes, a whole little forest of them. Thirty or forty paces away, one was canted over at forty-five degrees as if someone had tried to work it free or was still setting it in place. I was shaking uncontrollably now, jaws clenched painfully tight, but I needed to know what the slanted marker was. A sort of perverse fascination had come over me, and a little voice whispering in my head said that I knew very well what the name on the plaque was – because it was mine.

I stepped closer. A hollow had been chipped out of the ice in front of the marker. There was, indeed, no body, just that person-sized hollow. The ice went deep: at least a metre, impossible to say how much beyond that. I stepped closer still, to read the lettering, the pain in my cheeks sharp from the windchill.

The name wasn't mine. The sign said *Evangelina Mormont*.

The hand placed on my shoulder made me jump with alarm. I lost my footing, slid, fell to the glassy surface.

Hardknott-Lewis was standing over me. He did not appear to be affected by the cold. There was something odd about his features; his body blurred as it moved, smearing across the world, but his expression, when he stood still, was his usual quiet calm.

"Danesh, forgive me. I lost you for a moment there."

He held out a hand. Once its molecules had solidified, I grabbed hold to haul myself up.

"Thanks," I said. My face was so frozen that it came out as little more than a meaningless syllable.

"You appear to be struggling," he said, his voice oddly distant.

"It's cold," I said.

His gaze cast around, his features taking a few moments to catch up with his head. "Yes, forgive me. I have become somewhat inured to the effects of this place over the years. I should have prepared you better."

"Cold," I repeated, wanting to be sure we stuck to the essential facts of the situation.

"Here, take my hand again. I will return us to…"

Colour and warmth burst back in. The tiles of the curving tunnels were around me again. Bliss at simply being alive flooded through me.

"… London."

Hardknott-Lewis had my hand gripped firmly in his. "Are you okay, Danesh?"

I had my arms hugged around myself for warmth. I slowly uncoiled, studied my fingertips. I expected them to be blue, purple, bone-white: none of the good colours for fingers. Instead, they were reassuringly normal; pinky-brown.

"Better now," I said

"You perceived the dimension as a cold place?"

"I saw a plain of ice, stretching away for ever. The people there were trapped in the ice, buried in it. Isn't that what you saw?"

"Oblivion has no fixed physical properties, and each person perceives it in their own way. Ice and frozen wastes are a common-enough interpretation, whereas others see the dunes of an unending desert, the imprisoned buried beneath the shifting sands."

"What do you see?"

"For some reason, for me, it is a forest. Certain of the trees are not trees, if you see what I mean, but people, their arms stretched wide. They are unable to move, as if their flesh has been turned to wood."

"But their eyes are open."

"Yes, always that."

"I saw the hole in the ice where Mormont was dug out."

"For me, that particular tree has been uprooted, but the effect is the same. One or more people entered Oblivion, knowing where she was, and extracted her."

"Who is Johannes Devereaux?"

A brief moment of confusion flashed across his features. "Ah, no one important, at least not to us. That area has been used by the Office to entomb its troublemakers and miscreants for several centuries. Devereaux was placed there in the Victorian age, I believe."

My mind was beginning to work again a little more efficiently now. For one thing, I hadn't been consigned to Oblivion. I'd been shown it, but then pulled back out.

That was good. Although, was it some sort of warning to me to mend my ways?

"The people in there: they're aware of what's going on?"

"I believe so, perhaps on some subconscious level. You must understand that no one ever comes out of Oblivion, so we have not had the opportunity to ask anyone about their experiences."

"No one until Warder pulled Mormont out."

"Just so. Although, as you experienced, the environment of Oblivion is inimical to life. Would Warder have been able to last long enough to extract Mormont? I am not sure. I am really not sure."

"Who, then?"

"Others in English Wizardry. Others in the Office, perhaps."

"Lincoln said he thought Warder might have been acting under Mormont's control."

Hardknott-Lewis frowned. "It is not impossible, but it comes down to what is likely. Any mind can be controlled by someone who is sufficiently potent, but it is much easier to get someone to do something if they are already sympathetic or amenable. There are simply fewer barriers to batter down. Mormont – or someone – may well have influenced Warder, but I doubt they turned him into the opposite of what he really was. The effort of that … why bother? Simpler to find someone who is already thinking along similar lines and make a few quiet suggestions."

His words made me feel a little better – but only a little. It was obvious that Lincoln had liked Warder, and that visible grief and anger had brought home to me what I'd done at Faebrook Folly. I had killed his friend, in a way that contravened just about every tenet of magus law. If Warder had been innocent, it would have made my crime a hundred times worse. Bad enough that I wasn't sure it was a secret I could continue to carry around with me. The story I was telling myself was this: *he got what he deserved* – that and its close relative *I did what I had to do*.

Was it possible I was wrong? Until things had turned sour, I'd enjoyed Warder's company. That was the truth of it. Lincoln could have been a friend, too – we probably had a fair bit in common – but he appeared to hate me because of everything that had happened.

These troubling thoughts spiralled in my mind. The damned Office and its strictures – why did it have to make everything so difficult? Perhaps it was partly anger at being thrown into Oblivion without adequate preparation. I could have died in there – or been trapped. Rage surged through me – a rage not unlike that I'd felt at Faebrook Folly in the moment I'd killed Warder. This time, mercifully, I suppressed it. Hardknott-Lewis himself stood right in front of me. Even if I could have slain him – highly doubtful – there'd be no escaping such a crime committed on Office property when it was known we were alone together.

The Office were to blame for what I'd done, though, at least partly. If I'd known about my abilities, if someone had taken me aside and shown me how to control them, then Warder might be alive today. But, of course, that was never going to happen. I said nothing, made no move, but the injustice of it seethed away inside me. The damned Office and its anti-magical obsession. Its *hypocritical* anti-magical obsession.

I said nothing, and Hardknott-Lewis said nothing, although I was conscious of him studying me intently, as if reading my thoughts. It occurred to me that I hadn't responded, hadn't said anything for several moments.

"Did you say you had discovered something relevant to the succubus case?" I asked.

"If you're sure you are up to it? I'd like you to see something else before we head to Whitehall."

Whatever was going on, I needed to know more. Whatever the rights and wrongs of the Office's approach to magic use, something was threatening the people of Cardiff, and maybe people more widely. One way or another, that needed to be stopped.

"I'm fine. No harm done."

"Excellent, follow me." He strode off down the corridor, moving at his usual brisk pace. He always seemed to be hurrying somewhere. He talked to me over his shoulder as went. He didn't appear to be hampered by the gouges in his back, although there was no way they could be healed yet.

"Aldwych is also used as a storage facility. In fact, the possessed statuary used to be kept here, before the numbers outgrew the place. A sizable collection of other artefacts is still stored at the station, though, as well as some of the older records. It is rather a shame you weren't granted access when you wrote your thesis; you might have uncovered some useful additions to your findings."

He stopped at another doorway, this one conventionally-sized and sealed with a heavy steel door. The Crow took out a key, then hesitated.

"Our London colleagues do not know I have a copy of this key. I was given it some time ago."

"You're the Lord High Witchfinder of All Wales, one of the seven Keyholders of the Star Chamber. They're not going to refuse you access."

"No, true, but it is possible someone might … move things around if they knew I did have easy access, or even attempt to obstruct us. So far as anyone knows, I am simply here to give you a glimpse of where Mormont was."

Once again, he was letting me in on his fears about conspiracies. Once again, I couldn't tell if he was doing so because he was trusting me, testing me or warning me.

I looked around, searching for the video cameras set in the high corners.

The Crow understood my thinking. "There are none down here. Only on the entrance above us."

"Convenient."

"Yes, isn't it?"

He unlocked the door and we went inside. The curved walls and ceiling inside suggested this was another disused tube tunnel. A string of fluorescent lights ran down the ceiling, flickering on in a line with audible *pings* as Hardknott-Lewis flicked a switch. There were no rails on the ground: instead, the space had been filled with steel shelving running in long lines down either side. Sealed plastic boxes of varying sizes filled the shelves, each numbered. From somewhere in the walls, I could hear the thrum of machinery, keeping the air dry, perhaps. This far underground, there had to be the risk of damp air harming the artefacts.

The Crow strode twenty paces down the room and crouched to open a box on the lowest shelf. He unclipped locks and pulled out some sketches encased in protective plastic sheeting.

"These were drawn in the 1870s by an East End cleric who was ... troubled by visitations." He handed the drawings over. They were succubi, there could be no doubt. A succession of female forms, scantily clad, their breasts and thighs on display in a way that I didn't normally associate with British Victorians. They were all in very suggestive poses – assuming you found mouths full of too many very sharp teeth and a forked tongue suggestive.

There were also a couple of grainy and blurred photographs, hiding more than they revealed, although one depicted the supposed face of the demon in crisp detail; its eyes wide and its lips parted in apparent ecstasy.

"How the hell did he manage to take photographs?" The technology in those days was obviously primitive, requiring long exposure times – which in turn required that subjects didn't move.

"There has been much debate about whether the whole

thing was faked. To my mind, the blurriness and graininess adds to the pictures' authenticity."

"But this cleric still might have fabricated the whole thing. He might have been sublimating his suppressed sexual desires into morally-approved channels." Oh yes, I'd paid attention in psych lectures.

"These entities closely resemble those that have attacked me. Very, very closely. Normally I might have dismissed them as prurient nonsense, yes, but under the circumstances I thought it might be a good idea to delve deeper into this case."

"Perhaps you and this cleric were both reacting to images you've been exposed to. You were both seeing what you expected to see."

"Perhaps."

I read the notes typed on the back of the sketches. "Revd Eli Williamsburg. What do we know about him?"

"Not a great deal. He preached in a small chapel near the docks, although he was something of a missionary too, taking his message into the taverns and brothels along the Thames, as well as into the hulks of the decommissioned ships they used as prisons. A brave man, I would say. From what I can tell, he came into conflict with one Cathal O'Donnell, whom he condemned for *encouraging and enabling the mortal sin of harlotry*."

"He procured women."

"And girls. And boys. I imagine there was much money to be made from the ships that docked in London from all over the world."

"I don't see how the succubi came to be involved."

"According to the Office's own records, O'Donnell had been a sailor himself as a younger man. He had acquired – stolen, I think we can say – various treasures from ports around the world. One was called the Chalice of Lilith Unrepentant, which he took from a temple of sorts in Morocco or Algeria. The artefact's origins are unclear, but it's certainly ancient, Mesopotamian or Assyrian. Are you familiar with the Lilith stories?"

I wasn't.

"A most interesting figure in our mythological and magical history. In some texts, she was the original partner of Adam. Refusing to accept his authority over her, she walked out of Eden – a move, I have to say, I rather admire. Perhaps because of this act, she is often depicted as a demon, the embodiment of rampant female sexuality. And then, perhaps because of that, she is often associated with succubi and incubi."

"The chalice can be used in some form of summoning rite?"

"Used correctly, filled with the relevant fluids and with the right syllables declaimed, it could summon succubi into our world if the sources are to be believed. O'Donnell thought this would be an amusing way to exact his revenge on Reverend Williamsburg."

I tried to look serious – it *was* serious – but a small part of me found the story amusing, too. Williamsburg had been a good man and O'Donnell not, sure, but I also wondered which of the two I'd have liked more if I'd met them.

"What happened?"

"The Office at that time, as you know, was somewhat ineffective, and it had a regrettable tendency to focus on magus law crimes harming only the rich and powerful. It was a different age, of course, but the victims here were deemed less important. By the time the Office intervened, Williamsburg had fallen under the thrall of a succubus and had taken to preaching to his flock about the, ah, joys of carnal activity. Raised a few eyebrows, as you can probably imagine. I have read a few of his sermons, and they are certainly … vivid. By this time, he had been under attack for some months. O'Donnell, meanwhile, largely ignorant in the rites and rituals he was dabbling in, was also suffering. He hadn't worked the incantations properly. Each attack upon Williamsburg took its toll on O'Donnell, too, draining him a little. By the time we were involved, they were both far gone, locked irrevocably in their spiral of revenge."

"Did they die?"

"They are both in Oblivion, close by each other as it happens."

"And the chalice?"

He nodded, as if approving of my logic. "Yes, the chalice. That is the important point. The Office seized it and stored it for later investigation. There was some talk of destroying it, but of course there we come to the usual dilemma: if we destroy, do we lose knowledge that might one day be vital? In any case, the chalice was hidden away. Eventually, after the war it was moved here, to this very vault."

He returned the sketches to their box and fastened it back up.

"They have kept meticulous records. The chalice is stored in container J/42/3."

"You've studied it?"

"Let me show you."

He led me down the shelves to an alcove that might once have been where another railway line joined. More shelves stretched away into the gloom. Did Lady Coldwater know about this place? There didn't seem to be anyone around like her, making sure things didn't fall into the wrong hands. Or the right hands, come to that.

The box we were looking for was on the highest shelf about twenty yards down. I reached up and slid the black box in question off the top shelf with my fingertips.

I expected it to be heavy, but I could hold it easily. I set it on the ground and the Crow opened up. He obviously knew what was going to be inside, and I had a pretty good idea by that point, too.

I shone my phone light inside. The box was empty. The Chalice of Lilith Unrepentant was gone.

11 – 13 Downing Street

Slept poorly again. Awoke at 3:00 am and could not return to my slumbers. In an attempt to exhaust my body and find oblivion, I left the house and ran through the streets for an hour, but it had little effect. I know why: these troubled dreams; the disturbing images that are waiting for me as soon as I close my eyes. They are a reaction to the demonic entities we have been battling recently, I'm sure, some post-traumatic psychological reaction. They are vivid, though. Their physical, sexual intensity can be … disturbing.

–Campbell Hardknott-Lewis, Lord High Witchfinder of All Wales, *private journal*, 2019

I searched the box in case there were any hidden compartments, but of course there weren't. This was not some cheap magician's prop such as El Encantador might have used to conceal a rabbit or a dove.

I peered up at the Crow, looming over me. "Have you ever seen the chalice?"

"It was not here when I first came to look. I have searched for it everywhere I could think of, obviously including Faebrook Folly, but there is no sign of it. My assumption is that Peter Warder removed it from its box at some point, but where he took it, I have no idea."

"We must know when he took it, at least. You said the records they keep are meticulous."

"Let me show you that. It is another puzzling detail."

I returned the empty box to its high shelf, and we retraced our steps to the vault entrance. The container nearest the door had no label on it, but inside was a surprisingly old-fashioned ledger, detailing each object brought into and out of the repository. The entries on the first page, scrawled in purple ink, told me that the book had been in use since the 1950s.

"The system is not quite as archaic as it seems," said the Crow, perhaps seeing my expression. "They also trace each object with an RFID tag. Warder could not simply remove the chalice without it being spotted."

Hardknott-Lewis turned to the last completed page in the ledger, then turned back a page. He ran his finger up the column of entries.

"Here. The chalice was removed for investigation and cleaning a little over two years ago. The entry is signed by Warder."

"He was taking a huge risk. The RFID tags must be logged in a database as the objects are brought in and out."

"Yes, except, according to the electronic records, the chalice was, indeed, returned a week later. Here." He showed me the ledger entry a few lines down, once again signed by Warder.

"He removed the tag, brought that back, and just hoped no one would notice that the chalice was missing."

"Just so," said the Crow. "I do not believe that it was a huge risk. Who would come and look?"

"You did."

"I did, true, but perhaps most people would not have made the connection. Remember, they didn't think I even had a key. If someone did notice, Warder could simply claim ignorance, say he dutifully brought the chalice back and placed it in its container. He was clever; he removed and returned numerous items ostensibly for analysis and cleaning at around this time, and all the others are safely back here. No one could accuse him of systematically ransacking the repository."

I studied the lines in the ledger, looking for some relevant detail. The obvious one was staring me in the face.

"Wait, the date," I said. "The chalice was removed over two years ago, yet you said the attacks upon you were recent."

The Crow returned the ledger to its box. "Tell me, Danesh, do you maintain a personal journal?"

Who the hell did that? This wasn't the Victorian age.

"I don't, no."

"Ah, well, if I may, I recommend the practice. I record my thoughts and reflections every night, setting down every significant event, or simply those matters that appear to me to be significant. I find the discipline a most useful exercise for working my ideas into straight lines. And the process, it helps me sleep, I find."

"Is it safe to record your thoughts, though?"

"I use a cipher of my own devising so that only I can read it."

"And your journal from two years ago tells you something relevant?"

We stepped out of the repository and he locked the door behind us. We headed back towards the Oblivion portal and the lift up to the surface. It took him a few moments to find the right words. Our footsteps echoed off the tiled walls as we went, punctuating the silences like the dots of an ellipsis…

"After recent events, I looked back over my notes from previous months, and began to see a wider pattern to the attacks I described to you. They have become much more physical of late, as you have seen. I said that they were weaker before, and I now believe that I have, in fact, been under assault for very nearly two years. It was remiss of me not to have done something about it previously."

I had to ask. "You said the earlier attacks were like vivid dreams. I assume there was a … sexual side to them?"

"Our sex drive is, of course, fundamentally intertwined with our nature, so I genuinely thought little of it. Sex as metaphor, sex as symbol: I told myself that this was what was going on. I didn't once consider that it was sex being used by a third-party as a weapon against me. As a way of weakening or discrediting me."

We had decided to walk to the Star Chamber meeting. The original plan had been to meet at the Possessed

Statue Warehouse that I recalled so fondly from my previous exploits in London. It was suitably out of the way and anonymous, and it also had plenty of room. For some reason, plans had been altered at the last moment, and now we were gathering at Earl Grey's house in Downing Street. Given Hardknott-Lewis's relentless walking pace, we would be there in twenty minutes. It was strange to be walking along familiar, busy streets, weaving in and out of the crowds, red buses whooshing past, all the while discussing the finer details of the Lord High Witchfinder of All Wales's experiences of assault by a hypersexualized demon.

"Something's changed, then," I said. "The attacks upon you became stronger after Warder died."

"I think so. My belief now is that Warder was behind the original attempts to harm me with these succubi, but that he was not powerful enough or skilled enough to summon the demons properly. The chalice provides a focus for the conjuration, but the summoner must still do the work and get the spells right. The demons he was able to call forth remained ethereal, or he could only bind weak ones."

I thought about that. "Right, so, and with Warder dead, someone a lot more capable and powerful has taken over."

"I assume so. This meeting of the Star Chamber is, in part, an attempt to answer the question of who that might be. You recall I explained to you that I had an English colleague who had possibly experienced something similar? We have been discussing matters, and that now definitely appears to be the case. The question is, how widely do the attacks go? These are not, as you are perhaps experiencing, easy matters to discuss, but discuss them we must. If someone is attempting to cripple the leadership of the Office of the Witchfinder General, then we need to address the situation urgently."

"This English colleague will be at the meeting?"

"What I am telling you must go no further, but yes, he will be there. It is Mason Greentree. It was he I was talking to in Herefordshire. He has a rather nice weekend cottage there, only ten miles from Martha Ndidi's house, as it happens."

Right. Mason Greentree was the Lord High Witchfinder of all England, the Crow's equivalent across the border. The fact that Hardknott-Lewis was confiding in me – and the fact that he'd provided a perfectly reasonable reason for the Office's high command to meet that had nothing to do with my misdemeanours – was not lost on me. Perhaps I was in the clear after all. I breathed a little easier as we walked along Whitehall. The sun peered out from the cloud it had been skulking behind all day and shone on me for a moment. The grand, white facades of the fine buildings along Whitehall briefly *glowed*, I swear.

"What do you want me to do?" I asked.

"Convocations of the Star Chamber are, in many senses, no different to any other sorts of meetings. The real decisions, the actually useful exchanges of information, happen beforehand, or afterwards, or in the tea break. I want you to, well, would you say network? I believe that is considered a verb these days. All seven Keyholders will be in the chamber, but we will all have brought along advisors and acolytes. You will be left to wait around outside. I would be grateful if you could find out anything useful from the others during that time."

"It sounds as if you're not sure who you can trust in the Office hierarchy."

We walked in silence for a moment, the Crow swerving off the pavement to grant someone in a wheelchair safe passage.

"Honestly?" he said when he was back beside me. "I would trust each and every one of them with my life, and have done so many times, but the simple fact is that they may not want to admit to their fellow Keyholders anything … embarrassing. I, for example, will find it most uncomfortable to be frank about my experiences with the succubi that have attacked me. But a trusted colleague that they work with every day – a person such as yourself in my case – that may be a different matter."

Was he laying it on too thick? Possibly.

"I'll see what I can do," I said.

I'd never entered Downing Street before. Not many people have. Of course, there's a lot of security, and the odd little *cul de sac* of old houses in the heart of London where the Prime Minister resides, and from where many of the decisions affecting the UK are made, is shielded from the outside world by high steel gates and car bomb bollards and a small platoon of armed police officers with blank expressions. Not that I blame them; they've seen some bad stuff in recent years. I had stood at those gates as a boy on a school trip to Westminster, peering through the gaps, and I'd strolled past often enough on my way to and from the river. Now I was being admitted inside.

We strode along the pavement past Number 10, beneath a lamp suspended from a black iron arch, directly in front of that austere black door familiar from so many news broadcasts, when the door, unexpectedly, opened. The armed police officer standing on guard outside appeared to be aware someone was coming out, the message presumably whispered into his earpiece. He peered inside the building, nodding that it was safe to emerge, and a tall man dressed in black robes appeared on the pavement directly in front of us. His hair was grey and he sported a full Biblical prophet beard. His features were vaguely familiar, although I couldn't put a name to them. Around his neck was a large silver crucifix. Two acolytes, a young man and a young woman, both in very sensible suits, followed in his trail. Both were laden down with armfuls of binders and papers.

The robed man hesitated at the sight of the two of us. One of his bushy eyebrows shot up. His gaze had flicked across me, but he appeared to know Hardknott-Lewis judging by the disapproving scowl the man cast at the Crow.

His voice was little more than a whisper, as if he didn't want anyone to overhear his words. "Hardknott-Lewis. Here you are again."

"Fighting the good fight," Hardknott-Lewis said in reply, his voice louder. Deliberately so. There was a hardness in his tones that I recognized. It was one he generally reserved for magus law criminals. Necromancers and summoners and clairvoyants.

"Of course, of course," the robed man said. "And, you're sure you're fully up to speed on what constitutes *good* and what *evil*, yes? No confusion there? They can be tricky concepts to tie down. I'm always happy to provide you with some guidance."

Hardknott-Lewis's politeness was as brittle as a sliver of ice on a puddle of water. "No confusion at all from me. But, please, should you ever feel *you* are in need of guidance, you know where to find me."

The robed man looked as though he wanted to say more, but one of his acolytes laid her hand on his forearm, whispered something to him. He nodded.

"Well, forgive me, we have pressing matters to attend to. I'm sure we'll meet again."

"I'm sure we will."

The robed man strode off saying nothing more. The two acolytes in his wake frowned daggers at us, but didn't speak.

We walked too, completing the short walk down to Number 12.

"Who was that?"

"That was the Archbishop of Canterbury."

That was where I'd seen him. "Oh, it was? Right. Aren't you supposed to refer to him as *Your Grace* or something?"

"The situation is … delicate. The Office does not recognize the right of the archbishops of the Church of England to sit in parliament as a matter of right."

That threw me. Another aspect of our work that had passed me by.

"It doesn't?"

We stopped outside Number 12 while the officer guarding it knocked and awaited a response from within.

"It doesn't," said the Crow, speaking quietly now so

that only I would hear. "In truth, we have a somewhat troubled relationship with the established church. Of course, we were once firm allies, united against the diabolic and so forth. These days, well, we in the Office oppose all supernaturalism, and the church comes under that heading, does it not? Private worship is one thing, perhaps, but we have tried very hard – and so far failed – to have the twenty-six Lords Spiritual removed from the upper chamber. As things stand, the UK parliament contains that number of unelected representatives, there only because of their belief in certain transcendent or supernatural entities. It is a strange state of affairs in a modern democracy."

"He seemed to know who you are, what you do."

"Yes, all the archbishops are in the know. They, in turn, have often tried to have us disbanded. Cast out, if you like. We oppose their presence in parliament, and they are aware of the fact and lobby to have us dissolved. They find our knowledge and our activities distasteful. The irony is that they say we have no place in the modern, twenty-first century state. We cannot fight them too openly as we do not wish to be publicly denounced."

"I had no idea."

"Well, no. One of many things we don't like to talk about, of course."

The door to Number 12 was finally opened, and the police officer stepped aside to grant us access.

The interior was oddly shabby, the décor of a mid-century townhouse that had been allowed to slowly fade and scuff. There were gilded chandeliers hanging from the ceiling and there were portraits of politicians and diplomats and Generals scowling from the walls. I could smell *years* of wood-polish and dust in the air. There was something typically British about the whole place: it was understated, backwards-looking, a bit shabby. I wasn't taken in for a moment; it was all part of a cunning and ruthlessly-conceived plan. Look and sound archaic, perhaps even a bit of a joke, and people won't notice the high-tech military state operating behind the scenes. I got it. It was an approach we in the Office also employed, in our own quiet way.

Number 13 Downing Street doesn't actually exist – officially speaking. It isn't on any of the maps. If you look the address up in any of the histories, they'll tell you that it was subsumed into what is now 12 Downing Street (two doors down from the Prime Minister) in 1876. As so often, this is simply the Office's preferred version of events. 13 is very definitely still there, although there's no austere black door with the number on it in white for all the world to see – at least, not on the outside. To get into Number 13, you go in through Number 12, and then, half-way along a wood-panelled corridor is an unremarkable door that says, simply, *13* on it.

We passed through that hallowed portal now.

The corridor that was revealed looked no different to the one outside: richly-carpeted, everything slightly faded. Different dead white men stared down at us from the portraits, though: individuals I recognized from the Crow's office and the few Office history books I'd studied. Or, well, *skimmed*. These weren't Generals and diplomats; they were former Witchfinders General.

We passed a flight of stairs leading up, presumably, to Earl Grey's private quarters. Somewhere there'd be steps down to a cellar, too: it was said that a private tunnel linked Number 13 with Number 10. The Office wasn't technically a department of the UK state – we were too semi-detached – and the Witchfinder General didn't have a seat in cabinet, but if the PM needed to consult with the Office on some supernatural threat facing the UK, Earl Grey could be summoned without having to use the street outside and potentially arousing the suspicions of any lurking reporters. There'd been various episodes in recent history when, according to Office rumour, that tunnel had been used a lot. During World War II, for example, when the V1s and V2s rained down on London during the Blitz, there'd also been attacks of a more supernatural nature. Some rockets had delivered seething packs of malevolent spirits rather than conventional explosives.

A hubbub of voices murmured from a room around the corner. The varnished wooden door we needed to pass through had a brass sign on it, bearing, simply, the letters *ABRA*.

Hardknott-Lewis obviously caught me looking puzzled by them. "A weak attempt at humour by some civil servant, I've always assumed."

"I don't … ah, right, like, *abracadabra*?"

"Which, obviously, is not actually any kind of real-world incantation. You're familiar with COBRA, I assume?"

"The emergency committee that meets to discuss urgent matters of national threat."

"Just so. It is simply a room up the road in Whitehall, COBRA standing for Cabinet Office Briefing Room A. This is our equivalent, a suitably vague name despite the attempt at levity. This is Alternative Briefing Room A."

"Right. And is there a CADABRA anywhere?"

"If there is, I've never seen it. Although, now that I think about it, we do have an annual meeting in here that we refer to as the Contingencies and Decisions committee."

It took me a moment to work that out in my head. "Hilarious."

"I'm afraid that there have been times when we in the Office of the Witchfinder General have struggled to be taken seriously by those in the more mundane branches of government. Perhaps it is for the best."

The Crow pushed open the door. Two distinct sets of people stood inside, sipping at coffee from china cups and nibbling at the little triangular sandwiches and the bland biscuits that had been provided. One group consisted of the Keyholders of the Star Chamber: those who ran the various sections of the Office. The other, clustered on the other side of the room, contained the various advisors and acolytes and minions the Keyholders had brought along. My people.

I recognized the Keyholders: nearest was Mason Greentree, in charge of England, an academic-looking man with a bald head and a pair of delicate Gandhi glasses. He was so skinny he looked like he'd snap in a high breeze. Or even if he leaned over too sharply.

Then there was Ian Majkowski of Scotland, perhaps the youngest of the group at pushing fifty. He'd retained his ridiculously good film star looks despite his advancing years: high cheekbones, a strong jaw, luxuriant hair that he occasionally flicked back out of his eyes with a jerk of his head. Some people were just lucky.

Next to him was the Irishman Mac Ferrier. He was a large man in every way: tall, wide and personality-wise. You could imagine him standing in the middle of a crowded bar, holding court, roaring with laughter as he recounted some hilarious anecdote or other. He was, supposedly, profoundly intelligent, one of those people who seemed to have an informed opinion on any subject you brought up.

Slightly behind them all stood Thomas Quirk, responsible for the various scattered isles and scraps of land that didn't fit anywhere else. He was the tallest of the group, standing head and shoulders over the others. He had a slight stoop, as if from constantly leaning down to hear the words of those around him. Despite his age – 60 something maybe? – he also had a full mop of hair, scattered wildly around his head as though he were permanently standing in an offshore gale.

Talvin Epenesa was there too: he covered *Overseas Domains*, a somewhat reductive term that, basically, meant all of the rest of the world – especially those parts that had once been part of the British Empire and that were now in the Commonwealth. His constituency was hundreds, thousands of times bigger than any of the others, but the Office being what it was, he was generally considered the last among equals in the hierarchy. There was something shabby and dusty about him; he had the look of an exasperated schoolteacher from a second-rank secondary school – or perhaps an accountant who can't quite believe the depreciation rates on the balance sheet he's been given. These faded librarian looks were deceptive; I knew he was a ferocious combatant when it came to facing down revenants and demonic presences. He *hated* them; took their very existence as a personal affront.

With the Crow (Wales, obviously) joining them, that made six: the only one missing from the group was Earl Grey himself, responsible for *All Britain and the British Isles* and the superior of everyone else in the room. The Keyholders were, I noted once again, all white men of a certain age. Even Epenesa, with his promising-sounding name, fitted that mould. Maybe the Office wasn't so different to every other powerful body in the land, but I wasn't convinced. Perhaps the lack of oversight that we enjoyed made it easier for the old guard to protect their positions of privilege.

The other group in the room was more encouraging in that regard. There were women *and* men, people of colour, a guy in a wheelchair. Lincoln was there, standing among them, his poltergeist presumably quietened for the moment. One of the Scottish team had come out as gay a year or so back and no one had batted an eyelid. I'd mentioned the fact to Olwen, whose sister, I knew, was trans. Her response had been, *We're far too busy battling real monsters to go round inventing our own*. Perhaps the Office was, slowly, making progress. Even in the Office it's the twenty-first century, although, sometimes, it feels like it's still the seventeenth. Perhaps in twenty years' time, some of these individuals would be among the all-powerful seven gathering for Star Chamber hearings.

Maybe. And maybe, miraculously, it would be the white males in the group who happened to be *the best person for the job* when it came to the selection process, and the Office really was institutionally, maybe even literally, stuck in the dark ages. Hardknott-Lewis I trusted, in this regard at least, but the others, the whole hierarchy of the Office? Not so much.

While the Crow went to engage with his fellow Keyholders, I ambled over to join the younger set in the other corner. I picked up a cup of black coffee from a nearby table. It was dismally weak, but I'd steeled myself for the grim prospect.

We acolytes knew each other by name from reading our various case reports, and one or two I recognized from joint Office operations and Office parties. We chatted idly for a time, breaking the ice and making lame jokes. We were all so used to being wary around people we didn't work with every day that it always took time for us to open up, even with people we knew we could trust.

After five minutes of this, the Crow crossed the divide to touch my elbow and let me know they were going into session. There was no mistaking the meaningful look in his eye: *find out what you can*. The temptation to ask whether they were going to be discussing me at all was a powerful one. I resisted manfully.

The Keyholders of the Star Chamber filed into the inner sanctum where they would meet. I caught a glimpse of an oak-panelled interior, seven chairs set in a circle upon a black-and-white mosaic tiled floor. It looked like some courtroom from Victorian days, grim and austere.

Beyond the chamber lay a yet-more dimly lit anteroom, in which I caught a glimpse of two other figures, apparently locked in some urgent conversation. One I recognized: it was Earl Grey himself, Her Majesty's Witchfinder General. I'd never actually spoken to him, and I doubted he'd have a clue who I was without someone whispering in his ear, but his features were obviously familiar. If we'd had a public face, he'd have been it. In any other government department of a similar size, he would be the one popping up on television every few months to tell the public it was all fine, everything was under control. I had attended two or three of his new starter lectures in my early days in the Office, and his quiet, conversational manner had impressed me enormously. He'd talked about facing down the nightmares and horrors he'd battled with all the drama with which I might describe cooking a meal. Actually, probably with *less* drama: I'd so far failed to inherit my mother's or my grandmother's abilities in the kitchen, and if I attempted anything complex, things could get a little … fraught.

The other figure, meanwhile, I didn't know: a much older man I thought, and considerably taller than Earl Grey. In the dim glow, something to do with the way the single light in the room was behind him, his white face seemed almost translucent. For the briefest moment I thought it was the Archbishop of Canterbury again; this figure wore similar flowing robes, deepest black. This man's head, however, was completely hairless. He also had some pendant or symbol hung around his neck, but I couldn't make out what it was. The two men were almost squaring up to each other, and I had the clear impression, in that brief moment, that they were arguing. Earl Grey was pointing something out with a jabbing finger. The older man was scowling, arms crossed. He shook his head as if to dismiss whatever the Witchfinder General was saying. Then I lost sight of them as the others passed through the outer doorway.

Once they were all inside, a functionary wound a red slip of silk around the handles of the double doors in a sideways figure of eight, an infinity symbol, symbolically sealing the room off from outside intrusion. It didn't look like my plan to corner Earl Grey and have a quiet word about the Crow's possible complicity in his succubus attack was going to work out. I'd see what they discussed in open convocation: if Hardknott-Lewis was anything like as open with them as he had been with me, the extent of his involvement would be clear enough to all the Keyholders. Not much I could add to the debate.

I turned back to Lincoln and was about to speak when his phone started buzzing. His Office phone, I could tell: low-tech, old spec, not very cool. Lincoln frowned as he read some message.

"What is it?" I asked.

He scowled, although whether it was because of me or the words on his phone, I didn't know.

"Trouble," he said, not looking up.

I persisted. The Crow would have been proud of me.

"Bad trouble?"

Lincoln sighed and glanced at me. He started to speak

but then stopped himself.

"Maybe it's something I have experience of," I said.

His voice was a low murmur when he finally spoke, like he was trying to work something out.

"Keep the faith."

"Um, I'm, sorry?"

He translated for me. "The threat; it's a keep the faith. A Code 18."

Right. More rhyming slang: *keep the faith*, *wraith*. A Code 18 covered any spectral or indistinct presence glimpsed inside smoke, cloud or fog. In the lovely, sunny climate we enjoy in South Wales they're surprisingly common, although they tend to be benign, indistinct, and easy to pass off as figments of the overactive Celtic imagination.

Lincoln slipped his phone back into his suit pocket.

"I need to go," he said.

"Where is it?"

"Nearby. Down on Westminster Bridge."

That was very nearby – and disconcertingly public. A possibility occurred to me. "Want me to come with? Two-person rule and so on?"

"This is a London Office matter."

"Right, and you're as understaffed as we are. More so since you lost – " I caught myself before I spoke Warder's name. "More so with recent losses, right? I'm Wales, sure, but I can legally operate anywhere in the UK. We all can. You know this. Besides, I'm a London boy at heart, born and bred."

He didn't like it, I could tell, but there was no escaping my iron logic. He had his doubts about me, but maybe things were no longer quite so black and white. Or maybe he'd been instructed to watch me as closely as I was him.

His face was expressionless as he looked at me. "You sure?"

"Sure."

He shrugged. "Okay, let's go."

Together, we left the building.

12 – Moments of Clarity

> Fog everywhere. Fog up the river, where it flows
> among green aits and meadows; fog down the river,
> where it rolls defiled among the tiers of shipping
> and the waterside pollutions of a great (and dirty)
> city. Fog on the Essex marshes, fog on the Kentish
> heights. Fog creeping into the cabooses of collier-
> brigs; fog lying out on the yards, and hovering in
> the rigging of great ships; fog drooping on the
> gunwales of barges and small boats. Fog in the eyes
> and throats of ancient Greenwich pensioners,
> wheezing by the firesides of their wards; fog in the
> stem and bowl of the afternoon pipe of the wrathful
> skipper, down in his close cabin; fog cruelly
> pinching the toes and fingers of his shivering little
> 'prentice boy on deck.
>
> –Charles Dickens, *Bleak House*, 1853

London has always been susceptible to fogs and smogs. True fact that they taught us all at primary school: it's effectively a coastal town as the Thames is tidal all the way up to Teddington Lock. The sea and river mists combined with heavy industrial and domestic smoke in the past meant that London used to suffer from *pea souper* fogs so thick that thousands died. The filth got into people's lungs and stuck there. At its worst, your actual street urchins had to be employed to carry flaming torches to lead people around the streets, take them back to their houses – or maybe into some dank alley where the gang of hoodlums was waiting. In Victorian times, the incidence of diseases like cholera and typhoid was blamed on the foul miasma that Londoners were breathing in – and coughing out.

It's better these days, although cars, lorries and buses have stepped up to fill the void in our pollution levels left behind by the Clean Air Acts. What's less well-known is that the mists harbour other dangers too – mysterious faces and indistinct figures glimpsed in the fogs and smogs – and while these are also less prevalent, they are most definitely still there. Either these are magical entities who live within miasmas, as fish need water to swim in, or else the smoke and mist simply forms a convenient canvas upon which passing spirits can manifest. Whatever the truth of it, there are many references to them in the (Office-redacted) history. Londoners in the 1950s named them *smokewraiths* and, more prosaically, *mistfuckers*, and while we in the Office have successfully debunked such notions as the *obvious nonsense* that they aren't, we remain alert to the risks. Not only do such wraiths scare the living hell out of people, we also have reports of angrier variants causing people direct harm and of some individuals – often children – being *taken*. They walk into a bank of mist and are never seen again.

Walking into a bank of mist, meanwhile, was exactly what Lincoln and I were about to do. We raced together down Parliament Street for the bridge. I could feel the air getting colder and damper on my face as we neared the river. I glanced aside at him, tried to engage with him as we hurried along.

"Do you have a plan or do we just charge in?"

He had a determined look in his eye. "I'll go in, you stay back and relay intel to base." His voice was leaden in the heavy air. Detail around us was already fading away as the air thickened.

"I'm going in too," I said. "No knowing what we'll find in there."

He shrugged, like it was of little importance. I tried again.

"Do you think this is random or is someone doing this? Is this an attack?"

That got a reaction, a calculating glance thrown at me.

"What make you say *attack*?"

I stopped running with the bridge directly up ahead. The ornate walls and gothic glasswork of the Elizabeth Tower – Big Ben to you, me and everyone else in the world – loomed overhead. They were weirdly indistinct, though; I had the odd sensation that I was on a stage or a filmset, and that the walls and buildings around me were simply painted onto the backdrop.

"Because we've been under attack in Cardiff," I said. "Deliberate and powerful magical attacks."

A throng of people had collected around the bridge, people from all over the world merrily taking snaps on their phones of the fog. We had to push our way through. We just had to assume that no one was paying any attention to what we were saying – or that they'd dismiss it as more of the craziness you hear on London's streets.

There was a calculating look in Lincoln's eye. "An attack?"

"We've seen definite suggestions of a coordinated effort to undermine us in Wales," I said. "Certain entities have been brought to bear upon us to weaken us. Maybe, even destroy us."

"What entities?"

"Bad entities. Is it possible you've seen something similar here? That this goes wider?"

He looked like he was going to say something, then thought better of it.

"We get stuff like this all the time. This? Probably a false alarm. People see faces in the mist and imagine the ghosts have come to eat them."

When we reached the river, Westminster Bridge was gone – swallowed whole by the rolling cloud of fog coming off the Thames. As well as the crowd of onlookers, there was a traffic jam around the entrance, cars and buses held up by the red lights that glowed through the haze as if they were flaming torches. Across the river I could see the upper half of the London Eye peering out over the bank of mist. In between was … grey. The effect was weirdly localised: a hundred metres upstream or downstream, the air was clear. No doubt a meteorologist could give you a perfectly rational explanation as to why – but I had theories of my own. The air as I inhaled it was heavy with moisture; there was a solidity to it that made breathing more like eating. Even my movements were sluggish as I waded onto the bridge, the leaden weight of the air slowing me down.

Within a few steps, we were on our own: London faded away and we were moving through a hazy bubble. The universe consisted of me, Lincoln and a circle of tarmac around our feet. It was as if I were in a computer game and the hardware wasn't powerful enough to maintain an adequate draw-distance. The sun was nothing more than a circle of brighter haze within the mist. Then even that was gone. The bridge was devoid of vehicles; presumably the traffic flow controllers had spotted the developing problem and had switched the lights to red at both ends before things got too snarled up. I was grateful: it meant there were fewer people around to witness anything uncanny, and we also didn't need all those diesel and petrol fumes adding to the smog.

My mother liked to describe cold winds as *lazy winds* because they went right through you rather than bothering to go around. It was a phrase that I recalled had always delighted my father, and he liked to use it to describe just about any slight breeze he encountered. The air was completely still today: but we were experiencing what my mother might have called a lazy fog. It also didn't bother to go around us: instead, it seemed to seep through my skin to turn my bones to ice. The tips of my fingers were already going white, and that isn't good if they're supposed to be a delicate olive brown.

I was about to comment upon the cold to Lincoln when we heard muffled cries coming out of the fog ahead of us.

We froze – metaphorically and, increasingly, literally. I caught Lincoln's calculating look. Without either of us speaking, we each drew our Office weapons and stepped forwards, into the unknown.

A man charged out of the gloom, his features suddenly

clear right in front of us. A businessman judging by his suit and tie, his face twisted into an expression of terror. He was screaming words that made no sense, and in his hand, he carried a laptop case which he was flailing ineffectually around, as if he was using it as a weapon to bat away unseen assailants.

We let him go. Thirty yards further on, I nearly tripped over a figure lying on the ground. For the briefest moment, I thought someone had dropped a pile of old clothes on the road, but I twigged pretty quickly that wasn't it.

She was another office worker, impossible to say if she was alive or dead. I knelt down, ready to give CPR while Lincoln stood guard. But as soon as I saw her face, I knew it was futile. Her skin wasn't just blue, it was rimed in frost, as if she'd been immersed in frozen water for hours. Low moans and whispers seeped out of the mists, seeming to dance and swirl around us, but she wasn't going to make any sounds every again.

I stood back up. "Okay. We're definitely not alone in here."

"Yeah, I…"

Lincoln didn't complete his sentence as the fog in front of him became suddenly more solid, rushing at him. I glimpsed a head attached to a hazy, limbless body, the mouth impossibly wide and full of hundreds of pointed teeth.

Do you know what a Jenny Haniver is? The Seacastle book has a section on them, and they were vaguely familiar from my induction. Once there'd been a proper cryptozoological department in the Office – the *Monster Hunters*, a bit like the Nazi Hunters – but cuts had meant we had to do that job, too, now. The story we've had accepted is that the creatures are just the desiccated bodies of rays and skates made to look like weird, haunty sea-creatures – because some of them, the copies, are. The originals, though, the malign spirits that sailors once knew all about, are real enough. Go look them up, they're deeply hideous.

That's what these wraiths resembled: the malign ghosts of Jenny Hanivers. Summoned, maybe, from the unlit depths of the North Sea. Although I was bang in central London, I was suddenly very conscious that I was over tidal water and that the air was thick with moisture. Perhaps that had made this particular act of summoning easier, given it a focus. There was something of the cold depths in the creatures' swimming movements, in their deep moaning as they swam around. These were entities of the lightless void. I felt the muscles in my limbs thicken and slow a notch. My core muscles reacted by starting to shiver in an attempt to keep me warm. Maybe it was just the temperature, and maybe it was some deep-seated reaction to these entities.

Lincoln raised his weapon to fire, but he was too slow. The wraith hit him in the head, seemed to swim *through* his skull. It slowed slightly as it went, as if wriggling its way through the cavities and lobes of his brain. As it passed through him, it gave off a high-pitched screech that I felt in my teeth. There was hunger in it, and also delight. A creature from the depths devouring his heat and life.

Lincoln dropped to the ground like a sack of rice thrown off a cargo boat. I took aim at the wraith but it was gone, melting back into the fog. I saw it – or another one – writhe out of the mist like a malign eel to my side, but it also vanished before I could react.

I stepped backwards, but I'd become disorientated in the fog. I was no longer sure which way *backwards* was. Perhaps if Big Ben had chosen to strike at that moment, I could have orientated myself – but the odd thing was that I could no longer hear the sounds of the city: no background hum of vehicles, no emergency vehicle sirens, nothing. Weirdly, what I could hear, very clearly, was the gurgle and rush of the water passing somewhere beneath my feet. The air tasted of brine and seaweed.

I found one of the white lines in the road and followed it in what I hoped was the direction of the centre of the bridge. Another indistinct figure emerged from the mist, this one a shape about my own height. There was something tree-like in its pose: the arms held wide like branches. For some reason, it made me think of the Crow's vision of Oblivion. It was stationary, but I began to pick up the murmur of magic being worked; a steady stream of incantatory vowels. I switched my Office phone to start collecting audio in case the syllables proved to be evidential. Or in case I didn't survive and my colleagues needed some clue about what had happened.

Gun in one hand, blade in the other, I took another step forward. I was suddenly in light, a bubble of clear air, the walls of fog held back. And, standing at its centre, arms held wide, a figure wearing the sort of robes supposedly beloved of wizards everywhere, at least if you believed the movies.

The summoner of the smokewraiths, no doubt about it. He was a man, I thought, but it was hard to be completely sure: the robes were white and flowing and covered his torso and limbs completely, right down to the black leather boots on his feet. The robes covered his face, also: he was wearing something like the traditional pointed hat with a wide brim, but it had a flap of cloth, a mask, sewn into it, so that only his eyes were visible through little holes. The garb managed to look both ridiculous and deeply sinister at the same time. Imagine Gandalf had joined the Ku Klux Klan and become a very different sort of Grand Wizard – that was the look. Such clothes had been described to us before, of course – from the images plucked by Gilroy out of the dead minds of both Evan Cornwallis and Martha Ndidi.

Just to make it absolutely clear, there was also a symbol on the front of the man's robes: a stylized oak tree with seven stars arrayed around it. There could be no doubt.

English Wizardry.

On the ground around the man were three more victims. They were alive but writhing in agony, curled up in foetal huddles. Each had two or three of the Jenny

Haniver smokewraiths winding in and out of their bodies, feeding and feeding on them. Each of the three gave off grunts and whimpers of pain and distress, sounds far below the level of intelligible speech.

I took another step forwards while my thumb dialled in a standard ballistic round on my Office handgun. No need to mess around with anything magical against a flesh-and-blood human. Assuming that was what was underneath the robes.

"Arms by your side and get down on the ground," I shouted. If any civilians were nearby and overheard, they might not think anything spooky was going on.

The figure's voice was muffled behind the mask covering his face. A man's voice, though, deep and slightly rough, as if he was an older person.

"Get down on the ground yourself, half-breed scum. The gutter is where you belong, on the ground with these worms, beneath the feet of the true-born Englishman."

The user moved his hands through a rapid series of complex motions and more wraiths were suddenly all around me, looping out of the fog to swarm across my body, fly into my face. My finger twitched on the trigger of my weapon, but I didn't fire. No knowing where the round would go without me being able to take careful aim, not unless I could get right up to him.

The guttural sounds from the three victims had lessened a little as he talked. I'd taken his attention off his victims.

"Who are you," I shouted. "Why are you doing this?"

"You know who we are. This land is corrupted, infected. Overrun. We are bringing it back to itself, returning it to the old ways. This is a warning and a lesson."

It was fair to say that none of the three victims would have ticked the *White British* box on the census form. Whether they were locals out for a walk or tourists seeing the sights, I had no idea. They'd simply been in the wrong place at the wrong time.

I kept him talking, moved a step closer. A couple more paces and I could risk a shot. "Your *old ways* never existed. They're a fantasy. None of that shit in your head is real. I'm going to tell you one more time. Put your arms down and dismiss this magic. Send these wraiths back to the water they came from."

I was getting to him, riling him maybe. The mist spirits still drifted around the three victims in a halo, but they were no longer attacking.

The user's voice was a growl. "Witchfinder lackey; you will be destroyed when we come to power in this land. When the natural order is restored and all the degenerates are removed."

Keeping my eyes focused on his, I took another step forwards. Close enough. In one rapid motion, I raised my gun to my sight-line and squeezed the trigger.

I wasn't quick enough; he'd seen it coming. Wraiths were suddenly a seething ball knotting themselves around my right forearm, freezing my muscles, sucking out their strength. The icy contact of the creatures was so intense that it felt like burning. Maybe if I hadn't had the Lady's ring on my finger the effect would have been worse, but as it was, I dropped the gun to the ground. I still had my knife, though. It was in my left hand, my weaker hand, but I could put it to use. I threw myself at him, lunging for his chest, the oak tree logo providing a convenient target.

He anticipated that, too. A wall of force, some spell, threw me to the ground, my back thumping hard into the tarmac. Was this what he'd used to pin down his victims so the wraiths could attack? Had to be: the knot of hideous demons that had frozen my hand so effectively were swirling around my head now, as if choosing an orifice to battle their way through to get to my brain. There were too many of them. I swung at them wildly with my clothcutter blade and caught one, dissipating it back to mist. That was good: they were summoned entities, pulled from elsewhere to be there on the bridge, in the mist. Two, three, four more took its place, though. I could feel their contact as the worst brain-freeze ever. Still lying on my back on the ground, I tried to crawl away, get back to the light, off the bridge. It was no use. The wizard took a step towards me and the bubble of light, our private little globe theatre, moved with us. He made a little flicking movement with his hands, and this time the creatures came for my left hand, numbing the blade from my fingers, leaving me weaponless.

He stood over me. "Do you see, now? Do you understand? This oak, it is not simply a tree. It is a depiction of the natural order. There is a hierarchy. There are those at the top and there are those born to be lower down, made to support those above them. And then there are those that should be buried, to feed the tree. That is the way it should be. In that way, all knowing our places, we all survive."

I saw his fingers flex as he performed the prestidigitations that his magic required, corralling the mistwraiths to feast on my mind.

Funny how life goes. There I was in basically zero-visibility; the fog from the river so heavy I could see nothing, the world outside our bubble nothing more than grey – and I saw everything. A moment of clarity. I couldn't fight this user and the creatures he was controlling with my Office training and my gadgets. The whole thing was ridiculous. I needed to fight magic with magic. I had abilities and I was risking my life by not using them.

And, as with Warder, I wanted to do this. And again, as with Warder, my opponent appeared to have no idea what I was capable of. With Mormont and Warder gone, there was no one to pass on the information to the rest of English Wizardry. Even if there had been, the wizard standing over me presumably had no idea who I was, and wouldn't have expected an operative from Cardiff to be there in central London. Maybe he didn't even see me as an individual, worthy of his close attention.

I felt the fire kindle, then begin to rage within me. It grew rapidly – like opening the valve on a Bunsen burner and turning the benign, pottering flame into a jet of roaring blue energy.

It seethed inside me, and the sensation was suddenly alarming. My attack on Warder had manifested in the real world as heat, which was perhaps why my inner eye was seeing the energy as fire. As before, I seemed to feel the blood in my veins boil, my bones char from the conflagration. I had to expel it, urgently, before it consumed me. This time, maybe, I had a little more control over what sensation I was doing, the timing of it, but I had no real idea about how to keep the mounting energy safely contained, or whether there was a way of letting the flame channel safely away without being expressed.

I held up my hand, palm facing upwards. Perhaps the wizard thought it was an unconscious act of self-defence, nothing more. The mistake was his undoing. A boiling red line of flame, so intense that it was almost solid, blasted from my hand and into his chest. It hurled him backwards like a rag doll, his limbs flailing as he thumped into the tarmac of the bridge.

Instantly, the mistwraiths were gone, returning to whatever depths they'd been summoned from, or fading back into the substrate of the foggy air.

I stood, clutching my right hand, the hand I'd used to work the magic, in my left. My flesh was hot as if it were sunburned, but there were no marks upon me to show that anything had happened. There was still a coil of rage smouldering inside me, but it didn't feel like it was in danger of raging out of control at any moment. It was like … the embers of a bonfire, the ash and an occasional red spark, rather than the fire itself.

I walked over to the English Wizardry user, lying where I'd hurled him. His back and limbs were ricked at broken angles. He wasn't moving, wasn't breathing. I kicked him once, just to see if there was a reaction, then lifted back his mask, put the back of my hand near his mouth and lips, feeling for a breath.

Nothing. I had killed another English Wizardry operative.

Or, to put it another way, another person.

13 – Progeny

Moreover, to beget a child is the act of a living body, but devils cannot bestow life upon the bodies they assume; because life formally proceeds only from the soul, and the act of generation is the act of the physical organs which have bodily life. Therefore bodies which are assumed in this way cannot either beget or bear.

–Henricus Institoris, *Malleus Maleficarum*, 1487

I stood back up, trying to decide what I should do. The man's features were twisted in agony and perhaps shock at what had been done to him, but I was sure I didn't recognize him. I took some shots of his face in case I didn't get another chance when my colleagues from the Office and the regulars arrived at the scene to tidy up.

The three victims he'd been tormenting were still alive, slowly uncurling themselves from their agonies and blinking in wide-eyed alarm.

"What happened?" one asked, an Asian-looking guy with a strong Scottish accent. "Who the fuck was that?"

"What do you remember?" I asked.

"I don't…" The guy looked at the other two victims, then around at the scene: the fog, the bridge. I could almost see his brain trying and failing to reconcile what he'd witnessed with what he knew was possible.

"I was attacked. I think. This guy come out of nowhere, all shouty and scary. After that it's all a bit vague. He was wearing, like, crazy white robes, like a monk or a ghost or something. And there were all these creatures, vicious wee ghosts, their heads full of bastard sharp teeth snapping at me."

"We'll get you looked at. You banged your head on the

ground; your memories are probably a bit mixed up."

"There was a guy," he insisted.

"There was. He's over there, he's been neutralized. But there were obviously no – what did you say? – vicious ghosts."

Often with these things it's important to get your preferred delusions, your official version of events, in as early as possible. Plant the seeds so they can grow.

He stared over at the wizard, then up at me. "Are you the police?"

"Something like that. I'll go and get them, and an ambulance. Stay here while I look at the others, okay?"

"Right you are, yep," he said, as if I'd simply told him to sit on a river bank somewhere to admire the view.

The other two victims were unconscious. There wasn't much I could do for them. Medics of the Office or of the traditional varieties were needed. I found Lincoln a little farther away. The wisps of mist were very definitely dissipating now. Normal reality came crashing back in as I knelt down beside him: the blares of horns and the rumble of vehicles and the murmur of the crowds. Big Ben chose that moment to chime the quarter hour.

Lincoln's eyes flickered open. "Are we alive?" he asked. "Did we win?"

"Yes, and I think so," I replied.

"What happened?"

I decided not to tell him the truth. It was quite an easy decision to make.

"I got lucky. I hit one wraith with my clothcutter round, timed it so well that two of the others got pulled in, too, down the plughole back into the aether. It was a hell of a shot; I am hugely disappointed you didn't see it with your own eyes." I made a mental note to myself to discharge a clothcutter round somewhere quiet later, just in case anyone asked to look at my gun to confirm my story. The lack of a bullet at the scene – there's a physical slug that carries the ensorcellment – would be easy enough to explain. It was somewhere at the bottom of the Thames.

"Sorry. I'll try not to be so unconscious next time. Was anyone directing the attack?"

I gave him my hand to haul him up to his feet.

"There was a user controlling the wraiths. Once he'd been neutralized, they faded away."

"You shot him, too?"

I needed a different explanation there as there would obviously be no bullet entry wound on his body. What there *would* be was a lingering magical trace of the spell I'd thrown at him.

I improvised – as, ironically, we're trained to do.

"He threw some fire sorcery at me, pretty potent. Luckily my Stebsen's kicked in for once and deflected it. Sent it right back at him."

As usual, I wasn't carrying mine. The belt containing it was at home, somewhere in my sock drawer. I was assuming Lincoln wasn't going to check.

Lincoln's eyes went wide in surprise. "You got lucky."

"My guess is he was in too much of a hurry to work his hoodoo properly."

I could see he was a puzzled by my story, but he shrugged his shoulders and appeared to accept it. The safe elimination of the threat was the main issue, and he maybe wasn't going to raise too much of a fuss given that he'd been knocked out and I'd had to tidy up. I just had to hope – as with Warder – that no one thought to Assay the user and get his version of events.

"Anyone else killed?" he asked.

"Just the woman you saw, I think."

"Right."

People were suddenly appearing in the mist around us: normal confused, abrasive Londoners, gor bless 'em. I was relieved to see uniformed police officers too. We'd need them to take charge, keep the crowds back from what was a crime scene. I obviously didn't recognize any of the officers, but Lincoln appeared to know one. He went over to explain, making several gestures towards the body and the victims.

Finally, he came away.

"Come on, we can go. They have it under control."

"That officer was in the know?"

"I've worked with her before. Let's say she's in the suspicion and leave it at that."

We didn't have the benefit of the gizmos they have in the films, where you press a button and everyone's troublesome memories are instantly wiped from their brains. Fortunately, people are good at not believing stuff that doesn't fit into their pre-existing view of the universe. Their default position is: wraiths and the undead don't exist, therefore they *can't* exist, and this ghostly presence currently trying to suck out my soul is just my crazy imagination running riot. We help the process along as best we can, hinting at mass hallucinations or psychoactive chemical leaks, but our main weapon is social conditioning. A belief in fairies: everyone knows that's just for kids, right?

"Those three victims saw something," I said. "They'll need careful handling."

"They'll be looked after."

"What's your preferred rational explanation?"

"We'll say it was gang violence. This close to Westminster, maybe even another terrorist atrocity."

Up ahead, more and more buses and cars were roaring into life. Crime scene notwithstanding, they'd want to get the London traffic flowing again as quickly as possible, maybe by opening up one side of the bridge to traffic. I was suddenly conscious that we were standing in the middle of the road.

"Come on, let's get back to Downing Street."

We crossed back to the pavement, hopping over the barrier that separates the traffic from the pedestrians. The crowds completely ignored us. I gripped hold of one of the ornate lamps that decorate the bridge. Leaning over the low parapet, I could see the waters of the Thames emerging from the fog. Normality – whatever that was – was returning.

"Thanks for what you did," said Lincoln as we strode back towards parliament. "Those things were powerful."

"It was English Wizardry," I said. "They were behind it."

"How do you know?"

I recounted what I'd seen and heard. I gave him a burst of the audio I'd grabbed too. Not too much, though. And I made a note to delete the rest of it in case anyone wondered why my gunshot hadn't been recorded.

Lincoln said, "If there's one thing I hate more than a racist bastard, it's a magical racist bastard."

"Yeah. They're definitely the *worst* sort of racist bastard."

Another thought struck him. He glanced at me before speaking, unsure, maybe, of what he wanted to say, or how to go about saying it.

"In Oxfordshire, with Peter. You really were fighting them, weren't you?"

He'd thought – what – that Warder was a good guy and that I'd been part of some plot to kill him? That I was on the side of English Wizardry, despite my Asian ancestry, because I secretly despised my father's side of the family?

"I was," I said. "I'm sorry, but Peter was one of them. I don't believe he was thralled in any way; I think I saw the real him. He *hated* me." I filled him in on the things Warder had said to me; his precise words.

Lincoln took a moment to absorb it.

He nodded his head. "Damn."

"Yeah," I said. "I'm sure you've heard all that shit before, too many times, but from someone you thought was a friend, someone supposedly decent and reasonable … it's heart-breaking."

"I'd convinced myself you lied about what happened," he said. "That Hardknott-Lewis was secretly on their side and that you were following his orders like a good little soldier."

"I can assure you that no one in the Welsh Office are on the side of English Wizardry. Not me, not the Crow, not anyone."

"The Crow?"

"Ah. Don't tell him I call him that."

Lincoln looked amused. "The Crow, yeah. I can see that."

"Was there anything more to your suspicions about us? Beyond not wanting to believe your friend was an evil bastard, I mean?"

I could almost see him picking carefully through his thoughts. "Greentree … I'm close to him. We all are; we're a close-knit group. And there have been attacks made upon him, attacks we're trying to understand. There's been some doubt about where they might be coming from, who's involved."

I took the plunge. "A succubus?"

That stopped him in his tracks. A banker-type holding a conversation on her phone swore loudly as she swerved around us, barely breaking the flow of the instructions she was relaying to some distant lackey.

Lincoln ignored her. The suspicion on his face was clear. "What makes you say *succubus*?"

"We've seen attempts by a highly sexualized demonic entity to undermine the Office in Cardiff."

"Wait, what? Hardknott-Lewis?"

He sounded amazed – which meant he was either a brilliant actor, or he had nothing to do with what was going on.

"Hardknott-Lewis," I said. "The Crow."

"I don't believe it. There's no way he'd be vulnerable to the sins of the flesh. He's made out of stone or something."

"He's been attacked," I said. "Trust me, I've seen the evidence."

"He has the bites too?"

"He has claw marks. Mason Greentree has also been attacked?"

Lincoln hesitated only a moment longer. "Look, between you and me, yes. I've also seen the evidence; these attacks are vicious."

"Have you identified any associated outbreaks of summoning runes?"

"The fuck? How can runes *break out*?"

"We've also seen an infestation of runes locked in a cycle of exponential growth. Our theory is that the location was the one used to perform the ritual that pulled the succubus into our world."

"Runes are tricky bastards," Lincoln said. "You know for sure they were what brought Hardknott-Lewis's succubus into the world?"

"It's a working theory. The close proximity in time and space suggests a connection."

"We've seen nothing like that," Lincoln said. "But that doesn't mean much. London isn't Cardiff; it's *big*; we can't monitor every location."

He was right, of course. Also, patronisingly dismissive of other cities. I couldn't really complain: that had once been me. And maybe, if English Wizardry were working on these runes, deploying them as a sort of slow magical bomb, they wouldn't attack London. Cities in the *provinces* were much more likely to be targeted.

"Just … be on the lookout," I said. "The runes are vicious and they spread. They may be alive in some way. Trust me, you don't want them getting out of hand in a city that's so large and important."

He glanced aside at me, saw that I was being sarcastic. He laughed.

"Fair point, bro."

"Wales, England," I said. "The question is how much wider this goes. Our assumption is that English Wizardry is behind it, but we have no proof of that. What about Earl Grey?"

Lincoln shrugged.

"No idea."

"He's not part of your close-knit team?"

"Nah, it doesn't work like that. He's in London 'cos, sorry, it's the centre, but he's not one of us day-to-day. I see about as much of him as you do."

"Hardknott-Lewis came here today to try and work out how widespread these attacks are."

"Yeah. As has Greentree."

"Better get back and see what they've found out, then," I said.

The Star Chamber convocation droned on for another two hours. I went in search of coffee and food but all we'd been provided with was tea and slices of Victoria Sponge. The Crow had wryly mentioned to me before that the British establishment basically ran on tea and cake – a fact that I wasn't sure if I was reassured by or depressed about.

12 Downing Street shares a walled garden with its neighbours, Numbers 10 and 11. There was no one around, no high-level prime-ministerial summits going on amongst the roses as far as I could tell, so I found a bench and sat quietly to decompress.

12 Downing Street shares a walled garden with its neighbours, Numbers 10 and 11. There was no one around, no high-level prime-ministerial summit going on amongst the roses as far as I could tell, so I found a bench and sat quietly to decompress. The space was hushed behind its high walls, the city distant. The Crow, I saw, appeared to be wrong about the tea and cake: a dead wine bottle lurked in the shrubbery near my feet, and there was another wedged end-on into a bush as if someone had tried to conceal it.

No one approached me or came to ask who I was.

Eventually, the meeting finally over, I found Hardknott-Lewis standing in front of one of the portraits of former Witchfinders General that line one of the building's staircases. He was staring at it, but his fixed gaze suggested his thoughts were elsewhere, not seeing the painting.

The work was from the 20th century, I'd say, its style light and breezy. The little gold plaque at the bottom of the frame said *Emrys Strickland Robinson, 1875 – 1926*. The figure twinkling out of the painting, a smile on his face as if the artist had just told an amusing joke, was vaguely familiar; I was fairly sure Hardknott-Lewis had a picture of the same individual on his walls back in the Black Tower. The same unruly fuzz of springy hair, the same boyish features.

I moved to perch beside the Crow. "A former Witchfinder General?"

"Ah, Danesh, there you are." He seemed to see the painting he was standing in front of for the first time. "Yes, yes, Emyrs Robinson. As the name suggests, a Welshman. The first and, so far, only Witchfinder General from our country as it happens. So many holders of his office have been inadequate individuals, I'm afraid: flawed, weak, even corrupt. He, I'm glad to say, was one of the good ones. Something of a personal hero, in fact. Are you familiar with him?"

Many books have been written on the history of the Office – all suppressed, of course. There are copies to be found in libraries looked after by people like Lady Coldwater, but nowhere else. As an operative, I was encouraged to look into our past, understand the threats we'd faced over the years. Doing so wasn't made easy by our librarian being so protective of her wards. I'm not going to lie, though: I mainly didn't know about Robinson because I hadn't bothered to learn.

"He's … familiar," I said.

"The name means *immortal*. Somewhat ironic, given what happened."

"Exactly what did happen?" I asked.

"Well, many things, as I am sure you are aware. He was perhaps best known for facing down the Wiedergängertrupp threat in World War I."

"I'm not sure I recall the details," I said, frowning as if accessing the memories from my extensive (but actually non-existent) reading.

Hardknott-Lewis placed a schoolmasterly hand on my arm. "Don't fret, this is not a history test. The Wiedergängertrupps were reanimated soldiers deployed by German necromancers during the worst of the fighting in the trenches. *Wiedergängertrupp* means something like *solider who walks again*, if my German is correct. I suppose the idea had some appeal. The poor slaughtered boys were already dead: why not reanimate their corpses and send them over the top to attempt to take another few feet of mud?"

I hadn't heard of this. Not surprisingly, it wasn't an

episode that had reached the standard history text books.

"Robinson turned them back?"

"He and a small group of Office operatives who were attached to the British Army. They crossed into no man's land when a Wiedergängertrupp incursion was detected, at huge personal risk to themselves. I am sure I don't need to spell out the dangers they faced: gunfire, shells, barbed wire, and that is setting aside the horrors and traumas they must have witnessed. It wasn't always possible to retrieve the wounded. They were terrible killing fields; perhaps it was almost … enlightened to send soldiers that were already dead into such a maelstrom rather than all those young, terrified lads."

He seemed to recover himself from some other train of thought. "In any case, yes, Robinson and his small group criss-crossed no man's land deploying their defences, laying antirune mines, quite often resorting to hand-to-hand combat with their knives when they were overwhelmed. They had handguns filled with silver bullets and they carried clothcutter blades something like ours, which had some effect, although as the war dragged on the German necromancers learned to raise revenants resistant to our weapons. It was a classic arms race. Still, Robinson and his dwindling group fought on. They knew the risks, of course, and they also knew that they could never be recognized for all that they had done."

"I had no idea. Did our side ever attempt such a thing?"

"Actually, yes, we did, although not on such a large scale. There was a grouping in the British establishment who sought to use magical powers to defeat the enemy. One or two British necromancers were recruited to the cause, a man called Nicholas Semper being one, but they never achieved very much, and everything was hushed up afterwards."

"According to the painting, Robinson survived until 1926."

"It is somewhat ironic. He emerged physically unscathed from the war to return to his duties here, but was killed by an Englishman eight years later. Or, rather, not actually killed. Something far worse, in point of fact."

"What happened?"

Hardknott-Lewis turned his attention from the painting. "Forgive me, Danesh. If you aren't careful, you will get trapped here all day listening to me lecturing you about the past. Robinson's fate is a story for another day. In essence, he came up against the group who style themselves the Order of the British Vampire, and it did not go well."

The name was familiar from Office hearsay. If you'd asked me, I'd have said it was a joke, nothing more. A supposed clique of powerful vampires close to the heart of the British establishment, their members ancient and highly secretive. Standard conspiracy theory stuff.

"The Order are real?"

"Oh, yes, most definitely. One more very potent threat that we face, I am afraid. They were formed after World War I, although there had been groupings like them for centuries. As with so much that we face, they are hard to tackle. By definition, they operate in the darkness and the shadows. But they are there. Now, enough of Robinson's trials. I hear you have been out on manoeuvres. Tell me everything that happened."

I gave him a quick summary of events by the Thames.

The Crow looked troubled. "Such arrogance. They goad us deliberately. Are you convinced you detected the hand of English Wizardry in this?"

"They went out of their way to spell it out."

"The timing and location can't be coincidence. They picked a target near here, at a time when they knew we would all be in attendance, specifically discussing the attacks upon us. The Houses of Parliament have seen similar outrages for precisely the same reasons. An attempt to strike at the heart, to say to us, *even here in your fortresses, you aren't safe.*"

"We defeated them, though," I said.

Hardknott-Lewis sighed. "We did, yes, this time. The point has still been made."

"Apart from Lincoln, I didn't get much chance to tap

people up for information."

"No, understood. In fact, the others were rather more forthcoming than I had imagined. A measure of how concerned they are, I suppose. Once I opened up about my experiences, the stories came tumbling out. Some assaults have been stronger, some weaker. Once the immediate threat we face is resolved, we should attempt to rekindle closer ties with the other regions. We need to cooperate more closely if we are to defeat English Wizardry's assault on the Office. Perhaps it would be a good idea for someone such as yourself to go on rotation around the other departments. Ostensibly just for the job experience, of course, but actually in an attempt to ... piece everything together."

"But all seven of you have been attacked? We know that much at least?"

"All of us have been attacked, yes. It is likely that not everyone is revealing the full extent of the assaults they have suffered, but reading between the lines it appears that the attacks on Ian, Talvin and Mac were weak and soon stopped. Both Earl Grey and Thomas admitted to suffering the sorts of attacks I have been the victim of. Earl Grey's appear to have been particularly ruthless and cruel, but he is a strong-minded individual and has not, ah, *succumbed* in any way. Mason I wasn't sure about, but from what you have learned, it seems he is suffering too. Seven succubi for seven Keyholders: it is clear to me that English Wizardry are attempting to discredit or destroy the Office of the Witchfinder General. With our leadership incapacitated or compromised, we would be hopelessly crippled, unable to act to protect society from the horrors that we face. And they would have free rein to behave as they please."

Part of me thought: seven straight older men in charge and seven succubi, each superficially a young and alluring female, sent to tempt or impair them. It was, I could admit to myself, just a little satisfying. Would it have been the same if we'd been more diverse? It would obviously be a lot harder to steal gametes from a female

Keyholder. Or someone on the asexual spectrum? Maybe they'd be immune to the whole thing.

But, for all the doubts I had about the Office, I knew for sure that English Wizardry would be far worse. For one thing, they were not going to leave me alone to live a life of peace and contentment.

The Crow glanced over my shoulder, making sure no one else was within earshot. "There is something else, though. We scored another victory, I think. An important one. The last-minute change of venue was known only to very few of us, deliberately so. Yet our enemy seemed to know all about it."

He'd voiced doubts about the Office before, but this went further.

"Do you believe the Warlock is one of the seven?"

"If not a Keyholder, then someone very close to the inner circle: immediate advisors, perhaps, or I suppose it *could* be someone who happened to be working in Downing Street today, someone who knows who and what we are. There are one or two Civil Servants in the know. But for English Wizardry to muster this nearby attack so rapidly – I think we can assume that an individual here today was involved. What is more, I think their actions suggest a certain level of arrogance. An assumption that they wouldn't be found out. I wondered if they would be able to resist such a gathering."

"It could be coincidence."

"Do you really think so?"

I thought about that. "It might be someone in the thrall of the Warlock, betraying the Office but unable to help themselves. Maybe not even aware of what they're doing."

"It is possible although, for the record, I have been taking thaumometer readings since we entered the building and I am picking up nothing. It is more likely that the Warlock figure – even if they do not call themselves that – passed on instructions to their English Wizardry minions to act."

"Have you made any progress in working out who it

might be? There must be investigations going on in the other regions."

"I have nothing solid. I talked to each of the others individually, in confidence, and each is pursuing leads just as we are, but no one has made any great progress. These attacks … it is difficult to work out where they are coming from. And of course, when it comes to resourcing, well, you know what I am going to say."

"We're stretched thin."

"We are stretched thin."

He hesitated, debating with himself whether he should say something else. There was definitely a troubled look in his eye. A surge of panic fluttered through me again, but he was clearly involving me in his plans, confiding in me. It seemed I was in the clear – for now, at least.

I changed the subject as rapidly as I could.

"Isn't it odd that the attacks on three of the Keyholders stopped?"

"Odd why?"

"Odd as in … perhaps one of them is responsible for the whole thing and they went through the motions of arranging attacks on themselves to avoid suspicion."

The Crow thought about that. "If you were going to do that, you wouldn't stop short. You would claim to have suffered the worst of the assaults."

I obviously didn't say, *which is exactly what you did.* Instead, I went for, "Not if you didn't want people checking on your wounds. You've clearly been attacked. The evidence is there for all to see."

He looked troubled, his brow furrowed, but he nodded his head. "Keep the possibility in mind. Any other thoughts?"

"Just one: you explained about *cambions*, the offspring of the victim and the demon."

"Yes, although there is no evidence that such children exist here. Why do you mention them?"

"If these demons are attempting to acquire … genetic material, and the attacks on the three you mentioned stopped, then perhaps that suggests those particular incursions were successful. English Wizardry have what they wanted."

"That is troubling … but possible. Another line of enquiry worth pursuing."

"I'll get back to Cardiff first thing tomorrow," I said, "see if I can get anywhere with the runes. The signature in them may give us a clue to the user responsible. The warehouse, too. And the chalice: perhaps that will get us somewhere."

Hardknott-Lewis nodded. "I shall remain in London to investigate matters from this end. Keep me informed of what you find."

I made it back to my childhood home later than planned, getting on for nine o'clock. I'd texted ahead to let my mother know. She was getting good at replying promptly. *No problem, come when you can, love you.*

Inevitably, she'd cooked, but not the overwhelmingly epic banquets that she'd once spent all day preparing. I took that as a good sign. What there was, was delicious, and there was plenty for two of us. These days, since the intercession of Lady Coldwater and her mysterious colleagues, my mother spent more time on herself. She walked, she stitched, she had even picked up the guitar again, and was very nearly past the hesitant strumming and swearing under her breath stage when her fingers refused to do what she wanted. Very nearly.

We sat and ate parathas, dipping them into the assortment of dhals and sauces she'd conjured up – some of them, she freely admitted, defrosted that afternoon from the chest freezer in the garage. I'd peeped into the appliance, and it had been chock-a-block with Tupperware containers full of frozen home-made curries, all carefully labelled and dated. I'd closed the lid with a nod of approval. She was going to have to have a massive clear-out if she wanted to freeze a murder victim in there – there was barely a centimetre of room.

The important point was that she was looking after herself. Her appetite was definitely improving. She didn't spend most of her time living in the mists of the past, away with the fairies.

After we'd eaten, we sat and chatted over our chai, laughing over the little family jokes and shared memories that no one else in the whole world would have understood. I could almost imagine them there: the two missing individuals. My father and Az. If I closed my eyes, they were with us, sitting in the circle, sharing in the laughter.

She must have seen the look on my face.

"Oh, Danny, always so serious. Just like your father, always trying to fix the world. Did I do this to you? By not looking after you and your brother?"

"No, no, of course not. You didn't do anything wrong."

She set her teacup down. "You are careful out there, aren't you? What you do … there are risks. We of all people know there are risks."

We of all people. She didn't mean we British Asians, she meant we who come into contact with magic. Officially, she thought I was a civil servant in the Welsh government, working in the sphere of public health. I'd always imagined she knew more, or suspected more, but we didn't talk about it. I didn't want to worry her – or open up painful memories for her.

Now, though, she seemed completely fine, on the level. When we talked about Az, now, she was sad but not confused. She hadn't called me by his name for well over a month. She knew her boy was gone. It seemed also that she knew something of the supernatural dangers I faced, too.

"I'm careful," I said, feeling oddly like we were talking about contraception rather than the nightmarish threats of the ineffable. "We're well-trained, we work as a team." I obviously chose not to mention what had happened with Warder – or the Crow's suspicions about others among my colleagues.

However, my mum, being my mum, obviously had a sixth sense about what I wasn't saying.

"Have you experienced any of *that shit*?"

Now she did mean we as British Asians. *That shit* was family shorthand for prejudice, abuse, racism – something we obviously knew all about. My mother, a white woman falling in love with an Asian man, had experienced her own specific version of it. I, as the offspring of that union, had my variant, too. This stuff was all depressingly the same – but also unique to each and every one of us.

And did I? Day to day? Honestly, no, not so far as I knew. The people I worked with took me for who I was, nothing more, nothing less. But then, there was the small matter of English Wizardry and their version of magical history, their desire to expunge everything they perceived to be foreign, alien, unwelcome – which clearly included me. Having a shadowy and powerful cult of magical crazies after me most definitely came under the category of *that shit*.

But the fact that she was worrying about me was perhaps the best sign of all. She had been so locked up in herself, going around in the circles inside her head. But I didn't want her to worry. She needed to keep on healing. I gave her the Executive Summary.

"No."

She leaned over and gripped my hand. "Just … look after yourself. Losing you as well as Az and your father, well, it would be too much. I know the work you do is … vital; it keeps us all safe. Safe so we don't have to worry about it or even know about it. And I know I've struggled at times, with everything, but I feel so much better now. I feel like a fog's been lifted from my brain. And the main thing I see is *you*, my beautiful boy. If I lost you as well, I'd give up the ghost and be done with it all. I would."

"That's a pretty heavy thing to say."

She brushed that aside as if we were simply discussing the rain. "It's a simple fact."

I squeezed her hand back, then dropped to my knees to embrace her. There was the faintest scent of perfume on her neck too – another thing she hadn't bothered with for a long time.

"I'm careful," I repeated. "You're going to have to keep on feeding me, I'm afraid."

"Always," she said. "Always."

I sat back on my chair and looked at her. Sometimes she wore Indian clothes, the sort of colourful dresses my father had so liked, but mostly she wore jeans, leggings, tee-shirts, blouses. She was wearing these now. I was pleased about that, too; she hadn't gone to obsessive lengths to dress up, get everything perfect.

"Your new friends from Gravesend," I prompted. "You're getting on well with them?"

A light began to glow in my mother's face. Animation. Enthusiasm. It was wonderful to see. "Oh yes, we get up to all sorts. Nothing too terrible, I mean it's mainly embroidery, but, you know, we have fun."

Did she know who they were? Did she know anything about the Pale Sisters and what they did? The truth was, I didn't care too much. Whatever they were doing, whatever sly healing magic they were knitting with her, I wanted them to carry on doing it. I didn't care what magus law said, or what my oath to the Office said – this countermagic was what my mother needed. Needed and deserved.

"Oh," she said then. "I nearly forgot. Another memory came back to me."

She rose and crossed the room to a pile of binders stacked upon the sideboard. Once she might have spent hours searching for the particular scrap of paper she wanted to lay her hands on. Now, she went directly to it.

"I've been drawing again, too."

She held out a sheet of sketch paper. On it was the figure of a man in a long winter coat. I knew who it had to be. She'd mentioned him in the fragment of memory she'd scribbled down late the previous year. *Short man, long coat, his face invisible ... filled with fury, demon eyes, face invisible.* The man who'd killed Az and inflicted the curse on my mother, scrambling her thoughts into nonsense.

They were nonsense no more. This time, she'd

sketched in the man's features, too. Taken care over them, getting them very clear: the sharp nose, the round eyes, the thin line of the mouth.

"Do you recognize him?" she asked.

I shook my head. I did not, but this was a memory from two decades previously.

She moved a little closer, as if there were people nearby who might overhear. "I thought that was likely. But then I thought, you know, that there might be spells you could use. Incantations or the like to identify him. That is the sort of thing you do, isn't it?"

14 – The People in the Basement

No good may ever come from the recitation of the
dweomers and rites the use of which we are sworn
to stamp out. They are evil, and evil always begets
evil. Even may a practitioner's intentions be noble,
still they will be corrupted. By uttering these
charms and glamours, the very charms and
glamours uttered will take on life and have their
own way. They will take control of the very mouth
that spake them – turning the person, corrupting
them. However strong the temptation to wield a fire
to douse a fire, such must always be avoided.

–Sister Agneish Faygold, *Accounts*, 1686

Back at my desk the following morning, I spent a happy
half hour filling in reports on everything that had taken
place in the smoke, checking on progress while I'd been
away, and kicking off new lines of enquiry.

Hardknott-Lewis's comments about acolytes had made
me think. We were all encouraged to keep notes on each
other as part of the whole *semper vigilans* thing he was so
keen on. Always vigilant. I'd started off with the best of
intentions, but I'd slipped. The more and more I
considered my colleagues as friends, the less inclined I
was to maintain secret dossiers on them. Who did that?
The troubling thought had been that they were keeping
notes on me, but I didn't sweat it these days. Much.

Still, thinking about Warder and whether someone
could have spotted his activities before he'd gone too far,
I revisited what I had. The documents I'd checked into
MORIARTY were supposedly completely secure and

unreadable to anyone else – but I'd encrypted them as well, just in case. I'd even used proper strong passwords, each one different, like you're supposed to.

Hardknott-Lewis? Betrayal was basically inconceivable. He was the Office personified. As my mother might have said, if he was compromised we could all go home. Kerrigan? Ditto: he was the muscle to match the Crow's brains. Digbeth? I'd actually been concerned about him when I spotted there was a person with the same surname active in English Wizardry in the middle of the twentieth century. But I'd done a bit of digging and found no family connections between the two. So far as I could tell, it was coincidence. Wouldn't he have changed his identity if he wanted to conceal who his forebears were? Like I say, Digbeth preferred the quiet life; he was a plodder rather than a firebrand. You need people like that, though.

Olwen. I'd also been briefly suspicious about her when she suddenly cut her previously long hair during the eye collector episode. I'd imagined all manner of outlandish explanations: she'd gotten it burned during some illicit dalliance with the forces of evil and had to hack it off to hide the evidence. She'd used the hair as a component of some act of ritual summoning. Then she admitted to simply fancying a change of look as Christmas approached, and I felt pretty ridiculous.

Lady Coldwater? Completely compromised and completely upfront about it. She was what she was. McLeland? Again, I had nothing against him, no reason to doubt his devotion to the cause. He was solid, dependable. Gilroy? Not really Office, of course. As a necromancer, he was fatally compromised, but he made no attempt to conceal what he was.

There were other officers around, including a group who concentrated on North Wales and that I didn't have much contact with. They didn't get involved in our affairs too much, either.

I closed the documents. I wasn't going to get anywhere. Aside from the Librarian, the only operative for whom I had clear evidence of unlawful collusion with the unnatural powers was one Danesh Shahzan, and I wasn't going to turn *him* in. Despite everything, he was one of the good guys. Wasn't he?

I'd taken the opportunity to dig through plans for the warehouse in the nearby archive of the city's planning department. There'd been a lot to delve into: the whole area of Butetown and the docks – Tiger Bay – had been developed extensively during the industrial revolution, then completely redeveloped around the turn of the twenty-first century, land filled in, many buildings demolished, and the creation of a new freshwater lake from the dammed waters of the rivers Ely and Taff.

The area I was particularly interested in was covered by multiple plans, stepping backwards in time. It felt a little like archaeology as I uncovered each deeper, older layer. The warehouse that now stood, then an earlier, smaller building erected for the same purpose, then a small, oblong chapel. As I went back through time, details became sketchier, the lines of the drawings less precise, the measurements vaguer.

On the oldest layer they had, the plans barely more than a rough sketch with little attempt to get the dimensions or the alignments correct, there was only a single round room depicted. There was no date on this diagram, but the archivist had hazarded a guess at the sixteenth century (so well before the docks), although she also mused about it being *maybe much older, perhaps pre-Christian*. So far as I could tell, it was beneath the current warehouse sub-basement, or perhaps off to one side. There'd been that weird little arched doorway, of course. Had that once led to this ancient space? I assumed the room had gone, now, filled in as part of the various redevelopments. The only explanation as to what it had been was the single word *Crypt* scrawled in someone's handwriting on the drawing.

Crypt. It was, well, cryptic. The word suggests burials, but it really only denotes an underground vault beneath a church. Or, more loosely, a vault, or anything concealed: it derives, ultimately from the Greek *kruptos*, meaning hidden.

Etymology now. Sometimes I worried I was turning into Hardknott-Lewis.

Dutifully, I scanned the diagrams I'd photocopied into MORIARTY. Maybe they'd be useful. There was a binder in my bag that was accumulating a nice collection of sketches: alongside the succubi that the Crow rendered, there was now the drawing that my mother had made of Az's attacker. Life, I reflected, would be so much easier if they invented phones with cameras built into them that everyone could simply carry everywhere with them. But that wasn't Hardknott-Lewis's style, and twenty years previously, it hadn't been my mother's, either.

I also scanned the new sketch in and kicked off a fuzzy image-matching search. The software hadn't turned up anything useful on the succubi, but maybe the man my mother had drawn would come up with a hit on some magical perp we had in the system. People could change their appearances – either magically or by all the cunning tricks seen in the films, like growing a beard – but our software was good enough to find even the most tenuous of connections.

I also uploaded the mugshots I'd taken of the wizard on the bridge to try and get an ID there. While those jobs were running, I caught up on my messages and alerts within MORIARTY. The system had started out as a way for the various branches of the Office to coordinate major investigations – and from there it had grown and spread like an outbreak of evil runes. *Feature creep* the developers called it if you asked them, usually with a pained expression on their faces. Now we used the system for just about everything we did – email, word processing, calendars, you name it. Earl Grey was, apparently, very keen on us not relying on software we didn't own and control.

I skimmed through the tidy-up notes on the Westminster Bridge incident. The three surviving victims were all doing fine, no long-term magical, physical or psychological injuries apparent. They'd all been, as the reports put it, *satisfactorily debriefed* by the London Office, meaning that the approved false story had been subtly suggested to them, and they'd left convinced that a fundamentalist religious sect had carried out the attack, and not, obviously, a wizard.

The woman who'd died had been identified as Jasmine Smith-Tang, a British Chinese lawyer. Married, no children. As with the three survivors, there was nothing on her in our or the police's systems. They were all simple cases of *wrong place, wrong time*.

The wizard himself had been identified as one Thomson Fulger, a stock market trader and father of two by day. He didn't appear to be a particularly good stock market trader, judging by his modest house. I guess they can't all be megarich masters of the universe – or maybe he was just good at flying under the radar. He was, as they say, known to the Office as there'd been a couple of ritual summonings broken up in the noughties at which he'd been, supposedly, nothing more than a bystander. He wasn't on any active threat list, and it hadn't been known that he was an adept. Someone, the report concluded rather unhelpfully, has presumably been training him in the spells required to carry out his attack.

Worryingly, there was talk of an Assay – not because anyone was suspicious about his death so far as I could tell, but because they wanted to know what he knew about the attacks. Assayed souls can lie as readily and happily as the rest of us, but their testimony is often given credence on the simple basis that they have nothing left to lose. If they did speak to the departing soul of Fulger, something that could have already happened, he was not going to hide the fact that he was magically zapped by an Office operative. Especially one of my racial persuasion. I glanced around me, expecting to pick up suspicious glances from Olwen and Digbeth, the other two in the office right then, but no one even looked at me.

Maybe I was safe.

Next on the pile of things was the Assay of Maude Woebegone, which had come back early that morning. I skimmed through it, then studied it more closely, baffled by what I was reading. It made no sense. It hadn't revealed anything directly useful, so I sent a secure note to Zubrasky informing her of the fact. We'd run background checks on the contacts in Maude's phone, but none of them had come back as suspicious. The police, I knew, would be speaking to her friends and family, relaying the grim news.

Was she another case of *wrong place, wrong time*? The Assay results troubled me, though, filled me with an odd sense of dread that I couldn't put my finger on. In the end I decided to get the answers I needed from the horse's mouth, and went into the basement to have a little chat with Gilroy.

"What now?" I heard him bellowing from his lair even before he appeared around the corner of his inner doorway, face full of purple fury. He was dressed in a baggy grey tracksuit, a choice which I calculated was more to do with comfort than because he'd been working out. There were food stains down his front, old and dried.

I felt a bit bad about Gilroy: I'd assumed he was a racist evil magician scumbag that we kept around because he was useful. Turned out, though, that he was a non-racist evil magician scumbag that we kept around because he was useful, which made him infinitely more acceptable. Okay, sure, my bad for making assumptions about him because of his florid appearance. I get the irony. He'd been amused and disgusted at the sight of me – but not, as I now knew, because of my Asian heritage, but because he'd known my grandfather and had fought alongside him against both English Wizardry *and* the Office back in the day. The cellar we kept him in was comfortable, but it was still a cellar. A prison.

"I read your report on Maude Woebegone," I said.

"What about it?"

"Is there any doubt about what you found?"

"Course there's no fucking doubt. Would you prefer it if I'd made something up, proved to you how useful I am?"

"Obviously not. I just thought, perhaps with the time delay, you might have been … mistaken." It was the wrong word to choose, but half-way through the sentence I panicked and couldn't think of an alternative.

"Mistaken? You think I'm fucking mistaken? And you thought you'd swan down here to throw that at me, did you?"

"Assays work best when death is recent, you explained this to me yourself. Maude had been gone for a week. Her soul might have … dissipated."

"Look, bastard features, I know what I found and my report is accurate. Even after a week there'd be a vestige, an echo, even if it was too far gone to get any sense out of. She was different. She had no soul. It wasn't there. It had been ripped from her, the connection to her body severed. She was a husk. An empty vessel."

The police report knew nothing about that, of course. There was no Coroner's verdict on her death yet, but the police seemed to be assuming death by natural causes, given the lack of any marks on the body and the complete absence of toxins in her system. There'd been some speculation about suicide, but no one had been able to work out quite how she could have killed herself. What they didn't know, of course, was that her life essence had been ripped from her body.

"How is that possible?"

"How the fuck do you think it's possible? Evil magic, isn't it? Does this come as a surprise to you? Hadn't you noticed what it is you're fighting?"

I thought about him working alongside my grandfather. It helped me to remain calm with him. Just about.

"I don't understand the magic involved, or how that could work. I'd be grateful if you could explain it to me."

"If I do, will you leave me the fuck alone?"

"I promise."

He gave me the explanation. It's possible to work magic that acts like a guillotine, completely severing the connection between body and soul. It's a heavyweight enchantment, the sort of thing only a powerful adept can work. Brutal, too. Maude's body became an empty shell, a meat machine, and would simply have stopped, like a phone with its battery pulled out. Her soul, her identity: that would have drifted around, detached and confused, probably in searing agony. You've heard of phantom limb syndrome? This would be a case of phantom *body* syndrome. The thought was not pleasant.

"What would have happened to her?" I asked Gilroy. "To her disembodied essence, I mean."

I braced myself for another volley of invective, but the question stopped him. His voice was a whisper rather than a shout as he replied.

"She'll fade away eventually, lost and broken."

"How long will it take? Could we still contact her if we managed to track her down?"

Disembodied souls like this were one source of the entities we call ghosts, although that's a vague term covering a multitude of different phenomena.

"A soul anchored to a body fades quickly. An untethered one, even more so. Forget it, she's gone."

"But is it worth a try? If we took you back to the scene of her death, you might catch an echo of her, lingering on."

"For fuck's sake."

"What?"

"This isn't pleasant for me, you know. I don't enjoy swimming around in all that grief and anger and confusion. This isn't *fun*."

"No, sorry. I understand."

"Do you?"

"Probably not, no. Can you do it, though?"

"Maybe. I can fucking try if you ask nicely."

"Please?" I said.

"No. Fuck off."

He was enjoying himself, causing what trouble he was able to. I couldn't blame him. I decided to try a different approach.

"She was found in a hotel, you know. A nice one, actually, down on the harbour. The *Gwesty'r Ddraig Goch*.

You won't know it, but it's smart. Very comfortable beds, I believe. Great views, attentive room service."

"I'm sure she must have been really happy right up to the point where she died."

I pressed on. "If she was mindwalking, her soul could have been, what up to thirty metres away? Fifty?"

I saw the moment when his eyes narrowed, very slightly. He'd finally grasped what I was getting at.

"More if she was powerful. Her essence might have wandered into any room in that hotel if she was headhopping."

"That's a thing?"

"Sure, if you're bored."

"And, to seek for an echo of her, I assume you'd have to spend some time in each possible location?"

"Night's best," he said. "The long quiet and the darkness are … conducive."

"If we put you in there, you'd remain under very close control," I said.

"Yeah, yeah, I fucking get it. Do you have any idea how much I miss a view? Do you know what it's like to stare at the same walls every fucking day?"

I didn't, but I doubted I'd have remained as sane as he had over the years. And, sure, if we did this, he had no incentive to actually find anything in any hurry. If he strung it out, he could take weeks and weeks over it, demanding to be relocated in each room for a night or two while he searched. I could hear him making his demands now. *I think I caught an echo of something on the penthouse floor. You have to put me up there.*

Again, I couldn't blame him. All the years he'd been locked away, denied his freedoms, and what had he ever done? Committed magus law crimes, sure, but what had he done that was *evil*? What crimes had he committed that were anywhere near as bad as mine? Maybe he deserved this little glimpse of freedom. And maybe, if he felt generous, if there even was anything to find, he'd let me know about it.

Whether we could afford it was another thing.

Cooperation from the hotel would go a certain way if we played the *ongoing investigations* card, but at some point, they'd balk at us simply trying out each of their rooms in the vague hope of catching a killer in ways that we couldn't spell out.

"I'll talk to Hardknott-Lewis, see if there's a budget," I said. "If he agrees, you know he'll tag you, don't you? You'll be under constant surveillance."

"No fucking change there, then," said Gilroy with his customary gratitude and charm.

I added another demand to the deal: that he teach me about magic use, give me some guidance at least. He could speak to the dead, and for all anyone knew I could too. The Lady had said he had little ability with magical combat, but he had to know *something* that might be useful.

His response was typically forthright. "That is not fucking going to happen, boy. What would Hardknott-Lewis do if he heard I'd been training you? I'd be hurled kicking and screaming into Oblivion on the spot."

He had a point. And, I wasn't completely sure I wanted to open up to him anyway. If he became my mentor, he'd inevitably find out things about me. He might be on my side when it came to opposing the rule of the Office – if that was what I was doing – but I figured he also wasn't above using any information I gave him as leverage to help himself.

Which I couldn't blame him for at all.

Leaving Gilroy, I climbed the stairs back up to ground level – then turned to descend by the other flight of steps, the one leading down into the book vault.

Lady Coldwater was exactly where I'd left her early the previous day – a fact that sent a flutter of alarm panicking through me. I could make out her silhouette in the glow from her desk lamp, but she wasn't moving. She was slumped backwards in her chair, a scuffed, red leather-bound book clutched to her breast as if it were the most precious thing in the world to her. Had she simply never got up, succumbing to her injuries, spellburned by the runes that had crept up her limbs? And if so, had I been the last one to see her alive? Should I have insisted on helping her? And, had the last thing she'd said to me – words I couldn't even recall now – been her last utterance on Earth?

Then my trained detective's eye picked out a couple of other details. Firstly, she'd changed outfit since I'd last seen her: now she was wearing a pretty, floral dress, the sort a lady of her years might be expected to wear on, say, a trip to a village fete. It was a choice, I'd always assumed, that she went for out of irony.

The second thing I noticed a I got closer was that her eyeballs were moving: flicking rapidly from side to side. Asleep? It seemed unlikely: she had a little camp bed that she used when she wanted to sleep near her books – a bed that, for all I knew, she slept in every night. Also, her pose did not look comfortable. There was something taut, stressed, in the arch of her back, the way she clutched the book so tightly to herself. If she were in the throes of some nightmare, I doubted she'd have remained sitting upright in her wooden chair.

I was nearly at her desk now. The floor beneath my foot creaked, as it always did. I'd finally worked out what that was all about: the Lady had set it up so she would know if anyone was down there. The floor was intentionally noisy, although it was subtler than that: different floorboards creaked in slightly different ways, making different notes. I'd put it down to a need for maintenance at first, but that wasn't it at all. The entire floor was like a musical instrument, and someone able to play it could sit in the dark and *know* where the intruder was. And I was damn sure Lady Coldwater had practised and practised exactly that.

I stepped forwards again, and a creak that was perhaps a quarter tone higher than the previous note sounded from the floor. The effect on the Lady was immediate. With a startled gasp she jerked forwards, like someone forcing their way up from the depths of some lake and sucking in a first, desperate breath.

She'd used a flat-bladed dagger as a bookmark in one of the tomes piled around her, fortress-like, upon her desk. She clearly decided I was a bigger threat than the annoyance of losing her page and grabbed it even as she stood, sending her wooden chair spinning backwards on its little wheels. There was a look of both fury and fear in her eye, a look I'd seen once or twice before and that usually didn't bode well for someone or something.

Mercifully, before she could spring to the attack, she clocked who I was.

"Danesh. You're becoming a regular visitor."

"Are you okay?"

"I am perfectly well, thank you."

"Do you mind if I sit?"

I could see that she wanted to say no, but some other thought overrode the impulse.

"Well, it is a library."

The admission was almost shocking. We thought of it as a library, sure, but to her it was more of a fortress.

I sat. It's a good way of de-escalating any threatening situation. Okay, not *any* threatening situation. Any where the bad guy is of the human persuasion and isn't cursed, possessed or batshit evil.

"I wanted to thank you again for my mother," I said.

The Lady lowered the knife and placed it back on the desk, next to the black leather notebook in which she'd been writing notes about something in purple ink. I deliberately didn't look at the words she'd written. She also set down the red tome she'd been clutching. She pulled her chair back to the desk and also sat. She ran her fingers through her long, grey hair to smooth it into order.

"Can you see an improvement?"

"A huge improvement. She's more or less back to being herself again."

"She may never fully recover."

"I understand."

"There may be days when she regresses. You will need to be patient."

"Yes."

Her gaze dropped to the notes she'd been making. She frowned at the words she'd written out, as if surprised to see them there.

"And, I hope that the efforts of our friends in Gravesend have shown you that not all magic is evil in nature. Magic is magic; it's the people who use it, the uses they put it to, that are so often the problem."

"What's being done to her … it *is* definitely magical in nature?" I guess I'd clung to the hope that it was something more, you know, sciencey.

"The Gravesend chapter of the Pale Sisters are using an array of psychic enchantments to slowly and gently unravel the curse that has been left to worm its way through your mother's brain. It's as magical as you can get. Are you shocked by this?"

She was peering at me intently through her reading glasses as she spoke. The bald assertion of illegal magic use was there between us.

"No, no."

"As I say, it is a slow and delicate procedure. There will be days when it seems no progress is being made, but the trend will be in the right direction. If they are allowed to continue their work uninterrupted."

We both knew that I wasn't going to call her out for what she was saying. Instead, I did what anyone would do and changed the subject.

"Just now, when I came in, you seemed to be in some kind of trance. Have you recovered from the runes?"

"It wasn't a trance. I was communing."

Communing was like communicating, but in a way that contravenes magus law.

"With who?"

"*Whom*. Why do you want to know?"

"I didn't know what was happening to you. It looked like you were suffering some sort of attack. I'm allowed to be worried for you."

She turned her attention back to her notebook, unscrewed the gold cap off her fountain pen, wrote maybe one word, then abruptly set the pen down again.

She removed her reading glasses, letting them dangle by the gold chain around her neck.

"That's … the thing is, I know I'm not always much of a team player. I find it hard to trust the rest of you. I regret it sometimes. You all think I'm terrifying, but I don't want to be terrifying. Mostly I want to be left alone."

It was the most she'd ever revealed to me about her feelings.

"Whatever you or I may think of the Office, the fact is you're one of us," I said. "We all look out for each other. If we don't, then we don't have a chance."

She studied me for a moment as if I was a strange insect making fascinating noises. Then she looked down, nodding her head.

"The truth is," she said, "I was attempting to converse with the bookwyrm."

I glanced at the scuffed, red leather tome she'd been clutching. Presumably the illustrated dragon had harvested everything it needed from my phone and had returned to take up residence in the more comfortable surroundings of a vellum-paged volume.

"It's in there?"

"It is."

"Has it worked something out about the runes?"

"I have no idea; it wouldn't talk to me."

"Why not?"

"They are capricious and haughty entities. They like to hoard their information just as a fairy-tale dragon hoards gold and jewels. They're concerned with acquiring and protecting knowledge and have little concern for those on the outside who might wish to make use of that information."

If she saw any irony in her words, she didn't show it. I chose not to mention it.

"So, what do we do?"

"I will keep trying. Was there anything else?"

I had the clear impression she was trying, really trying, to be civil and chatty. She didn't quite have it right, though. Like she'd read about someone doing that rather than experiencing it directly.

"Some things happened in London."

"My experience of London is that things are always happening there."

"One of the things was that I was attacked by a shoal of magical cryptids summoned by an English Wizardry adept using river fog to give the creatures form."

She thought about that. "The creatures were malign?"

"Most definitely. One person died, in addition to the attacker. Didn't you see the news?"

She waved that question away as if it was unimportant.

"How was that little debacle explained on the television?"

"We certainly didn't tell anyone the truth."

"Of course not," she replied, and it was hard to miss the acid dripping through her voice. "We can't have people going around and simply telling the truth, can we?"

I felt like she was missing the main point I was making. "The thing is, when I was attacked, and when I very nearly died, I came to the conclusion, the realisation, that what I need is training."

One of her eyebrows very definitely rose a couple of millimetres.

"Training?"

"I need to know what I'm doing. I need to know how to control my … powers, these urges within me."

"Are you telling me that you used magic to defeat this user?"

She knew all about me – or quite a lot about me, at least. She had actually tasted my blood to work out that I had magical potential. She knew about my mother, and maybe she'd guessed more that she wasn't admitting. Still, it felt hard to admit to the truth.

"I'm not sure what happened. That's part of the problem. There's something in me, sure, a burning energy. I'm worried it's going to take someone's head off. Maybe *my* head. I need to know what I'm doing."

Her expression hadn't changed. "You want me to train

you in how to use offensive magic?"

When she put it like that, it suddenly sounded like madness. Admitting anything openly was dangerous for either of us. But she was learning to trust me; she'd opened up to me. And, I was sure she knew a lot more magic than she'd admitted or revealed. With her to guide me I could become adept in using magic for a good cause: fighting evil, healing people, generally bringing light to the world. A brief training montage flashed through my brain. I'd come down here for lessons every day. It would be gruelling at first, and there'd be moments when I'd get frustrated and angry and want to give up, but she'd make me persevere. There would be inspiring speeches. And in the end, I'd get there.

"No," she said.

"No?"

"No. Absolutely not."

"Can I ask why?"

"Isn't it obvious? What you're asking for is dangerous, destructive magic."

"Magic that I need to use to defend myself. To fight people like English Wizardry."

"Don't you know anything about me, Danesh? Don't you know what the Pale Sisters are?"

"You aren't afraid to use magic where it is called for."

"Magic is a broad term. There are many different sorts, and many more uses to which it can be put. We don't simply *use magic*. We employ a certain set of spells, yes, but only ever to incorrupt, uncurse, unravel, as with your mother. But that isn't at all what you're asking for, is it?"

"I don't know what I'm asking for. I don't know anything."

She considered me for a long moment. When she spoke again, her voice was low. "You used destructive magic, death magic. Am I right?"

"I wanted to incapacitate, not kill."

"Harm is harm. Once you know how to incapacitate, killing becomes easier too. I'm sorry, I can't help you. We in the Sisters don't always agree with the Office, naturally, but in this we do. It is because of this understanding that I am able to be here. Some magic is never and can never be allowed. It is fundamentally wrong."

"And if I use such magic to defeat someone evil?"

"And who is to say who has right on their side? And who is to say where it will end? The next time you see the need to wield such spells it will seem just a little easier, a little more tempting. And so it will proceed until it becomes your habit."

"No. That isn't…"

"Yes. I will not help you in this, Danesh. If you insist on wielding such powers you make an enemy of the Pale Sisters *and* the Office of the Witchfinder General. There are no grey areas."

I stood. The glint of menace was back in her eye, and it was clear our heart-to-heart wasn't going to go any further. The two people in the building who I knew for sure could wield magic had both refused to guide me, and there was nothing I could do about it.

15 – Forbidden Magical Artefacts

The Assizes of Suffolk in the eighteenth century granted the Office of the Witchfinder General the power to employ "demonic powers" so long as their use is "reasonable" and "made only to defeat some yet greater supernatural threat." No attempt was made in the wording of the assizes to measure or grade such threats, however – making the question of whether it is acceptable to fight fire with fire a troublingly subjective one. It is a small gap through which, doubtlessly, many nameless horrors have crept or slithered over the centuries.

–Mirabelle Glee, *Magus Law*, 1982

I was halfway back to the door up to ground level when I remembered the other thing I'd come down to ask the Lady about. The temptation to just keep on walking, leave it for another day, was very strong. But I didn't have too many other lines of enquiry that were getting me anywhere.

Her stare was as warm and welcoming as the icicles hanging from a barbed-wire fence as I approached her again.

"Sorry, I need to do some research, too," I said, hoping the request to do normal library things might placate her.

The frost in her voice was enough to make me wish I'd brought a nice warm coat to wear.

"Into what?"

"There's an artefact that might be relevant to everything that's going on. I need to know more about it."

"What artefact?"

"It's called the Chalice of Lilith Unrepentant. Do you know of it?"

The little shudder of revulsion that passed across her features told me exactly what she thought about the object.

"That object is safely locked away in the vaults of the London Office."

"Actually, that's not true. It *was* there, but now it isn't."

She looked genuinely stunned. "What?"

"It's true. I saw the empty container."

"That cannot be. That artefact is cursed, malign. It should have been destroyed. We *demanded* that it be destroyed when it was recovered. We were assured that it was safe and could never be used."

I recounted the full details of what the Crow and I had learned in the ghost station. She actually held her head in her hands as I gave her the story, as if I were passing on the news of the death of someone close.

When I was finished, she stared into the shadowy depths of her library for a time. It occurred to me that she spent her days surrounded by artefacts and tomes that she despised, that she probably wished to destroy. That couldn't be easy.

"Peter Warder took the object?" she said.

"I assume so. There was no sign of it at Faebrook Folly, not that I knew to look out for it at the time, but we've obviously scoured the place since. Where the thing is now, I have no idea."

"We must recover it. This time, we must destroy it before anyone talks about locking it safely away. You talked about succubi before; I assume the chalice was used to summon such an entity?"

"I believe so. In fact, not just one."

"*Two* of them?"

"Seven."

The sound she made at that was somewhere between a moan and a swear word.

"Who? Who is using it? Warder is dead."

"That's what we don't know. That's what I'm trying to

find out. Someone from English Wizardry."

"There is nothing remotely parochial about the sorcery that object taps into, but I don't suppose that little contradiction will stop them for a moment."

"I need to know what the chalice does, how it operates."

This, apparently, was magical knowledge that she was prepared to share with me. She stood, all wiry energy again.

"There are books we need to consult, volumes I haven't bothered to read for decades because I assumed I didn't need to."

"Are they here?"

She didn't respond. Instead, she charged off, her floral dress rustling like a nest of hissing snakes as I trotted to keep up with her.

An hour later, I stood on the flat part of the roof of the City Hall, the impressively baroque building that houses Cardiff's local government – and, tucked away at the back, our own rather shabby rooms. The roof is a good place to come and stand and think without all the distractions of computers and alerts and, you know, people talking to you. So far as I knew, I wasn't actually supposed to be up there, but there's a little doorway that isn't locked at the top of a steep flight of steps that no one had explicitly told me I wasn't allowed to use, so I took that to be good enough. The exit was part of the building's fire evacuation plans and so was never locked. A sign on it said, *This Door Is Alarmed*. After what I'd learned, I knew how it felt.

The grand and really rather pretty Clock Tower rose over me. Apparently, there'd been some talk of the Crow migrating to it a decade or so earlier – it was much taller than the Black Tower of the castle, where he currently perched – but the ringing of the bells every quarter hour had put him off. I couldn't blame him. And, somehow, the more austere Black Tower seemed much more his sort of thing.

Cardiff lay arrayed around me: the shops, the offices, the roads. The waters of Cardiff Bay and *Môr Hafren*, the Bristol Channel as I might once have said, in the distance. It all looked reassuringly normal. Crowds crowded the streets. Cars and vans and buses and bicycles competed for space on the roads. I found myself studying the buildings, fearful of glimpsing the scribble of runes crawling across them, but I was too far away to pick out detail. It was a drab, late winter's day, the flat light seeming to come from every point in the sky, as if it were nothing more than a canopy thrown over the world.

Another wailing sound lifted off the maze of streets and arcades stretched out around me, then. It rose to a pitch and died immediately, as if some stalking beast were calling to its fellows. The call sent a cold shiver through me. I'd heard that voice before, of course. The cry of the cyhyraeth as it foretells of death. What had the Crow said? *The victim hears it three times on three separate days, and on the third day it's the end.* This was the second day I'd heard the sound, but that didn't mean anything. I'd been in London; for all I know the call had been echoing around the streets while I was gone, warning its victim of their fate.

The call came again, slower and lower, but unmistakable. Was it possible it was the innocent siren of some emergency vehicle or car alarm setting off unwelcome associations in my head? I told myself that had to be the case. The Lady and I had despatched the wraith, sent it back through its portal. We had defeated it.

Except, I knew that wasn't true. There was the sound, loud over the city rooftops. No machine made such a sound. What we'd done – it hadn't been enough. We sent the cyhyraeth back, but it had returned. It had to return, had to fulfil its fate. It had been set on someone's tail and had re-entered our dimension to carry that fate out, because that was what it did, what it was.

And, if I was the victim? At least I knew I had a little time. There would be another day, the third day. For now, I was safe.

I tried to put the wail out of my thoughts. I had other things to tackle.

Lady Coldwater had shown me what details she had on the workings of the chalice. It hadn't made for pleasant reading. Details were beginning to slot into place in my mind, the scraps of information I'd picked up in London and now this. I needed to speak to Hardknott-Lewis, but he wasn't responding to calls – a fact that was, in itself, troubling. Whatever his doubts about me, whatever it was he was doing, he very much needed to know what I'd learned. There were larger matters at stake than the troubles of one lowly witchfinder.

I tried his number again, got sent to voicemail again. Was it possible the dire warnings we'd uncovered from the Sister Agneish Faygold account had come to pass, with Hardknott-Lewis as the victim? The details were somewhat lurid, the language archaic, but the meaning was clear enough. Perhaps the possibility of his death should have come as a relief: after all, if he did harbour suspicions about me, then his death might put me in a safer position. Yet, here I was, doing everything I could think of to prevent that happening.

Okay. I had to assume Hardknott-Lewis was alive and well somewhere. Maybe he'd pursued some demonic presence into a hellish dimension of reality where there was no phone signal. Maybe he was simply back in Herefordshire with Mason Greentree. Whatever the truth of it, it would have to wait. There were two places I needed to go next. One was official Office business, the sort of thing the Crow could have no issue with. The other, the thing I was going to do first – that was almost exactly the opposite.

The storage room where we keep our racks of Armitage Hobbles and boxes of bullets for our handguns and all the rest of our m/tech paraphernalia was right next to the broom cupboard – the door that became a portal to Oblivion when the universe was persuaded to arrange itself in the requisite way. It was the storage room I needed, but I couldn't resist peeping through the Oblivion door as I passed. I was still trying to work out exactly out how the switch was engineered: whether it simply happened at certain times or had to be magically activated. I gained no clue: instead of that infinite icy plain with its frozen souls buried in their permafrost, I got only mops and brushes and the smell of disinfectant.

The storage room was obviously kept locked – but I had checked out the key on the perfectly innocent pretext of needing to fill up the magazine of my handgun after the fight on Westminster Bridge. I had quietly dropped my unused clothcutter round, the one that I'd claimed to Lincoln I'd used on the smokewraiths, into the Taff early that morning, where I hoped it would remain until the end of days. I'd also deleted the recording I'd taken of events on the bridge. No one could ever know what I'd done.

My gun refilled, I checked outside that there was no one else around one more time – and then found the object I'd actually come to borrow. Because, of course, it isn't stealing if you intend to bring it back afterwards.

The artefact in question was kept disassembled in a cardboard box sealed with brown tape and the cryptic letters *G Proj* scrawled on its side in red marker pen. Lifting up the flaps, I peered in at the odd assortment of components: cluttered semicircles of metal, struts, a telescope-like tube heavy with glass lenses and a spiked ratchet thing with a sprung lever for setting … something. Bolts and ball-bearings rattled around in the bottom of the box. There were, inevitably, no instructions on how to assemble it. It was like the worst flat-pack furniture construction ever. But I had once seen a diagram of the object when it was fully assembled, and I had a rough idea of how to operate it.

It would have to do. I carefully lifted each component out of the box and slid them into my backpack, wrapping them in some old tee-shirts I'd brought with me to stop the objects clanking incriminatingly as I carried them. The backpack was heavy when I had everything inside – it would be immediately obvious to anyone that I was lugging some weighty object around – but I just had to hope my natural charm and confidence would see me through.

Yeah, right.

Our security isn't completely lax: we have a book we're supposed to use to log items out and in. I cunningly defeated the system by the simple measure of not mentioning the large magical artefact I was illegally removing. I knew for a fact that we didn't have everything RFID tagged like they did in London, which helped. I did note down my new clothcutter round, checked that everything looked just as I'd left it, the *G Proj* box back on its shelf, then turned out the lights and left.

My heart walloped away in my chest as I made my way back through our offices. If my theft was discovered, if anyone challenged me, I was going to have a damn tricky time explaining what I was doing. The tee-shirts I'd wrapped the components in weren't doing a great job of muffling the sounds: each step brought a tiny clatter of clinks from my backpack. I tried to walk as if I didn't have a care in the world – which, obviously, immediately made me walk in a completely unnatural and suspicious way.

I made it as far as the exterior doors before anyone saw me. Digbeth was coming in as I approached. There was no way I could hide without it looking very strange indeed.

He immediately got to the heart of the matter.

"Hey, Danesh. That looks heavy."

At least it was Digbeth and not someone more suspicious like Hardknott-Lewis. Like I say, my impression of Digbeth was that he'd do anything for a quiet life, and wasn't going to go out of his way to make trouble for himself.

"Yeah," I said, reeling off the joke I'd prepared, "just stealing all our magical artefacts to sell on the black market."

Digbeth, fortunately, found that amusing.

"Excellent. Don't forget your colleagues slaving away here if you make a killing, right?"

I grinned my agreement and tried to step past him without jiggling my backpack in any way. He didn't appear to think I was up to anything suspicious, which was good, but he'd seen me and he'd no doubt recall the fact if anyone noticed the object I'd removed was missing.

It was too late to worry about it now.

I drove across the city and up Cathedral Road, looking for a parking spot near to the two properties that Sally Spender had used: her house where I'd encountered the Pestilential Presence and the flat she'd occupied across the road to watch her house and see who turned up. Both properties had remained unoccupied so far as I knew – although the utility bills and the rent on the flat were still being paid by someone. The copy of *Dorian Gray* that Sally had sent to me clearly told me she was alive and had returned after battling Evangelina Mormont through the Faebrook Folly portal. The subtlety of the message also told me that she'd gone back into hiding, no doubt to protect herself and thè mysterious Myrddin – a man I now knew to be Arthur Stonewall, the figure whom English Wizardry called the *Destroyer*. They wanted to kill Stonewall, we in the Office wanted to capture him and, no doubt, send him to Oblivion for the rest of eternity. It was hardly surprising that he'd remained in the shadows.

I decided to try the flat first: it was less well-known that she'd used it, making it a more likely setting for the scheme I planned. It was entirely likely nothing would come of it and that I was walking down another blind alley – but Sally had been smart, and there had to be a chance she'd foreseen how events would unfold. Of course, it was entirely possible I was deluding myself that she'd want to pass me a secret message in those circumstances, but I was willing to give it a try.

And, after all, what better way to hide a secret message than to leave it safely in the past?

I had keys to her flat acquired through proper, official investigatory channels. Inside, everything was just as I'd left it two weeks previously: the same scatter of books and magazines, the TV remote left at an angle on the coffee table. The air was cold, the heating not running. I'd emptied the fridge, turned it off and propped the door open, and no one had returned to restock it. I ran my finger along one of her bookshelves. It came away with a layer of dust. There was no sign of anyone having been there since I'd communed with Sally before our jaunt to Oxfordshire.

I moved the coffee table from the centre of the room and set about constructing our sole remaining Grafton Projector.

They're weird, steampunky contraptions, flaky and unreliable in operation, with limited range – but when they worked, they could be invaluable. Really, it was surprising we didn't use them more frequently. Except, we didn't know the secret of how to build them and the contraptions were hard to come by. The one I was now assembling was the only one we had. We'd recovered it from the attic of a deceased magical adept on Anglesey four or five years earlier, although we'd had others over the decades according to the records I'd read. The devices also have the annoying tendency to explode into a cloud of magical fire and shattered glass when activated. And, of course, they're magical in nature, meaning that we would employ them only when we absolutely had to. Probably not even then, if Hardknott-Lewis had anything to do with it.

It took me an hour to slot together the various parts to match the image of the completed device I had in my head. When it was complete, the mechanism resembled a cross between a telescope and an orrery, the whole thing set upon a lopsided stand, the lenses pointing off at odd angles, seemingly at nothing particular. Despite being magical in nature – my thaumometer picked up a clear pulse from it – the device was also clockwork. An elaborate silver key had to be wound to store energy in the machine's springs. There was a lever to set to the right value on the cog-like spiked ratchet thingy, and there was even a scale marked on it, but it made no sense to me. It started out with Roman numerals (I, II, III, IIII), then went to Arabic numerals, then backwards letters, and finally to symbols I didn't recognize at all. The gradations weren't evenly spaced, but I couldn't discern any reason why.

Using all my skill and experience as a witchfinder – essentially, guessing – I set the dial to roughly the middle and pushed the catch to engage the springs. The device whirred and grumbled, the entire head of the device spinning around on its axis, faster and faster. If I hadn't pulled my hand away quickly it would have taken my finger off.

I stood in the middle of the room, next to the device, and watched. Whatever the rune I'd set the gauge to, it was working. Colour was leeching out of the room, and the once-solid walls had taken on a slightly misty remoteness as if I were seeing a recording of them.

Which, in a sense, I was. I watched as an image of myself disassembled the Grafton Projector, ghosting around me, before carefully returning the components to the backpack. I then walked backwards to the door. The device was showing me time in its area of effect slowly unravelling.

I stood and watched, waiting for anything to move. The room around me faded as the images moved back to sunrise. I stood in darkness for a time, not daring to step away from the protective circle created by the machine. Eventually, light returned: the previous evening filtering in through the windows. Nothing in the room had altered in any way. The Projector was fully up to speed now, the minutes and hours unwinding with greater and greater rapidity. Day became night became day, and still nothing changed or appeared. No one had been in Sally's flat in the past week.

The images were beginning to fade: flattening out to a uniform greyness, like a tarnished old mirror that has lost its shine. Grafton Projectors only let you look backwards so far. A few months at the most. After that, all you get is greyness. Whether this is a limitation of the devices or something built into the fundamental nature of the universe, I have no idea.

When the device had wound down, I gave it one more shot, this time with the dial turned up to what I assumed was maximum.

The projector was even more vicious this time, snapping into an angry buzz the moment I released the catch. It took a flap of skin off my fingertip. The room around me began to move backwards through the days with much greater rapidity, so much so that I soon lost count. Weeks then whole months flicked by. I caught a glimpse of myself passing through the room on a prior visit, but other than that there was nothing until I hit my encounter with Sally Spender's astral projection into the room and our first meeting. We'd left for Oxfordshire and our date with Evangelina Mormont and Peter Warder, and she'd never returned.

Again, soon after, the images faded into murky silver, all details gone. I was back in the present with a forbidden magical artefact and no answers.

I really needed to get the device back into its box and pick up the work I was supposed to be doing, before anyone noticed what I was up to. But I'd come this far. It was clear there was nothing of interest in the flat, but that still left her house. I had the key for that, too, and the security code for the alarm, so I wouldn't have to mess around with a holdfast. There were more rooms in the house, so sweeping it could take a long time – but I figured I knew where she might have left a message. Assuming she'd even done so.

I folded up the contraption as much as it would go and covered it up with a plastic carrier bag from the kitchen, in case anyone noticed me crossing Cathedral Road. The house was as silent and undisturbed as the flat had been, although there was a much bigger pile of flyers and utility bills behind the door, making it harder to even get inside.

Fortunately, no Pestilential Presence was there this time.

I peeped briefly inside the rooms on the ground and first floor, just in case there was something I needed to know about, then made my way through the low, narrow doorway at the end of the passageway. It looked like it would contain nothing more exciting than an airing cupboard, but the cramped, steep set of steps winding upwards into the loft space were exactly as I recalled.

I stood in the centre of Sally Spender's studio, surrounded by her paintings and sketches, some on easels, most leaning against the walls. The scenes were all competent but dull: mountains, lakes, forests. It was fair to say I didn't see the appeal of such artwork: a painting could never compete with the real thing, so why bother?

But I hadn't come to consider the artistic merits of her work. I set the Grafton back up in the middle of the room, wound its springs, set the control lever to full-fat and, warily, withdrawing my wounded finger as rapidly as I could, flicked the device into life.

I watched for a full minute, night and day and night flickering by like those scenes from the film of *The Time Machine*. A pungent smell of burning metal also rose from the device, stronger and stronger, and something deep within its workings buzzed like a furious hornet. Whether it was supposed to make that sound, or was on the point of exploding, I didn't know.

Then, just as all detail was bleaching away, I saw it. One of the paintings changed. In the present, it was a watercolour depicting the Sugar Loaf above Abergavenny in sun-washed blues and greens. This image was suddenly replaced by a plain white canvas with words daubed upon it in bold, black letters. There was a brief moment – so perhaps she'd stood stock still for an hour or more – when I got a clear glimpse of her face, her amused smile, there next to it.

"Sally, you beauty," I whispered.

I'd been right. She'd left this message here for me – or for someone at least. I took a snap of the words on my phone, but also committed them to memory in case it turned out not to be possible to take photos of the past when revealed in the field of an illicit Grafton Projector. Even as I did so, the images withdrew into the mist and were gone. The magical device whirred to a halt with a *clunk* and the present day returned – complete with the painting of the landscape and the lingering stench of burnt-out Grafton Projector machinery.

Was it the same canvas painted over? Left there in case someone really wanted to dig deep to track her down? An X-ray scan of the painting might reveal the words. Or had she guessed or predicted that someone with access to a Projector would come by after everything had died down to peer into the past? Judging by the timing of it, I reckoned she'd left the message before any of the events surrounding the Borderlands Writing Group and the thing with the eyes had happened. Or, maybe as it was all kicking off and she knew *something* was going to befall her, one way or another.

Whichever, the message was clear. I even had it clearly captured on my phone. She'd left the address visible for a couple of days on display in her attic, just to be really sure. An address, one not previously known to me, but local too.

I now knew where Sally Spender was.

16 – Seeds

Of all the denizens of the circles of Hell catalogued in this book, perhaps none is more feared among those of a high-minded sensibility than the succubae. These accursed and malign imps delight in bedevilling and deranging their unfortunate victims until madness or even death overcome them. The succubus is a malign perversion of all that is noble and chaste in woman: they are lascivious temptresses, their carnal hunger unquenchable, their immodesty despicable. They make no attempt to hide their physical charms away; quite the contrary. Other demons harrow and wound the body, and while succubae are capable of such, their taint is so much worse, for they cut and rend the very soul of those who encounter them. Once in their grasp, few men can withstand their advances. Instead, they must repeat, over and over, the very act that saps them of their strength, sanity and life.

–The Reverend Jebediah Snow, *A True Study of Imps and Daemons*, 1836

"Danesh. Where are you?"

The Crow finally phoned me even as I was lifting my backpack into the boot of my Mini. The bag made a loud clanking sound as I set it down. Was Hardknott-Lewis capable of recognizing the sound made by a stolen and disassembled Grafton Projector in a bag over a phone connection?

Probably not. Emphasis on *probably*. My relief that he was alive and well was tempered with all my usual anxieties. I gave him the official line.

"Olwen came up with a lead on the warehouse while I was in London. I'm heading across Cardiff to see a guy now."

"Be careful. He might be part of the conspiracy."

"I think he's just a guy. He showed someone round the warehouse a couple of weeks ago, someone making odd requests, apparently. He doesn't know much more than that."

"Just be careful. It might be a trap."

I slammed the door of the Mini's boot shut.

"Sir, are you okay? Forgive me, but you sound a little … strained."

There was a pause.

"It is possible that a certain amount of paranoia has crept into my mind. Although, in my defence, not unreasonably."

There were things I needed to tell the Crow, facts that had emerged about the chalice and the workings of the sorcery from my researches in the Vault. It explained why I'd been quietly worried at the Crow's lack of response. But, a little thrill of dread was trickling through my stomach. It would be just like the Crow to sound calm and matter-of-fact in some life-threatening situation.

"Something's happened to you in London?"

"There have been no more attacks, not upon me at any rate. Mason, though … I am afraid to report that he hasn't survived the latest assault upon him."

"Mason Greentree is dead?"

"He is, most assuredly. I am sitting by his body as I speak to you. There are quite definitely no signs of life."

"What attacked him?" I asked, although it was, in hindsight, a stupid question.

"The entity that we have previously discussed. The marks upon his neck, torso and loins – bites and claw-marks – they are diagnostic, I would say, of a vicious attack by a succubus-like demon. There is also video."

"What? How so?"

"Greentree expected further intrusions. He mentioned to me he had set up a hidden camera in his bedroom to record anything that happened. Do you want to see the footage?"

Watching something like that felt wrong. Intrusive.

"Does it get us anywhere?"

"I don't know. I thought, given your expertise, it might show you something that I have missed. I have uploaded it to MORIARTY as it is clearly material evidence. I will send you the link. Take a look."

Intrusive, unsettling, but sometimes it has to be done. I lowered my phone to find the link he'd sent. After a few seconds of swirly buffering graphic, I began to see the pictures.

They were black-and-white: it was dark in Greentree's room; he'd clearly used an infra-red camera. I could see him lying on his bed, very still, his chest rising and falling slowly. He was alone. The time counter at the bottom of the frame said it was 2:15 AM. A faint, grey light filtered in from some curtained windows half out of the frame.

Then there was a blaze of light in the corner of the frame, a sort of scribble of movement, confusing, hard to focus on, and then there was another figure there.

It was a succubus, there could be no doubt. It was very definitely female – in an exaggerated, hypersexualized way. It wore no clothes, and it crept towards the bed where Greentree slept in a cat-like, overly-seductive way. I could see it opening its mouth, the forked tongue flicking out to lick its lips, but there was no sound. The creature swept its hands over the curves of its own body, across breasts and belly and buttocks, making a sort of flame-like writhing motion as it did so.

It stood over Greentree. By some means, he became aware of the demon's presence; he started awake and tried to push himself up the bed, away from it. At the same time, he appeared unable to resist, some invisible force holding him down, pinning him to the bed. The succubus continued to writhe and wind in its exaggerated way, but with one hand it also grasped the quilt on Greentree's bed and threw it aside to reveal his naked form. His wiry body was bright with white heat on the infra-red recording.

I could see Greentree's mouth working as he held up his arms in an attempt to stave off the creature. His expression was one of horror, but also, I thought, fury. The technology made his eyes white globes of light, which probably didn't help. I couldn't work out what he was saying: perhaps it was the syllables of some protective spell; more likely, he was simply instructing, beseeching the demon to leave him alone. Maybe just screaming.

The succubus, in response, shook her head slowly and passed a finger across Greentree's mouth, telling him to be quiet. Greentree appeared to be powerless to resist. There had to be some enchantment going on; he could have leapt away, confronted the entity, but still he lay there. The muscles of his limbs and abdomen flexed and strained as if he were undergoing electric shocks. The succubus's finger moved down to his chest, his belly to stroke his penis – which, very clearly, was responding.

The succubus climbed onto the bed to straddle Greentree. It pinned him down, arms and body, and although Greentree struggled a little now, he appeared to be too weak to throw off the demon. The succubus lowered its head, letting its long hair play across Greentree's chest as the two writhed together, the succubus sometimes arching its head upwards in apparent ecstasy, sometimes lowering its mouth with its jagged teeth to Greentree's flesh. I could see the wounds upon Greentree's body from these bites, and from the rakes of the entity's talon-like claws, by the heat of the blood that welled out. Still, Greentree appeared to be unable to fight back with any conviction, as if he were lost inside a dream he couldn't wake up from. Or was he welcoming what was happening to him? He might object intellectually, even emotionally, but it was hard to escape the evidence of his body's complicity in what was happening. Was that what was happening here?

The clenching and straining of his leg muscles reached

a crescendo as he climaxed. I thought that was going to be the end of it, but the demon, lashing its head around, paused for only a moment before continuing its writhing and grinding on top of Greentree's body.

A few seconds of this, and the graphic video stopped. I put my phone back to my ear.

"It goes on like this for over two hours," Hardknott-Lewis said when I told him I'd watched. "By the end of it there were abrasions and lesions all over him. His penis and testicles were little more than a bloody mess. Forgive me, but they looked like someone had attempted to chew them off."

"Is that what killed him? Loss of blood?"

"It is hard to be completely sure. Physical exhaustion would have contributed, too. Possibly his heart eventually gave out from the relentless effort. He was not a young man."

"Couldn't he have fought harder, though? Resisted? It's hard to interpret the video, but isn't it possible he welcomed what was happening to him on some level?"

The Crow took a moment to respond. "The demons … they exert a sort of sorcerous influence that has the effect of rendering their victim physically willing. Akin to a magical Viagra if you will. It plays on instincts deep within us, instincts that our higher selves might feel revulsion at."

He was, clearly, talking from personal experience. Still, I wasn't completely convinced.

"Saying that, forgive me, it could be interpreted as a convenient way of claiming innocence, of shifting the blame."

"If this were a human woman, then I would obviously agree with you. But this is a demonic entity in quasi-female form. This was an attack. Greentree had suffered less powerful ones previously, but they were taking their toll on him, grinding him down. I was worried about him. You should know, also, that he found the sex act distasteful. I tell you this in complete confidence, obviously. He had suffered some unwelcome advances as a young man and preferred to remain abstinent. These assaults were particularly onerous for him."

"He did what he could to protect himself? With wards and locks and the like I mean?"

"He used all the weaponry and defences at our disposal. He hoped it would be enough, but clearly it was not. Were you able to discern anything useful from the creatures and its actions?"

"It looked identical to the sketches you drew."

"Similar but not the same, I would say. Of course, the physical form adopted by demons might vary. As I say, I believe seven of these creatures have been summoned, a heptad. This one was Greentree's."

"And now it has his semen."

"Yes."

"With Greentree dead, only you, Earl Grey and Thomas Quirk are still suffering these attacks, yes?"

"That is my understanding."

"You said the assaults on Ian Majkowski, Talvin Epenesa and Mac Farrier had subsided because they were weak, but that wasn't it at all. I know now – those attacks stopped because they were successful."

The Crow took a moment to absorb that before responding

"Ian, Talvin and Mac … their demons succeeded. Our enemies acquired their seed too."

Seed was like *congress* and *loins* – words that probably only Hardknott-Lewis would have used in that context.

"I believe so. I unearthed some evidence of the chalice's usage in the eighteenth century. I really need to sit down with you and go through it, but in essence, the attacks get more and more vicious until they're successful, or the victim is killed in the assault. The demons, once properly summoned and bound: they won't take no for an answer."

"My," the Crow said, "Well, I am not sure either of those outcomes is particularly appealing. Let us at least allow a third option: that the attacks are rebuffed and the demons sent back to their own domain. Poor Mason did not manage it, but that does not mean it isn't possible. Have you learned anything about the grand plan of our attackers? What their specific intentions are?"

"That's what I'd like to go through with you. It looks more and more like a coordinated attempt to discredit or cripple the Office's operations across the United Kingdom. This magic English Wizardry are using … it's pretty troubling."

"Involving cambions? The offspring of these … interactions?"

He was always sharp. I didn't know if he had children, but there was a note of some deep sadness in his voice that I hadn't heard before. He really despised the evil that he spent his days battling. In this particular case, it was hard not to feel the same way.

"I've learned some details of the rituals and the sorcery," I said. "The cambions are significant: their existence gives the users responsible for the magic certain powers."

"Forgive me, I know I used the word first, but shall we start calling them babies?" the Crow said, quietly. "People? That is what they are."

"Yes. So, the babies resulting from these rites – from what I've learned, they can be used. Exploited to harm and destroy the parents. The strong connection between offspring and parent allows the sorcerer to control one and bring harm to the other."

"Such evil," he said, bitterly. "The attacks on us are bad enough, of course, but to abuse innocents like that. To *make* them as tools. It is unimaginable."

"Except, that's precisely what English Wizardry have imagined. With seven offspring from these rituals under their control, they could exert complete control over the Office. They could pull the strings, control you in any way they wanted. Send you mad, give you paranoid delusions. Make you blind to their actions. Kill you if you refused to comply."

"Mason knew all that, I suspect. He fought back. He wasn't the strongest of men, nor the fittest, but when his hackles were up, he could be ferocious."

"At least we can be sure he wasn't the one responsible."

"In other circumstance, I might have thought his demise makes for the perfect alibi," said the Crow, "but there really can be no doubt whatsoever that's he's dead."

"It's definitely him? Not some manner of doppelganger?"

"It's him. Some of the scars on his body and limbs: I know exactly when he acquired them, what creature it was that inflicted them, because I was there. I bound some of those wounds. No sorcerous copy could ever be so perfect. It's him. We'd been friends for thirty-five years."

"I'm sorry." I couldn't think of anything else to say.

"Thank you," said the Crow. His voice was as even as ever, but I saw it had taken him a moment to be able to do it.

"Have you made any progress at all in working out who might be behind all this?" I asked.

"Whoever this sorcerer is, they are clever and they are subtle, hiding in the shadows."

"Or hiding in plain sight."

"That is possible, too," the Crow conceded.

"Will you Assay Greentree?"

Hardknott-Lewis sighed. "I think not; despite his aversion to the sex act, he was married, and I am not sure revealing the details of his last moments are going to help anyone."

"Do the others in the English Office know what's happened? Lincoln said they were a close group. They deserve to know the truth."

"I will make sure of it."

"There's someone else involved in all this," I said. "The old texts were predictably silent on the matter. The Keyholders are, or at least *were*, all men, and the whole thing is very definitely straight and binary. Somewhere, though, there must be seven women. Mothers. The incantations call for them. The babies have to be *born to woman* in order for the rituals to work. The book I read talked … well, it actually describes the women as *vessels*. Which, yeah. I suppose they may be fully involved, knowing what they're doing. Devotees of the cause, say. I think it's more likely they're being coerced, though, used without knowing what's really going on."

"Seven women," said the Crow.

"Yes."

"From your research, does the sorcery allow for magical exploitation of both parents?"

"It was vague on the point. My guess would be yes."

"Mine, too. Your investigations, Danesh – please pursue them with all alacrity. Follow the leads that have come to light in Cardiff. I shall remain in London and continue to try to identify who might be responsible from this end. If our enemies' plans succeed, the Office will be incapacitated for some time. We may never recover from the damage – which I am sure is precisely what they want to happen."

Thoughts were queueing up in my head like the traffic squeezing into the Brynglas tunnel.

"There's something I don't get: if this is English Wizardry as we assume, why are they attacking all the Keyholders? Wales, Scotland, the Isles, the overseas territories: why would they care?"

"Two reasons, I think. One, the Star Chamber is constituted so that the other Keyholders step in with temporary jurisdiction over a domain when its Keyholder is incapacitated or dies. Consequently, they want to control or harm all of us at once."

"And the other reason?"

"Do I need to spell it out? There is a history here. I am sure I do not need to give you any lessons about the merits of the British Empire. The assumption of superiority, of a right to control: I think that is very evident in their actions."

"What I said before – maybe I'm looking at this the wrong way. The attacks on Ian Majkowski, Talvin Epenesa and Mac Farrier: if they stopped so quickly, might that actually suggest one of those three is behind it?"

The rapidity of his response suggested that his thoughts had run along similar lines.

"I just find it so hard to believe. I do not know any of them as well as I knew Mason, but they are all utterly trustworthy."

"You said yourself someone in the inner circle had to be responsible. Someone there in Downing Street that day."

The Crow sighed. He sounded weary.

"All I really know at this point is that it is not me or poor Mason who is responsible. I am convinced someone who was here that day arranged that little piece of theatre on Westminster Bridge. Someone is goading us, laughing at us. We must find out who, urgently."

"I'll go see this guy, see what he knows."

"Excellent, Danesh. It is a relief to know I can trust you. But, please, be very, very careful. They are attempting to knock out the leadership, but that doesn't mean they will not come for others, too. Individuals they have particular reason to despise."

"I'll be careful. You, too, sir."

"Oh, and Danesh. This request for Gilroy to be sent to the hotel where Maude Woebegone died. Is it strictly necessary?"

"I think there's a chance he can give us something useful."

"I do not like it."

"No, I understand. But I don't think he's evil. Just a criminal."

There was a long pause while the Crow considered my words.

"Is there really no other way?"

"None I can see."

"Very well, I suppose we have no choice. I have this troubling sense that things are slipping, that we are becoming too lax. But if it helps us track down bigger enemies…"

"Yes, sir. Thank you."

He rang off and I breathed. I was still standing on Cathedral Road, traffic squeezing between the two lines of parked cars. It was already getting late: Sally's house was in shadows, although the low winter sun bathed the houses on the other side of the street in a yellow glow.

I'd planned to return the disassembled Grafton Projector to the store room, cover my tracks, but it would have to wait. The Crow was right: I did need to be careful, and Sally seemed to be the only one capable of giving me the guidance I really needed. But first, the warehouse guy; there surely couldn't be any danger to me going there.

Preston Jones was a balding man in maybe his late forties. I'd checked him out on our systems and the police databases and found no red flags at all. He sat behind a desk in a shabby office overlooking Newport docks. Over the top of red brick offices and houses, the vast, spidery body of the Newport Transporter Bridge bestrode the landscape like some vast skeletal monster dreamt up by the fevered mind of a fantasy writer.

The sign on Jones's door said *Principality Impex*. A stained filter coffee machine sat on a tray upon a filing cabinet in the corner, a little touch that warmed me to him. The office was small and square, the walls breeze-blocks painted in an ill-advised egg-yolk yellow, but, however unlovely his surroundings, he hadn't lost all dignity and hope and started drinking the instant stuff. The walls were also marked with dots of Blu Tack arranged in rectangles: the remains of pictures put up by some previous occupant. On his desk was a wired mouse and keyboard. His screen was one of those deep CRT ones that they'd used in, I don't know, Victorian times.

At his invitation, I sat down. He immediately asked me the question people always want to come out with but never do.

"Are you the police?"

"I'm from a related branch of the law-enforcement

authorities. If I learn anything that requires action from the regular police, I will, of course, pass the information across."

It was a response designed to give the impression that I was some kind of undercover, secret service agent. Which wasn't so very wide of the mark.

Jones held my gaze for a moment. He looked like he was going to question me further, then gave a little shrug and pressed a few buttons on his rattly old keyboard.

"You had some questions to ask me?" he said.

"I'm interested in an individual you showed around the Mermaid Warehouse in Cardiff Bay two weeks ago. January 3rd, I believe."

"Mermaid, mermaid," he said. Another staccato burst of keyboard gunfire followed. "Yes, here we are, just checking my notes. Yes, yes. Odd request, I suppose, but a customer is a customer. Quiet time of the year, so he stuck in my memory."

"What was odd about him?"

"Nothing, nothing at all. Seemed like a perfectly normal bloke. It was what he wanted: normally we rent out the warehouses to store goods for import or export, obviously, but that wasn't it at all. He said he was looking for a performance space."

"As in the theatre?"

"I assume so. Not really my thing, if I'm honest with you, give me the rugby any day of the week. But he said he wanted to put on a dramatic performance and that the backdrop of the building would be perfect for what he had in mind. He may even have said it had *ambiance*. Not a word that crops up much in my line of work."

He didn't know that I'd been to the building. At our request, the police had kept it cordoned off as a crime scene since the Librarian and I had gone inside to tackle the runes, and everything was being kept quiet under the pretext of not endangering an ongoing case.

"Did he give you a name?"

"A company name. Gwydion Productions."

"Does that name mean anything to you?"

"Nope."

"Did you get any contact details?"

"He gave me a card with a phone number on it. Said he'd be in touch."

"Did he get back to you?"

"People say they'll contact you, then they don't. Happens a lot. Can't say I was surprised. Health and Safety, isn't it? Place could be a death-trap with a couple of hundred people in there if a fire broke out."

I decided not to tell him how else the place could be a death-trap.

"Did you try the number?"

"Couple of times. The first go it didn't get me through to anyone, like the number wasn't even registered. The second time I reached a very puzzled Scottish lady who had no idea what I was talking about. I Googled the company name, but it doesn't appear to exist. To be honest, the whole thing felt a bit unbelievable. He didn't really seem to know what he was talking about."

"So, what did you think was going on?"

"I assumed, maybe, a competitor was trying to sound us out? Or maybe something criminal, illegal goods being brought into the country."

"Does that happen?"

He looked a little wary, I thought. There had to be times when he skirted around the law.

"Sometimes people bring in drugs or other illegal items using seemingly legitimate goods as cover. We obviously try hard to spot anything like that."

"But you didn't tell the police about this case?"

"Tell them what? There's literally nothing to show them."

"I'm surprised the warehouse was empty. A building of that size."

Jones looked a little rueful. "No one needs warehouses these days. Just-in-time supply chains, containerized transportation: warehouses are an anachronism. That's why they get converted to expensive flats and museums."

"And performance spaces," I said.

"Anything, if they're prepared to pay."

"Did he have access to the building while you weren't with him at any point?"

"He didn't have a key if that's what you mean."

"But he might have seen you entering security codes. Maybe taken a copy of your key while you weren't looking."

Jones bristled at that. "I'm always extremely careful. What are you saying?"

I did my best to placate him. "Only that some of these people are extremely clever and manipulative. You've done nothing wrong, I'm sure. I'm not interested in any sort of Health and Safety transgression if that's what you're worried about." Well, perhaps *some* health and safety transgressions – but none that he needed to know about.

"No, well. I suppose it's possible he may have noticed the code as I entered it."

"And the key?"

Jones nodded his head, sifting through the thoughts in his mind. "I suppose that's possible, too. What exactly has happened in there? The insurers get itchy if they hear word of anything funny going on. I'm losing money every day I can't use the place."

I doubted that was true, but I didn't say so.

"We'll be finished in there soon, I assure you. I can't say anything more. Don't want to endanger an ongoing case."

"Of course, of course."

"Can you describe this man to me?"

"Like I say, nothing remarkable about him. Just a bloke. Old, a bit thin like he'd been ill, maybe. He was very pale. I could see the shapes of his bones beneath his skin. Hair going thin, same as the rest of us."

"Can I show you some pictures? See if any look like him?"

Jones shrugged. I laid out the pictures I'd brought with me, dealing them one at a time like a magician working a trick. *Is this your card? This?*

I showed him, in no particular order: all seven Keyholders of the Office of the Witchfinder General (including the Crow), Thomson Fulger, Peter Warder (who, okay, was dead and had been so at the time of the meeting, but still), Lincoln along with all the other male acolytes who'd been there in Downing Street. Also, Kerrigan, Digbeth, McLeland and Gilroy from the Office. I even threw DI Evans in there, taking a picture of him off the police HR system. And, for laughs, a picture of the Archbishop of Canterbury. Because, best to cover all the bases.

At each, Jones simply frowned and shook his head. Even when he came to the Archbishop of Canterbury.

"He definitely wasn't any of these blokes."

"Do you recognize any of them?"

"Should I?"

The Church of England would be disappointed. "Not necessarily. Please, take another look, just to be sure."

"I told you," said Jones, "I don't know any of them. I have a good memory for faces. You need that in my line of work. I've never spoken to any of these people."

"Do you have CCTV footage of him at all? Something we could get an image off?"

"We're an import export business, not a high-security prison."

I changed tack. "This performance he was planning. Did he give you any details? Whether he'd need a stage or props, that sort of thing?"

"Not my area of expertise. I left him to look around the place."

"Did he go into the basement?"

Again, he stonewalled me. "I don't know. Probably."

"What about his accent? Where was he from?"

Jones shrugged in the way people have when their patience is running out. "He had a perfectly normal accent. Swansea maybe. Somewhere in South Wales, anyway."

"He was Welsh? You're sure?"

Jones gave me a withering look but chose not to

respond. Fair enough. It was a stupid question. But it gave me a bigger problem, one that messed with my world view: what the hell was a Welshman doing in English Wizardry? Okay, maybe he didn't know anything about them and was simply being paid to find a venue.

Or maybe he agreed with them and was a fully paid-up member. People, in my experience, can be weird.

A call came in from Lincoln as I drove back into Cardiff. It's an odd stretch of road: scrubby greenery and massive, decaying industrial remains competing. At one point, there's a cavernous old factory building inside which a massive claw on a crane plucks the husks of dead cars from small mountain ranges of wrecks for recycling. At the same time, there are often horses wandering around on the roads outside, as if that little area of ground never did get the hang of moving forwards in time along with everywhere else.

The Bluetooth on my car picked up the call so I could talk and drive.

"Danesh, hey. How's it going?"

"Still fighting the fight. How's the media smokescreen progressing?"

He laughed. "For once the term is literally apt. They've bought our story of a terrorist outrage taking place under cover of a freak river fog."

"I assume you know about Mason Greentree?"

"Do you?"

"Hardknott-Lewis is there. He told me all about it."

In London, Lincoln exhaled loudly. It sounded like a strong wind gusting through my car in Cardiff.

"Yeah, everyone's pretty freaked-out about it. I liked the guy; we all did. I thought he was indestructible, you know?"

"I'm sorry. There doesn't seem to be much doubt this is an escalation in the succubus attacks."

"Seems like it. Did the Crow say he'd also seen more vicious assaults?"

Now my nickname for Hardknott-Lewis was being

bandied around by others. There was no way it wouldn't reach him sooner or later. Hopefully he wouldn't realise I'd coined the name.

"He didn't say, but I think we have to assume that's either already happening or is going to happen. Have you got anywhere, found any leads I need to know about?"

Lincoln's next words sent a pang of panic thumping through me.

"That's why I'm calling you. You probably know that, before he was killed, Mason sanctioned an Assay on Fulger, yeah? We just got the results back from our tame necromancer."

17 – Mists

And as they sat thus, behold, a peal of thunder, and
with the violence of the thunderstorm, there came a
fall of mist, so thick that not one of them could see
the other. And after the mist it became light all
around. And when they looked towards the place
where they were wont to see cattle, and herds, and
dwellings, they saw nothing now, neither house,
nor beast, nor smoke, nor fire, nor man, nor
dwelling; but the houses of the Court empty, and
desert, and uninhabited, without either man or beast
within them. And truly all their companions were
lost to them, without their knowing aught of what
had befallen them, save those four only...

–The Mabinogion

I heard myself playing along, asking Lincoln the question
any loyal and honest Office operative would ask.

"Did you get anything useful?"

At the same time, the panic was thumping through me.
It was bad enough that the Assay of Thomson Fulger
would show that I'd lied about my clothcutter round
being discharged. Worse, clearly, was the fact that it
would also show me using unnatural sorcerous powers to
slay him. There was no chance they'd miss it: the
memories of the dead faded as they got older, but this
would be the freshest impression in Fulgur's dying brain.
And, if they knew the truth about me, they'd be coming
for me. This call from Lincoln was – what – a friendly
warning from a fellow-operative? A chance to condemn
me for my actions?

But that wasn't it at all. His next words sent sweet joy
through my troubled mind.

"His brain was fogged. We got nothing at all off him."

"Fogged."

"Yeah. Ironic, really. You've seen that in Cardiff?"

I was still reeling, adjusting.

"I … no, I don't think so."

"He was a suicide summoner; he knew there had to be a good chance he wasn't going to get away. He had some heavy-duty incantation inside his brain, futzing his thought-patterns. The Assay got, like, white noise, nothing more."

I tried really hard to sound disappointed. A small part of me was, in truth. I really wanted to know who Fulger had been working with.

"Damn. I didn't know they could do that."

"Yeah. We're seeing it more and more. It's like a curse that eats away at your brain, sends you doolally in the long run. But, in the short run, it completely hides your memories from anyone trying to listen in. Users we chase love using it; if their guy gets caught, they're completely in the clear."

I was still driving. I realised I'd negotiated several roundabouts and sets of traffic-lights without being consciously aware of them.

"Do you figure Fulger worked this curse on himself, or is someone else involved?"

"We've picked his life apart in the past twenty-four hours, studied everything about him. He was a user, yeah, but I don't think he was a very capable one. We have a few old accounts of his attempts to experiment in the forbidden while at Oxford. Pretty much everything he tried failed. Not in an *unwittingly-summoning-the-devil* way either. Just in a basically sucking kind of way."

"Oxford as in Oxford University?"

"One of the good ole boys, that's for sure. Rich family; you know how it goes."

"Anything to tie him to Peter Warder?"

"Nah, we obviously looked into that. Fulger was at Oxford twenty years before Peter, in a completely different college. Fulger studied English Literature, Peter

Art History. Hard to draw a direct connection between them."

"Then we're no further forward. He was a foot-soldier, nothing more. Whoever is summoning these succubi, this Warlock, used him to mount the Westminster Bridge attack and made very sure nobody else in the conspiracy could be identified."

"Yeah. Yeah, probably."

There was a little note of pleasure in Lincoln's voice. He had *something*. Fulger wasn't a complete dead end, I was sure of it.

"Why only probably?" I asked.

"Fulger was careful. His house had no signs of any illegal activity under magus law. I mean, he was so careful he was boring. Even the books on his shelves; there was nothing we could object to. It was all, like, golf and shit."

"But you got something."

"We found some interesting messages on a tablet."

"Saying what?"

"No idea. End-to-end encrypted."

"Right, so, the IP address at the other end? That tells you something."

Lincoln laughed. "Bro, that is so not how the internet works, you do know that right? People rarely have fixed or useful addresses. We got the IP, sure, but it was proxied and VPN'd to shit. Impossible to tie it to anyone or anywhere. Except…"

"What?"

"Couple of times we managed to geolocate the address. That stuff is vague, yeah? Doesn't tell you where the other person is, just where their access point onto the internet is. But, these two times, the location was South Wales. Cardiff area."

"But you can't give me anything more precise."

"That's all we have."

"Then I don't get it. It's interesting, but doesn't really tell us anything."

"It's the timing of the messages. I don't know how she

was doing it, but it can't be coincidence."

"She? You mean … Mormont?"

"Mormont. I assume she was training him, prepping him for the attack. Maybe even walking him through the incantations, I don't know. But they talked a lot – and then, the day we took her out of her cell and put her into Oblivion. The very *hour*. The messages stopped."

"Could be coincidence. Could be chatter *about* Mormont between Fulgur and an unknown third party."

He wasn't finished yet, though. "Then, late last year, the messages start up again. Round about the time we believe she was pulled from Oblivion."

"Okay, but again…"

"Then they stop again, and we can tie *that* time up very closely to known events. The messages cease when you and the user Sally Spender get to Faebrook Folly. To the very hour Mormont was thrown through the portal into dimensions unknown."

"Okay," I said, "but that's still not proof Fulger was talking to Mormont."

"Right, bro, sure. But here's the thing. Two weeks later, the messages kick off again."

"Two weeks after Mormont's death."

"You got it."

"How do you know it was the same person if the IP addresses are unreliable?"

"We don't, but Fulger only ever seemed to communicate with one person on this channel. Dude, it cannot be coincidence."

"Except that Mormont is dead."

"Do we know that for sure?" Lincoln asked.

Did we? Sally hadn't specifically told me that. But then, she hadn't specifically told me anything.

"We know she didn't come back through the Faebrook Folly portal. We monitored that very carefully until we sealed it up permanently."

"Okay, well, I'm just putting this on your radar. Is there anything you can do to check out the possibility?"

"I'll see what I can do."

"Good, bro, because with Mason taken, any of us could be next. I do not want to be the one they come for."

"The runes," I said. "Did you find any like those I described?"

"Nah, we've looked over known sites of recent activity. There's nothing like that here."

"Interesting. Okay, thanks. I'll let you know if I find anything out."

"Sure thing, bro. And be careful, yeah? No knowing who they're coming for next."

Back in the office, I caught up on developments on MORIARTY. Thomson Fulger was in our records, but only with the details Lincoln had already provided. He was a loner, a bit of a car obsessive, with no other strong connections we could usefully pursue. The man my mother had sketched appeared to match no one we knew about – or, at least, it loosely matched too many people to be useful.

There'd been no further magical activity at the warehouse, and Zubrasky had ordered that the building could be used again. There would be no ongoing investigations unless we in the Office chose to pursue them. There'd been no sign of any infestation of the malevolent runes, either in Cardiff or anywhere else in the country. There was lots of chatter among Office members about the death of Mason Greentree, but no one had come up with any solid leads as to who was behind it.

I'd left a scan of CCTV feeds in the area of the warehouse running, and that did turn something up. Jones had explained he had no cameras on the building itself, but sometimes nearby devices pick up a scrap of something interesting. One had now. The camera software had dutifully filtered out the suspicious pixels before the public got to see them, but we had the raw footage. I'd given the software my library of images to scan for, and a camera on the corner of a bar two hundred metres away had come up with a good match on one of them.

I watched the footage now. An empty street, the tyres of cars in frame, a dog trotting by. In the distance, I could see the corner of the warehouse, the blank brick wall of its side. Suddenly there was a figure on the screen, frozen briefly by the low frame rate. She – it – was skimpily dressed; if I hadn't known better, I might have mistaken it for a young woman out on a hen do (which can get pretty wild in Cardiff; I was frequently amazed at how Cardiff's revellers don't appear to feel the cold.) It was alone, though, and didn't have any of the usual hen party paraphernalia. The L-plates and the rest of it.

Also, I'd seen that figure before – or one very similar. It glanced up at the camera and there it was, peering out of the murky grey of the frame directly at me. The mouth full of too-many jagged teeth, the forked tongue. The hungry smile.

A succubus, walking the streets of Cardiff. The timestamp said 04:37. Was it on its way back from another of its nightly visits to the Crow? Perhaps.

I watched as the demon ambled down the road. It stopped at the warehouse wall, and in the next frame it was gone, as if it had simply stepped through the bricks. I watched for another ten minutes, but nothing else happened. At least it proved my theory that the warehouse was the centre of all the summoning activity. Or one of them, at least: I checked the video from other nights and picked up nothing. If I ran out of leads, perhaps I'd have to resort to lurking around the warehouse in the dead of night in the hope of encountering the succubus myself – and maybe the person responsible for summoning it.

I ran a search on Gwydion Productions and, like Jones, found nothing at all. There should have been something: a domain name registered, something at Companies House. I rang the number and also reached a puzzled and somewhat irate Scottish lady. A few brief questions made it clear she had no idea about a supposed theatre production in a Cardiff warehouse, and that we really, really had to stop fucking bothering her, alright? Clearly, whoever Jones's visitor had been, the thing with the production company was a façade.

Olwen was on the phones and McLeland had his head in some books, but Kerrigan and the rest were in the field. Digbeth was out with Gilroy, getting him set up at the Red Dragon Hotel and the Crow was still in London. It gave me a good opportunity to return the Grafton Projector to its proper place. I retraced my steps to my parked car and took the clanking, tinkling backpack out of the boot. Then, once again working on my nonchalant walk, ambled back inside to return the device to storage.

I was decanting the contraption's components back into their box when I heard footsteps approaching in the corridor outside. Hard, abrupt *clacks* on the hard floor: whoever was coming was in a hurry. I didn't have time to put everything into the box or back into my bag.

I stood, hoping to conceal my actions even as the door opened.

Lady Coldwater stood in the frame. "Danesh! Where have you been? Come on, hurry. We must go."

"I don't…"

Her gaze flicked across the disassembled projector. I don't know whether she thought I was taking it or returning it. She didn't appear to care either way.

"Never mind, no time. It's finally consented to talk. Come, you should hear what it has to say."

She turned and left. After a moment's calculation, I hurriedly finished placing the parts of the projector into their box, terrified I might crack the lenses in the device, knock something vital out of whack. But if I had, no one would know I was responsible. Hopefully.

I closed the box, returned it to its shelf, then raced after her.

I caught up with her at her desk on Level -1, the pool of light at the centre of the floor, the radiating lines of the book shelves. This time, I didn't make any attempt to tread carefully and limit the symphony of squeaks and creaks from the floor.

"Lady Coldwater, I…"

"Hush, hush. Here, come here. Place your hands on the book and close your eyes."

The same scuffed, red leather book lay on the desk: the one with the bookwyrm residing conceptually within its pages. She already had one hand set upon its cover, as if she were about to make some solemn vow upon it.

"I don't know what to do," I said. "This magic … I have no idea how it works."

She grabbed my wrist and placed my hand next to hers on the book. The leather was parched dry, like old bone, the touch of it on my skin scratchy. Her voice went from its usual strident snap to a hushed whisper.

"Close your eyes and *see*. Follow my lead; you can do this. You wanted my help so here we are."

Keeping my hand in place on the book, I manoeuvred onto a chair, closed my eyes and tried to see.

I was definitely … somewhere. I could still feel the chair beneath me, smell the papery, dusty scents of books and their covers, the polish on the wooden floor, but I also had the strong sense of standing somewhere outside, gulfs of space around me. A cold chill in the air was sharp on my cheekbones even though I knew I was in the climate-controlled warmth of the Vault. I also picked up the tang of pine trees and, from somewhere, the white-noise tinkle of running water. I kept my eyes closed so as not to dispel the illusion – or whatever it was.

I couldn't see anything except for mist. It was a situation I was beginning to get very familiar with. A fulgent light glowed around me, but it wasn't coming from anywhere in particular. It was the mists themselves that shone with a pearlescent illumination.

Something touched my hand, faint as a breath of wind. I resisted the urge to pull away, open my eyes. The sensation came again, someone seizing hold of my fingers. The mist lifted a little and I saw Lady Coldwater standing beside me. Her voice was oddly thin and remote as she spoke.

"Very good. I knew you could do it. Follow me to the dragon's lair."

"I don't … where are we?"

"We're exactly where we were. This world around us; it's in the mind of the bookwyrm. I told you, they don't occupy the same physical universe as we do. They dwell in the realm of ideas. This is its overblown idea of where it should live, ridiculous creature that it is. This is how it sees itself."

"Where is it?"

"In the cave up ahead."

As she spoke, the mists lifted some more, and I saw I was standing high up in a range of jagged mountains, their peaks covered in snow that sparkled where the sun, bursting through the fog, picked them out. The air felt colder and colder, sucking the heat out of me, just as it had in Oblivion. Directly in front of us, a steep and narrow path leading up to it, there was a cave entrance.

"Most of the time that entrance is not there," said the Librarian. "This is the creature's way of making it known that we may approach."

"Is it dangerous?"

"Not in the conventional sense. It is dangerous because of what it knows. It can't physically harm us."

"But it could work magic," I said. "It's a sorcerous creature."

Lady Coldwater conceded the point with a nod of her head. "Perhaps. It hasn't harmed me so far, at least. Mostly it's just annoyingly aloof."

We climbed the path. The illusion of our surroundings was impressively real. The air was cold in my lungs when I breathed it in, misty when I exhaled it. Sunlight sparkled off the white peaks of the mountains, although the picture wasn't complete. When I scanned the deep blue sky to find the sun, there was no sign of it.

The cave entrance was a triangle of darkness in the white world, but up close I picked up a faint red glow coming out of it, the light flickering as if from a fire. Something down there rumbled rhythmically, like the mountain itself were breathing.

There was a brief resistance as we stepped inside,

pushing through invisible veils, and then we were edging down the passageway into the heart of the mountain. Even though I knew this was all a pretence, it was hard not to tread warily. I could feel my heart pounding in my chest. I was breathing deeper too, as if I'd been running. Perhaps thinner air was also a part of the bookwyrm's magical construction.

Finally, the passageway began to flatten out. A final twist, and the chamber filling the mountain came into view. A vast four-legged dragon, its flanks red and purple, slumbered atop a mountain range of gems and jewels. Coils of smoke rose from its nostrils, and its sides heaved in and out as it breathed. It had to know we were there, but it was making a show of its indifference. We were truly tiny standing in front of it: mice cowering in front of a Bengal tiger. Red light flickered from torches set all around the walls. The setting was clearly ridiculous: who lit the torches? How did such a vast creature get in and out?

The dragon shifted its body, stretching itself out like a sunbathing cat. In doing so, it set off avalanches in the mountains of gems and I saw, then, that these were not mere precious stones like some dragon hoard from a fantasy novel. Encased within each stone ran a series of runes, letters, symbols, many of them in alphabets I didn't recognize. This treasure wasn't one of mere precious stone; it was one of ideas, sentences, insights. Each of these gems represented a discovery made by the bookwyrm over its long life. This was its treasure. The scale of it was incredible – greater, surely, than any library of books. The dragon slumbered amid mountains of knowledge. I picked one up, a faceted purple stone at my foot, and peered into its depths. A whisper of speech reached me as I saw the rush of incomprehensible words deep within the stone. I glimpsed faces, too, the line of a cityscape. I recognized none of them.

"Set that back where you found it, little creature."

The bookwyrm's voice was a rumble of thunder, shaking the walls around me.

"What is this city?" I asked, trying to make my voice as loud as I could in the cavernous space. "What language are these words written in?"

"They are none of your concern. Words read in a book long ago in a very different world to yours."

The Lady stepped forwards, casting me a glance of disapproval at my time wasting.

"You said you had found something on the phone, bookwyrm?"

"A most interesting device; in its own way it is a library, is it not?"

"In a way."

"The number of ideas and writings available to me on this network it appears to have access to; I could live there happily for a long time."

"Tell me what you have found and I will consider allowing you to travel there," the Lady said.

"Give me what I want and I will tell you what I have found."

"How do I know you have found anything?"

"Why would I lie? My knowledge is vast and I never forget anything. Your concerns are irrelevant to me."

The dragon breathed, more smoke pluming from its long snout. It bared its teeth: long rows of pointed teeth. The Lady, though, wasn't taken in by any of it.

"I have no time for this, bookwyrm. I have given you access to many books, and you know I have many others in my possession. I will do the right thing as I always have. I will ensure that you never run out of sustenance while you are in my care."

The dragon snaked its long head closer. I had to work hard to remind myself that this was an illusion, a conjuration. The dragon could not eat us alive if it so chose.

Could it?

"Very well," it said at last. "You have been fair to me. By your foot is a small green gem. That is what you seek."

I searched around and found a green jewel among the mounds of coins and gemstones.

"This one?" I asked.

"That one."

I peered into it. Once again there were letters, swirling lines of them. I thought they resembled the runes from the warehouse a little.

"How do we read what it says?" I asked.

"You can't," said the dragon. "No doubt you lack the knowledge required for the language and the script used. Fortunately, I speak every tongue and I can translate for you."

"Your wisdom is boundless," said the Lady. "Please tell us what you know."

The dragon waited a moment more, enjoying its position of power.

"This is a single page transcribed from a larger journal. The journal is old in your terms, some three-hundred years."

"Have you read this journal?"

"I have not; it has never been made available to me. But I have consumed the single page transcribed in the journal of a later writer. If you have the original, then perhaps you will be able to find the answers you need."

"How do you know this journal is the one we need?"

"The runes you provided for me to consider are the components of a poorly-constructed summoning incantation, inscribed by someone who either did not know what they were doing or who didn't care. Perhaps the spell didn't work, or it may have worked too well, spiralling out of control."

"We know all that," the Lady said.

"Then you will also know there is a cartouche in the runes. It is intermingled with warding runes by which, I believe, the sorcerer sought to ensure that he or she wasn't devoured by the creature summoned."

"You recognize the cartouche?" I asked.

"It is identical to one written down in the journal."

"What use to us is that? This must be the signature of someone who lived hundreds of years ago."

"And you assume they must be dead by now? You

know very little, human. You may be correct and you may not, but the fact remains that such spells as these are very jealously guarded, passed in secret from adept to adept. It seems to me highly likely that whoever worked this summoning spell was either the original sorcerer from three hundred years ago, or had access to the original wizard's private notes."

"What is the name of this journal?" the Librarian asked.

"It has no name. It's a private diary. But I can tell you who wrote it, and perhaps from that you can find what you need. Unless, of course, you already know the book I am referring to? Perhaps it was one of you who unleashed this magic, not realising that some of the runes were a signature and not essential to the working of the spell?"

"If that were the case, why would we be asking you for help?" the Librarian said.

"Very well, I believe you seek the private journal of Owain Williams, a sorcerer active in your eighteenth century. Do you have his collection of journals?"

"I might," the Librarian said. "Where did this man live?"

"A remote farmstead in a place called the Black Mountains, if the notes I have read are correct. You still call them that, do you not?"

We did. I had been walking in them often, getting away from the stresses of my work life. They were lovely hills, bleak on a wild day, glorious on a sunny one.

"Owain Williams," the Lady said. "Are you sure that's the name?"

"Of course, I'm sure. His name is in the incantation, clear as day to anyone with the knowledge to decipher the runes used."

"Can you tell us anything else?" I asked.

"Such as what? There is little else to learn from this fragment. An attempt was made to entice a cyhyraeth into your world. A successful attempt, no doubt."

"We are grateful to you," said the Lady. "As ever, your knowledge is boundless and invaluable."

The bookwyrm sank its head back onto its mountain of

gems. "Yes, I'm sure that's true. Now, leave me in peace. I have much to read, much more to learn."

The Lady put her hand in my arm and drew me away. "We should leave while we can. We don't want to get trapped in the creature's mind if it closes the doors again."

"Is that possible?" I asked.

"I don't know. I've never liked to find out."

We retraced our steps back up the winding passageway. Cold, white light shone up ahead, brighter and brighter. Finally, we stood back on the icy mountainside. A whole wide world of jagged peaks stretched around us.

"How do we get back to Cardiff?" I asked.

"Wait a moment. All this will fade away, and we will be returned."

"Have you conversed with the bookwyrm often?"

"Once or twice. The knowledge it carries in its mind is dangerous. I do what I can to contain it while giving it more books to consume."

"You're not really going to let it wander off into the internet, are you?"

"As I say, I believe that may already have happened with another such entity. This one, though, I know for sure harbours vast reserves of dangerous magical knowledge. I will do all that I can to ensure it remains where it is, safely locked away in our Vault."

Just as she had promised, the hard lines of the mountains began to blur into mist. The icy air was replaced by warmer, softer atmosphere and the smell of books and wood-polish. In a moment, we were back where we'd always been: Level -1 of the Vault.

"Incredible," I said.

"Dangerous," the Lady said. "The books in my care down here – you see why I protect them now? Prevent them being taken out and used?"

"This journal of Owain Williams – do you have it?"

She paused for a moment, glanced up as if she carried her entire catalogue of books in her head.

"I know the name," she said. "I assume it's the same

person. His collection of journals came into our care early last century. I believe I can find the volume."

"Will you let me see it?"

"No."

"Will you give the bookwyrm access to the complete book?"

"Certainly not. Not if I can help it. In any case, I doubt it will tell us anything else of use. Now it is up to you to find out about this Owain Williams. Find out how a summoning spell from the eighteenth century ended up plastered across the walls of a Cardiff warehouse in the modern day."

"I'll do what I can," I said.

"Excellent. And when you find anything out, be sure to tell me all about it. This arcane knowledge is clearly still out there when we thought it was contained. We must do everything we can to remove it from public knowledge."

"Everything?" I asked.

"Everything," the Lady replied. "Absolutely everything."

18 – Bella Mine

Maleficos non patieris vivere.
> –the motto of Her Majesty's Office of the
> Witchfinder General

The address Sally had written on her canvas turned out to be a modern and thoroughly anonymous bungalow on the outskirts of Cardiff. How many properties did she own? Three that I knew about now. There had to be a hundred ways illegal magic use could be turned to the mundane task of making money. You didn't even need to resort to extortion or blackmail. A bit of clairvoyance and lotteries or horse races could turn a vast profit, so much so that you'd mainly have to be careful not to attract attention. Maybe her family simply had money – but somehow, I doubted it.

I rang the doorbell and waited. The curtains were closed in all the windows and there was no car parked outside. Was she even there? No one came to the door. Perhaps she hadn't survived her off-world battle with Evangelina Mormont after all, and the copy of *Dorian Gray* I'd received had been sent by a friend as part of some pre-arranged pact. I looked around as I waited, wary of imagined eyes watching me through blinds.

The small garden between me and the road was gravelled over, low-maintenance. No plants to prune, no lawn to cut. A few low weeds grew out of the cracks here and there, but everything looked clean enough, well-maintained. Although, *unused* might have been a better word. A low, grey light suffused the scene, as if the sun simply couldn't be bothered to properly rise and begin the work of shining that morning.

It was the day after I'd learned the name Owain

Williams from the bookwyrm. I'd looked into him as much as I could the previous evening, skimming through the few details that had been scanned into the archives on MORIARTY from old newspapers and the like. There wasn't much, and I had to read between the lines – between the words – to guess at the truth. One story in a paper called the *Black Mountain Reporter* referred to him as *a most unlucky homesteader, for his beasts suffer many afflictions, and Mr Williams is often to be seen in the market purchasing fresh livestock*. Which maybe was accurate and he wasn't a very good farmer, but maybe described a sorcerer burning through a large number of animal sacrifices.

Another piece, thirteen years later, reported briefly on his death. *No mourners attended the interment*, it said simply. *Mr Williams was a recluse, his family all having already passed on or left the area some time ago.*

There were hidden stories there, I was sure, events not being spoken about. It all meant I was keener than ever to track down whoever was using his sorcery – and to get help with wielding my own.

I put my face to the frosted glass of the front door and tried to see inside. There was an indistinct mass of white on the floor that might have been a Seething Blob preparing to suck me in to my death, but was probably just the traditional pile of letters, papers and fliers.

Next to the door, under a bay window, was a green delivery locker for companies to drop off parcels. Down the side of the building, in a little alleyway, stood two wheelie bins, one black, for rubbish, one blue, for glass. I wasn't above peering inside. The latter was empty but there was a tied-off bin bag in the black one. Someone had been there that week. A few metres down the passageway, a boiler exhaust flue vented a plume of smoke into the air. The heating or, at least, the hot water was on inside.

I tried the bell again, and this time got a reply. A detached voice came to me through a tiny grille I hadn't previously spotted. A woman's voice, quavering and weak.

"Can I help you?"

Was this the right place? I felt like I was intruding on an old lady's privacy. She might be terrified of strangers coming to her door.

Still, I put my lips close to the grille. "I'm looking for Bella Mine. Is she here?"

"Bella Mine?"

That was the name Sally had put on the address on the canvas revealed by the Grafton Projector. For all I knew, it was her real name. In truth, I had no idea of her true identity. She'd put herself into my phone under *Goddess*, but I was pretty sure that was a pseudonym. I really didn't know anything about her – but the thought of meeting her again was sending a thrill of anticipation through me, like butterflies before a leap off a high ledge. I'm not going to lie.

Zubrasky I admired because, well, she was an attractive, intelligent and highly-capable woman, perhaps a bit out of my league. Her green eyes and red hair were dazzling, and the way her body moved beneath her stab vest made my heart pulse – and other parts of me. Sally, though – Sally, I'd fallen in love with. When I thought of her, I fantasized about holding her hand, and of telling her all my secret fears and hopes. She was even more unattainable given who and what she was, but there was no point denying it. Zubrasky, inciteful as ever, had been right about my feelings for her.

"Bella Mine, yes," I said. "Does she live here? Do you know her?"

"Who is looking for her?"

"My name is Danesh Shahzan. I'm a … friend?"

"Is that what you are?"

"I … yes. I think so."

"You don't sound very sure."

"To be honest, I'm not very sure."

There was a dry, wheezy laugh from the grille that collapsed into a cough.

When she'd recovered, she said, "But you came anyway?"

"Did Bella mention me? Could I perhaps come inside and wait for her?"

There was a pause, and then a thick buzzer sounded from the wall. The lock on the front door clunked open.

The tinny voice from the grille said, "Come in."

The interior might have been any suburban bungalow anywhere in the country: magnolia walls, pastel carpets, every surface polished or painted. No clutter though, no pictures or knickknacks on shelves. No shoes or muddy boots by the door. It didn't feel like a lived-in home at all. It felt almost like one of those show houses they have on new developments, for customers to see what it could be like to live there.

It was a blank canvas.

"Hello?" I called out, "Shall I just come in?"

The voice summoning me down the hallway was hoarse.

"I'm in here."

"Shall I take my shoes off?"

"If you like."

The first room I passed – the sitting room overlooking the road – was empty. It had armchairs and a coffee table and a television but it didn't look like anyone had stepped inside it for some time. It looked like people had once been sitting there, quietly doing the crossword or reading a book, and they'd been *taken*. No, not that: it looked like a film set for anyone peeping through the window. A façade. A normal, boring room in which no one happened to be at the moment.

"I'm in the back," came the voice. Again, it collapsed into a splutter of coughs, then recovered. "There's no one else here. Just you and me."

It seemed an odd thing to say, but I followed the voice down the little hallway. A kitchen was directly ahead, the surfaces and appliances pristine as if everything had just been unboxed and placed there. The voice was coming from another door between me and the kitchen.

I peered round the corner. An old woman lay in a bed that took up most of the room, her small face and shock of grey hair peering out at me, so it seemed, from the depths of her blankets and pillows.

It looked like a hospital bed, a metal frame with motors built into it to allow it to be raised and lowered. A control with five or six buttons on it snaked out on a cable to rest by the pillow. A drip on a stand, a vitals monitor and a steel-framed commode with a white plastic seat were set up around the bed. All the paraphernalia of infirmity. I smelled disinfectant, fustiness and the faint tang of urine. The remains of a meal lay on a chest of drawers, next to a telephone, a tablet and a pile of books. A window provided a view of a small square of garden, the wider world shielded by high trees.

"Excuse me for intruding," I said. "Do you know where Bella is?"

The woman looked frail, almost fading away, but the smile on her wrinkled, grey face was suddenly bright. "You received my copy of Dorian Gray then? I'm disappointed it took you so long to track me down."

"Sally?"

"How did you do it – X-ray the painting?"

"I had access to a Grafton Projector. I saw the message before you painted over it."

She nodded her head in appreciation. "Very good. I hope you were careful; those things have a habit of exploding."

"I was careful."

"I hope you didn't turn it all the way up to the twenty-three moons setting."

"Obviously not. That would be madness."

"I'm surprised you're allowed to use such a nasty sorcerous contraption. *Unnatural*, they are."

"We use them when we have to."

"How much does a line have to blur before it stops being a line?"

"I'm sorry?"

"Never mind. Help me sit up, will you?"

I hooked my hands under her arms and pulled her into a more upright position. Her body was feather-light, stick-thin. The movement cost her; she closed her eyes, grimaced for a moment as if something inside her was tearing, before unleashing her amused smile on me again.

"Better, thank you. It gets so uncomfortable staying in one position for so long."

I didn't know what to say for a moment. The vital young woman I'd accompanied to Faebrook Folly – was *this* the real her? Powerful users could alter their appearances, we were told, even extend the length of their lives. Perhaps this Bella Mine was her true identity.

"You probably have questions," she said. "Could you pass me a glass of water before I answer them?"

I refilled her plastic jug from the kitchen tap, then poured her a fresh glass of water. When she took it, her hand shook, setting up a tiny storm of waves in the drink. Her skin was mottled. At the same time, there was something in her eyes I recognized. That familiar glint of mischief and defiance.

She sipped at the water. "Ah, better. Thank you."

"Are you … ill?" I asked.

"You want to know why I look so old, but you're too polite to ask."

"I don't know how old you really are. For all I know this is the real you."

"It's very impolite to ask a woman about her age."

"Yes, sorry."

She was playing with me, enjoying my discomfort.

"The truth is, the Sally you met last year was more or less the real me. Not the name, but the general appearance."

"Then … what happened?"

"Evangelina Mormont happened. Perhaps if the Office didn't exist and we could battle evil like her more openly, this wouldn't have been the result, but there we are."

I sat down in the upholstered, winged chair beside the bed. "She did this to you?"

"It was partly her and partly the dimension we passed into. Some planes suck out your life, the Oblivion dimension being only one of them. Places like that literally suck out your soul, as you must know. Linger for long enough and you don't come out."

"At Faebrook Folly, you did something to the portal. I saw you add a rune to those around it."

She grinned, enjoying the appreciation of her skill. "A simple trick, like adding a character to a web address. The secret is to know what to add, of course. Since I planned to jump through too, I had to make very sure I didn't end up somewhere inviable."

"You knew you were taking her to a place you could both die."

She closed her eyes for a moment as if remembering the pain of where she'd been. "That was the calculation: I was prepared and I figured she wasn't. It was a gruelling ordeal, a matter of stamina as much as magical artistry. Having your life force drained from you like that: there's an agony to it. The sorcery she threw at me as we battled was cruel, but it was our surroundings that did the real damage to both of us. In the end, it was close. Very close."

"But you did win. You returned and the Sorceress is dead."

"With Myrddin's help, I predominated."

"You're absolutely sure of that?" I asked.

She tilted her head onto one side to consider me. "You look sceptical."

"Recent events have made me sceptical. Everything we've seen of late suggests the intercession of a powerful user acting for English Wizardry. Our knowledge of their membership is patchy, but Mormont is an obvious candidate."

"What about the one in charge?" asked Sally. "The Warlock?"

"It's possible they're responsible," I replied, "although he or she seems to stay in the shadows. Do you have any idea who it is?"

Sally shook her head. "Not a clue. I've heard the name, of course, but nothing more. I thought you'd know."

"No."

"Tell me about these recent events," she said.

"What have you heard?"

"Nothing. Since my return I've been … recuperating. I lose track of the days. Weeks, too, come to that."

"Will you recover fully?"

"Oh, you should have seen me a month ago. A shivering little scrap of bone I was. Death's door was wide open and me with one foot on the other side. Sometimes I think it was only the agonies running through my bones that kept me pinned to existence. But, yes, I am slowly returning to myself. The damage unwinds. Six months or so, a year perhaps, and I believe I'll be back to how I was. More or less. Probably even more beautiful and glorious."

"Who looks after you, makes you food?"

"No one. No one knows I'm here apart from you. On my good days I get up and about, feed myself, wash my body. On the bad days, well, there's not much I can do but lie here and … endure."

"If I'd known I'd have come."

"To arrest me for crimes under magus law?"

"To help you. You're the victim here."

"Perhaps. Never liked to think of myself as that. But, tell me what has been going on in the world. Assume I know nothing."

I filled her in on recent events: the summoning of the seven succubi and the wraith-like cyhyraeth. I left out names and details as appropriate. It was apparent from her attention that a lot of it was news to her.

"Well," she said when I'd finished. "A cyhyraeth. Nasty bastards. Was it brought into our world to scare someone do you think?"

"The one I met was brutal, even without the effect of the runes. If you ask me, they don't just portend death they bring it about, like spectral assassins. It's like, the fate they've foretold has to be fulfilled and they'll damn-well make sure it *is* fulfilled if the universe fails to comply."

Sally nodded, as if that made sense to her. "Then there's the succubi. No doubt about them. Oh, they seem like a lot of fun at first, them and incubi, but they'll destroy you in the end. I've seen it happen. Vicious things they are, too, playing on people's weaknesses. But I can tell you that whoever is responsible for all this summoning activity, these assaults upon the Office, it isn't Mormont."

"You're absolutely sure about that?"

"Yes. With Myrddin's help, I defeated her."

"You can use his real name. Arthur Stonewall. I was there when Mormont gave the fact away, remember?"

"She did? You were?"

Her memory was clearly still patchy.

"At Faebrook Folly, during the showdown. Stonewall is English Wizardry's *Destroyer*, their *Abaddon*. The leader of your rebel alliance must be an incredibly powerful user in his own right. He's, what, one hundred and fifty years old by now?"

"Something like that. Direct help from him is rare, though. He also likes to stay in the shadows as much as possible. English Wizardry would do anything to remove him from the board."

"Yet he followed you into the other dimension?"

"No, not that. He foresaw that a showdown with Mormont was likely at some point. Three years ago, he gave me a soul maze amulet attuned to her. She needed to be weakened before I could use it and I needed to get close to her, but the item allowed me to drain her essence, capture her soul. Once I'd used it, her body was just a lifeless husk. An empty vessel."

Vessel. I'd heard that phrase used before.

"Where is this amulet now?"

Bella – Sally – lifted her hand, pointing with a shaking finger across the room at a chest of drawers.

"It's there. The necklace with the gaudy purple stone on it."

Next to a jewellery box stood a gold-coloured stand in the shape of a tree, bangles and necklaces hanging from its branches. One of the chains did, indeed, have a large purple jewel hanging from it.

"That's Mormont right there," said Sally. "Trapped in that gem. Once I'm back to myself and I can work the magic, I'll destroy the stone and her life energy will be gone. No coming back from that."

"You should have destroyed it straight away."

"She can hardly escape, and I wanted her to watch me recovering from our battle, regaining my strength and beauty. And, also, I thought I might … talk to her a little before I despatched her. Extract knowledge of our foes from her."

"Wait, she can perceive the outside world? She's aware of us now?"

"Someone of her power? Yes, most likely. I haven't had the strength to delve into the stone and see what she's up to, but I imagine she's over there listening to every word we say right now. She'll be seething with frustration and fury, and there isn't a single damn thing the evil bitch can do about it."

I found it hard to take my eyes off the gemstone. The thought of Evangelina Mormont trapped inside there, listening to everything we said was unsettling.

"She's escaped impossible situations before," I said. "Oblivion for one thing."

"There's no escape; her essence is trapped in the soul maze. And, besides, her body is lying in a broken heap upon the black sand of a distant realm on the far side of the aether. Even if she could somehow escape the amulet, the journey across the void would be impossible. She'd end up wandering the grey infinity for the rest of time in search of her own bones, lost and alone. Which is a tempting fate for her, actually."

"We should destroy the stone," I said. "I don't want to take any chances with her."

Sally looked amused. Her chuckle turned into another bout of racking coughs.

When she'd recovered, she said, "Are you going to confiscate it from me, witchfinder?"

"I'm asking you for it. We can't take any chances with Mormont."

"Fine, fine. Take it if you must. Destroy it and we'll be done with her. Your librarian will know what to do even if you don't. But learn what you can, first. Interrogate her. Maybe she can even lead you to the Warlock."

"Thank you." I rose and plucked the amulet off the stand. It seemed to resist, briefly, but it was probably just my imagination. The chain getting tangled up with one of the others.

"What will you do now?" she asked.

"Pursue whoever did summon these entities into the world."

She shook her head. The pink of her scalp was visible beneath her uncombed grey hair.

"Why do you even care if someone is trying to destroy the Office?"

"These evils, the runes and the demons: they endanger real people. A petty war between the Office and your Borderland Reading Group hardly matters in the grand scheme of things. And besides, I think they're coming for me whether I'm part of the Office or not."

"The *Borderland Reading Group*?"

"That's what you called yourselves, remember? Martha Ndidi and Oliver Auchter and the rest of you. Have you forgotten your comrades so quickly?"

"No, Danesh. I haven't forgotten them at all. The name we adopted, perhaps, because it was never important. Tell me, what happened to Oliver? Is he safe?"

"He is, but I genuinely don't know where. The Librarian took care of him. The Pale Sisters."

"Ah, good, good. I don't fully understand how she is allowed to operate within the Office, but you can trust her. He will be safe enough for now. The reading group, though; it was just a joke. We don't really call ourselves that. Not amongst ourselves, I mean."

"What do you call yourselves?"

"The Unnatural."

"Why would you call yourselves that?"

She half-chuckled, half-coughed. "It's a classic example of reclaiming a term of abuse. I'm sure you can think of other examples. It's taken from your own mission statement. You recognize it, obviously. *Protecting the public from the unnatural since 1645*, yes? We took the name for ourselves as a badge of pride."

"Right. I see."

"You in the Office talk about suppressing unnatural impulses. You do realise how that sounds if you try applying it to other aspects of human nature, don't you?"

I did, of course.

"I'm not responsible for any of these names or mottos," I said. "I'm not responsible for calling you that."

"*You*?" she said. "You mean *us*, surely? You're one of us. Tell me, how are the blackouts? The weird episodes of dislocation you suffer from?"

"You know about them?"

The grin that spread across her face told me the truth of it. She hadn't.

"A lucky guess. I do know what sort of symptoms you can have if you try to suppress your true nature. I've seen it before: psychological effects like depression, even odd physical things like back pain or lethargy. I figured there'd be something for a sensitive lad like you."

A sensitive lad? That was hardly the adjective I'd have hoped for. There was also no denying that I'd suffered no such episodes of late. Not since I'd admitted to myself, at least, that I was a user. There'd been grim, feverish flashbacks to the deaths of Peter Warder and Thomson Fulger – to the moment when I'd slaughtered the two of them – but they were different. They were my mind reliving traumatic events. The moments of sickening disorientation – moments that I now thought of as my incipient magical ability trying to burst through into my consciousness – had gone.

Sally hadn't finished with me, though.

"Then there's your other little motto, isn't there? *Thou shalt not suffer a witch to live.* That's an absolute charmer, isn't it? You work for a brutal, misogynistic pillar of the patriarchy, and you're better than that, Danesh."

"It's a quote from the Old Testament. It doesn't mean anything in the modern world."

"And yet, there it is, still in use. Do you know what the line was originally? In the Latin?"

"I'm sure you're going to tell me."

"I am. *Maleficos non patieris vivere*. It's written on the Office's crest. The key word, though, is *maleficos*. It means evildoer, baddie. *You shall not suffer an evildoer to live* – which, okay, is a bit eye-for-an-eye in the modern world, but it's something we could probably all sympathise with. Somehow, though, the word became translated as *witch*. As dangerous, evil woman. Funny how that happens. Is this *really* what you want to be part of?"

I tried to reply, but stopped myself. What she said – it made some sense. But I didn't have the head space for it, just then.

"Look, I get what you're saying, but now isn't the time. There's too much else going on."

"So why did you come here, exactly?"

"I wanted to know what had happened to you."

"All this going on, and you stretched so thin, and you came to drop in on a friend to see how I was doing?"

"I knew you were back because of the book you sent, but I had no way of knowing what state you were in. And, okay, I wanted your help, too. I needed to be sure that Mormont is out of the picture."

"And now you know she is, yet you're still here."

I took the plunge. "I was worried about you. The time we spent together … it meant something to me. I missed you."

I saw that she was about to fire back some sarcastic comment, then stopped herself. There was a moment of silence as we both considered the words I'd spoken.

When she responded, her words were soft, little more than a whisper. "I'm glad that you came. It has been a lonely few months."

"I can come again. Fetch your things, empty the commode."

"Ooh, romantic."

"I'm serious. Do you want me back?"

"As Danesh or as a witchfinder?"

"Just as a friend."

"I'd like that."

"There, ah, there is something else I need help with though."

"Hah! I knew it. Go on."

"It's just, like you say, I'm one of you. I have powers and abilities. I admit that now. Every now and then, in moments of stress, I lash out, and these impulses … I have no control over them. They're dangerous, for others and for me. I need guidance. I need a mentor like you or Myrddin to guide me."

"That happened at Faebrook Folly, yes?"

"It did."

"There have been other times?"

"There have."

"Then, yes, you need help. No one should face what you're going through alone. Once, before the Office and all the rest of it, people like us banded together, helped each other. Now, though, it's dangerous. Very dangerous. The Unnatural – yes, in normal circumstances, we would help you. But, given who and what you are, and given how many people we've lost, it's not going to happen, sorry. I'm in no shape to do very much, and if you think I'm going to tell you were Myrddin is, then you're sadly mistaken. You're a user in need of a guiding hand, but you're also an operative of the Office, attempting to infiltrate us for all I know."

"I'm not attempting to infiltrate you."

"Which, of course, is exactly what you would say. Speak to Lady Coldwater."

"She wouldn't help. There is no one else I can turn to."

She considered me for a moment, then looked down. "I can't help you, Danesh. I'm sorry, it's too dangerous. You must see that. If things were different, if the Office didn't oppress us all, I'd do what I could for you, but that isn't the world we live in. If we knew you were on our side, if we knew you were secretly acting against Hardknott-Lewis, then it might be different. But can we know that?"

"I understand."

"It's a shame the Mystical Council was disbanded. Seems to me that would have been the perfect home for you."

"The Mystical Council?"

"You must know what that is."

"I've never heard of it."

She shook her head. "When the Office rewrites history, it really rewrites history. Ask Hardknott-Lewis; I'm sure he'd love to tell you all about it."

I tried another angle. There had to be someone who could give me what I needed.

"Okay, so, Stonewall is your leader. You and Auchter are members of these *Unnatural*, and Evan Cornwallis and Martha Ndidi were until they were killed. Who else is involved? There has to be someone who could give me the direction I need."

"I'm sorry, but I'm hardly going to give you names, am I?"

"Was Maude Woebegone one of you?"

"I have no idea who that is. And why do you say *was*? Has she been killed, too?"

"I believe so." I'd assumed she was someone like Sally: a user fighting back against Mormont and English Wizardry. Maybe that wasn't right at all.

"Who was she?"

"I can't reveal the details of an ongoing investigation, especially to a known user."

"Just damn well tell me."

And I did. It was little enough: someone or something had ripped out Maude Woebegone's soul. The similarity to the fate Sally had inflicted upon Mormont was clear – and troubling. Still, Sally appeared to know nothing about it. She claimed ignorance, and from the pained look of disgust on her face as I recounted what we'd learned, I believed her.

"You see?" she said. "This is where it takes you. This is where your *burn the witch* bullshit takes you."

"You don't know that. The Office had nothing to do with Maude's death."

"How do you know?"

"Because we're doing everything we can to investigate it. To bring those responsible to justice."

She waved my protestations away. "Directly or indirectly, you're implicated. Maybe not just you, but you're part of the picture, aren't you? It's all related."

She looked suddenly drained from our long conversation. She seemed to sink back into her pillow.

"Can I get you anything else before I go?" I asked.

"Let me sleep. That's all, let me sleep."

"I can take the amulet?" I asked.

But she was already unconscious.

19 – The Family Ghost

The cyhyraeth … (probably from the noun *cyhyr* "muscle, tendon; flesh" + the termination *-aeth*, meaning "skeleton, a thing of mere flesh and bone", "spectre", "death-portent", "wraith"), is a ghostly spirit in Welsh mythology, a disembodied moaning voice that sounds before a person's death.

–Wikipedia

I carried the amulet back to my car with all the reverence of a royal flunky carrying the crown jewels – or maybe a bomb disposal officer carrying a suspect device that could explode at any moment.

I didn't know much about such amulets – I'd skim-read a few details but had never come into contact with one before – and I was fairly sure simply dropping it wasn't going to smash the stone and release the malevolent, screeching spirit of the Sorceress back into the world. But I also wasn't going to take that chance. There were probably … rituals. Back in the Mini, I slid the item into a clear plastic evidence bag. It wasn't going to help a damn in protecting me if she did escape, but the act of sealing the bag made me feel a little bit better.

I placed the amulet on the passenger seat of the car and headed back to base. Weird how carefully I drove knowing that an emergency stop might send the gem with the soul of Evangelina Mormont trapped inside clattering into the footwell. Perhaps they should give such an amulet to everyone learning to drive, to encourage them to be careful.

I found myself talking to it as I negotiated the twisty, turny traffic lanes of central Cardiff. You might even say *rambled.* Perhaps it was a way of coping with the anxiety of having her there.

"So, who is it, then? This Warlock. Who is so powerful and fearsome that even the mighty Evangelina Mormont takes orders from them? No answer? Well, never mind. I'm going to destroy you now, you do know that, don't you? You'll be the third member of English Wizardry I've accounted for. Peter Warder was the first. Do you remember him, or was he just a useful idiot, a servant who revered you and who carried out your orders? I liked him; I really did. Perhaps if you hadn't gotten your claws into him, he might have turned out alright. But you corrupted him and I had to kill him.

"Thomson Fulger, too. Yes, he's dead as well. Did you know that? I also killed him. Another expendable foot-soldier in your battle: a little more powerful, perhaps, capable of actually working magic, but not very effectively. I'm sure you had to coach him and control him until you wanted to scream. Did you convince him he was powerful, a mighty wizard, to get him to do what he did? Still, he's dead too. Another member of English Wizardry ticked off from my list. Once that stone you're trapped within is smashed to pieces, that'll be three of you.

"Yes, I'm admitting the truth to you: I'm a user. I've committed several major crimes under magus law. If Hardknott-Lewis and Earl Grey knew the truth about me, I'd be in a frozen grave in Oblivion. I'm a user who has somehow ended up as an operative in the Office, and that's a pretty fucked-up situation to be in, and I'm also English, but none of that means I'm on your side. Not for a single moment. I despise you and everything you stand for. Quite what the future holds for me, I'm not sure. I genuinely don't know what Hardknott-Lewis knows about me. I like him, in all honesty. He's a good man. He's misguided, I see that now, but he can't be that bad if you're his enemy, can he?

"Then there's Evan Cornwallis and Martha Ndidi and all those other unfortunates you killed and stole the eyes from in your futile attempt to track down Stonewall. How does it feel to have gone to all that effort and be foiled? How does it feel to have me, of all people, acting as your executioner?"

She didn't reply. The stone remained unmoved in its bag on the seat of my car. My little speech over – I had no idea where it had come from – I parked back near our offices and carried Evangelina Mormont's trapped soul inside to be destroyed.

The Lady appeared to have some inkling about where I'd been and what I was carrying into the office. For once, she met me at the door to the Vault. There was a look of clear hunger in her eyes as she studied the amulet. I filled her in on what it contained.

Lady Coldwater held the object up to her eye, twisting it around. "Evangelina Mormont is really in here?"

"And probably able to hear everything we say."

"Well, well. How did you acquire it?"

"Best I don't say. A reliable source, as we investigators say."

"And the chalice? Were you able to recover that?"

"Still no sign, I'm afraid."

"Keep looking. We have to make sure no one makes any further use of that evil object. The more I read about it, the less I like it."

"You'll destroy the amulet?" I asked.

"Oh yes. The amulet and Mormont along with it. There are rites that need to be carried out, incantations and the like. It will take a while, but I'll begin them now."

"Is there any danger she'll escape?"

"You said that her body is far from this plane, unreachable?"

"So I'm told."

"Then we may proceed. A few hours, and we can finally see the end of her."

I couldn't help asking. "You despise the use of death magic. You wouldn't teach me anything."

Her eyes were still on the amulet. "This is different. She's already been killed, she just refuses to accept it."

She glanced up to look at me. "And … perhaps there are grey areas. Very small grey areas. For one such as her."

"What happened to *who is to say who has right on their side?* You said when you refused to help me: use such magic and it becomes a habit."

"I did say that, yes."

"Perhaps now you'll concede I'm on the right side and give me the training I need. I've given you Evangelina Mormont."

"Perhaps," she said. "I'll give it some thought. I will."

She changed the subject. "Did you get to the bottom of the Owain Williams mystery yet?"

"That's the next matter I'm going to look into."

"Make sure that you do. I've delved into his journals. A seriously nasty piece of work he was."

"Anything I should know about?"

Her words confirmed everything I'd inferred from the newspaper articles.

"Evil is mundane. Mundane and repetitive. Three hundred years ago, Owain Williams used and abused those around him for his own ends. Animals, his family members, his own children: he saw them all simply as useful ingredients and components for his sorcery, nothing more. He was wicked, utterly wicked, and that means the spells he crafted, these runes, are wicked. We must make sure they never see the light of day again. Or the dark of night, come to that. Find out who is using them and stop them, Danesh."

"I will. I…"

I stopped talking as realisation dawned within me. Why hadn't I seen it earlier? The name was a common one, of course, especially in Wales. Williams. There are people called that everywhere. Still, two of them in one investigation. Was I seeing patterns where there were none, or had I missed a vital connection?

"What?" said the Lady. "What have you worked out?"

"I have to go," I said. "Investigations to pursue. Destroy the amulet and perhaps tonight we can all sleep soundly for once."

The Lady snorted her amusement. "I don't ever sleep soundly. Always best to have one eye open in my experience."

Back at my desk, the first thing I did was pull up a picture of El Encantador – Hywel Williams – from his web site and put it side by side on the screen with the one line-drawing we had on MORIARTY of Owain Williams, scanned in from one of his journals. I squinted at the two images, looking for a family resemblance. There was possibly some similarity, but maybe it was wishful thinking on my part. It wasn't helped by the fact that Hywel was pictured in a ridiculous wizard outfit, eyes blazing with faux magical light, while Owain was drawn from three-quarter perspective, sketched in austere black pencil lines. His features had all the sternness of a hellfire and damnation preacher.

There was also the rough outline of the face I'd glimpsed in the runes: the target, I'd assumed, of the incantation. I had no physical image of that, only my memory. Which wasn't very scientific – I could convince myself that both of the faces on the screen in front of me bore a resemblance to that magical visage.

I ran both images through our facial recognition algorithms and got a pretty high match, a little over sixty percent. That at least suggested I might be on the right lines. Maybe the connection wasn't only in the surnames.

I rang Kerrigan. He was somewhere out and about in the wilds of the Brecon Beacons, where there'd been talk of a flock of sheep acting strangely. Someone had reported them lining up to spell huge words right across a hillside – almost certainly a prank, obviously, but worth checking out. Because we'd look really stupid if it turned out to be true.

To my surprise, he had signal, and I got right through to him. His phone exaggerated the whistling of the wind as he spoke – or else, he was on top of a mountain as he shouted his responses.

"Do you still have that video you took of the wizard we went to see?" I asked.

"If you need to work out how to do the tricks, there's plenty of videos on YouTube, you know."

"I need to check something out from his performance."

"Seriously?"

"It's a theory, nothing more."

"I'll send you a link to my cloud backup. Come on, though, Danesh, you saw him. The guy's a joke. My auntie Mabel would make a more believable wizard than he would, and she's dead."

"You're probably right," I said. "Except, maybe that's exactly what he wants us to think."

There was a pause on the other end while the wind howled around for a bit.

"You mean he's actually a powerful wizard hiding in plain sight as a crap children's wizard? That's devious, Danesh, very devious. I like your thinking."

"We didn't suspect him at all, did we? We decided he was a joke even as he stood there *telling us* he was casting spells."

"Yeah, I suppose."

"It's probably nothing, a coincidence, but I need to be sure."

"Okay, well. Just don't discount our initial theory. That he's just a bad stage entertainer with a sparkly cloak and a pointy hat with a compartment for hiding doves."

The footage was shaky and poorly-shot: Kerrigan had clearly held his phone at an angle while filming, making it look like Hywel Williams – El Encantador – was performing halfway up a hillside. I hadn't paid particularly close attention during the actual performance. Now, I watched his face and his hand movements more closely, slowing the video down at times, stepping through the frames. I thought there was a hunted expression on his face at times. A wariness. If it wasn't for my suspicions, I'd have put it down to having to stand up in front of a room full of excited and noisy children and entertain them – a prospect which would certainly have filled me with horror. Give me a brush with a nice gibbering revenant from the dimensions of despair any day.

There was a moment halfway through the performance that I played back several times. Williams was attempting to perform a simple trick involving a white rabbit, making it disappear and reappear in unlikely places. It was actually pretty skilfully done, although it was too subtle for his audience, who clearly wanted something more exciting, perhaps involving explosions.

I caught the look of exasperation in his eye. I'd noticed it at the time now that I thought about it, but I'd put it down to frustration at having to work the kids' party circuit when he'd maybe dreamed of bigger and better things, stage shows and TV series. Now, though, I wasn't so sure. He was working some pretty skilful trickery, carrying out vanishes that he'd clearly practised over and over. The children in his audience were laughing, but not at him. They were talking among themselves, play fighting.

I caught the moment when his frustration boiled over. There was nothing overt, nothing in his actions, but I could see it in his eyes beneath the rim of his ridiculous wizard's hat. His lips moved silently, a rapid series of syllables, and he *did* something. I was sure of it. One of the poor, supine rabbits (there were clearly several, all identical), disappeared from the table. He made a swishing motion with his hands in front of the creature to give the vanish some drama – but also to cover up what was really going on. Stepping from frame to frame I could see it very clearly – but then, I knew what I was looking for. Briefly, the rabbit's body was limned with a faint blue glow, and then it was gone.

I tried to lip read the syllables he'd muttered but I couldn't make them out. It didn't matter. I knew a real spell when I saw one. We're trained for stuff like that.

"Hywel Williams, you sneaky bastard," I said out loud.

All this time, he'd been here in Cardiff, publicly calling himself a wizard and no doubt laughing while I chased wild leads. I'd assumed some shadowy figure like

Mormont was my foe, and here he was, this ridiculous stage wizard. I studied the pictures on his web site, all the ridiculous hocus-pocus nonsense. It was brilliant in its amateurism. He'd even, by all that is unholy, used Comic Sans. Maybe Mormont had been brought back to instruct him, guide him in some particular ritual magic, and maybe she hadn't – but it was Williams who was responsible. It had to be. Maybe it had been *his* burner phone that Thomson Fulger had been ringing, seeking help on the intricacies of summoning smokewraiths.

If my theories were correct, Williams was a powerful English Wizardry adept. He'd summoned his demons and his horrors and unleashed the succubus onto Hardknott-Lewis's trail and done who-knew-what else. The fact that he was Welsh puzzled me a little. Why would he be a member of English Wizardry? The racial supremacy bullshit they peddled extended to basically everyone who wasn't (a) white and (b) born in the country they probably call Albion – specifically the bit of it we now think of as England.

I did some background research, pulling in what details I could from the web as well as our own records and those held by the police. He had no convictions under magus, criminal or civil law. He was completely clean. It was beautifully done. He came from a long line of Williams who had lived in and around South Wales for centuries. Tracing such a common surname back through time wasn't going to be easy, but the extended family I could track down had certainly lived in houses and farms in and around the Black Mountains: the part of the world where Owain Williams, the known historical sorcerer, had lived. Somewhere, I was willing to bet, there was an old family house and an old family library, and a whole catalogue of incantations and summoning spells sitting there in ancient tomes. Books that the young Hywel had pored over and studied when he should have been reading comics and books about his favourite rugby players and looking in wonder at pornography.

I also managed to trace his immediate forebears from

an old newspaper article on one of his performances. His father was Welsh, but his mother was English. His father had died when Hywel was young – a situation I had some sympathy with – and his mother had brought him up. Had there been tension there, resentment? Had his mother turned him against his Welsh background, setting him on an intellectual path that, eventually, took him to membership of English Wizardry. He might have been a valuable asset to them: a token Welshman, operating behind enemy lines.

I also found a picture of him with his son: a young lad, eight or nine, who sometimes helped him with his tricks. I'd seen him before, too: the boy from the supposed transportation that Kerrigan and I had witnessed. The one whom Kerrigan had blithely assured me was a twin, dressed identically for the purposes of the illusion.

The embarrassing truth was that Williams did not have twins. He had only one child. Kerrigan and I, two highly-trained witchfinders, had sat and watched Williams magically transport his son through space, in clear breach of all the statutes.

We'd even applauded.

I had one more thing to check before leaping into action. I had Preston Jones' number from my visit to his shabby little office at Newport Docks. He picked up straight away. The disappointment in his voice when it was me and not some actual customer was clear, but I pressed on.

"I'd like to send you another picture if I may."

"Do we have to do this now?"

"Please, it will only take a moment. Is the email address on your card the right one?"

"Yes, yes, if you must."

There was a pause while the mugshot of Hywel uploaded at my end and downloaded at his. I could hear Jones making frustrated little grunting noises as he waited.

"Is that the man who came to book the warehouse?" I asked eventually.

"No, no, I don't think so."

"It must be. Please, take another look."

"Nope, not him, definitely."

The whole elaborate theory I'd constructed came smashing down like a collapsing building.

Then Preston said, "This might be his son, though."

"What?"

"His son. There's a definite family resemblance."

"The man who came to see you was older?"

"Much older. But the face was the same, I think. The same eyes and mouth."

A disguise? It had to be possible: an attempt to conceal his identity. If he was used to performing on stage, he probably had some skill with make-up. He might even have used a magical glamour to alter his appearance, age himself to put people off his scent.

"Thanks, Preston. You've been really helpful."

"Enough, though, now, okay? I have a business to run here. We don't all get paid by the government to do nothing all day."

I let that slide. "Can I ask you one more favour? Then I promise I'll leave you in peace."

He sighed exaggeratedly. "What is it?"

"Is the warehouse still empty?"

"Times are tough, what can I tell you?"

"I'd like to gain access again. Can you give me the key?"

"Why would I do that?"

"It's for an operation. You should know that it's possible the fabric of the building could sustain some damage. If things don't go well."

"The police have a key. That's how you got in last time."

I did not want to have to explain to Zubrasky or Evans what I was up to.

"You wouldn't believe the bureaucracy involved in that," I said. "It would be much simpler if I could borrow yours."

"Why would I let you have it?"

"I'm a government employee, as you say. I'm completely indemnified. Any damage to your building and you'll be compensated. Very well compensated. You might even find that you don't have the cost and worry of an obsolete warehouse sitting on your books anymore. That has to be appealing, right?"

It took him several nanoseconds to reply. "Fine, fine, the building's yours. Do what you have to do. But any damage, and you pay for it, yes?"

"You have my word."

As I was leaving, a final question occurred to me.

"Do these keys unlock all the doors in the place?"

"Obviously."

"Last time I was there, down in the basement, there was a room I never went into. A stone archway and a tiny little door."

"That? No, there's nothing there. Used to be other rooms but it was all filled in and sealed up a hundred years ago when the building was redeveloped."

I wondered if they'd sealed the *other rooms* off for a reason. If, maybe, dark magic had been worked there at the epicentre of one of the Crow's magical nodes. If malevolent beings had a habit of passing through the veils there to trouble the people of Cardiff. I chose not to mention any of that to Jones.

"Thanks," I said. "I'll come and get the key now."

20 – Bae Tigr

It is our view that the demands of His Majesty's Office of the Witchfinder General should be ignored – and, indeed, that their recommendations gravely endanger the British people, especially given the current difficulties. The list of the achievements and triumphs worked by the Mystical Council in defence of the realm is long, and to deny the country this capacity out of prejudice and fear of matters poorly understood is the height of foolishness. I therefore urge you, Prime Minister, to set aside their imprecations – and, indeed, to give some thought to the question of whether a modern state such as Britain requires an Office of the Witchfinder General in the first place. The Council is not only capable of dealing with all the threats currently handled by the Office, it is also, by definition, very much more able to defeat those threats and to prevent them from ever recurring.

–Lancelot Honeydew, Mystical Council, private letter to Winston Churchill, 1943

Hywel William's cover became impressive the more I looked into it. It wasn't only his crap magician shtick; he was also, from the outside, clearly a good man. He volunteered for at least two charities that I could find, helping children with long-term and incurable medical conditions. He organized baking competitions to raise money and dressed up as Santa at Christmas. He was married and had the son that I'd seen during his act, and from the pictures I could find, he appeared to have numerous close friends. A less likely evil wizard it was hard to imagine.

Contacting him turned out to be less straightforward than I'd imagined. Given that he was trying to make a living as a stage wizard – or at least, appearing to do so – I would have expected phone numbers and social media links on his web site. Instead, amidst all the forced jollity and bad wizard puns, there was only a form to fill in, along with the promise that El Encantador would *get back to me as soon as he could!*

I filled out the form, mentioning my name. If he knew I was onto him, I figured, he'd be more likely to take the bait. I offered him a chance to meet up, couched as an innocent request to employ him for a show in case anyone not in the know fielded the request. If English Wizardry did have plans to kill me in some malicious and magical way, though, I was deliberately giving them a clear opportunity. They knew I was an adept, but my calculation was that Williams would think of himself as more than a match. He was clearly capable of summoning powerful entities, and all I'd managed was to unleash a poorly-controlled blast of magical energy at Peter Warder and Thomson Fulger. Williams probably laughed at such pathetic attempts to wield magic.

I paced and fretted for the rest of the day, hearing nothing back. I filled my time catching up on paperwork and more research on the figure my mother had sketched – which came up blank.

The following morning, finally, my phone rang, called from an unrecognized mobile number. I recognized the voice on the other end immediately from his stage performance: El Encantador, Hywel Williams.

He sounded oddly wary, no doubt conscious that he was walking into an Office trap. I hoped that the location I was proposing – the warehouse in the docks – would be too tempting for him. I was offering to meet up in their territory, in the very place where he'd used the runes of his forebear to summon the cyhyraeth that had so nearly destroyed me. Surely he'd feel sufficiently comfortable about meeting me there, of all places.

Instead, though, he sounded puzzled when I told him

where I wanted to meet.

"A warehouse at the docks?"

I played along. Perhaps there were people listening and he needed to maintain his cover.

"It's empty," I said. "I thought it might make a good venue for a party I'm thinking of throwing."

"A party?"

It was weird conversing in these polite terms with such an evil user. I kept up the pretence. Williams might think I didn't know the truth about him, didn't know his dark secret. For all he knew, his was just a name I'd come across, someone to ask a few questions of. He didn't know that I knew about his involvement in the summonings. I hoped. He might think I was simply going to ask him a few questions about a place where I'd witnessed some suspicious activity.

"A few friends, nothing more," I said. "Could we meet there to see if the location is suitable?"

He paused for a moment, perhaps conversing with someone else on mute.

"I have time now. Can you send me the address?"

I had to admit, he was a good actor. Anyone listening in would think he had no idea where Mermaid Warehouse even was. Still playing along, I texted him the address.

"See you there in an hour?" he said.

"An hour. I'll be there."

I thought about taking someone else along with me on my crazy attempt to trap him. Inevitably, though, there weren't many people around. The only other operative was the Lady, and I didn't want to interrupt her attempts to destroy the amulet containing the disembodied soul of Evangelina Mormont. On the other hand, I was sailing into dangerous waters, basically making myself bait in a trap for English Wizardry, and doing so without any training in the forbidden arts. But I also didn't want to delay. There had to be a good chance they'd accelerate their plans, especially since the killing of Mason Greentree. There also had to be a good chance they'd come for me after events on Westminster Bridge. Time to take the attack to them.

In the end, I left a log entry on MORIARTY explaining my intentions for anyone to find if they were interested. It would have to do. Olwen was at her station, womanning the phone line, and I could have requested she accompany me – but I didn't want her there to see if it came to me unleashing another magical attack against another English Wizardry adept.

I stepped out into a drizzly Cardiff day. Grey clouds had slumped out of the sky to engulf buildings and streets and people alike. Everything was the neutral, muddy colour of water after too many paint brushes have been washed in it. I strode rapidly past the castle and through the shopping centre, cutting through the arcades and down onto Lloyd George Avenue and the bay area.

It's hard to imagine, now, what the place must have been like once. It had a dangerous and notorious reputation back in the day, but that was maybe an outsider's view. It was also the first truly multicultural community in all of Wales, as ships arrived from the world over bringing with them languages and customs from across the seafaring globe. There'd been populations from fifty or more countries in the little corner of Wales, and while these groups had dispersed and mingled now, Cardiff, like all port cities I'd been to, retained an outward-lookingness, a sense of the wider world. It was a large part of the reason I liked the place.

I reached Mermaid Warehouse first. No sign of Hywel or anyone else. The police cordon was long-gone. Despite my earlier statements about the key, I was a little tempted to phone Zubrasky or Evans, summon up the reassuring presence of the *Heddlu*. I decided against it. They weren't going to be much help with what I was facing.

I let myself into the familiar interior of the warehouse using Jones's key and the access code. I half-expected the floor and walls to be crawling with living runes, sniffing me out, but the place was as quiet as the grave. The air was damp and musty. I made a quick reconnoitre, checking that all was in order, no sorcerous outbreaks or undead horrors lurking anywhere. It was all clean. Down on the sub-basement, I took the opportunity to test the old, half-height door that I'd never been through. It was, as Jones had said, a false door, leading nowhere. It wasn't locked, and behind the ancient wood of the door was a grey stone wall, nothing more. I tapped it, just to reassure myself that it was completely solid.

I waited for Hywel on the ground level. Whatever focus for magical power the building harboured, the effect was seemingly stronger underground. That was where the cyhyraeth had manifested, and where the runes had first been drawn upon the world. I set up a couple of discreet cameras in shadowy corners of the room to capture unfolding events, and prepared all the paraphernalia I'd brought with me to assist in the fight with Hywel Williams: my gun (standard round currently selected), my clothcutter blade and also the assortment of Armitage Hobbles, holdfasts, glimmers and touchstones that might be of use against whatever Williams threw at me. I still had the Lady's ring on my finger, and I was even wearing my belt with its Stebsen's Ward woven into it, just in case that helped in some way.

The plan was mainly to survive. Beyond that, capturing Williams alive so we could question him about his associates in English Wizardry was obviously the ideal. There had to be a chance he knew who the Warlock was. There was even a possibility *he* was the Warlock, controlling events from afar. But then, would his fellow English Wizardry headbangers accept a man from Wales giving them their orders? I suspected not.

Finally, I was ready. I waited in the half-shadows, grey light filtering in through the narrow windows. What form would the attack take? Would he manifest behind me, already unleashing some sorcerous attack? Would mists drift through the air, rich with wraiths come to drink my soul?

What came instead was utterly unexpected. I heard

footsteps approaching from outside, and then Hywel calling out.

"Hello? Is there anybody here?"

"Come inside," I called out. "I'm here. The door is open."

His silhouette filled the doorway and I snapped on my head torch to illuminate him. There could be no doubt it was him. He wore jeans and a fleece jacket, and sported a balaclava on his head rather than a wizard's hat, but there was no mistaking his features.

There was also no mistaking the expression on his face. Somehow, I saw, I had made a terrible miscalculation. Malevolence, fury, hatred – none of those were present in his features. Instead, quite clearly, I could see that he was utterly terrified.

21 – History

My esteemed predecessor Isaac Shackleton noted more than once in his private journals the presence of what we may call *magical nodes* – places upon or beneath the surface of the world that are especially dangerous and troublesome; where there is a long tradition of witchery, incantation, ritual summoning or other magical acts taking place. Whether these are points at which the veils between the worlds happen to be weak, or they are sites where the memories, spirits and *genii locorum* of prior events linger, I do not know. But these places need to be watched with an eagle's eye – if only we had sufficient resources to do so!

–Campbell Hardknott-Lewis, Lord High Witchfinder of All Wales, *private journal*, 2015

The fear was raw in Hywel's voice, too. "Are you working for him? Did he tell you to invite me here?"

I didn't move. His words threw me. What was this, some elaborate trick?

"Who?" I asked. "Are you talking about the Warlock?"

Williams still hadn't stepped inside. "I knew there was something strange going on. I should never have come here."

I pressed on with my line of questioning. "Who's giving *you* orders? Is it someone in the Office, controlling everything? Tell me who it is."

He finally seemed to hear my words. Now there was confusion on his face. He held up his hand to try and shield the light and see my features.

"The Office? What does the Office have to do with

anything? When have they ever done anything to help anyone?"

Confused, I grasped for the facts. "You're a user. I saw one of your performances. You pretend to be a bad stage magician but you're really something very, very different. The cyhyraeth you summoned; it nearly killed me. What was the plan, let the runes spread across the city? Were you trying to kill everyone or fuel some greater act of sorcery?"

"What do you know about the runes?" he said. "And the cyhyraeth – you've seen one? He manifested one?"

This was getting me nowhere. I lowered the torch beam so that it wasn't shining in his eyes. Was he trying to confuse me while he worked some deception? If he was, he was doing a good job.

"Are you claiming that it wasn't you who summoned the wraith? It must have been you. The cartouche of your forebear was embedded in the runes. You used the old spell you inherited, brought that entity through the veils. Right here, in this building."

He looked shocked, like I'd physically hit him.

"Here?"

"When I was last in this room, the runes were spiralling out of control, covering the walls and the floor. We contained them, barely. But you know all this. You must know all this."

"The sigils worked. I feared they would. He succeeded in bringing a cyhyraeth through. I've heard the wailing sounds over the rooftops, twice now, and I told myself it was nothing. But really, I knew. It's a harbinger of death. It's foretelling *my* death. He brought it here to kill me."

"Kill *you*?"

"Yes, obviously. What did you think, that it had come for you?"

"You keep saying *he*. Who's he?"

"I can't … I have to go. I have to get away from here. This place, it's unquiet. I can feel it. I should never have come here. All this time, and I had no idea this was so close. Oh, how I despise him. Don't you see? I've tried to stop him, spent my life trying to stop him, but he's too powerful, damn him."

"Who? Who are you talking about?"

"Owain."

"Owain Williams?"

"That bastard. He should have been stopped a long time ago."

My thoughts raced. "You're talking about your forebear. That makes no sense."

"Why does it have to make sense? I…"

A mournful wailing noise cut off Hywel's words. It bounced off the walls, filled the world. It was hard to tell where it was coming from. Nowhere and everywhere.

The look of shock and fear on Hywel's face was unmistakable. "It's here. It's come for me."

"No," I said. "We despatched it, sent it back. It can't be here."

"It has unfinished business. Three times its cry is heard before it takes the soul it's come for. I have to get away. I have to try and outrun it."

"We'll fight it. Whatever's going on here, if one of those things is here, we need to destroy it."

"It's useless. It's my fate. He's finally won."

"Then, what have you got to lose from trying? I'm from the Office. We can fight this thing together."

"If you're from the Office, then you're powerless to help."

I was walking towards him now, putting less distance between us. I needed to understand what was going on here.

"I have … certain abilities most of my colleagues don't."

"They won't be enough."

"They might. What's the alternative: run and keep running?"

Hywel ran his fingers through his hair in a gesture of desperation. He *needed* to flee, get away from this horror set on his trail. But he also knew running wasn't going to help.

We were standing close together now, the grey light from outside illuminating the room a small way. The wail sounded again, louder, like a wind whipping itself up into a storm. I could tell it was definitely coming up from below, now.

"Where?" he said. "Where's the crucible?"

"I don't know what that is."

"It's what he calls them. He spent his time finding them: places he can work his summonings, places he is strong. There must be one here."

"Downstairs. If this thing is coming back through, it'll be there."

He was torn by indecision, but finally he nodded. Underneath his fear, there was a steeliness I hadn't noticed before. He had battled his demons for a long, long time.

"Okay. Enough running."

We edged our way downstairs to the sub-basement, my torch illuminating the way. But I already knew what we were going to find: the rustling, chittering sound I remembered grew louder and louder as we descended the two flights of steps. The runes were already creeping up the rough stones of the second set: twisting, writhing forms, questing upwards.

In the centre of the room, the cyhyraeth was back. As before, I could sense the malign magic winding off the entity as a sickness in my gut. The smells of rotting flesh and burning metal were unmistakable. The tattered flesh of the entity writhed as if it were desperately trying to assemble itself from random scraps. This time, it had a face. A semblance of a face, at least, but a face I recognized.

It bore, unmistakably, the likeness of Hywel on its own visage. It turned in a circle, seeming to sniff, and when it found Williams standing next to me, something like an evil smile cracked across its face, the wound-like gash it had for a mouth almost splitting its features. The keening wail coming from it raised a note, scraping across my nerves like fingernails scraping on a blackboard. I seemed to hear the sound in my brain as vicious spikes of metal.

I raised my gun, selecting a clothcutter round with my thumb, and fired. The shot hit, and the entity reacted, wailing in alarm and pain. But it remained material, resisting the pull of its own dimension. Its hunger to fulfil its destiny was too strong.

"Get behind me," I shouted to Hywel.

He completely ignored me and stepped forwards himself. "No. It doesn't care about you. It's come for me."

He was right, I saw that. The creature held out its arms – let's call them that – and wavered its way towards Hywel, like any mother intent on sweeping up a long-lost child. The entity *yearned* for him.

For a moment, I thought Hywel was accepting his fate, giving in. But he hadn't come totally unprepared. No doubt a lifetime of pursuit had ensured that. He worked some magic, his mouth working just as it had on the video, his hands sculpting complicated shapes in the air, as if he were drawing runes of his own.

Magical energy like billowing mist sprayed from his hands to engulf the cyhyraeth.

The creature's voice took on a further edge of alarm and hatred. I took the opportunity to fire, unleashing all my rounds at it while it was weak. Some of them would merely inflict physical damage, but others – the silver bullet and the holdfast round in particular – might have a more magical effect. Each round knocked it back with a howl, but still it clung onto its presence in our world.

A shudder ran through it as it shook off the misty bonds wrapping around it from Hywel's spell. It was furious now. The runes on the floor pulsed and writhed more rapidly as the cyhyraeth, breaking free, lurched forwards again, directly for Hywel.

But he'd been expecting that. His first attack was a feint while he prepared his second. He raised both arms and then, with a rapid dashing motion, directed two spells at the floor, one on each side of the entity. Hywel grunted in pain as he worked his magic.

The wailing from the cyhyraeth took on an exultant

note. It thought Hywel had missed. But that wasn't it. He must have practised the magic so many times – had that stage trick involving his son been related? Some benign version of the same spell?

The malign runes reacted immediately to the two spots on the floor, flowing away from one and towards the other, like the poles on a magnet, or like water flowing down to a sinkhole.

The cyhyraeth felt the tug of it too: it lashed its misshapen head around and, straining against the pull of the portal opened up by Hywel, inched forwards.

It hungered for him. It loved him. And Hywel, out of tricks, stepped backwards. The horror was clear in his wide eyes. He had expended his magical powers, and it wasn't enough. He was beaten. The creature had him, and he would never get away.

I had a brief moment. The entity was utterly focused on its quarry, paying me no attention. Deliberately this time, dropping my gun, I raised my hands and prepared to unleash a stream of magical force. It was inelegant, no doubt, and poorly worked, but I put all my fear and revulsion into it. I'd done so before. This time it was a little – a little – more controlled. To some extent I was in charge of it rather than being picked up and carried away on the flood.

I unleashed my spell even as the cyhyraeth reached for Hywel. The full force of the magic hit the entity square in the chest, ragdolling it backwards. Directly towards the drain portal that Hywel had opened.

The runes were spiralling down into it now, their chittering note rising and rising in pitch. The cyhyraeth joined them, suddenly unable to escape the gravitational pull. It gibbered and howled, but to no effect.

A few moments of struggle, and it succumbed. Once again it, and the runes that had summoned it, were gone. After a moment, I crossed the floor to look at the spots where Hywel had cast his magic. There was no sign of the portal or the runes. I walked on solid, stone floor, nothing more.

"You're a user," Hywel said from behind me.

"You noticed that."

"But you're from the Office. All these years I've been fighting him, and you've never helped. I've had to fight you, too."

"Yes."

"How is that possible?"

"It's possible. Where did we send that thing?"

"Back where it came from."

"Permanently?"

Hywel breathed in, breathed out. "I think so. Its destiny is fulfilled. Three times it sounded and crossed into our world. It failed, but it won't come again, unless Owain summons another."

"Owain, right. Are you really claiming he's still alive? He'd be hundreds of years old."

"Getting on for three hundred. Whether you'd consider him *alive*, I don't know, depends on your definition. But he's certainly active."

"That's not possible."

"I've spent my whole life fighting him, as did my parents and their parents. Owain is our family's curse, the blight on all our lives, and you do not get to simply dismiss all that heartache by saying it isn't possible. I don't care what you think."

Even in the low light I could see that his face was flushed red with anger.

"Then tell me," I said. "Tell me how it's possible."

"Why should I?"

"Perhaps I can help."

"I doubt it. Are you going to arrest me now?"

"Please, just tell me."

He took another deep breath, swept his hand through his hair. "You must know about Owain."

"Assume I don't."

"He was born in 1732, on a farm in the Black Mountains. A good man at first, helping folk where he could. There was a scattered community, and our family had a tradition of being cunning men and women, working simple spells to help with illness and expelling evil spirits and the like. It wasn't enough for Owain, though. He … dabbled. Whether something whispered into his ear or he opened the doorway out of curiosity, I don't know, but he found a way to step from our world into the domain of the *Tylwyth Teg*."

"The Tylwyth Teg?"

"The fairy folk, as you might say. But a particularly vicious and malevolent nation of them. The *Gwyllion* his notes call them. They corrupted him. For what end I don't know, maybe just mischief-making, but to achieve what he did, Owain became a twisted, evil man."

"What exactly did he achieve?"

"He opened the doorway for the Tylwyth Teg by sacrificing his child, used the spilled blood of his boy in the incantations. The blood of his line is irrevocably tied up in the sorcery. That's how it works. That's been the source of the trouble all along. He's been quiet for some time, and we were beginning to hope he'd gone, that his age had finally caught up on him. Clearly that's not the case. If anything, it seems he's been preparing for something big. Building up to it."

"What?"

"We have no idea."

"If he killed his own son all that time ago, how are you here?"

"He didn't know his wife was pregnant when he did what he did. Another was born, my forebear. By that time, my family had fled in horror from Owain. We've fought him all this time, across the generations, trying to destroy him just as he tries to destroy us. Only our blood, the blood of his line, can seal the breach up again, reverse the magic, and he knows it. He spent hundreds of years trying to slaughter us and our children."

I thought of the man Preston Jones had described. *He was very pale. I could see the shapes of his bones beneath his skin.*

"How can he be so old?"

"A gift of the Tylwyth Teg. Owain is no longer human.

He's something more and something less: a thing that looks like a person but with bile instead of blood pumping in his veins."

"Where is he?"

"In the shadows. In the darkness. We don't know. We have chased him and been chased by him all this time, but we don't know where he resides. He has been defeated here, but he will try again. He won't stop until all his family are dead."

I nodded, trying to take it all in.

"Does the Office know about any of this?" I asked.

"It must do; this has been going on for a long time. So, what are you going to do? Arrest me? Put me into Oblivion? Sometimes I think that might be for the best. It would drive Owain insane knowing I was forever out of his reach."

"I'm not going to do that to you. I'm not going to do anything. You should leave. You've done nothing wrong that I can see. Between us, somehow, we need to defeat this Owain, but locking you up isn't going to help."

"You're letting me go?"

"I am. Just … be careful. And stop using real magic in your stage act. Keep your head down until we know how to deal with this properly. Don't disappear. We'll come and find you when we're ready."

"You can't defeat him. He's too powerful."

"Perhaps. We'll see. You should go now before anyone else comes."

He looked like he wanted to say something else, but instead nodded and turned away.

I stopped him as he climbed the stairs back up to the Cardiff day.

"Why the succubi, though? Why did he go to all that trouble to discredit and defeat the Office?"

"Succubi?"

"The seven succubi he summoned them to attack the Keyholders. Does he really fear us that much?"

Hywel looked genuinely puzzled. "I don't … Owain knows no magic for summoning succubi that I'm aware of. There's nothing in his journals or spellbooks, nothing to suggest he's even interested in the entities."

"It must have been him. The attacks; they've been vicious, all across the country."

"Owain has been operating here, all along. Pursuing the remnants of his family. He has little interest in other parts of the country. I'm sorry, but it wasn't him. It can't be him."

"It must be."

"No, I don't think so. Odd as it may sound, he would have found such entities distasteful."

"But…"

My phone buzzed before I could complete my sentence. The signal was weak, the voice on the other end muffled and fuzzy, but I recognized the number.

"Gilroy? What is it?"

"I found her."

"Found who? I don't…"

"Who the fuck do you think? Maude Woebegone. I found her terrified little soul flitting about the hotel, just like we thought. She's scattered and confused, but she's seen things, boy. She's seen things."

I waved Hywel away. He needed to hide, prepare his defences. His forebear had been thwarted and wasn't going to be happy.

"Seen what?" I said into the phone.

"Who killed her. Who summoned the succubi. Who's right there with you, about to kill you."

"Who?"

"Evangelina Mormont."

"She can't be here. She *isn't* here."

There was a squall of white noise, then Gilroy's voice came through loud and clear again.

"She is. She's somewhere very nearby. Maude flits around the aether, lost and confused like a moth in the city lights, but she's seen enough to piece it together. Mormont's body was recently brought back to our plane. The Sorceress is alive again. Maude saw it happen."

"Where?"

"Near. You need to find her, boy, find her and stop her now."

"Maude…"

"Don't worry about her. I'll give her the peace she needs. You worry about Mormont."

I hung up. In the little sub-basement, nothing moved. Then I picked up the red glow. It hadn't been there before, and now it was. A red glow around the little arched doorway. The doorway that led nowhere.

I reloaded my gun and then, holding it ready, I tried the handle again.

22 – Something Wicked

By the pricking of my thumbs, something wicked
this way comes….
      –Shakespeare, *Macbeth*, Act 4, Scene 1, 1606

Instead of a blank wall, there was a room there. A chamber. Details slowly presented themselves by the low light of flickering candles.

The stone walls sloped inwards as though I was within a kiln or a great oven. On the floor, a star had been marked out within an encompassing circle. A seven-pointed star. Candles were set out at apparently-random points around the star, and symbols had been inscribed on the floor. Complex runes from the forbidden alphabets.

At each of the seven points of the star, an iron cauldron the size of a large cooking pot sat upon the floor. Those that I could see, the nearest three, had some sort of red-purple liquid bubbling within them, although there was no source of heat evident. In the centre of the circle, unmistakable, set upon a low stone plinth, was the Chalice of Lilith Unrepentant. The candle flames glinted from its polished brass surfaces, sending odd shadows dancing and leaping around the walls. The air was heady with burning herbs, sweet and bitter at the same time.

Evangelina Mormont stepped from the shadows of the room. The smile was bright on her face.

"Really, this is becoming tiresome. You've done well for someone of your inferior breed, but it obviously has to stop now."

"You aren't dead," I said.

"Very good! You spotted that. And, to answer your other question, yes, I do."

"Do what?"

"The question you asked me when I was in your car, inconveniently trapped inside Myrddin's amulet. Yes, I do know who the Warlock is. And, no, I'm not going to tell you."

"Then perhaps you don't really know."

"Oh, I know who he is very well. But I don't want you to have the satisfaction of having the question answered. I want you to die with it still on your limited little mind."

"That makes no sense. If you heard my question, then you really were trapped in the amulet. Yet, here you are, using the chalice, summoning the succubi. You've been working this magic for weeks."

She smiled as if I were endearingly ridiculous, like some pet performing tricks. "You see the world in such simple, binary ways. Inside the amulet or not inside the amulet? Good or evil, black or white, friend or enemy. What a dull little life you lead. I was both. A part of my mind was captured, it is true, made to suffer the tedium of watching that Spender woman struggling to cling to her boring life. Fortunately, she's too incompetent to work the amulet magic properly, and most of my mind was left inside my body. Or perhaps the incompetence lies with Stonewall, her precious mentor. I've been perfectly capable of functioning with what I had, and now I am fully restored I can complete my task. I suppose I should thank you for coming to my rescue. My knight in shining armour."

"You're *restored*?"

"More incompetence. Your Lady Coldwater isn't as adept at handling magical artefacts as she believes, either. Rather than destroying that part of my essence, she released it." Mormont laughed a crazy little laugh, then it cut out immediately. "Amusing, really."

Her words sent a jolt of anxiety through me. "What happened to her?"

Mormont shrugged her indifference to the question. "Does it matter? She's weak, a nobody. A foolish old woman. One really despises the misguided amateur, especially when they're a traitor to their own kind."

I hit Mormont with more questions while I desperately

tried to think of a way to fight her. Sally had used Myrddin's amulet, but I didn't even have that. Mormont clearly knew I was a user now, too, so I didn't have any element of surprise.

"What is this place we're in? How is it here when it wasn't?"

She looked about the round stone chamber with its odd, curving walls. "Come, I'm sure you've worked it out. There are fixed points in the aether. Islands, specks of grit. This place is a bubble, an intersection, inside other dimensions as much as ours. A place where the walls are thin and stepping between the worlds is easier. It has a presence in many locations in our world, too. It's here, it's in London. Many places."

"Which is why you used the place to summon the succubi."

"Bless you, you do understand. Location, knowledge, power, they all intersect. This entrance was sealed off, but reopening it was simply a matter of possessing the knowledge and the power required. Which, fortunately, I do."

"Who brought you back here?"

"Who do you think? The Warlock, obviously. He found me and he carried me across the aether, used this place to restore me and I then used it to call up the succubi. The chalice helps: it is a potent object. Knowing how to use it properly, what liquids to fill it with and what incantations to weave around it, helped. But this place, yes. It is special. A place of power."

I didn't like to ask precisely what the liquids were.

"Which is why the adjacent room was used to summon the cyhyraeth."

"The magic leaks out into the surrounding area. I have watched with amusement while this local pursues his little family feud, confusing you and taking up your time."

"What happens if I simply kick the chalice over?"

"I'll kill you before you set foot inside the circle. Obviously. A member of the lesser breeds can't be allowed to sully what I have worked here."

I stepped around the edge of the room, taking care not to cross the line. For now.

"Not all your succubi have succeeded in their tasks."

"He has resisted so far. It won't last."

"One of your targets was killed."

A brief flash of annoyance crossed her features. "A setback, nothing more. The death of Greentree means the cambion produced from him won't have the same blood hold over whoever replaces him, but we can still use it. Chaos and death within the Office are absolutely fine. It's precisely what we're trying to achieve, isn't it?"

"The sorcery you are working: do you really think it will give you control over the Keyholders, allow you to manipulate them as you desire?"

"Weaken them, discredit them, embarrass them. Yes. Delicious, isn't it? Without the Office there will be nobody to oppose us. The Keyholders will be our puppets to play with."

I'd seen all seven points of the star, now, studied the whole circle.

"Were there others before these? Children brought into life?"

"You'll see."

Five cauldrons contained bubbling liquids. Two – which had to be those for the Crow and Earl Grey, as there'd been a note on MORIARTY the day before to say that the attacks on Thomas Quirk had stopped – were empty. I'd come in time. If I could stop her.

"Look at you!" Mormont said. "I can see you trying to work out a way to win. Really, it's too much. You're *nothing*. You're a cockroach. You are going to die in here and no one will ever know what happened to you. Hardknott-Lewis will be so sad at losing his little project, his would-be son. Your poor mother, too: another loss will surely be too much for her."

As an experiment, I slowly lifted my gun, watching for a reaction for her. She didn't move. The wide smile on her beautiful face didn't crack.

I aimed for her body and fired.

The only reaction was the briefest raising of one eyebrow. She let the bullet hit her in the chest. The smile didn't waver. Blood didn't flow. She reached into the entry-wound as casually as if she were delving into a pocket for her phone and pulled the projectile out of her tissues. A single gob of viscous blood dripped off it. With a simple shrug, she let the slug fall to the ground. It tinkled on the stone floor.

"Happy now?" she asked. "Or are you going to throw some other weapon at me. Your ridiculous Office that only likes *nice* magic. Soon, you'll all be swept away, and true English spellcraft will be restored to its position of superiority. The magic my people have worked in the woods and meadows since before time, walking hand-in-hand with the Green Man. You, though. You're different, aren't you? You're not even a very good Office adept. Are you going to unleash one of your childish bursts of magic at me? Your father was the same, thinking he was my equal. I broke him, too."

I very nearly attacked. I restrained myself. Which demonstrated admirable self-control, but didn't give me a way out. The fire within, though. It was growing and growing in fury.

"What do you know about my father?"

"I know that he died like the dog he was. Whining and grovelling."

I was on the far side of the room from the entrance now. Mormont, standing inside the circle, had slowly rotated to watch me. Perhaps she hadn't even been aware of it and perhaps she didn't care either way, but her back was to the door.

Sometimes the strong and powerful make the mistake of dismissing anything seemingly too weak or inconsequential to trouble them. It's a failing. Mormont had made that mistake now. Over her shoulder, clearly visible in the low doorway, I caught a glimpse of Lady Coldwater. She'd read my log entry on MORIARTY, or guessed where I was, and she'd come. Around her neck, unmistakably, was the amulet that the portion of

Mormont's soul had been trapped in. Whatever the Sorceress had done to escape, it hadn't killed the Librarian. Did Mormont assume that it had? Perhaps.

I did my best to keep my gaze firmly on Mormont's face.

"The cambions to be born from this sorcery: who are the seven mothers? What is happening to them?"

A fond, maternalistic glow came into her features. Or, at least, a twisted version of one. Had she always been mad or had recent events turned her?

"There are no others; *I* am the mother. They will all be mine, born of my body, and they will be under my thrall. My own little soldiers to do their mother's bidding. How they'll love me and worship me. How happy they'll be with their lives."

The Librarian had disappeared again, perhaps preparing something in that other room. That had to be it. I kept Mormont talking.

"And how does it feel taking orders from the Warlock? You've suffered years of incarceration and struggle, had no life, and all because some shadowy figure is controlling you. If you ask me, he's sitting somewhere and laughing."

Again, a flash of annoyance crossed her features. She *did* resent how she was used. Perhaps she had quiet plans for the Warlock, once she was done with the Office. Which gave me a troubling thought: if I could, by some means, defeat Mormont, was I doing precisely what the Warlock wanted? Removing a threat?

Whatever. Really, you can go mad trying to work this stuff out. First things first.

I dropped my handgun and, in what I liked to think was one fluid motion, plucked my clothcutter from its scabbard and arrowed the blade at her head.

It skittered off her like a pencil thrown at a sheet of glass.

I tried two holdfasts set for immediate activation. Again, Mormont swatted them away, bored by each puny attack. The holdfasts had no effect. She waited patiently between each attack, utterly unconcerned, fascinated only to see what trick I would attempt next.

Which was precisely what I wanted to happen. For those brief moments, while she had fun demonstrating how pathetic I was, she wasn't paying attention to the doorway. Or maybe she was but didn't consider that threat real. The Librarian knew a bit of magic, maybe, but she was no match for the Sorceress. She couldn't throw any spells that would endanger her.

Lady Coldwater had seen what I was doing, too. She acted, stepping silently into the room behind Mormont's back.

Something had happened to her, though. She walked stiff-legged, as though bones inside her were broken, as if each step was an agony. Mormont had harmed her when that part of her soul was released from the amulet. I'd feared the Lady had been killed – but, clearly, she had been sorely wounded.

Despite what it cost her, she crept forwards. Still Mormont's attention was on me, waiting for me to unleash my next futile onslaught.

Lady Coldwater stepped inside the circle, got to within two paces, before Mormont, with a bored swish of her hand, worked some spell and plucked the Lady off the ground, sweeping her round so she was next to me. The Sorceress held the Librarian in mid-air, helpless, considering her, before letting her drop to the ground with a thump and a cry of agony from the Lady.

Mormont was considerably older than Lady Coldwater. I knew for a fact that the Sorceress had been active in English Wizardry in the 1930s. Her long life and current appearance had little to do with good diet and her skin care regime, and a lot to do with the sorcerous leeching of life from others.

The difference between them seemed to amuse Mormont. "Pathetic old crone. What did you plan to do, skewer me with a knitting needle? Work some of your *healing* magic on me?"

The Lady groaned. She was trying to work her way back

to her feet, despite the pain. She climbed to her knees. For a moment, the briefest moment, she was turned away from Mormont, looking at me. I caught the glance she threw at me. I'd seen it before. It said, simply, one thing.

Now. Attack now.

I attacked. The coiling, raging fire had been growing within me throughout the fight, raging more strongly with each dismissive taunt. My control was getting better. A little better. With a pained cry of my own, I threw everything I had at Mormont, bathing her in flame, engulfing her.

She staggered backwards. I'd inflicted that much harm on her. But it wouldn't be enough, I saw immediately. Mormont remained upright in the heart of the conflagration, deflecting it, waiting for it to dissipate.

For that moment, though, that brief moment, she was fully focused on the effort and on me.

Lady Coldwater struck. All her broken clumsiness was gone. She pulled a long, curving blade from the leg of her trousers – that was why she'd been walking stiffly – and, even as my magical flame petered out and died, leapt at Mormont.

Moving with a dancer's strength and speed, she struck, burying the blade in Mormont's chest.

The look on the Sorceress's face was one of utmost surprise. She really had believed the Lady was a frail, broken old woman. Wisps of smoke coiled off her hair. I had inflicted that much harm on her.

"I didn't bring a knitting needle," Lady Coldwater said.

"But…" Mormont said. Then she crumpled to the ground, her eyes closed.

Lady Coldwater knelt beside the Sorceress. "Quickly, help me. We have to capture her soul before she comes round. She caught me off-guard last time, and I'm not going to let that happen again. She's been weakened by everything that has happened. We have a moment now."

"Tell me what to do."

"Hold her head still while I work the magic. We'll only get one attempt at this."

Lady Coldwater held the amulet to Mormont's forehead and began to mumble an incantation. It seemed to go on for a long, long time. Mormont's head grew hotter, as if her brains were on fire, but I didn't let go of her. Expressions of anger and confusion were rushing across the Sorceress's features. She was resurfacing. We had to be quick.

"Hurry," I said.

The Lady cast me a look of irritation but didn't pause in her intoning.

Then Mormont's eyes flickered open, and I saw that she knew what we were doing.

The arrogance was gone from her voice. "No. Not like this. Not by your hand."

"It's over now," I said. "For you and, soon, for the Warlock and all the rest of you. I'm going to make sure of it."

"No."

She stirred and began to rise. But her strength was gone. Too much had been drained from her. Sally had weakened her, and I had weakened her and now the Librarian was sucking out her soul. Finally, she couldn't resist. Her last look, before her soul fled her body for the final time, was one of unalloyed hatred for me.

There were words, too. A whisper.

"Mongrel scum. You know nothing. Go to Oblivion and see."

I could have ignored her. Maybe I should have.

"See what?"

"See who else has been lying there all this time."

What the hell did that mean? Her last sound, before her eyes closed again, was a bitter laugh, as if all of her long life had been a bore, a disappointment.

Lady Coldwater studied the amulet, peering into its depths. "She's trapped inside, all of her now. I'll destroy it without releasing her. No mistakes this time. She's not coming back from this."

"I thought she must have killed you."

"Oh, she tried."

"Thank you for coming when you did."

The Lady stood. "I have high hopes for you. It would be a shame if you died now."

"Do what you have to do. I'll tidy up here."

She stuffed the amulet containing Evangelina Mormont into her pocket and left, ducking through the low arch of the doorway. I slumped against the old stone wall and let my breathing calm. I sat there for five minutes, maybe ten, just breathing.

Nothing moved.

The fumes from the candle, the air of the place, the stress of what I'd been through: it was making my head throb. I really needed a cup of coffee. A good, strong cup, bitter enough to cut through the fug in my head.

It occurred to me I probably should leave before the weird little transdimensional room drifted off into the aether and left me stranded on the far side of forever. I stood. I didn't want to be on my own anymore, and certainly not with the lifeless corpse of Evangelina Mormont and those bubbling cauldrons and the runes of that heptagram.

And then I realised that I wasn't alone. Someone else was outside.

23 – Crow's-Foot

… Open, locks, whoever knocks.
   –Shakespeare, *Macbeth*, Act 4, Scene 1, 1606

From the adjacent chamber, I heard the sound of footsteps picking their way down the stone stairs.

The tread was slow and deliberate. Whoever it was took their time, as if they were deliberately drawing out the tension. They knew, perhaps, that I was trapped in there with no way out. Grit crunched under their heel. The individual – there was definitely only one person – paused briefly as if considering something, or listening intently, then continued, coming nearer, always nearer.

I stood, readying myself. Who knew I was there? Was this the Warlock, come to take his revenge for destroying Mormont? I found I was holding my breath as the footsteps paused outside the inner sanctum.

A figure stood framed by the small arch. He stooped and stepped forwards, and it was the Crow. Campbell Percy Hardknott-Lewis KCB DL, Lord High Witchfinder of All Wales.

He paused for a moment to take in the scene. It occurred to me that he was wearing the same hat and clothes he'd worn that evening he'd come to visit me in my flat. The evening he'd shown me the fresh scars on his back.

He acknowledged me with a dip of his head, then crossed the room to crouch beside the lifeless form of Evangelina Mormont. How long had he been in the area? If he'd been nearby during the fight, he'd surely have picked up the magical discharges of our battle. Even if he hadn't heard or seen anything, the fact of Mormont's body was clear proof. There were no users like Sally around this time, which meant the conclusion he would come to was both obvious and accurate: I had thrown magic at the Sorceress. Perhaps he knew about Lady Coldwater's involvement, and perhaps he didn't, but he knew about mine.

He also knew that mundane weapons like bullets and blades would not have been enough.

Finally, he spoke.

"She is dead, then. We have made sure of that, at least."

"Yes," I said. "Did you know she was still alive?"

"I did not, although the possibility had occurred to me. Powerful adepts have ways of cheating death do they not? We have seen it before with her."

He walked slowly around the circle, stopping at each point of the seven-pointed star inscribed within. He knelt to examine the seven cauldrons and the roiling red-purple liquid five of them contained. He seemed to listen to each of them, maybe even sniff. He also passed a thaumometer over them. At each stop, a frown furrowed his forehead. His distaste and disgust were clear.

"They had five of the seven embryos," he said finally, "ready for whatever foul sorcery they planned to work with the chalice. They needed only two more."

"The succubi set upon you and Earl Grey," I said.

"We resisted the longest. If the Witchfinder General and I had also fallen, they could have begun their work, and by now, perhaps, we would all be dead. Dead or worse: enthralled to English Wizardry, incapable of resisting their dominion. We came close to disaster here. Very close."

"We should destroy the chalice," I said. "Lady Coldwater wished we'd already done so. Now is the time."

The Crow crouched beside the ornate chalice set in the centre of the star, studying it without touching it. The candles set around it made deformed shadows dance from its base.

"Yes, I think so. The temptation, always, is to retain such artefacts, learn what we may from them, but then that puts them in temptation's way. It needs only someone like Peter Warder and a powerful adept like Mormont to unravel all our work. I will see to it that the Chalice of Lilith Unrepentant is melted down and its constituent material diluted and scattered irrevocably. There must be no possibility of it being used again."

"There are still the embryos," I said. "I know something of how the sorcery works. They are magically maintained in these cauldrons. Destroy the chalice, and they will die."

"Do we know who the mothers are?"

"Mormont. They are all Mormont's."

"Ah. We are fortunate that our enemies waited and did not bring any of the five into full life. The existence of a cambion, a living being birthed from our seed by these sorcerous means: these would have been powerful and dangerous entities."

"They would also have been babies," I said. "Innocent. None of us can be blamed for our background or where we come from."

The Crow looked into my eyes for a moment. The candles sent a distant white light flickering there.

He looked away. "Just so, Danesh. We must prevent the suffering of innocents. If we in the Office do not do that, then we do not deserve to survive. But the contents of these five cauldrons: the question is, what do we do with them? Are they beings or are they clumps of cells? Do they deserve to live?"

"They cannot live," I said. "I don't mean morally, I mean physically. Without the magical effects of the chalice, they aren't viable. It all has to be destroyed."

He looked troubled by the thought, but eventually he nodded his head.

"That is what you think we should do?"

"It is."

He sighed. "Very well. It troubles me, but it is also what we agreed in the Star Chamber. More grey areas. Sometimes it is not a matter of doing the right thing so much as finding the least wrong. I will ensure that everything in this room is destroyed."

"Can we be sure these plans haven't already been enacted? Elsewhere, perhaps? There may be other such children already out there."

"It is hard to be sure of anything. I thought we had already defeated her, but here she is. She was weakened after Faebrook Folly, but not fatally. Once she was brought back, she took control of the summonings. The Chalice of Lilith Unrepentant stolen by English Wizardry was given to her. Others in their ranks, Thomson Fulger perhaps, had used it but had succeeded only in drawing weak demons through the veils: creatures I and at least some of the others were able to resist. The entities she called up and bound, however, were a very different proposition. Too fearsome for poor Mason. I am under no illusions: they would have been too much for me, too, sooner or later. I would have died or become enslaved. I have you to thank for my salvation."

"For both our sakes, I'm glad to see the back of her."

"Forgive me, though," he said, "but I have to ask. Exactly how did you defeat her? She was an immensely powerful magical adept. Weakened, yes, but still potent."

It was an excellent point. I chose not to tell him the truth. Yet again. I had no desire to explain the Lady's role in events, and he didn't need to know about mine either.

"I think the summoning magic she'd been working drained her further. When it came to it, she didn't put up much of a fight. You can see the sword blow, the gunshot wound. In the end, she had no defence against my Office handgun."

"Ah, excellent. One hates to see anyone killed, of course, but in this case, there is a certain amount of relief. The sword, though – it is hardly standard equipment."

He would surely be able to detect the magic running through the blade. "I borrowed it off Lady Coldwater. She was reluctant to let me have it."

"Ah, I see. It is gratifying to see that you have been keeping up with your fencing."

"Mormont is definitely not coming back from this. Is she?"

"No, I think not. I can detect no sign of life in her. I will see to it that her body is destroyed. She will be burned to ashes, and then there can be no doubt."

"She claimed she wasn't the Warlock."

A wry little smile passed across his face. "I don't suppose she revealed the true identity of our opponent? Who it is giving her orders?"

"Is it you?" I heard myself say. "Are you the Warlock?"

He considered my words for a moment, then smiled. "Well done, Danesh. Excellent work."

"You admit it? Just like that?"

"Me the Warlock? No, no, of course not. The idea is ridiculous. I have no magical ability and I hardly approve of their mission. The pre-eminence of the English tradition over everything else; the approval of the *right* sort of magic over the *wrong* – these are all anathema to me. No, I am not the Warlock. But I congratulate you absolutely for your open-mindedness and your fearlessness. They are both qualities that I saw in you at the start."

"But if you were the Warlock, you would say that."

"If I were the Warlock, would I even bother to have this conversation? I would have you here alone and in my power. I would not hesitate to slaughter you with some murderous curse where you stand. Yet, happily, I have not done so."

"You were in Downing Street that day; you could have arranged the attack on Westminster Bridge. You told me that yourself. You could have been the one messaging Thomson Fulger, timing everything carefully to frame Mormont. You were definitely in Cardiff at the time. You might be keeping me alive because you have some other plan for me."

He held up his hand as if to deflect my words. "All excellent points, but I give you my promise that I am not this individual. My commitment to protecting the public from the unnatural is absolute and unswerving. You have seen the wounds upon my back. But if they are not enough, then I can only congratulate you and tell you to maintain your suspicions. *Semper vigilans*. Be wary of everyone. I *want* you to be suspicious of me. And that, perhaps, more than anything, is good evidence of my innocence."

"Perhaps so," I said. "The Office failed, though. She was in our power, held in Oblivion, and we let her go."

"Not everyone is to be trusted, I agree. Can we move on, you and I, or have you lost all trust in me?"

Had I? No, I couldn't believe he was anything other than the incorruptible Lord High Witchfinder of All Wales. Perhaps my doubts about him were a way of deflecting the doubts about me that I strongly suspected he harboured. And perhaps that was a subject best avoided completely.

And also, if I was to remain in the Office, working secretly for the Unnatural, I needed to remain in the Crow's good books.

"We can move on," I said. "Tell me, who were the Mystical Council?"

The look of surprise on his features was hard to miss. "Where did you hear that name?"

"It came up in conversation."

He frowned, as if having to pick his words very carefully. "I suppose you *should* know about them. We do not like to talk about them in polite company and repeating their story is well, discouraged, but it is important to know one's history at some point. Very well. They were a sister organization, in a way. This was in the nineteenth and twentieth centuries. They were like us, but they were also the opposite of us."

"What do you mean?"

"They were an arm of the state, a semi-autonomous law enforcement body charged with controlling and monitoring the supernatural realm. But their methods were very different. Very, very different."

"They used magic to fight magic."

"They did. They employed the forbidden powers to defeat threats to the state, but also to pursue the political interests of the state. A sort of magical secret service.

Sometimes, in an attempt to align them with other branches of the secret services, they were referred to as *MI0*. I told you about the attempts to raise undead soldiers in World War I, the necromancer Nicholas Semper."

"Semper was part of this Mystical Council."

"Well, he was something of a freelancer, but they were controlling him. Handling him, as I believe the term goes. The truth is, there are numerous examples of us using strong magic to intervene in wider political and military events throughout the world, often with dire consequences. As you can imagine, the Council and the Office were often in conflict."

"Conflict that the Office won."

"In the end, our voices were heard and the Council was disbanded as part of the widespread social and political changes following World War II. Many in the twentieth century wanted to turn their back on the supernatural and the mystical, of course. The triumph of the Office over the Council became inevitable. I am confused, though – why are you interested in this?"

"No reason; I wasn't sure if they were relevant to current events. Clearly not."

He considered me for a moment, then nodded his head as if some suspicion had been confirmed, or some decision made. "Did Mormont give you any clues at all about the true identity of the Warlock?"

"She refused to. She did say *him*."

"Interesting. A man, then, unless she was deliberately throwing us off the scent. I genuinely do not know who this Warlock is, but I do know they must be formidable if Evangelina Mormont was prepared to take orders from them. We must redouble our efforts. This defeat will only have made them more determined, I fear."

Whoever was behind the attacks, they weren't going to stop. Mormont was gone, but the shadowy individual giving her orders wasn't going to give up. And if they'd hated me before, they were going to be seriously pissed off at me now.

"Tell me, Danesh," the Crow said. "In the outer

chamber, unless I'm very much mistaken, powerful magics were recently employed. I was under the impression that all the malevolent sigils had been destroyed. Was that incorrect?"

I hesitated. What should I tell him? Hywel Williams was certainly a potent sorcerer, strong enough to be of significant concern to the Office. My guess was that he had contravened magus law repeatedly. But had he done anything *wrong*? I now saw he was nothing to do with English Wizardry. His battles with his malign forebear were something we should concern ourselves with – but if Hardknott-Lewis knew the truth, he was not going to simply let Hywel pursue his family feud in peace, and my suspicion was that Hywel was better suited than anyone to counter Owain.

And then there was the simple truth that I had let Hywel go.

"More of Mormont's work," I said. "The cyhyraeth. She was attempting to manifest other entities to attack us. The succubi were only a part of the plan."

Was there the slightest note of surprise in his voice when he replied? "Mormont was responsible for the runes? She summoned the wraiths?"

"Who else?" I asked.

He looked into my eyes, and he *saw* me. He knew. Knew I wasn't giving him the full picture, knew what I was. Maybe he hadn't told anyone else. Maybe he had only just admitted it to himself, or maybe he'd known for a long time. But he knew.

"Ah, Danesh," he said simply.

And in that moment I understood, finally, that I had to leave the Office. I could admit it to myself. My position was untenable. All the damage the organization caused by denying people their nature, hounding them and pursuing them for doing nothing wrong. It had to stop. I had to do what I could to make it stop. I could no longer reject who and what I was.

The Crow, however, was shaking his head, a look of wry amusement on his features.

"I had this conversation often with Lady Coldwater, in the early days."

"What conversation?"

"In the end, we decided we were more united than we were divided. What is the saying? *The enemy of my enemy is my friend,* yes? She and I disagree on many things, but we see eye to eye on the larger matters. Our enemies are still out there. The Warlock and all the other threats we face. You and I – it is possible we may disagree about, let us say, the means, but I am sure we could agree about ends. We have to destroy these people, do we not? We have to at least try to stop them."

"I don't…"

He held up his hand.

"Please. You should know I have decided it is time you were promoted from Acolyte. I want to make you an Adept in Her Majesty's Office of the Witchfinder General. You have earned it. Will you accept? It means more money, if that is important to you. More than that, it implies a greater degree of trust. A belief in you and everything that you have done. The enemies we face – can we face them together?"

He knew what I was, but he still wanted me to be a part of the Office. That, in itself, was remarkable. We lived and worked in the shadows, the grey areas, but the truth was we were also weak. The Office deliberately made itself weak by refusing to employ magic to fight magic. Perhaps I was just one more compromise he had no choice but to make. He didn't only want to keep a watch on me. He needed me.

I thought about Sally and her suggestions for what I should do, join the Unnatural, gain the trust of Myrddin. I thought about the Librarian. I thought about Gilroy, locked away for so many years in his prison. I thought about my mother and about Az. I thought about English Wizardry and the Sorceress and the Warlock. I couldn't fight every evil, but I could fight some of them.

And once the Warlock was defeated and English Wizardry were consigned to history, what better way to bring down the Office than to be part of it, fighting it from the inside?

"I'll be in the office first thing tomorrow," I said. "Then we can make a start."

END

Acknowledgements

As ever, my thanks to my wonderful wife and our two daughters. All of this is for you. My eternal gratitude also to Elsewhen Press for believing in these books, and for producing them with such care, attention and good humour. I'm delighted to be a part of the Elsewhen family.

As with *The Eye Collectors*, I'd like to extend a special thank you to "The Whisperer", my contact in the Welsh Division of the Office of the Witchfinder General, without whom details of the Office's inner workings couldn't have been brought into the light. My thanks, also, to Dr Miriam Seacastle for helping me with key details of the weird and, indeed, wyrd creatures that live in the shadows around us.

Elsewhen Press

delivering outstanding new talents in speculative fiction

Visit the Elsewhen Press website at elsewhen.press for the latest
information on all of our titles, authors and events; to read our blog;
find out where to buy our books and ebooks; or to place an order.

Sign up for the Elsewhen Press InFlight Newsletter at
elsewhen.press/newsletter

Coming soon

𝕽𝖊𝖉 𝔇𝖗𝖆𝖌𝖔𝖓

A Bestiary of Modern Britain
Dr Miriam Seacastle
2022 FACSIMILE EDITION

Elsewhen Press are pleased to be able to produce this facsimile of the 1999 illustrated, limited edition privately published by the author but since unobtainable.

"Dr Seacastle's … Bestiary was the product of a great deal of solid research and investigation. It is a short volume … but there is much in the book that is precise. Not only that, she makes several rather inciteful remarks about actions taken by Her Majesty's Office of the Witchfinder General over the decades."
— **Simon Kewin**, author and OWG scholar

The original edition has all but disappeared, but we temporarily gained access to a copy from the library of the Cardiff Office of the Witchfinder General, from which we have been able to create this facsimile edition.

"A must-have for historians, students, and those interested in the OWG or indeed protecting modern Britain." – **Sally Spender**

This invaluable collector's item will be available Spring 2022.

THE EYE COLLECTORS

A STORY OF
HER MAJESTY'S OFFICE OF THE WITCHFINDER GENERAL
PROTECTING THE PUBLIC FROM THE UNNATURAL SINCE 1645

When Danesh Shahzan gets called to a crime scene, it's usually because the police suspect not just foul play but unnatural forces at play.

Danesh is an Acolyte in Her Majesty's Office of the Witchfinder General, a shadowy arm of the British government fighting supernatural threats to the realm. This time, he's been called in by Detective Inspector Nikola Zubrasky to investigate a murder in Cardiff. The victim had been placed inside a runic circle and their eyes carefully removed from their head. Danesh soon confirms that magical forces are at work. Concerned that there may be more victims to come, he and DI Zubrasky establish a wary collaboration as they each pursue the investigation within the constraints of their respective organisations. Soon Danesh learns that there may be much wider implications to what is taking place and that somehow he has an unexpected connection. He also realises something about himself that he can never admit to the people with whom he works…

"Think *Dirk Gently* meets *Good Omens*!"

ISBN: 9781911409748 (epub, kindle) / 9781911409649 (288pp paperback)

Visit bit.ly/TheEyeCollectors

HOWUL
A LIFE'S JOURNEY

DAVID SHANNON

"Un-put-down-able! A classic hero's journey, deftly handled. I was surprised by every twist and turn, the plotting was superb, and the engagement of all the senses – I could smell those flowers and herbs. A tour de force"
– LINDSAY NICHOLSON MBE

Books are dangerous

People in Blanow think that books are dangerous: they fill your head with drivel, make poor firewood and cannot be eaten (even in an emergency).

This book is about Howul. He sees things differently: fires are dangerous; people are dangerous; books are just books.

Howul secretly writes down what goes on around him in Blanow. How its people treat foreigners, treat his daughter, treat him. None of it is pretty. Worse still, everything here keeps trying to kill him: rats, snakes, diseases, roof slates, the weather, the sea. That he survives must mean something. He wants to find out what. By trying to do this, he gets himself thrown out of Blanow… and so his journey begins.

Like all gripping stories, *HOWUL* is about the bad things people do to each other and what to do if they happen to you. Some people use sticks to stay safe. Some use guns. Words are the weapons that Howul uses most. He makes them sharp. He makes them hurt.

Of course books are dangerous.

ISBN: 9781911409908 (epub, kindle) / 9781911409809 (200pp paperback)

Visit bit.ly/HOWUL

Working Weekend

Penelope Hill

Sometimes authenticity sucks!

Marcus Holland, European Folklore expert and award-winning writer of Horror and Fantasy fiction, is guest of honour at the CoffinCon convention being held in an old gothic mansion-turned-hotel. He's looking forward to the weekend, as he's hoping for a break from the pressures of work, the enthusiasm of his agent and the demands of his ex-wife. There's to be a midnight masque, a Real Ale bar, and the convention committee have even arranged to have a 'real' vampire wandering the halls, to help add to the atmosphere.

From the moment Marcus arrives he starts to feel uneasy, but can't quite put his finger on the reason why. Although he soon comes to realise what is wrong, he knows he can't broadcast his concerns without being thought insane. Far from being a relaxing break he will be working harder than ever in order to safeguard his friends and fans.

ISBN: 9781911409717 (epub, kindle) / 9781911409618 (240pp paperback)

Visit bit.ly/WorkingWeekend

FAR FAR BEYOND BERLIN

CRAIG MEIGHAN

Even geniuses need practice

Not everything goes to plan at the first attempt… In Da Vinci's downstairs loo hung his first, borderline insulting, versions of the Mona Lisa. Michelangelo's back garden was chock-a-block full of ugly lumps of misshapen marble. Even Einstein committed a great 'blunder' in his first go at General Relativity. God is no different, this universe may be his masterpiece, but there were many failed versions before it – and they're still out there.

Far Far Beyond Berlin is a fantasy novel, which tells the story of a lonely, disillusioned government worker's adventures after being stranded in a faraway universe – Joy World: God's first, disastrous attempt at creation.

God's previous universes, a chain of 6 now-abandoned worlds, are linked by a series of portals. Our jaded hero must travel back through them, past the remaining dangers and bizarre stragglers. He'll join forces with a jolly, eccentric and visually arresting, crew of sailors on a mysteriously flooded world. He'll battle killer robots and play parlour games against a clingy supercomputer, with his life hanging in the balance. He'll become a teleportation connoisseur; he will argue with a virtual goose – it sure beats photocopying.

Meanwhile, high above in the heavens, an increasingly flustered God tries to manage the situation with His best friend Satan; His less famous son, Jeff; and His ludicrously angry angel of death, a creature named Fate. They know that a human loose in the portal network is a calamity that could have apocalyptic consequences in seven different universes. Fate is dispatched to find and kill the poor man before the whole place goes up in a puff of smoke; if he can just control his temper…

ISBN: 9781911409922 (epub, kindle) / 9781911409823 (336pp paperback)

Visit bit.ly/FarFarBeyondBerlin

The Magic Fix

Mark Montanaro

The Known World needs a fix or things could get very ugly (even uglier than an Ogre!)

"Did we win the battle?" asked King Wyndham.
"Well it depends how you define winning," answered Longfield, one of the King's royal commanders.

In fact, the Humans are fighting a losing battle with the Trolls. Meanwhile the Ogres are up to something, which probably isn't good. Could one flying unicorn bring about peace in the Known World? No, obviously not.

But maybe a group of rebels have the answer. Or perhaps the answer lies with a young Pixie with one remarkable gift. Does the Elvish Oracle have the answer? Who knows? And, even if she did, would anyone understand her cryptic answers (we all know what Oracles are like!)

The Known World is in danger of being rent in twain, and twain-rending is never good!

Did I mention the dragon? No? Ah… well… there's also a dragon.

ISBN: 9781911409731 (epub, kindle) / 9781911409632 (240pp paperback)

Visit bit.ly/TheMagicFix

THE WORLD IS AT WAR, AGAIN
SIMON LOWE

**The World is at War, again.
New technology has been abandoned.
A period of Great Regression is under way.**

In suburbia, low level Agent Assassins Maria and Marco Fandanelli are given a surprise promotion as "Things Aren't Going Too Well With The War". Leaving their son Peter behind, they set sail on the luxury cruise-liner Water Lily City, hoping an important mission might save their careers and their marriage.

Dilapidated and derelict, Panbury Hall is not what Peter expected from boarding school. Together, with his celebrity dorm buddy, he adjusts to a new life that involves double dates, ginger vodka, Fine Art face painting and kidnapping, as they attempt to uncover the mystery of Panbury Hall.

Despite being a member of the Misorov Agent Assassin dynasty, Chewti is a reluctant AA. She only joined the Family Business to track down her cousin Nadia, the rogue AA who killed her mother. Really, she wanted to be a school teacher. So when Nadia is spotted loitering in the grounds of Panbury Hall, the opportunity to avenge her mother's death and have her dream job is too tempting to turn down.

The World is at War, again blends genre and expectation as characters take on an extravagant, often comic search for identity and meaning in unusual times.

ISBN: 9781911409939 (eBook) / 9781911409830 (296pp paperback)

Visit bit.ly/TheWorldIsAtWarAgain

ABOUT SIMON KEWIN

Simon Kewin is a pseudonym used by an infinite number of monkeys who operate from a secret location deep in the English countryside. Every now and then they produce a manuscript that reads as a complete novel with a beginning, a middle and an end. Sometimes even in that order.

The Simon Kewin persona devised by the monkeys was born on the misty Isle of Man in the middle of the Irish Sea, at around the time The Beatles were twisting and shouting. He moved to the UK as a teenager, where he still resides. He is the author of over a hundred published short stories and poems, as well as a growing number of novels. In addition to fiction, he also writes computer software. The key thing, he finds, is not to get the two mixed up.

He has a first class honours degree in English Literature, is married, and has two daughters.

Printed in Great Britain
by Amazon